ALPHAS NEVER HIDE

Willow Lake Supernaturals

Book 5

LORI AMES

Alphas Never Hide by Lori Ames

Published by November Snow
Copyright © 2025 by S.L. Paton. All rights reserved.
Digital edition / 2025 - ISBN 978-1-989764-78-7
Print edition / 2025 - ISBN 978-1-989764-79-4
Large Print edition / 2025 - ISBN 978-1-989764-90-9

Cover by: S.L. Paton
Beta Reading by: Kirk Waite at Rare Bird Beta Reading & Courtney
Bassett

Thank you for respecting the hard work of this author.
loriames.com

ALPHAS NEVER HIDE

WILLOW LAKE SUPERNATURALS BOOK 5

The wolf who refuses to be Alpha.

Hayden Walker might be trapped in Willow Lake by guilt and duty, but he's no one's alpha. It doesn't matter how many times people call him Alpha, with a capital A like it's his name, he just isn't—just ask his last pack. They had no problem rejecting him to follow his traitorous brother, Robbie, twelve years ago.

Hayden thought he'd come to terms with what happened back then, but it turns out some things don't get easier to accept with time. After discovering his brother's latest sinister activities, Hayden can't hide from the truth anymore. He has to stop him, particularly when Ryley Bell, his fated mate, is his brother's latest victim.

Hayden can't let his brother harm anyone else. Robbie won't take anyone else from him. Not again. Never again.

Tags: MM Fated Mates Paranormal Romance, a wolf who refuses to be Alpha, a faun who doesn't put up with his mate's nonsense, let's pretend a kick in the face is a sign of love at first sight, the Eternal Magic is a persistent diva, the confrontation between brothers we've all been waiting for, he has a pack whether he wants one or not, he will also get his happily-ever-after whether he wants one or not, wolves should listen to their clever mates, and, most importantly, not all fauns play flutes.

Content Warning

Generally, I would not characterize my books as the kind that will rip your heart out and stomp on it until you cry, however they do have some content that people may find uncomfortable or triggering.

Note: This list contains spoilers.

Content warnings include: sexual content, swearing, violence, one main character reacts violently to the other main character out of fear at beginning, patricide and matricide (off page / prior to start of book), abduction, reference to torture (off page), attempted fratricide and threats of murder, child abuse (emotional / off page / prior to start of book), injuries, car accident, trafficking of supernatural people, supernatural people in cages.

Chapter One

HAYDEN

Whenever someone made the mistake of calling me Alpha —with a capital A like it was my fucking name, even though it damn well wasn't—I always corrected them. Immediately.

I was not Willow Lake's alpha, capitalized or not. Not now. Not ever. And the people who worked for me in my own damn garage should definitely know better than that. My name was Hayden Walker. That was it. Nothing more.

"So, what do you say, Alpha? You coming to the pub for a drink tonight? Jeremy is teaching us about human sports." Buddy smirked, because seriously? Supes might not know much about human holidays and traditions, but sports we understood. "And the new kid in the kitchen is doing a steak special tonight." Buddy grinned at me as he wiped his grease-covered hands on a rag.

I'd already corrected Buddy about the whole alpha business twice this afternoon.

This time I growled.

My other employees cringed at the sound. Most people did, because they all thought I was the damn alpha of their pack, and they didn't want to displease me. And that thought made me growl louder.

But Buddy merely lifted an eyebrow. He wasn't the least intimidated. The bastard knew I wouldn't bite him. He'd been working for me at the garage the longest and had seen me through worse moods than this. That he was still here always surprised me.

And talking about the *new kid* and his supper special was the last thing he should have said to tempt me into coming out tonight. Of course, he didn't know how every time I saw the new guy all I thought about was how fucked up things had gotten this past summer.

Because the new kid?

His name was Brodie. I'd learned everything I could about him without appearing too obsessed. Thankfully, Van, our hellhound Chief of Police, had given his file to me without question. And Gage, our local demon guardian, nodded approvingly whenever I went to the inn to spend time with Brodie and Dakota, the other kid who'd been found with him. Because Van and Gage, like Buddy, thought I was driven by my instincts as alpha of this place.

But they were wrong.

I'd needed to know about him and his friend because they were the ones we'd saved from my brother's land out in the hills west of town. They were a constant reminder of how epically I'd failed, and how desperately I needed to make things right. Because if I'd been more of an alpha, those kids wouldn't have had to be saved. They wouldn't have even been in that situation.

Still, I was glad to hear Brodie was settling in. But if everyone was fine and safe in Willow Lake, I had other things I needed to do.

"Why would I want to learn about human sports? Jake puts sports up on the TVs at the pub all the time," I said. "What is there to learn?"

"Fuck if I know. He obviously thinks we live under a rock or have shunned everything mundane our whole lives or something, but the steaks should be good. So, are you coming or what?"

"No," I said.

"Ah, come on. You haven't been out with us in weeks."

"I'm busy." I turned my back to him and tidied my tools.

I didn't have to see Buddy's face to know he was rolling his eyes and shaking his head.

"Alice is going to think you're avoiding her," the persistent asshole said.

Alice was Buddy's girlfriend. She was a sweet supe who worked at the pub a few nights a week. When she'd agreed to go on their first date this past summer, Buddy had been too distracted to work. I had to stick him at the reception desk for the day, so he didn't get himself killed. He even smiled through all the ribbing the guys gave him, because *she was the one*. They'd been dating a few months now, and it looked like they were on their way to becoming chosen mates. I was happy he'd found someone. I was always happy when one of my pack—

Now I'd gone off thinking of everyone as my pack, too.

"No, she won't," I snapped. "If you don't bring it up, she won't notice if I'm there or not."

"That's a lie and we both know it."

Yeah. He was probably right.

At least Buddy finally figured out I was done with this conversation, because he quit pestering me. When he and the others left, I didn't lock up right away. This place was almost as much of a den to me as the place I slept every night. The familiar scents of gear oil, fresh grease, and new tires always calmed me. And, right now, I needed calm.

This was home. My refuge when I needed one. Even before I started working here, I'd sneak over and watch the mechanics work. I'd begged Georgina, the old owner, for a job when I was barely fourteen years old.

My parents hadn't known what to think about my passion for cars and trucks and anything with a motor, but they still supported me. All they asked was that I not let my work at the garage interfere with learning how to lead our pack.

Ha! What a waste of time that had been. My training as a mechanic had served me a hell of a lot better.

I shouldn't have bothered with all that pack crap, because all my parents' dreams for the future—for me, for themselves, for the town—faded away after their deaths. The only good to come from that time in my life was when old Georgina had offered the shop to me when she retired. It was like she'd known I needed something to ground me and keep me busy.

The day Georgina's Garage became Hayden's Garage, I'd even been happy. Almost.

From that moment forward, I'd done my best to be Hayden, the mechanic. Not the previous alpha's heir or the guy who refused to be Alpha. Just Hayden.

Now I was skipping down memory lane again like a kid going to the ice cream shop.

I pushed the memories away. The damn things had been haunting me lately. Until this past summer, I would have said I'd come to terms with my past, but life sometimes had a way of proving you wrong. I scrubbed my hands over my face and wished I could scrub away all the shit in my head at the same time.

I turned out the lights in the service area and made my way to my office. The tiny, cluttered room wasn't much of a space. My desk was covered with invoices and the same desktop computer Georgina had used when she owned the place. And I was pretty sure the thing had been old even then. But it still did what I needed, so I saw no need to change it.

I was adamant about keeping the service bays reasonably clean and tidy—well, as clean and tidy as a space like that could be. And I paid a local husband-and-wife team to clean the washrooms, the front desk area, and the waiting room, so those were always presentable, too. But I couldn't remember the last time I'd dragged a mop across the floor in here.

It was looking a little grungy to be honest, so I did my best not to look.

I stripped out of my stained and ratty overalls and hung

them on a hook behind the office door. I should toss them, but I just hadn't had the time to order more.

Things would settle down. As soon as I found Robbie, everything would be back to normal. I hoped.

A quick sniff of my pits told me I needed a shower, but I didn't want to waste time. I needed to get out of here. I'd be fine for another couple of hours. It wasn't like I was expecting to see anyone, anyway. I'd shower when I got back.

With one last cursory check of the empty shop, I shut off the rest of the lights and locked up. I exited through the back door to the fenced lot where we stored the cars we kept overnight. In the far corner, behind a stack of used tires, was the old travel trailer I called home. The thing looked like a piece of shit because it was one. The only thing I fixed and checked regularly was the caulking at the seams. I didn't need a lot to be comfortable, but I preferred to be dry.

I hadn't ever told anyone I lived back here, but I suspected Van knew.

I gazed longingly at the small corner of the trailer I could see from here. All I wanted was to go in there, get shitfaced, and pass out. Except no one in town sold magically enhanced whisky anymore, and the human-strength alcohol did fuck all to get me drunk. Ulric, the old owner of the pub, had sold the high-test stuff as off-sales, but he was dead more than a year now and whatever stash he'd had was long gone. I'd hoped now that Jake had found out about supernatural things he'd start ordering more again, but he hadn't yet.

So, the only thing left to do tonight was hunt.

Since the attack on Robbie's pack a month or so back, I'd been out every night looking for leads, trying to find my damn brother. Instinct told me I was missing something, but what? Right. If I knew the answer to that question, then I wouldn't feel like I'd missed something, would I? Still, I had a niggling feeling the answer was right there in front of me.

He wasn't dead. I was sure of that because the same instinct that told me I was missing something obvious also told me my brother was still alive. I just had to find him. The drive to hunt him down was all that was keeping me going right now. I *had* to find him before he hurt anyone else. I needed to do it for myself, for those poor kids he'd trapped and caged, for all the people in my pack—

Nope. Not going there. I was doing it because it was the right thing to do.

I'd planned to go out there again tonight, but my feet refused to carry me to my truck, which could only mean one thing. The Eternal Magic had different plans for me tonight.

"Son of a—" I groaned and rubbed my eyes with the heels of my hands. Why couldn't she leave me alone?

I lifted my face and sniffed the area for strangers or non-magical people. No one should be able to see me back here, but I still checked anyway. Not finding anything amiss, I let a partial shift roll over me as I took on my Anubis form. I hated wasting time like this, but the Eternal Magic was becoming increasingly pissy with me. Lately, she only deigned to communicate with me when I tapped into the magic of my wolf.

When I was a pup, people said they could sense a

strong alpha power inside me. It'd taken me a long time to figure out what they were talking about. My dad, who'd been the alpha of the only pack I'd ever been a part of, had tried explaining it to me. In the end, I figured it all boiled down to an innate need to take care of those in our pack, having a closer connection to the Eternal Magic through our animal side than the average shifter, and being able to merge those two things into our alpha power.

Alpha power was some woo-woo shit the Eternal Magic gave to us to help us look after our pack that essentially made us a conduit for all things magical. If a shifter had trouble shifting, we could help them access their magic and shift. If a shifter was anxious, we could help them connect with the powerful calm of the Eternal Magic. Any time someone needed to tap into the Eternal Magic, alphas were your one-stop shop solution.

Not every wolf had alpha power. It wasn't something you could learn. The Eternal Magic either blessed you with it or she didn't. At least that was my interpretation of what my dad had said when I was a pup. At the time, it made me feel special. Of course, it also made my brother jealous, but I hadn't figured that out until it was too late. What was it they said about hindsight?

And the other thing I'd discovered over the years? The Eternal Magic hated when her gifts were ignored. But she could fuck off because I didn't want to be alpha. She'd accept it, eventually.

I daydreamed about the Eternal Magic finally accepting defeat and stripping me of this ridiculous alpha power and giving it to some other wolf. Then she could start pestering someone else for a change. Alpha power was more of a pain in the ass than anything else.

And, no, the back of my neck wasn't getting itchy at the thought of someone else becoming Alpha of Willow Lake and stepping in to take care of the pack. I'd be perfectly fine with it. Happy even. Seriously. The true alpha, whoever they were, would come soon and take over. I was a stand-in until they showed up. A stand-in. A pale imitation of what the real alpha would be. I swallowed around the weird lump in my throat.

I hoped I wasn't coming down with anything. It'd be just like the Eternal Magic to mess with me by giving me a cold, like a weak, mundane human.

Whatever. I didn't know why I was thinking about all that, anyway. It didn't matter right now. A new alpha wasn't about to step into the role tonight.

I pushed all the wayward thoughts from my head and concentrated on the message from the Eternal Magic. Damn it. It looked like I wouldn't be driving out to the hills west of town tonight like I planned. My obnoxious alpha instinct, which I wished I could scrape out of my head, insisted I stick closer to home.

This would be yet another wasted night.

Why couldn't I catch a damn break and finish this whole thing with Robbie? Oh well. What the Eternal Magic wanted, the Eternal Magic got. She was a whiny, demanding tyrant.

I let my partial shift drop. I cast one last look at my truck, before resigning myself to checking the perimeter of the pack lands—not *my* pack lands, to be clear. Just *the* pack lands.

I would like to pretend I was obsessing over the whole alpha crap tonight because Buddy had stirred things up at closing time, but the truth was, I'd been obsessing about all this for months now. It was like a virus I couldn't shake or a persistent rash. Unfortunately, Doc Roberts didn't have a cure for this ailment.

All right. I'd wasted enough time already. Tonight was going to be an absolute waste, but I needed to finish this so I could get back and get rested for tomorrow night's hunt.

I stretched until every bone seemed to crack, and every muscle screamed in protest. A yawn tried to slip free, but I smothered the damn thing. There'd be time to sleep later.

I crossed the back of the lot. As soon as I was through the gate, it swung shut and locked automatically. I'd long ago planted thick, evergreen shrubs back here to protect the area year-round from curious eyes, but I still sniffed the air to make sure no one was close.

Shifting and heading out to the perimeter would be a lot easier if I developed the land I'd purchased a few years ago on the outskirts of town. I'd be closer to the woods and further away from mundane neighbors. But I couldn't make myself do it. Instead, I had to hide behind an evergreen shrub to shift and hope no do-gooder human shot me as I trotted through town on my way to the woods. I could imagine how excited they'd be to take out the big, bad wolf like they were in a children's story.

Honestly, human stories were the bane of supes everywhere.

Once I confirmed I was alone, I let my full shift wash over me. My transition to my wolf was more sluggish than normal, but it still came faster for me than most shifters. It was all part of being the *almost* alpha in Willow Lake. Usually, I hated yet another sign of the Eternal Magic's fingers in my life, but right now I appreciated it. I needed every advantage to deal with my brother like I should have done all those years ago.

I shook out my fur and stepped away from the long shadows of the thick shrubs and into the early evening sunlight. This time of year, the days were getting steadily shorter, but sunset was still hours away. Having longer days, even at this time of year, was one of the perks of living this far north. I appreciated those extra hours now because by the time solstice came around, it'd be dark damn near all day. That's what it always felt like anyway.

Now that I'd fully shifted, the itch to check the territory was worse. It didn't feel like a threat, but something wasn't right. I lifted my face to the sky. It would be so damn easy to howl and call the supernatural Willow Lakers to me so we could investigate it together. Instead, I trotted through the back alleys of Willow Lake alone. It didn't take long to hit the tree line on the outskirts of town. Willow Lake wasn't that big.

My paws crunched over dry, brittle plants as I followed the familiar route. Most of the grasses and forbs had burnt up under the heat wave earlier in the summer and had never fully recovered. Now, with fall invading the landscape, there was no hope for soft green growth again until spring.

In the few days since I'd last run this path, we'd had a couple of hard frosts, and the change of season had become more pronounced. I used to wonder what it'd be like further south, where fall lasted longer, and frosts didn't come in September. But I'd come to appreciate the beauty of this place. It was my home.

The warmth of the late afternoon heat still hung in the air, but it was fading fast. The scents of dying plants and rotting leaves had grown stronger over the last few weeks and most of the larch and aspen trees were changing to golden yellow, a stunning contrast to the dark green pine trees. Those vibrant colors never stayed for long here, not like they did in other parts of the country or further south. Pretty soon a big wind would crash down the mountainside and yank all these pretty yellow leaves off their branches, then in the blink of an eye, snow would be dumping down on us.

In the summer when I'd first started hunting for Robbie, I didn't think it'd take this long to find him. Now, I wasn't sure everything would wrap up before winter came. I grimaced. I really didn't want to keep doing this through snow and blizzards, too.

Wolf shifters didn't share all the traits of our animal counterparts, but even our wild animal comrades would agree curling up in front of a heater while listening to the wind howl outside, knowing you were safe and warm under a heap of blankets and all our fur, was pure bliss. When I was a pup, my parents would wake up Robbie and me whenever a blizzard hit. They'd bring us back to their bedroom. Dad would build a fire in the hearth while Mom made a cozy nest in front of the fireplace from the blankets that smelled like my parents because she'd stripped them from their bed. When everything was ready, we'd all shift and settle in to sleep, with Robbie and me safe and warm curled up between our parents.

I wasn't sure I'd felt that warm in years.

And I sure as shit wouldn't be warm this winter if I had to keep going out hunting for my asshole brother. If Robbie had taken off for the winter, I'd never know. I could be out there for months with nothing to show for it. I didn't think he would leave, though. As much as he pretended to be better than the rest of us, he was as connected to this land as I was. It was how we were raised, although the lessons had become a warped and twisted mess when they hit his head.

I prayed Mom and Dad had never found out what he'd become before they died.

Shit. Why did I keep thinking about my parents tonight? Robbie, yeah, I knew why I was thinking about *him*, but the dead should be resting.

Pain squeezed around my heart, and I pushed into it, letting it wash over me. It reminded me I was alive. That I had a purpose. One I'd put off for far too long.

When I finished the perimeter and hadn't come across anything, the Eternal Magic urged me to turn away from town. I wasn't done yet, it seemed. I ran another circle along the perimeter, and then another. Each time, the circle got wider, and I was further away from my territory, but my damn alpha instinct kept prodding me on. The sun had disappeared long ago, slipping away beyond the tips of the mountains in the west. And now a starry sky twinkled overhead.

If it was closer to the full moon, maybe the moonlight would have shown whatever the Eternal Magic wanted me to find. But we were on the eve of the new moon and starlight was as good as it got.

When I reached the most westerly part of the route for the fourth time, I couldn't go any further. I flopped down with a huff. My paws burned and my muscles quivered. I had half a mind to curl up and sleep out here for the night.

Why was the Eternal Magic making me do this? Was she toying with me? Punishing me?

Robbie's old burnt-out pack lands were further to the west. I should have been out there, not here. I had absolutely nothing to show for tonight.

Not a single fucking—

The scent of blood stirred through the air. As battered as my paws were, it wasn't my blood. I lifted my nose and inhaled deeply. The injured person? Animal? Whatever it was, it was to the west of me. It had to be close, given that the wind was pushing most scents away from me.

I rolled to get my feet under me again, but I kept low. Adrenaline swept away my fatigue. I inhaled again, dissecting the scent for more clues. I couldn't tell if I was smelling a person or an animal. The scents were all mixed together. Staying crouched close to the ground, I crawled forward slowly.

Chapter Two

HAYDEN

"Son of a fucking, cloven-hoofed dick weasel." The muttered words cut off with a thud and a groan, like someone had fallen and hurt themselves.

It'd been a handful of minutes since I'd started tracking the scent of blood, so I paused and listened.

"Fucking bucking duck," the person continued. "Why hasn't anyone perfected transporters yet? I could really handle getting beamed the fuck up about now."

They obviously hadn't detected my presence yet. I sniffed the air again. The blood was concentrated here.

"Get the fuck up, Ryley," the mystery man said.

Was someone with him? I only scented one person and an unfamiliar animal-like scent, too. The mixture reminded me a bit of Isaac, the centaur who'd moved to town recently, or Levi, the local minotaur, but it wasn't quite the same. Weirdly, the scent, reminiscent of grass and sage and clover, intrigued me. It reminded me of hot summer afternoons when I ran the perimeter of the pack lands, particularly along the stretch that was more prairie than forest.

I crept closer.

They hadn't noticed me yet, and I wanted it to stay that way as long as possible. One step. Then another. I inched forward until I could make out limbs and fur and skin.

What was that?

Sprawled across the forest floor was the strangest creature I'd ever seen. He was undoubtedly a supernatural being, but I didn't know what kind. The bottom half looked like some kind of farm animal, but the top was human-ish except for the short, little nubby horns poking out through his dark brown hair.

Was he a centaur who had somehow lost his backside? Or a child-sized minotaur? No, minotaurs didn't shift like that. Was he stuck mid-shift?

I'd never seen a mid-shift problem like that before, so perfectly divided over the body. Although, my Anubis form, which had my head transition to a wolf and made subtle changes over the rest of my body, was similar. Was this the same, only in reverse?

Intrigued by the unusual sight, I stepped closer. A cluster of brittle leaves crackled under my paw. I froze, but it was too late. The supe lifted his head. My first thought was this was not a child. No, this was a full-grown supe. His wide eyes scanned the trees until they landed on me. His face contorted in anger, pain, and fear.

"Fuuuuck." He groaned and cast his gaze up toward the sky, as if begging for divine intervention. It was such a human gesture, because every supe knew the Eternal

Magic didn't live in the air. "Not another one. Are you replicating yourselves out here or something?"

I startled as he collapsed to his back. As I drew closer, I saw the source of the blood. His pale torso was covered in it. It flowed from scrapes and cuts and, fuck, were those bite marks, too?

What was he doing? Exposing his stomach to me was a submissive gesture, but his muttered words didn't sound submissive. His two little hoofed feet twitched in the air.

"Alright. Come on. Let's get this over with. Come and get me."

I edged closer, sniffing the ground for more clues about what was going on. "I smelled blood. Are you okay?"

"For Magic's sake," he muttered, like he couldn't believe I'd ask such a question. Even in the dim light, I could see his eyes roll. "Do I look okay to you?"

He sounded more irritated than pained, but between the eye rolling, the twitching, and the strange things he was saying, I wondered if he was having a hallucinatory seizure. His behavior wasn't normal.

"Come on already. Let's do this." His words dripped with impatience as he beckoned me closer.

"Are you okay?" I asked again as I neared him.

"Wouldn't you like to know," he grumbled. "What is taking you so long? Get your ass over here."

"Do you need help standing? Are you mid-shift?"

"What an asshole," he muttered, and I had no idea why. My questions were perfectly reasonable. He glared at me. "Yeah. Right. Sure. You should check my ankle. I think I twisted it."

Shit. If he'd broken it, he could be in shock. Was that

why he was acting so strangely? At least I could help with his ankle. Maybe then he'd settle. The place inside me where my alpha magic lived warmed as I gave in to the need to care for him.

The heavy scent of blood nearly obliterated the smell of everything else, but as I drew closer to the creature, I picked up other nuances. And there, under the rest, was a scent I'd recognize anywhere, even after all these years. Robbie. My damn brother's scent was all over this poor man. Knowing what I knew of my brother, I suspected he was responsible for those scrapes, bruises, and raw looking bites on the man's lean body.

My heart pounded as I glanced around at the woods again. I still didn't scent another supe, but this had to be a trap. And I was the dipshit who'd walked right into it.

"What are you waiting for? I don't have all night."

"Where is he?" I asked warily, scanning the woods. "Come on out, Robbie. Let's talk."

"My name's not Robbie, asshole. Which you would know if you'd asked me," the man said. "I'm Ryley. And could you quit yelling? Fuck only knows what you'll attract with all that racket."

I waited. No one charged at me from the shadows. I waited a little longer. Robbie had never been a patient guy. He must not be here. So, what did that mean? Was this Ryley guy another of Robbie's prisoners? Had he escaped?

If my suspicions were true, he was the best lead I'd come across.

Finally.

The Eternal Magic herself had delivered him right to me. If she expected an apology for all the bitching and complaining I'd been doing tonight, she'd have to wait. First, I needed to get this guy away from here and to safety as soon as possible. I shifted into my human form as I darted forward. The guy's legs twitched again. I didn't have a first aid kit with me, but I could strip off my T-shirt and use it to bind his ankle.

I reached for the foot he said was injured—

The supe's foot shot out, aiming straight for my eye. I dodged, but not quick enough to avoid it completely.

Thump. Thump. Thump.

His cloven hoof battered my face three times before I fell backward. As I collapsed, the back of my head struck a tree trunk. Fantastic. That was just what I needed after getting a hoof to the face.

"Watch where you put that thing. You could have blinded me." I slid my fingers over my cheek. They came away wet and bloody. The two points on his hoof were as sharp as knife blades. "Are you having a seizure?"

"You're still alive? Damn it. You must have a thick skull."

"You're trying to kill me?" My words were barely discernable through my growl. I blinked at the murderous stranger. "What the fuck, man?"

Ryley had grabbed onto a low hanging tree branch and was hauling himself to his feet. He didn't seem capable of putting weight on one of his feet, so he hadn't been lying about his injured ankle. When he got upright, he swayed and almost fell again. When he was finally steady, he scowled at me. If he had any kind of kinetic magic, like the kind humans gave their fictional superheroes, I'd be dead.

"Oh, don't sound so surprised. I'm not falling for it.

19

And I'm not going back with you." He raised his hands in the air and lifted his injured leg in a bizarre pose that reminded me of a praying mantis. I shouldn't think he looked cute like that. Like a little pup, trying to be all mean and menacing, while striking the strangest pose I'd ever seen. Yeah. I definitely wasn't thinking clearly. I probably had a brain injury. "If you try to make me, I'll go all Karate Kid on your ass."

"Huh?" My thoughts churned sluggishly through my throbbing head, but it didn't take much to figure out what the problem was. "I'm not one of those wolves."

He huffed. "Right. Like I'm going to believe that."

"I'm serious."

"So, what are you saying? You're just some rando wolf out for a stroll?" He lowered his arms and leg, then hobbled toward me. I inched away from him. I had no desire to be on the business end of those hooves again, so I figured my best plan was to stay out of kicking range.

I stared at his vicious hoof for a minute until I was sure he wouldn't strike me again. Then my gaze wandered up his body. Now that I saw him standing, he was taller than I'd first thought. He also reminded me of something or someone, but my head ached too much for me to figure it out right now. Was it from a movie or a TV show?

Even in my human form, my senses were strong enough to pick out a few details about him in the darkness of the forest. Beige-colored fur covered everything south of his waist. I didn't let my gaze linger down there, though. I didn't want him thinking I was trying to check out what he was packing between his legs, even if I couldn't see anything because of his fur.

In my quick glance, I noted how his bottom half was more animal-like, from the shape of his short legs to the hooves and his little stubby tail. His upper half was human, with two notable exceptions: those little stump-like horns sticking out through his brown hair, and eyes with creepy rectangular-shaped pupils.

"No, you're right. I'm not randomly strolling around," I said. "I'm looking for the wolves who captured you. Whatever you can tell me about them will help."

"Nope. I'm not falling for that. Why are you really here? You're just trying to distract me until they catch up, aren't you? Do I look gullible? And, while we're being all honest and shit, I should let you know you aren't taking me anywhere. Never."

"I'm not with them. I can help."

He sneered in disbelief. "If you aren't with those prick-crickets, how did you know I'd been captured, huh? You smell like you haven't had a bath in weeks, just like they do. I haven't had a shower in weeks, and I still smell better than you. Do you really think I'm going to fall for your lies?"

His voice had gotten louder and louder the longer he talked until he nearly shouted the last question. And prick-crickets? What in the name of Magic was a prick-cricket? This guy's swearing was truly bizarre. It was like he thought if he pushed a bunch of words together, that was enough, even if they didn't make sense.

"I don't smell that bad." I checked my pits again. He had a fair point. I was a little ranker than I'd thought. And my T-shirt had at least three oil stains, and my ripped jeans had more. I sighed and lifted my hands in a placating gesture. "Fine. I can see why you might be confused about me, but I swear I'm not with them. I'm the…" I swallowed. Nope. I couldn't say I was the Alpha of the Willow Lake pack. Lies would get me nowhere. "I live in Willow Lake. We're trying to catch those wolves and bring them to justice."

The guy stopped his wobbly approach. He put one hand against a tree to brace himself and the other on his hip. If his leg hadn't been injured, I suspected he would have been tapping his foot impatiently. "So I'm supposed to believe you're some kind of vigilante?"

"Can't we just say I'm here to help?"

The way his eyebrows lifted in obvious disbelief suggested that wouldn't be happening.

"Listen, how about you take my phone? You can go online and call the police or something. Sometimes the reception isn't the greatest out here, but you could try."

"And you're going to sit there quietly while I'm mucking about on your phone. Right. Sure. I believe you." He shook his head. "You really must think I'm an easy mark. I might not be a full supe, but that doesn't make me gullible. I've faced off against worse assholes than you."

"Listen to me for a minute." I wasn't sure if this was a mistake or not, but I wasn't getting anywhere with my other tactics. "I'm not saying this to scare you, but if my intention was to abduct you or hurt you, I could have done that by now. When I first approached, I wouldn't have gone for your feet. I would have gone for your jugular to kill or subdue you. And now? I could shift and knock you to the ground before you could duck behind that tree. But I'm not doing that." I paused and studied his reaction to my words while trying to figure out how to be as non-threatening as possible, particularly after saying all that. "Do you get what I'm saying?"

His face twisted, suggesting my logic wasn't impressing him. "You're saying I'm supposed to trust you because you haven't tried to kill me yet?"

"Pretty much, yes." I was used to being trusted. I didn't realize how much I took that trust for granted until I didn't have it.

"You must have really excelled at debate class in school." He frowned as he eyed me for one long moment. I felt the moment he decided to take a chance on me. The tension in the air eased. He reached out and wiggled his fingers. "Give me your phone."

I pulled my phone from my back pocket slowly, so he didn't think I was doing anything nefarious. My fingertip was still bloody from when I'd wiped my face, so it left a red streak across the surface when I unlocked the screen. I gently tossed my phone to him, still not keen on getting too close to his hooves.

My face was bleeding. Facial wounds were always such drama queens. And his hits had struck close to my eye, so the blasted thing was starting to swell. Nope. I didn't need another kick like that anytime soon.

"You know, you shouldn't show your pattern to anyone. Now I can unlock your phone any time and really mess things up for you," he said as he tapped on my phone. I couldn't see the screen, so I didn't know what he was doing. Maybe he was downloading viruses or installing spyware or all those other things Buddy had warned me about. I didn't really care. All I used it for was accepting calls from people in the pack, so it wouldn't be hard to replace it.

"Are you seriously giving me a lecture about phone security right now?"

"Well, it's true," he said. "Why don't you have more apps? These are factory basic. Where are your pictures? Your apps? Your socials? Your games? Are you sure you're legit? Because this is not normal."

I didn't think he needed an answer.

"Huh. So, we *are* close to Willow Lake. You weren't lying about that." He tapped on the screen a bit more. "Did you know you have the police station's phone number in your contact list as van? What is a van? Like an acronym or something? Villains Are Nicer? Or Victims and Numpties?"

"Van is the name of a friend. A hellhound. He's also the Chief of Police."

A few more taps. "Huh. Would you look at that? Supenet agrees with you. There is a hellhound in charge of the police in Willow Lake named Van Clark."

I barely stopped myself from saying I told you so.

Chapter Three

RYLEY

Was this guy for real? His phone suggested he was kind of pathetic. Sure, he looked handsome enough, but he needed a shower. Weren't there studies out there showing how good-looking people had an easier time making friends? Maybe I was misremembering because his phone told a different story.

He had a lot of contacts, but not a single picture of anything or anyone, not even a pet cat.

The other weird thing about him? Magic clung to the air all around him. I'd never felt anything like it. This was no average wolf shifter. So far, he wasn't using all that magic against me, but I didn't want to know what would happen if he changed his mind about me. I definitely wasn't ready to trust him, though, even if my gut was telling me I could. For now, I needed to gather as much information about him as I could, just in case the situation changed.

I studied him in my peripheral vision. My eyes in my human form couldn't see shit, but I wasn't in my human form at the moment. Excellent eyesight was one of the few heightened senses I'd inherited from my mom, but it only worked when I was in my faun form. Guys like this wolf always thought the Eternal Magic had gifted them with the best senses, but they had no idea about the way a faun's eyes functioned, which worked to my advantage right now.

His big wolf form had been intimidating with all those sharp teeth, and his human body was just as scary. He was muscular, but he didn't seem the type to work out at a gym, so he must do something physical for work. Based on the streak of grease or oil or whatever on his cheek and the stains on his clothes, I suspected he worked on machines. His eyes were a soft blue color. I couldn't identify the exact shade with only the stars for light—even a faun's sight had some limitations—but they were pretty. His dirty blond hair was a mess, standing up in all directions like he'd been pushing his fingers through it all day. He needed a haircut, and his stubble was well on its way to becoming a short beard.

If he didn't smell so bad, he might even be attractive. For a wolf.

Although, to be fair, I would have smelled a lot worse if I hadn't spent the whole of my captivity in my shifted form. It was one of the perks of being a shifter that every kid knew about. If you stayed shifted, you didn't need as many baths. As an adult, I loved showers, but my cage hadn't come with one. Having a long hot shower was one of the first things I'd do when I got back to civilization.

I clicked through his phone again, looking for hidden

apps or secret screens. There was nothing there. What kind of person left their phone empty? Not a grocery list? Or a music app? Or something favorited on their web browser? He didn't even have a picture of, well, anything. Why even have a smart phone if you were going to treat it like a landline?

He had to be a psychopath.

Wasn't that just typical of my luck? I'd escaped one psychopath only to be found by another.

I wasn't about to provoke the man who let me use his phone by asking questions like "are you a pathological liar" or "can you feel remorse" to confirm my suspicions. Nope. I didn't need to raise his ire by asking questions like that. Besides, only one in every thousand psychopaths gave in to the temptation to become a serial killer. Yeah, okay, that number was something I made up. I had no idea, but it made me feel better to believe very few psychopaths killed people.

In the meantime, I would play his game because I needed help, and this was my best shot. I resisted the overwhelming urge to sign in to my socials and my emails to check if I had any messages. I didn't want any of my information on his phone, although I doubted he'd know how to find it or use it. So, instead, I tapped the phone number for the police station. It rang and rang and…

Come on, come on, come on. Answer already.

Why was this taking so long? I needed to get away from this guy before he changed his mind about being nice to me. I also didn't want to stick around in these woods much longer. Those other shitty wolves shouldn't have discovered I was missing yet, but what if they had?

Honestly, escaping from them had been the only thing to go my way in ages. I wasn't about to trust my good luck to stick around. Not just yet. It could still turn on me any second now.

Someone answered my call. *Finally.*

"Where are you, Hayden?" Wherever this guy was, it was loud. "Buddy said you had something going on, but I don't believe it. Get your ass down here. Jeremy is talking about hockey and so far, no one's let him know we play shinny on the lake every winter. The questions the guys are asking are hilarious. He hasn't figured out they are pulling his leg yet."

I pulled the phone away to check the number. Yep. This was the number Supenet had listed for the police department. So...? "Is this the Willow Lake Police Department?"

A long pause followed my question. The ambient sound on his end cut off abruptly. "Who are you and where is Hayden?"

In the background, I could hear people whispering about an alpha.

"I'm fine, Van," the wolf I'd kicked—apparently his name was Hayden—called out. "But we need help."

"What's happened?" Van demanded. Even through the phone, his question resonated with thinly contained anger. "Put Hayden on the line."

Damn it. If I gave over the phone, I'd lose my advantage. So I ignored his request. "I need the police. Should I call 911?"

"Let me talk to Hayden. Are you holding him hostage?"

"Seriously?" I snorted. Like I could hold a big guy like him hostage. What a laugh. I couldn't even knock him out with my hoof, for Magic's sake.

"Seriously," the man said sharply.

"Fine." I reluctantly gave the phone to the wolf. I scowled at him to make sure he knew he needed to behave. I twitched my foot in his direction, just a little reminder that if he didn't help me, he'd get another kick. I'd aim for his nuts this time. Hayden leaned away from me and stared at my foot the same way my mother had once stared at a rattlesnake we'd stumbled across in the grass.

"I'm fine, Van," Hayden said.

I couldn't hear what the other guy said.

"You know I'm not lying. I was running the perimeter when I scented blood. I followed it to this… I don't know what he is."

I crossed my arms over my chest. "Seriously? I'm a faun or satyr. I prefer faun, which is the Roman name for my kind, but the Greek is fine. And what do you mean you don't know what I am? Fauns are everywhere. We're in mythology, *The Chronicles of Narnia*, *Carnival Row*, *The Mighty Hercules*…" I trailed off when he looked at me like I was speaking in tongues.

"He says he's a faun," Hayden said.

Van must have said something, because Hayden nodded. I wished my hearing was better but whatever. I'd learned to live with my shortcomings. "Yeah. I didn't know they existed either."

I stomped my hoof on the ground and regretted it. Pain shot up from my injured ankle and ping-ponged through every nerve in my body. I reached for the tree again to keep myself upright.

Son of a goat herder. That hurt.

"I need you to come get us."

Another mumble from the other side of the conversation had Hayden looking around. "Uh. We're west of town. Not as far as Robbie's old pack lands, but out that way."

I wiggled my fingers at him again. "Give me the phone."

"Hold on, Van, Ryley wants me to give him the phone." Hayden stretched out his arm, holding the phone out. I scooped it from his hand.

I clicked through his few basic apps until I found a map app. I put a pin in our location before talking into the phone again. "Can I send a text to you at this number, or do I need to use another?"

"This one is fine."

I sent the pin, then reluctantly returned the phone to the wolf. Hopefully if he knew the wolf was working with me, this Van guy wouldn't come in, guns blazing. And I really, really hoped all of this was legit. If this was some elaborate plan to trick me, I was going to be pissed. I didn't think this wolf had the know-how to set up a fake website for the Willow Lake PD or redirect calls, so I'd trust him. For now.

It wasn't like I had much choice. I couldn't get much further on my own. My leg could barely hold my weight, and I was feeling woozy. I didn't know if my light-headedness was because so much of my blood was outside my body instead of inside, or if I was in some kind of shock now. Either way, this was my best chance of getting out of these woods before the other bastard wolves came for me.

"You got it? Okay. We'll see you soon." Hayden looked at me. "And, Van, let Doc know Ryley will need to see him." Another mumble from the other end of the call. He shook his head, wincing as he moved. "No. Not me. I'm fine."

Whatever Van said next had Hayden frowning.

"Yeah, yeah, yeah. You can say you know I'm lying all you want, but you can also fuck off. I'm alive. That's good enough."

He ended the call with a huff. He shoved the phone in his pocket and leaned against a tree. His fingers tapped against his leg in a restless rhythm.

"They are coming, right?"

"Yes." He frowned. "We should start walking."

"It'll take them longer to find us if we move around."

"We shouldn't have called them," he muttered.

He dabbed at his still bleeding face again. When he saw more blood on his fingers, he stripped off his shirt. I did a double take. What was he doing?

I couldn't stop my gaze from drifting over his torso.

I shouldn't have. It was wildly inappropriate. After all he was bleeding because of me, but my eyes had their own agenda. And then my brain got in on the situation and purred a "Oh, hello. Yeah, baby." Which, really? Why did my brain sound like a slimeball?

But the guy looked good.

And I was a normal, healthy guy with a normal, healthy libido, so it was natural I'd notice. Anyone would look when presented with that chest and those arms and all those yummy muscles. But he went and ruined it by rubbing the shirt over his cheek. He was trying to wipe the blood from his face, but he was smearing it everywhere.

And my brain *still* thought he was sexy.

"I should be able to get us out of here," Hayden said as he continued to try to clean himself. "If you'd trusted me, we could have been on our way already."

"Isn't your pal the Chief of Police? It is literally his job to help people."

Hayden shook his head. "I didn't want them involved."

"Involved in what?" I scowled at him through narrowed eyes. He better not have double-crossed me.

"Hunting for Robbie."

"Who is Robbie?"

His gaze swept over my chest and all the wounds. He swallowed hard. "The wolf whose scent you carry."

I shuddered under the memory his words triggered. A wolf. His teeth dripping with saliva. The pain. The blood. His tongue lapping at my punctured skin. His fucked-up ideas about eating my magic through my blood.

Fresh anger flashed through me. I glanced down at my chest. Those bite marks better fade when I shifted. And I needed a gallon of antibiotics, because who knew what diseases that wolf carried? Supes weren't supposed to carry diseases, but who the fuck knew with that cannibal?

"You don't want them involved in finding the guy who did this? Is that what you're saying? Are you sure you aren't in cahoots with those other wolves?" I'd always loved that word. Cahoots. There weren't enough opportunities to use it in my day-to-day life. "Because it sounds like you're out here on your own because you want to join up with them without your pals in town knowing. Oh. Unless you're trying to get yourself killed."

"I won't die," he said with complete confidence. What a misguided fool. "It's safer if I do this on my own."

"You're such a cliché."

His frown deepened. "What do you mean?"

"You…" I waved my hand at him. "You're all, 'I'm a lone wolf.'" I'd dropped my voice in an amazingly accurate imitation of him. "Both literally and figuratively. 'I work alone.' Blah blah blah."

"I don't sound like that." His nostrils flared, and he clenched his teeth. "And it is for everyone's protection that I do this without involving the others."

"Right." This guy had me rolling my eyes so much and so hard they'd be falling out of my head soon. "And yet, a lowly faun knocked you on your ass. You think you could take on those other turd robbing jerks all on your own? You're a deluded ass. A deluded ass with a death wish. I need to get away from here. This place is teeming with your kind."

Although, even as I said those words, I found it comforting to have him here with me. I wasn't sure what that meant. He might be a deluded ass with a death wish, but I sensed I could trust him to keep me safe.

After my outburst, though, we waited in silence for help to arrive.

Chapter Four

HAYDEN

Ryley was wrong about me, but I didn't have to explain myself to him, even if part of me wanted to.

"What is that?" Ryley shrieked suddenly. His gaze darted from side to side and up and down.

My head was still fuzzy, so I hadn't seen what had alarmed him. I shot to my feet and braced for a fight. Had Robbie tracked Ryley here? If I was going to deal with my brother, I wished Ryley hadn't tried to leave a crater in my head. But tonight was not my night.

A massive black shadow blocked out the starry sky and I looked up. Oh. Now I understood. Thank Magic we weren't under attack. Now that I knew the threat wasn't a threat, I wobbled almost as much as Ryley, but pretended I was just moving to lean against a tree. I shouldn't have stood so quickly, because now I was dizzy on top of having a throbbing headache.

"Hi, Ogden," I called out to the newcomer. "We're down here."

I hadn't expected Van to show up with a posse, but I should have known better. I yanked my blood-stained shirt back on and waited for him to make his way to us. The leaves in the trees fluttered as the dragon's small wings stirred the air and sent a few of them spiraling to the ground.

"You know *that*? What is it? A dragon?" Ryley gestured to Ogden, whose long snake-like body was weaving between the trees as he descended to us.

As soon as Ogden was on the ground, the dragon sniffed the air.

"You're bleeding. Do I need to eat him?" Ogden asked me. His intense dragon's eyes blinked slowly as he eyed Ryley. Ryley let out a faint "meep" as he hobbled to safety behind me.

"Don't eat him," I said. "Is Van coming?"

"Soon," Ogden agreed. He pointed at Ryley with the tip of his tail. "Are you sure you can trust this one?"

I shrugged. "We'll know more when Van and Dillon get here, but my gut says yes."

"Of course I can be trusted," Ryley said indignantly. "The question is: Can I trust you?"

I didn't bother replying. We'd been over this already.

"They sent me ahead to check things out since they have to drive all the way around the lake and that'll take a few," Ogden said, ignoring Ryley's outburst. He'd obviously dismissed Ryley as a threat. He wrapped his long body into a coil, as if settling in to wait. "Can you text

Simon and let him know we're safe? My little kitty cat worries."

"You don't have to stay."

But before I could finish the words, he was already shaking his head. "We'll wait together, Alpha."

Ogden had only moved to Willow Lake recently, but the other Willow Lakers had already brainwashed him into thinking I was the local alpha.

"I'm not the alpha," I muttered, for the billionth time in my life. Actually, that would only work out to about a couple hundred thousand times a day for the last twelve years, so that number might be a bit light.

"Whatever you say, Alpha." Ogden batted his reptilian-like eyes at me.

I didn't bother correcting him again. My head hurt too much to argue. I sent the text to Simon, Ogden's mate, and got an immediate thumbs-up in response. "There. Simon knows you are with me."

I sat down and leaned against a tree trunk. Ryley sank down behind me and huddled against my back, keeping me squarely between himself and the dragon. It almost made me smile. Apparently he was now trusting me to keep him safe.

But I was too tired to manage even that. My muscles burned. My head ached. And a bone-deep weariness had me closing my eyes. Just for a minute. Was I exhausted because I'd been running all night, because I'd been hunting for Robbie for months, or because Van was going to demand answers to questions I didn't want to answer? I didn't know. It was probably all three.

At least with Ryley, we finally knew one thing for

certain. Robbie was still in the area. I'd figured as much, but Ryley was proof my gut was right.

I should shift and start tracking Ryley's route back to Robbie's hideout. Fuck, I was tired though. Maybe I'd rest a bit. Then, when I knew Ryley was safe with Van, I'd follow the faun's path through the woods. I could have Robbie in custody by morning.

That should make me happy, and it did, but it also…

There was a lot of shit going on in my head right now.

"Would he actually eat me?" Ryley whispered in my ear.

"Not tonight," I promised.

"It's for the best," Ogden agreed. "Simon would be mad if I was stuck in my dragon form for however long it took to digest you."

Ryley pressed close enough to me that I could feel him shiver in disgust. "You shouldn't say shit like that to people. I promise I'm leaving the area as soon as I figure out how. You don't need to threaten me."

A strange pang shot through my chest at his words. Fuck. What was that? I must be hungry. I hadn't eaten since I didn't know when.

I opened my eyes to see what Ogden's reaction would be to Ryley's words, but he ignored the faun's protest. Instead, he looked like he was admiring his long, sharp claws under the starlight. They were sparkly, like something had coated them with glitter.

"I'm so glad Willow Lake has a nail technician who is a supe," he said, as he held out his paw for me to admire. "This gel treatment is brilliant, don't you agree?"

Ryley snorted, but I felt the tension ease from his body.

I wanted to tell him not to underestimate Ogden, but admittedly it would probably be difficult to feel too threatened by a dragon who was busy praising his manicure. Or would it be a pedicure? Either way, I'd never bothered with either. A wolf's claws were his weapons. I wouldn't let anyone else touch them, especially not to cover them in fingernail polish.

Ogden dropped his gaze down to Ryley's feet. "You know, they do hooves too. Yours look like they've been through a grinder."

Ryley tucked his feet behind me and out of Ogden's sight.

"You'd be surprised how pretty they could make them look," Ogden continued, as if Ryley hadn't hidden his hooves. "Levi and Isaac didn't believe me either until I made them go with me."

Ryley smacked me on the arm. "You told me you didn't know any fauns."

"Ouch." He hadn't hit me hard enough to hurt me, but I cringed and rubbed my arm to tease him.

Ogden's gaze snapped over to us and a curl of smoke rolled out of his mouth.

"There is no way that hurt you," Ryley said. "Tell the dragon I didn't hurt you."

"This time," I agreed. "You didn't hurt me *this* time."

He folded his arms across his chest. "We've been over this. How was I supposed to know you weren't like the others? Now, answer my question. Were you lying about the whole faun thing?"

"I don't know any others," I said. "Levi and Isaac aren't fauns."

"A minotaur and a centaur," Ogden said, filling Ryley in. He'd relaxed again, after deciding Ryley hadn't injured me by hitting me. "And now, we have a faun. We'll have a little herd of hoofed supes soon."

"What the fuck? Do you realize how species-ist you sound when you group us together like that? Like we're livestock?" Ryley scowled and crossed his arms. "And for the record, you don't *have* me."

Ogden dipped his big dragon head. "Of course. I'm sorry. I misspoke. It's just you supes with hooves are quite rare. It seems notable that so many have come to Willow Lake."

Ryley tilted his head. "Fine. I guess that is unusual."

"Willow Lake is a special place," I said quietly, because it was true. My father had once said the Eternal Magic herself blessed Willow Lake and the supes who lived there. Not every supe was welcome, though. The Eternal Magic had a way of driving those unwanted supes away.

I'd often wondered if the Eternal Magic had driven Robbie to create a situation where he'd had no choice but to leave. It made as much sense as anything else.

I'd heard someone once describe Willow Lake as a Supernatural Utopia, but I didn't think that was it. Willow Lake had problems just like everywhere else, and we'd certainly had a lot of them over the last few months. But I'd always suspected what made us special was an enduring collective desire to respect the Eternal Magic and live harmoniously with different supes. That was the true magic of Willow Lake—its people. And, as a reward for embracing so many of her supernatural beings, the Eternal

Magic blessed us with more gifts, like fated mates and guardians.

The sound of a vehicle in the distance had both Ogden and me turning our heads.

"What? What's happening?" Ryley asked. He looked around, trying to see an invisible threat. Interesting. Ryley's hearing must be as dull as a human's.

Car doors slammed. A cacophony of chatter and footsteps tumbled toward us. I rubbed my forehead. If Robbie had been tracking Ryley here before, he wouldn't need to now. My would-be rescuers were making enough noise to wake every creature in the forest and scare everyone else away.

Ogden opened his mouth and flicked his tongue through the air.

"They're ours," he said, like I needed the confirmation.

"Yours?" Ryley asked. "You have a thing about ownership, don't you? Do you hoard people?"

Ogden rolled his eyes like Ryley was being ridiculous, but he still deigned to clarify by adding, "Our friends."

Light flickered through the trees as the others drew closer, so Van and Dillon must have been in their hellhound forms. My suspicions were confirmed when they burst through the last few trees separating us. Magical fire lapped over their inky black fur, but nothing around them caught fire. The fire from their hellhound forms filled the air with the scent of ash and smoke, so I couldn't distinguish between them based on their scents. Ash, the fire mage, clung to the back of one, though, so that must be Dillon. Ash wouldn't be able to touch Van's fires without injuring himself.

A few steps behind them was Adrian, a wolf who'd recently moved to town. He carried his mate, Jeremy, on his back.

Was riding each other like horses a mate thing? I couldn't imagine what it'd feel like, say, if Ryley climbed on my back, but I wished I had thought of that earlier. I could have carried Ryley out of here on my own and Van never would have needed to know about what'd happened.

Jeremy was busy talking to Ash, and neither of them had noticed us sitting in the shadows yet. Ryley, on the other hand, definitely noticed them. With each new arrival, he hunched lower and pressed harder against me.

"I didn't think I'd like riding on Adrian's back, but I'm changing my mind. It's pretty wild, and I bet we look amazing. Maybe this should be one of the competitions?" Jeremy suggested. "We should take a selfie and use it for promotion."

"I still don't understand how a discussion about hockey changed into Willow Lake holding its own Supernatural Track and Field Day," Ash muttered.

"Well, count me out of that riding competition. Centaurs aren't horses," Isaac said as he came last. In his centaur form, he towered over the others.

I didn't hear anyone else. Good. I didn't need everyone in the whole town out here. There were already too many people making way too much noise. When Dillon and Adrian quit walking, their mates sat up straighter and glanced around the area. They both had weak eyesight and probably couldn't see much past Van and Dillon's fiery fur. Ash waved his hand through the air and a glowing fireball appeared above us, bathing the area in its warm glow.

"Alpha!" Jeremy slid off his mate's back and dashed to me.

"Not the alpha," I corrected him.

Adrian shifted and grabbed for his mate as he scowled at Ryley, but Jeremy was too quick. I hadn't known Jeremy for more than a few months, but he treated me like he'd known me his whole life. He dropped to his knees and wrapped his arms around me.

For a guy who was mostly human, he had quite the bear hug. And he was definitely a hugger. I'd been on this side of one of his hugs a few times now. I still didn't like them.

"When Van got your call, we were all so worried," Jeremy said.

He pulled back and looked at me. "You look like shit, and you smell worse," he said. "What happened to your face? And your shirt? Shit. That's a lot of blood. Were you stabbed?"

Ryley huddled closer to my side, as if worried about what my friends might do to him when they found out he was the one who'd hurt me.

"Move away from them," Van commanded as he shifted into his human form.

"Who? Me?" Jeremy asked. "Or that guy?" Jeremy's gaze drifted over Ryley's body. "So cool. I have so many questions. Like, how do you balance on two hind legs like that? I know trick dogs can walk around a bit on their back legs, but not like always, right? They usually go around on four when they aren't performing. So I'm curious—"

"Jeremy," Adrian barked out.

"Fine, fine." Jeremy huffed.

"Now's not the time." The wolf tugged his mate away.

Jeremy frowned as he took out his notebook and started scribbling in it. Yeah. That was more like him. As Van approached us, he inhaled deeply, not bothering to hide what he was doing. Ryley swallowed.

"You smell like Robbie," Van said.

"He said the same thing." Ryley pointed at me. "But I never caught the guy's name. He was too busy gnawing on me for introductions. Like, seriously, who does that? I'm implementing a strict no-gnawing policy from here on out."

"Are you working with the wolves?" Van's gaze drifted over the faun, cataloguing the injuries. There were a lot of them, but they were mostly superficial. It was as if Robbie had wanted the injuries to look worse than they were, so Van's question didn't surprise me.

"Did you see this?" Ryley waved his hands over his chest. "Do you think I did this for fun?"

"Well?" Van prodded.

Ryley's jaw dropped open, and he crossed his arms. "What kind of question is that?"

"One I'd like the answer to," Van pressed.

"No," Ryley snapped. He stank of fear, but his hands were balled into fists and his leg was twitching like he was getting ready to kick again. "I'm not working with those ass-blankets. They abducted me. A while ago, I guess. It's definitely been longer than a week, but I lost track of time. But I finally escaped tonight and ran into this guy." He pointed at me.

"Thank you," Van said. His body visibly relaxed, so Ryley must have been telling the truth. Van would have known if he wasn't. It was one of the perks of being a hell-hound. I'd thought as much, but it was reassuring to have it confirmed. "We're going to take you into town, okay? Get your injuries looked at. You'll be safe."

A shiver rolled through Ryley. "I'm only trusting you because you and your friend over there are hellhounds."

"I know," Van said. "Now, let's get you and Hayden out of here."

"Who are the rest of these people?" Ryley asked. His gaze darted from person to person. He pressed closer to me again.

I did a round of introductions. I ended with, "You can trust them."

Ryley frowned. "Or not. Supes and I, we don't get along."

"What does that mean? I swear they aren't like Robbie."

"Yeah. Robbie's an asshole," Ryley agreed. "But most supes are."

Who the hell had hurt him? I growled low in my throat. He patted me on the arm.

"It's okay," Ryley said. "You've grown on me. I've decided you aren't like those other supes."

Considering earlier he'd been moaning about how he hadn't managed to kill me, that was practically a declaration of love. A warm sensation flowed through me, leaving a feeling of lightness in its wake. I don't know why I was so happy to have gained his trust, but I was.

"Hey!" Jeremy said. "I'm not an asshole and neither is Adrian."

"Thanks, bestie," Ash muttered.

"I mean, none of us are," Jeremy quickly amended.

"I guess we'll see," Ryley said. "It's not like I have a choice. Not if I want to get out of here."

"Speaking of which, can we finally leave?" Van asked. "Doc is waiting for Ryley and Hayden."

I straightened when he said my name. "What? No. I'm not returning to Willow Lake now. I'll find my own way back later."

"You're going to go see Doc Roberts." Van narrowed his flame-filled eyes at me as if daring me to disagree.

"No." I shook my head. "I'm fine. I'll shift and all this," I motioned at my face, "all of it will heal."

Van lifted an eyebrow.

I tried to lift one too, but my face was too swollen to move the way I wanted. I winced. Van's lips twitched as if he was trying not to smile because he thought I'd just proven his point.

"Fuck off," I muttered, but there wasn't any heat behind my words.

"Doc Roberts would have my head if I let you go running off with a head injury."

"This is the first lead we've had in months," I explained. "Robbie is out here. I need to find him."

"Dillon, Adrian, and I will follow the faun's scent."

I shook my head. "It needs to be me. He'll listen to me."

"Bullshit," Van said. "Robbie has never listened to you. He won't start now."

"But…"

"The three of us will assess the situation. If we need backup, we'll call for it, unlike you."

"I called you, didn't I?" I scowled.

"Only because you are both injured and couldn't get out of here on your own. I bet you hated calling me."

"Oh, he's got you there," Ryley said. "Although, to be clear, I was the one who called, not 'Mr. I'm a Lone Wolf' over here." He dropped his voice again, like he was trying to mimic me, but I'd never sounded like that a day in my life.

From the corner of my eye, I saw Ash's jaw drop open in surprise at Ryley's jab. Yeah. Only a select few supes dared to disagree with me, and they certainly didn't sass me. Not because I demanded obedience, but because of the alpha power thing. It made people uncomfortable to contradict the person they deemed to be their alpha.

I wasn't sure why Ryley wasn't intimidated by me or awed by my alpha power. But I think I kind of liked it.

Meanwhile, Van was staring at me, so I stared right back at him. To look away would mean I was submitting. My eyes watered. It didn't help that my face and the back of my head were throbbing, and my body ached from all the running I'd done after a long, busy day at the garage.

I blinked.

Damn it.

Chapter Five

RYLEY

"I'm telling you, I'm fine," Hayden grumbled. "I can shift."

"Absolutely not," Van said. "Doc said if you were injured, you weren't supposed to shift until he looked you over. And it's pretty damn obvious you're bleeding."

We all eyed the blood dribbling down Hayden's face. I'd always thought shifters, especially predatory shifters, healed quickly. I guessed not. Oops. The others glanced at my hooves. Yeah. It might be better not to dwell on how much the guy was leaking. It was time to change the topic.

"How far is the walk back?" My ankle ached. The trek out was going to be a bitch.

Van shot a look at Isaac. "Can you carry him?"

"Uh… What?" Isaac blinked, like he didn't understand the question.

"You heard me," Van said impatiently.

"If Isaac can't carry him, I'll shift and do it," Hayden said through a growl.

Van ignored Hayden.

"I never said I *couldn't* carry him," Isaac grumbled. "But I'm a centaur, not a horse."

Van stared the guy down with his fiery eyes. Man, those were creepy as fuck. It didn't surprise anyone when Isaac finally surrendered and agreed.

"Should I shift?" I asked.

"Doc said no shifting and that goes for you too." Van pointed his creepy eyes at me, and I held up my hands in surrender.

As soon as Isaac shifted, Van hoisted me onto the centaur's back. Hayden growled the whole time. What was his problem? It wasn't like he was the one trying to balance on top of Isaac.

"Oh," Jeremy murmured. "Maybe we should use a picture of them instead, you know, for the riding competition. Because it is impressive. Riding should definitely be a category."

"He's not riding me, I'm carrying him," Isaac protested.

I didn't see the difference.

I'd never ridden a horse before, so I couldn't say if riding a centaur was similar or not. But I was confident a horse wouldn't complain as much as this guy. It was awkward as hell straddling the centaur's back while I was still in my faun form. My bottom half resembled a goat, and goats weren't meant to have their legs splayed like this. Having my tail under me was also awkward. But I made it work with only a smidgeon of grumbling, unlike certain other people in our group—*cough*, Isaac, and *cough*, Hayden.

Once I was situated, I wiggled a little, testing how easy it would be to fall off. I kept my seat. So far, so good. I looked around. Huh. This wasn't so bad.

From his perch on Adrian, Jeremy was holding out a selfie stick, angling it like he was trying to get himself, his friend, me, and our rides, of course.

Having a phone pointed at me had me smiling by habit. I had one client who was always snapping selfies when we got together to discuss her projects. She plastered them all over her socials. It wasn't until Jeremy's flash went off that I realized what I'd done.

Being around supes usually made me want to run far, far away, but here I was smiling. I'd like to pretend I was comfortable around them for normal reasons. After all, Isaac reminded me a bit of Conny with his long hair, his hooves, and his youthful energy. But I suspected I was in shock.

Then we were on our way.

Having Isaac's body move under me was a bizarre feeling. I mean I'd ridden guys before—ha!—but it hadn't been like this. For one thing, I had no interest in the centaur. Not even a little itty bit. I blamed it on having already seen Hayden without his shirt on tonight. Apparently, my libido could only fixate on one person at a time.

My body swayed and jiggled with Isaac's every step. His back muscles moved under my butt, which was weird. But the best part was being up so high? I could see so much more. It was brilliant. Epic, even.

I felt like I was a warrior riding off to battle. Except, well, if we were at war with someone, the last place I would want to be was on a horse or a centaur going toward trouble. Fauns were more flight than fight. That was one of the few things I had in common with my kind. Being around other supes made me want to climb up a mountain-side to escape.

Huh.

So why wasn't I making a break for higher ground? I'd felt a spike of worry when they first arrived, but it faded fast. Faster than it should have. I hadn't been with this many supes since I left my herd, so what was going on? I glanced between them, wondering where my fear had wandered off to. My gaze landed on Hayden. Sure, I'd kicked him, intending to kill or at least maim him, but paradoxically I'd also come to trust him, possibly more than I trusted the hellhounds.

What in the Magic was that all about?

Stockholm syndrome shouldn't have kicked in yet. I'd only known the guy for little more than an hour or two. So, what in the name of goats everywhere was happening right now? Was it all because of Hayden? And, if it was, what did it mean?

"His foot can't be that bad," Isaac grumbled to himself as he clomped through the trees. "He got this far, didn't he?"

I patted his back, eager to distract myself from my absurd thoughts about the grumpy wolf shifter. "There, there. Be a good centaur."

Isaac swatted at me. Beside me, Hayden's growl deep-ened. I looked down from my mighty perch at Hayden, who was walking alongside us. His eye—only the one because the other had swollen shut—flashed with the golden light of his wolf. Why was he getting so worked up? Was it because his friends were making him go back to town? Whatever. He'd get over it.

Isaac's long blond hair flowed down his back, and I couldn't resist running my fingers through it. I used to braid my baby brother Conny's hair all the time. I missed that.

"What are you doing back there?" Isaac shook his head as if my touch tickled him.

"Hold still," I said. I gathered his hair into my hands and divided it into three bunches.

Isaac did not hold still, so I yanked a little to get him to behave, which earned me another of Hayden's growls. How curious. Why would me manhandling someone else be a problem for him?

"It'll look great when I'm done, I promise. Although if I had more time, it'd look better." I plaited his hair into a Dutch braid.

"Are you done yet?" Isaac asked, but he didn't try to pull his hair out of my hands again.

Our trek through the woods to their vehicle was longer than expected. I should have gone for a more complicated braid. Maybe next time.

"We would have been there already if I had shifted," Hayden mumbled as he kept pace beside me and Isaac. Everyone ignored him.

We made a strange procession through the woods. The fire mage, who was riding his hellhound mate, was in front and cast glowing balls into the air to illuminate our path.

Isaac, Hayden, and I were next. Behind us was the human riding a wolf, and at the rear was the other hellhound. The hungry dragon with the pretty claws had flown off, saying he'd let the doctor know what kinds of injuries to expect, so he was prepared. We were like a little convoy of misfit supernatural beings.

When we finally arrived at the SUV, Isaac sat his ass down on the road, sending me sliding down his back. I screeched and clung to his braid, so I didn't slide off his rump to the ground and get concussed like Hayden. Isaac shrieked in alarm as his head wrenched back, but it served him right.

"Get him off me," Isaac shouted as he batted at me to loosen my grip. He couldn't twist around enough to do any damage.

"We should give points for most memorable dismount," Jeremy whispered to Ash.

"Come here," Hayden said, scooping me off the centaur. "Let go of his hair, Ryley."

Isaac shifted as soon as I was off him, as if scared I'd try to climb back on him again.

"He started it," I insisted.

Although if I'd known the situation would end with me in Hayden's arms, I might not have protested so much. I might be thin, but I was solid, way heftier than a full-blooded faun, so Hayden manhandling me so easily was a bit of a turn on. Thanks to my human dad's contribution to my genes, I was bigger than most fauns and I always had been. No one had carried me around since I could walk on my own. Being in Hayden's arms was an unusual sensation, but I didn't hate it. The only thing I couldn't figure out was what to do with my own arms, so I crossed them over my chest.

"You were on my back because they said you couldn't walk here. We're here now." Isaac stared at me like he was daring me to contradict him.

"Enough," Van said. He'd already shifted into his human form and was digging in his pocket. He pulled out a set of keys and tossed them to Ash. "Get the faun and Hayden to Doc Roberts. Don't let Hayden talk you into anything else. Don't let him get out of the truck until he's at Xander's. And stay there to confirm what the doctor says."

"For fuck's sake," Hayden muttered.

Van jabbed his finger at the wolf. "We both know you want to hunt tonight but that's not happening unless Doc okays it. You got it?"

Hayden gritted his teeth.

"You guys ready?" Van asked Adrian and Dillon, both of whom were still in their animal forms.

They nodded.

"Let's go."

"Be careful." Ash dropped a kiss on his hellhound mate's fiery head.

"Should I come with you?" Jeremy asked.

"No. Take care of the alpha," Dillon said.

That made Hayden grunt and clench his teeth harder. Van dropped his hand on Hayden's shoulder and squeezed.

"We're going to do some recon. If we find anything, I'll let you know."

"Fine. Let's go," Hayden said. It was a wonder he

could squeeze out the words with how tightly he clenched his teeth.

"Shot gun!" Jeremy shouted.

Hayden stomped to the front passenger door and wrenched it open.

"Hey! I said—" Jeremy's voice dropped to a mumble as Hayden shot him a withering glare and climbed into the front seat, "—shot gun."

"Why does Ash get to drive?" Isaac complained as he held open the door to the back seat for me.

Jeremy had already claimed the seat by the door behind Hayden. It looked like I was sitting in the middle. I sighed and crawled in. Sitting in a car in my faun form was not any more comfortable than riding the centaur. My legs stuck out like weird little stumps, my tail was bent under my ass, and my horns, although not huge, were still big enough to hit the roof.

As soon as we were on our way, the human, who wasn't entirely mundane, pulled out a pen and a small coiled notebook from somewhere and eyed me curiously. "My name is Jeremy. I'm human-ish, but also the seventh son of a seventh son, so magic-ish too. Your name is Ryley, right? And your preferred way to describe yourself is a faun?"

The nib of his pen rested against the paper like he was ready to transcribe whatever I said. He studied me with an intensity that made me squirm, but when no one else was concerned with his questions, I nodded. He scribbled something in his book. I didn't know how he could see what he was writing in the dark, but that didn't deter him.

"So, part human, part goat?" He glanced down at my furry bottom half.

"Yes."

He pulled out his phone and before I knew what was happening, he tapped to activate his flashlight app and shot the light right into my eyes.

"What the fuck?" I knocked the phone away. Little rainbow-colored orbs danced in front of my eyes.

"You have pupils like a goat," Jeremy said, like it was the coolest thing he'd ever seen.

"You could have asked me! You didn't have to blind me." I rubbed my eyes.

"Try getting a hoof to the face, then you'll really know what it is like when someone tries to blind you," Hayden muttered.

"I said I was sorry."

"No, you didn't."

I thought back. He was right. Oops.

"Sorry," I said.

Hayden snorted like he didn't believe me.

"So," Jeremy started, drawing my attention back to him. "Are you faster in your shifted form? How do you run on only two hind legs? Do you hop? Would you go faster if you had one of those wheelchairs they make for differently abled dogs? You know, so you could lean your front half on the wheels and run with your back legs. I bet you could get some pretty good speed up."

I blinked at the strange man. "Pardon me?"

"Well, it looks like you escaped Robbie in your shifted form, so I was wondering why. It seems like you would be faster with longer human legs than two shorter goat-like legs."

I blinked at him some more.

"Unless your human legs are just as short…"

"Fine. You're right. My human legs are longer, which means I'm taller than this, too," I said, only because I couldn't handle anyone envisioning my long human torso on little stumpy human legs. The proportions would be all off. I didn't think I was a vain person, but it looked like I was. "They took my shoes, so I shifted. My hooves are sturdier than my bare feet."

He looked down at my hooves, which was easy considering how I was seated. They were sticking straight out in front of me. As a human, I didn't think he could see much in the shadowy darkness of the back seat, but his lingering gaze still made me squirm. I wasn't usually self-conscious about my shifted form, but suddenly I wanted to get in touch with the murderous dragon and book an appointment with his nail technician. If my hooves were buffed and shiny with a clear coat of polish, I might feel better about everyone looking at them.

"But you were limping."

"I messed up my ankle when I kicked the lock to break it."

At those words, everyone gasped.

"A lock?" Isaac asked.

I nodded. "They'd put me in a cage."

"Fucking Robbie," Hayden murmured.

I wasn't sure why he sounded so shocked and disturbed by the idea. He knew someone had held me against my will. What did he think they'd done to keep me there? Tell me to sit and stay like a dog? I was a faun, which meant I had some goat-like qualities. Determination was one of them, although my human dad had just called me stubborn. I wouldn't stay somewhere just because someone told me to.

"Hmm… I see…" Jeremy said eventually and made another note in his book. "That makes sense. Do you have a little loin cloth thing in your shifted form?"

Was he being serious? Or was he trying to lighten the mood? I glanced down. "Does it look like I'm wearing a loin cloth?"

"Levi told me he has a loin cloth, so I thought I'd ask," Jeremy said, sounding disappointed. "They could have taken it along with your shoes."

What had the dragon said about someone called Levi? I couldn't really remember. Now that I was reasonably safe, my energy was flagging. I didn't bother hiding my yawn when it hit me.

"Maybe ease up on the questions, Jer," Ash said from the front seat. "Ryley and Hayden have had quite a night. They're probably exhausted."

Jeremy let out a long sigh, but tucked his pen and notebook away.

A few minutes later, we passed a sign welcoming us to Willow Lake. No one spoke as Ash drove us through the deserted downtown streets before turning into a residential area. As we arrived at a regular-looking house on a regular-looking street, the garage door opened. Ash guided the vehicle right inside. As soon as the engine was off, the door slid down behind us, and a light came on.

A man in his pajamas approached us. He must have

been sleeping when they called to say they were bringing us to him. His hair was a wild mess of curls, and he had creases on his cheek from his pillow, like he'd fallen asleep while waiting for us to get here and had just woken up. Ash, Jeremy, and Isaac poured out of the vehicle, but Hayden and I stayed seated. The man leaned forward and peered through the passenger door window at Hayden.

"That's quite the shiner," the stranger said. Then he looked in the backseat at me. "Hi, you must be Ryley. I'm Xander."

"The doctor?" I eyed him, trying to figure out what kind of supe he was.

"You bet. At least until someone else wants to do it. Come inside and let's see what's going on." Xander motioned for me to exit the vehicle. "Come on, Hayden, you're coming too."

"I'm fine," Hayden muttered.

"We both know that isn't how this works," Xander said.

Suddenly it clicked. This guy was a sphinx shifter. I'd met a few when I lived with the herd. This guy wasn't like any of them, at least not a first blush. Most of them were so rigid and stiff they resembled that famous Egyptian statue.

Hayden huffed, but the doctor's gentle insistence got Hayden moving. As we walked into the house, Xander asked after Van. Ash filled him in on where the hellhound had gone.

"He's still out there?" His forehead creased, and he shook his head. "He might be a hellhound, but he isn't invincible. No one is, isn't that right, Alpha?"

Hayden scowled. "Not the alpha, Doc."

"Dillon and Adrian are with Van," Isaac said. He pulled out his phone and glanced at the screen. "They're supposed to let us know if they find anything. They checked in a few minutes ago with nothing new to report."

"Well, that's something, I suppose." Xander pursed his lips, but he didn't sound happy. He opened a door to a small exam room and motioned Hayden inside. The stubborn wolf didn't budge.

"Look at Ryley first," Hayden insisted.

No one was happy at his request, and I wondered about the whole alpha thing. Was he really the alpha here? If he was, the doctor should look at him first. I hated to think what would happen if the wound I'd given him got infected. I was used to supes being jerks, but I didn't need an angry mob of them coming after me with pitchforks.

"Make sure the alpha doesn't leave before I see him," Xander ordered the others before turning to me. "Let's check you over."

My medical went smoothly. The doctor was super friendly, and his bedside manner was excellent. He took swabs of the bite wounds, pictures of my chest, and measurements of my other injuries. He compared the lengths of my horns and my hooves, noting the differences. The worst of the damage came from when the bastards who'd stuck me in that damn cage had "taken samples" to see if they could sell bits of me on the magical black market. It was unsettling the shit people bought. Like, how could anyone truly believe a bear shifter's claw would protect them, or a succubus' tongue would make them more attractive? The wolves hadn't been impressed when I laughed at them for being deluded, because I was the least magical supe around. I was barely even a faun, something my old herd had reminded me of daily.

Unfortunately, they refused to take my word for it. They pinned me down and took hand-held cheese graters to my horns and hooves, while I'd let them know they were shit-snakes and swore to have the Eternal Magic curse them and their families. I just wished I could have carried through with the curse.

If I ever saw them again, their nuts were going to get up close and personal with my hooves. Their balls would swell up as big as Hayden's eye had, and it would be spectacular. They should consider themselves lucky I didn't have plans to take the damn grater to their family jewels. Sure, I'd thought about it, but I didn't think I could stomach touching those bastards there. And think of the mess. It'd be disgusting.

The doctor didn't mention finding Hayden's blood on my hoof, so hopefully there wasn't any. I didn't need him gathering evidence like that. I didn't want to end up in a supernatural prison for assaulting an alpha. He pressed here and there and everywhere as he assessed me for broken bones and such. In the end, he had me drink some kind of healing potion and asked me to shift a few times. By the time I was done, all the injuries were healed.

It was wonderful to be back in my human form again. My favorite burnt-orange T-shirt with the saying *This is not a red shirt* that I'd found at a Trekkie convention a few years ago had even survived the whole ordeal unscathed. Maybe it was a sign everything would be okay, like the Eternal Magic herself had declared I wasn't expendable. I sighed and stretched. Everything felt pretty good. Well, everything except my eyeglasses. The frame was bent and hadn't sat right on my face since they were damaged during my abduction. I pulled them off and tried to twist them into shape. It didn't work. Damn it. They felt all wrong. I'd have to buy another pair because I couldn't go without. My eyesight was amazing when I was shifted, but it sucked in my human form.

"Here, drink another of these," the doctor said, passing me a vial of the same elixir he had me drink before shifting. "It'll help replenish the magic you used when you shifted. And that's about all I can do for you. You'll want to eat lots of leafy greens over the next twenty-four hours, though, to bolster your magic a little more."

This time, when I drank down the potion, my nerves tingled as the magic zinged through me. In its wake, everything felt fan-frigging-tastic. My glasses weren't even bothering me as much as they had. "Do you sell that stuff? You'd make a killing."

"Nope. It's only administered under a doctor's supervision." Xander winked at me. He gave me funny little paper slippers to put over my socks since I didn't have shoes, and that was that.

Then it was Hayden's turn.

Hayden was in there a long time. When he and the doctor finally came out of the exam room, neither of them was smiling. The spot where I'd kicked him still looked messed up, although the swelling had gone down.

"I'll make up a bed," Xander was saying.

"He's staying?" Ash asked. He sounded shocked, and I

understood why. A shifter like Hayden shouldn't need medical supervision to recover from a little scrape.

"No, I'm not," Hayden argued. "I'm fine. It isn't the first time I've been knocked in the head."

Xander crossed his arms. "I have handcuffs for unruly patients. I will use them if I need to."

"Kinky," Isaac muttered, making Ash and Jeremy snicker.

"I'll rest better at home."

"Someone needs to be with you," Xander said, the first sign he was bending to Hayden's will.

I adjusted my glasses, then I stuck my hand up in the air like an eager child who knew the right answer to the teacher's question. "I'll do it."

Chapter Six

HAYDEN

Ryley's offer hung in the air between us.

Xander and I both looked at the faun. Before either of us could shoot him down, he stepped closer.

"What do I do?" Ryley asked. "Keep him awake or let him sleep? If he sleeps, do I need to wake him up every hour? Shine a light in his eyes to check his pupils? They are supposed to get bigger under the light, right? Or smaller? I can't remember. Do I need to make sure he's covered in ice to keep the swelling down?"

My head ached thinking about all the things he was mentioning. Wasn't it enough that he'd kicked me in the face? Did he have to sound so eager to torture me?

"That won't be necessary," Xander said. "He needs to rest, that's all. But if anything changes in his condition, bring him back here."

"We can all go back to the inn instead, if you prefer," Isaac offered.

Jeremy nodded. "Absolutely. I can text Jake and Gage and let them know. I know most wolves get weird about having strangers in their dens. Adrian doesn't, but he's never really had a den."

If I had to choose between having one person in my space versus going to the inn and having a whole horde of people staring at me and fussing over me, the choice was obvious. Like Jeremy said, I wasn't keen on having a stranger in my space, but it was the lesser of two evils.

"Ryley can come home with me," I blurted out. As soon as the words were out, reality struck. What was I thinking? Where would he sleep? We'd be tripping over one another in my trailer.

Before I could take back my offer, Ryley grinned and turned to the doctor. "Let's go over what I need to watch for again."

I rubbed the back of my neck. I should get us rooms at the Tarbeck Motel. Levi, who owned the place, and Simon, who worked security there, were a hell of a lot less nosy than the bunch at the Willow Lake Inn. Ryley and I could get adjoining rooms. Once he was sleeping, I could sneak out and meet up with Van and the others.

Isaac took me aside, while Ryley and Xander talked about me like I wasn't there. "Are you sure about this? Because I've already told Gage about Ryley, since I figured he'd need a place to stay and nowhere else has a vacancy. The Tarbeck is full for some kind of bear reunion."

"Bear reunion? Why did no one tell me?" Jeremy asked, whipping out his ever-present notebook again.

"Bears as in shifters or bears as in big hairy gay men? You know what, it doesn't matter. I'm there either way."

"Jeremy, maybe you should talk to Adrian first," Ash warned.

"It's for research," Jeremy said, like that was a valid excuse for wanting to ogle bears of either kind. "Who knows what I might find out? It might be exactly what I need for my next book. Oh, what do you think about a bear shifter falling for a regular old human bear? Can you imagine the sex? All those thick beefy limbs everywhere? Think about all the fur."

Xander cleared his throat, interrupting Jeremy's strange musings. "Ryley has my number. And, Hayden, don't make this difficult. You need the rest." I didn't know why he was so worked up about this. So what if my magic wasn't responding as quickly as it should? It would, it always did.

Before I knew it, Ash was dropping us off at my shop. When he questioned why I'd told him to go there instead of my house, I told him I had to grab my truck. Luckily, his hellhound mate wasn't there to hear my lie. But as he drove away, leaving me standing outside the garage with Ryley, I knew I'd made a horrible mistake. My concussion must have been as bad as Xander had made it sound, because I hadn't been thinking clearly when I agreed to this.

"Let's get your truck and get out of here," Ryley said, as he pushed his glasses up with one finger. He seemed to do that a lot. The glasses didn't look like they fit him very well, but maybe he liked them that way. "I'm wiped."

"Yeah," I said. "About that…"

"What?"

"This is where I live."

"Here? Where here?" Ryley eyed the storefront of my mechanic's shop. It was in better shape than the trailer out back, but even the shop was showing a bit of wear and tear. The paint was chipping, the sign was fading, and the window was cracked.

"I can take you to the inn," I offered. I could drop him off, then head straight out to find Van and the others. The perfect solution.

"Nope. We're doing this. I'm too tired to go anywhere else." He waved his hand through the air in an imperious gesture. "Take me to my room, Jeeves."

This was going to be a disaster.

I trudged around to the locked gate in the fence and punched in the code. Ryley was right on my heels as I walked through. The gate clanged shut behind us and the click told me the automatic lock had engaged. There was no backing out now.

The walk from one end of the yard to the other had never felt so long.

"Watch your step," I warned.

The yard light provided enough light that he shouldn't stumble into anything, but I didn't want the headache of having to take him back to Xander if he fell and hurt himself. My head ached enough already without suffering through another lecture from the doctor. I huffed out a sigh, recalling his reprimand when shifting hadn't fixed my ailments. I knew he meant well, but...

"You're strong, Hayden," Doc had said. "I can see that from the smoothness of your shift, but your magic levels are unbalanced. That's why it's taking longer for you to heal. Soon it'll impact other areas of your life too. Don't push this or you'll regret it. I'm not saying that to be an ass. I'm saying it because it's the truth."

"I'll eat a steak when I get home," I promised, knowing full well I didn't have any meat in my trailer and there were no stores open in Willow Lake at this time of night. But the hellhounds hadn't been around to hear my lie that time either.

Xander shook his head. "That won't cut it, I'm afraid. You haven't been looking after yourself. Your alpha energy has let you get away with the neglect longer than it would have if you were an average wolf shifter with average magic, but you've pushed it too far. There is still time to reverse this, but for tonight I'd like you to stay here."

And now, here I was, guiding a stranger to my den.

I should have stayed with Xander, just like one of those mysterious patients he housed on the second floor of his house, the ones no one ever talked about.

Was the Jahaller still up there? I bet he must be. I should have asked after him. After the neglect the small supe had suffered earlier this summer—again, all thanks to my brother—he would need the support of someone with alpha power. And if I could undo some of the damage Robbie caused, that'd be good. I needed to remember to ask Doc about him.

I supposed I would have seen the Jahaller if I'd stayed, but I was still glad I hadn't. And at least this way I'd be in my own bed tonight. I just wished I hadn't come home with a chaperone too.

Xander told me to come back in the morning so he could gauge my recovery, but I was banking on him forgetting that he wanted to see me again. The guy was a good doctor, but he was busy. He'd forget all about me once he started doing his rounds at the hospital or seeing patients. I wasn't dismissing his warnings. I would take care of it later, after I'd dealt with Robbie.

"Great place you've got here. Very, uh, used-car-lot chic," Ryley said. "It's like we're staying in a room at a theme park. It could be called Junkyard Jungle or Groovy Garage or Rusty Relaxation."

The trailer was unlocked, so I pulled open the door and stepped inside. To say I hadn't been expecting company was an understatement, but the place was reasonably tidy and in fair condition, considering its age. This wasn't a luxury motorhome like Gage used to call home. Mine was a regular trailer that had already been eight years old when I bought it twelve years ago. At the time, I hadn't expected to live in it this long, but I'd never needed more, so I'd never moved. It was functional. Sure, the place got a little cold in the winter. And most of the plastic fittings had become brittle and fragile in the last few years, so I'd either replaced them with duct tape or just gone without. But it worked for me.

Ryley came in behind me and shut the door.

I didn't look at him to gauge his reaction to the place. Instead, I went to the back of the trailer and grabbed two rolled up sleeping bags from a cubby under my bed. I'd never used them, so they should be clean enough. They might smell stale, but since he'd invited himself, he could take what I gave him. I set the bundles on the small kitchen counter before turning to the table. It hadn't been made into a bed since I bought the thing. I hoped nothing would break when I adjusted it.

"Can I help?"

"Just stay out of the way," I muttered. "Go have a shower or something. There is a clean towel on the rack over the toilet. Help yourself to whatever else you need."

"Tomorrow, can I borrow your phone again? I need to check on a couple of things."

"Where is yours?"

His face answered the question for me. Yeah. That had been a thoughtless thing to ask.

"Right. Of course. They took it." I scratched my cheek. Shit. I should have thought about him having a family or a mate. Of course they'd be worried. I didn't know why my chest tightened at the thought of Ryley having someone at home waiting for him. It must be empathy emanating from my alpha power or something. "Uh. Yeah. Did you need to call anyone tonight?"

He shook his head. "No, nothing like that. I just need to check my emails and things. Make sure the wolves didn't get into my bank accounts. It can wait. So, the shower is in there?" He motioned to the only interior door. "I've been dreaming about a shower for weeks."

"Yeah. Go ahead."

As soon as he disappeared into the closet-sized bathroom, I went hunting through my fridge for something to eat. As much as I tried to dismiss Doc's warning, it still rang in my ears. I scarfed down some leftover pepperoni pizza from the Flying Rowan, then I found a chunk of moldy cheese. How long had that been back there? I cut off the fuzzy green bit and downed what was left. None of that was ideal, but it was better than nothing. It also helped take my mind off Ryley being in my bathroom. Touching my things. Getting naked. Having hot water sluice over his skin. Using my soap all over his body. Drying his naked skin with my towels.

I was going to have to bleach them to get his scent out.

Shit. Was he going to be hungry, too? I opened my fridge again. As a faun, I suspected he'd need something green. I didn't have much in the way of vegetables. Would bread work? It was made from grains. The loaf was a couple of days old, but with a bunch of butter, it'd be edible.

When he stepped out of the bathroom, I pointed at the counter.

"There is bread there, if you want something. It isn't much, but it'll fill your stomach. Butter is in the fridge."

"Do you have peanut butter?"

I pointed at a cupboard. "Try in there."

If he wanted to eat, it was up to him to fix it. I wasn't catering to him.

But even as the thought hit me, the back of my neck started itching, as if I could feel my magic poke at me to step up and be a good alpha. It skittered along my spine, reminding me of all the times my parents had been disappointed in me. My father would not have approved of my interactions with Ryley so far. He'd always been determined to take care of everyone, treat everyone as a pack. And I did do that, usually.

I just…

Having him here, in my space, it was…

I wasn't the damn alpha. And no one was supposed to be here. It was my den. I never should have agreed to have him here.

Ignoring the impulse to jump in and prepare food for him, I turned my back to him to study the table. How did this work again? I flipped up the worn seat cushions to reveal the ledge where the table needed to fit. Right. I remembered how it worked now. A few minutes later, it was done. It looked damn uncomfortable, but it was a place to sleep. I grabbed one sleeping bag and shook it out. Then I tossed the other, still rolled up, to one end for Ryley to use as a pillow.

Done.

I looked around, expecting to find Ryley waiting impatiently, but he wasn't hovering at my side. I didn't remember hearing him go outside, so…

A soft snore made me spin toward my bed. Oh, fuck no. I stomped to the bed and found him tucked under *my* covers, with his damp head on *my* pillow, wearing one of *my* T-shirts. When had he gone digging through my stuff, and how hadn't I heard him?

My wolf instincts meant I was territorial. I normally heard every little thing, particularly in my den. The back of my neck should have bristled as soon as he tugged open the cupboard where I stored my clothes. My teeth should have snapped at him as soon as he touched my bed. My fucking bed. The heart of my den. But none of that had happened.

Was my magic absolutely FUBAR? Or was something else going on? It had to be my magic. I didn't want Doc to be right, but if he was, I needed to find Robbie and end this before anything more went wrong.

I cleared my throat to wake Ryley. Nothing.

I nudged him with my foot. Still nothing.

I poked him.

Finally, I grabbed his thin shoulder, which seemed so much smaller and more fragile now than it had when he'd been in his faun form, and shook him. Hard.

"Go away. Sleeping." He groaned and swatted half-heartedly at me. He pulled the blanket up higher and nuzzled into my pillow again.

Nope. That wasn't happening. He'd drool all over my pillow. And I didn't need his scent in my bed either.

Even if he smelled like something I wanted to lick.

Nope. He needed to get out of my bed. I whipped the blanket away and damn near swallowed my tongue. He wasn't wearing pants, but at least he wore boxers. Wait. Were those mine too?

What was even happening right now? Why was my wolf so calm?

He frowned and reached blindly for the blanket again.

"Out," I said.

"But I'm so comfy." He curled around my pillow.

"You aren't staying in my bed. Move."

But he was asleep again, making that cute little snuffling noise. He must be exhausted if he could drift off in the company of an angry alpha. I rubbed my aching head. All I wanted to do was crawl into bed and sleep, but I couldn't with him in there too.

Yes. The bed was big enough for both of us, but that wasn't the point.

I pried my pillow out of his arms. I shoved my hands under him and hauled him out of my bed. He hummed softly and pushed his face into my neck. His warm breath fluttered over my throat. The sensation tickled and teased my sensitive skin like a lover's caress.

Every part of my body was suddenly very aware of the man in my arms. I pressed my nose against his damp hair and breathed in until I could find his scent under the layers of my soap and shampoo.

I froze. What was I doing?

I carried him the couple of steps from my bed to the sleeping bags I'd put out for him. He didn't wake. Most shifters shared some traits with their natural animal counterpart. So, as a shifter who was like a goat, he should have bolted awake when he was being manhandled by someone who was essentially a predator. That he was still sound asleep must mean he trusted me to take care of him when he was vulnerable.

It had to be an alpha thing. Probably.

But now I felt even more responsible for him. Damn it. I stomped back to my bed and grabbed another sleeping bag from the cubbie. I threw it over him because I didn't see a way to wrangle him inside the zipped bag while he was sleeping. He hummed a contented sound and snuggled into the bundle I'd given him for a pillow.

Good. Done. It was time to sleep.

Except...

I'd planned to go out and help the others hunt for Robbie.

I checked my phone. Van knew I preferred phone calls to texts, but the bastard always texted anyway. I unlocked my phone. No new messages. Why was there no update yet? Had they found him? Or had he evaded them? The three out there had decent tracking skills, but I was better. If we were going to find Robbie, I needed to get out there. I had a duty to my... uh, neighbors.

I glanced at my bed. As tempting as it was, sleep wasn't happening tonight. I scrawled out a quick note for Ryley to find when he woke and set it on the counter by the sink where he'd left his glasses.

As soon as I opened the door, Ryley jolted upright.

"Where the fuck do you think you're going?"

Chapter Seven

RYLEY

The slippery sleeping bag that'd been covering me slithered to the floor and a gust of cool air from the open door rushed over my bare legs. I shivered. This was not how I wanted to wake up. Had I even grabbed more than ten minutes sleep?

I scowled at the damn wolf standing frozen in the open doorway.

"Well?" I demanded as I rubbed my eyes. I groped around for my glasses. Where had I left them? Ugh. I didn't have the energy for this.

"Go back to sleep," he said. "You're safe here."

"The doctor warned me you'd try something like this." I pointed toward the bed he'd been making up, but something wasn't right. I looked around. Hadn't I been sleeping in the bed over there? How had I ended up over here? He must have carried me here. Holy fuck a duckle. I must have been wiped right out if I hadn't felt him move me. I pointed to the bed he'd evicted me from. "Get your ass to bed."

"Just go back to sleep," Hayden said, easing the door shut a little, but not enough for it to snick closed. The bastard was still planning to escape and thought if he didn't have to touch the latch on the door, I wouldn't notice him leaving next time. "I'm right here. See?"

"No, I've changed my mind, don't go to bed," I said. "You should shower first. Then get in bed."

His jaw clenched. He really did have a nice jaw line, probably because he was always clenching his teeth. It was one of those chiseled ones I associated with human celebrities.

"Go on," I said, motioning to the bathroom. "Don't make me phone Xander."

His pale blue eyes narrowed. Then he walked into the bathroom without saying a word. As soon as he was out of sight, I got up and pulled the door closed all the way. I turned the lock, so he'd have one more obstacle to deal with before he could get out. I returned to the makeshift bed with the sleeping bags and pulled up the one that had dropped to the floor. Hayden's bed was a lot more comfortable, but it looked like I was stuck with this one for the night.

Whatever. I was tired enough I could sleep in the middle of a whole herd of flute playing fauns.

I listened to Hayden for a few minutes, relaxing only when I heard him turn the water on. Hopefully a warm shower would make him sleepy like it had me. It also wouldn't hurt him to clean up a bit. He needed someone to nag his ass if this was how he usually lived.

He certainly seemed fixated on getting back out to the woods, though—so fixated that it'd only be a matter of time before he tried to sneak out again. Thanks to the shifter side of my DNA, I remained alert for threats, even while asleep. He might have thought he could wait long enough for me to fall into a deep sleep so he could try his luck again, but that wouldn't work. With a smile on my face, I pulled the sleeping bag up to my ears and settled in for another nap.

I didn't know how long I was out for, but I was jolted from sleep to find Hayden with the exterior door open. Again.

"For fuck's sake," Hayden muttered. "You were sleeping."

I grinned at him.

"Go back to sleep," he said.

He looked better than he had before he'd gone into the bathroom. His face was clean of blood, and he'd changed out of his gore-stained shirt. This T-shirt fit snugly over his muscular body. Very nice indeed. And he'd traded his jeans for a fresh pair with fewer stains and holes. The coup de grâce, though? He smelled delicious.

I sighed. Yep. I'd been right. He cleaned up nicely.

"I'll be back in a bit."

"Nuh-uh." I shook my head and shoved off the sleeping bag. I looked around for my pants. Where had I put them? Oh, right. They were beside Hayden's bed.

"Where the fuck do you think you're going?" Hayden demanded when I walked toward his bed.

I laughed. "Hey, that's my line."

"You are not sleeping in my bed."

I ignored him and grabbed my pants. I didn't bother changing my shirt, or rather the T-shirt I'd borrowed from him. If we were going out to the woods again, it might help if I smelled a bit more like wolf and less like prey. I tugged on my pants. Damn it. I wished I had my shoes. I eyed Hayden's feet. He was wearing work boots, which I supposed was what he wore in his garage. An older, more worn-out pair of running shoes was in a pile in the corner by the bed. They'd be too big for me, but they'd be better than nothing. I reached for them.

"What are you doing?" Hayden demanded.

"If you are going, so am I." I pulled on one shoe and tightened the laces. I wiggled my toes. Yeah. Way too big. It was only a matter of time before I tripped over them and fell on my face. Oh well. I reached for the other one.

"No, you aren't."

"Yes." I shoved my foot in the shoe and tied it quickly before Hayden realized he could sprint to his truck and leave me in the dust. Instead, like a true gentleman, he waited for me to finish. He must have been exhausted to let the opportunity slip by, but weren't we all? I scrambled to my feet, ready to follow the ridiculous wolf wherever he thought he needed to go. A wave of dizziness whooshed over me. I reached for the countertop to steady myself and missed.

Oomph. *Thunk*. Ouch. Fucking shit weasel.

Hayden rushed over and kneeled at my side. "Are you okay? What happened?"

Instead of helping me off his linoleum floor, he pried open one of my eyelids so he could lean over and peer into it.

"What are you doing?" I swatted at him, and he let go of my eyelid.

"I was checking your pupils. I thought you might have some undiagnosed brain problem. And I heard something hit the cupboard. I thought it might have been your head."

"I'd roll my eyes, but you'd probably think I was having some other neurological issue. Do you know what to check for?"

He sat back. "They're supposed to react to light."

"In other words, you really don't know," I muttered. Yes, I was aware that I'd asked the doctor the same thing about Hayden's pupils. I shook out my hand. It smarted where I'd hit it against the cupboard, but I'd live. Then I held it out to him. "Help me up."

He did as I asked, getting to his feet and extending his hand. His hands were larger than mine, and stronger, too. I slipped my hand into his and shivered as his calluses rubbed over my smooth skin. The rough texture felt surprisingly reassuring, somehow. Strong hands like his would be good at keeping a person safe.

And I bet his hands would feel good in lots of different places.

As he hauled me to my feet, the way the muscles in his forearm tightened and flexed mesmerized me. I was such a sucker for a man's forearm. Honestly. Was there a porn channel dedicated to men rolling up their sleeves? If there was, Hayden should upload some videos. He'd make a killing.

Once on my feet, I swayed again. Most of the dizziness had passed, but I was still unsteady. That's what I got for not sleeping properly in weeks. And now this damn wolf was keeping me awake even longer.

Hayden's big hand cupped my elbow as he guided me to the closest seat, which happened to be his bed. He crouched in front of me. His wide shoulders filled the narrow walkway between the bathroom wall and the kitchen counter. His face was right in front of mine.

I couldn't help but look at him. Really look at him. The injury I'd given him earlier was mostly healed. The swelling had gone down and the mark where my hoof had cut through his skin was fading to a pale pink. Soon, that would be gone too.

And you know what?

He really was handsome, in a rugged way. Even back in the forest when he was grubby, I'd suspected he would be. I'd never been into those outdoorsy, build it, fix it, grease-under-their-nails men before. My typical dates were desk jockeys like me, but I could make an exception for this guy. We could have a little fling while I was here. Nothing permanent. Nothing serious. Just a bit of fun.

"Do I need to call Doc Roberts?" Hayden asked. A ripple of magic fluttered through the air, emanating from him. Everyone had called him alpha earlier, and I hadn't been sure what to think, but the alpha power he was throwing around right now confirmed it. Hayden was all alpha.

"I'm fine."

He raised an eyebrow.

"I'll be okay," I amended. "Nothing serious. I'm fine."

"Now I get why everyone was getting pissy with me

earlier when I said that," he muttered. His gaze caught on mine. "Can I touch you?"

"What?" I leaned away. "You want to feel me up? Now? I mean, sure, I might have possibly thought about having sex with you, but that's a weird way to ask."

Shouldn't he at least say he was attracted to me first? Something? We weren't hooking up in a bathroom stall at a club. We were in his bedroom, such that it was. Maybe he thought if he could jerk me off, I'd fall into a deeper sleep so he could finally sneak out.

"No," he said quickly, shaking his head. "Not like that. It's just that some people find comfort from my touch. Just to the back of your neck."

"Oh." I nodded. "I get it. Because you're the *alpha*."

He grimaced. "I'm not the alpha. I just…" He rubbed his forehead, like it held a genie who could magic up some other word. "Fine. I might have some alpha instincts. It is only temporary, until another person steps forward to be alpha."

I didn't think magic worked that way. The Eternal Magic didn't dole out power to people and take it back again when they said, "Thanks, but I'd rather not." I might only be a half-supe, and therefore not privy to all the insider knowledge, but as far as I knew, she didn't do refunds.

"So?" Hayden prodded.

"Yeah, sure. Why not?"

As Hayden rested one hand on my knee and reached for my neck with his other, my heart ticked a little faster. His rough fingertips slipped across the side of my neck, causing a wicked shiver to cascade through me. His mouth opened to reveal a sliver of his white teeth, and I wondered what they'd feel like pressed against my skin where he was touching me.

I shivered, but I wasn't sure why. Was I scared or turned on? Maybe a bit of both.

When Robbie had bitten me, I'd been horrified. But thankfully, the experience had been short-lived, and I'd survived worse torments in my old herd. So I wasn't fucked up over it, thank Magic, because I had better things to think about now, like those rumors about wolves being wickedly good fun in bed. All full of biting and knots and awesomeness. I'd never hooked up with a wolf before—I usually just stuck to humans who didn't have opinions about my hybrid genetics—but I was game to try almost anything once. And I knew, if Hayden bit me, it'd be everything I'd ever fantasized about.

His hand slid around until he cupped the back of my neck. He squeezed gently as he brought his forehead to mine. His scent was all around me. He was all I could see. He was only touching me in a few very PG places, but I could *feel* him everywhere.

His magic kicked up to the next gear.

Oh. That felt…

I couldn't think of the word. None of the ones flitting through my head were adequate to describe the sense of peace and belonging and wonder flowing through me.

My eyes fluttered shut as I leaned into him.

Chapter Eight

HAYDEN

My sex drive wasn't something I gave much thought to. Lots of men and women flirted with me and tried to get me into their beds, but I'd never been interested. They just wanted to get close to me because they thought I was Alpha with a capital A, and that equaled power and prestige.

I couldn't remember the last time I'd had sex or found someone interesting enough to want to get naked with them.

But right now? Listening to the sounds Ryley was making because my hands were on his body? My sex drive had gone from zero to sixty in record time. In a fair race, it would have beaten a Dodge Challenger SRT Demon 170, hands down.

As my alpha power flowed from me to him, I picked up more than he'd probably want me to see. Xander had warned I'd depleted my magic, but thankfully I still had enough to comfort Ryley. The alpha energy always had felt different, separate somehow, from my shifter magic, but I was choosing to pretend this magic was working because Xander was wrong.

And right now, my alpha energy was telling me Ryley was exhausted.

Because of course he was.

He'd been captured and caged and tortured. I didn't even know how long Robbie had held him prisoner, because I was an ass and hadn't asked. But I wouldn't remind Ryley of Robbie now, not when he was finally resting and relaxed again. There'd be time enough for that later when Van came to get his statement.

But I couldn't take him out to the woods with me tonight, not when he was like this. And he was being stubborn about me going on my own.

I inhaled deeply to settle my frustration before it could rise again. Robbie had been out there in those woods recently. He'd probably been out there since the attack on his pack lands. One more night wouldn't matter. But one night could make a world of difference to Ryley. He needed rest. He needed to let himself slip into a deep sleep, which I doubted he would if he thought I might sneak out again.

I waited for my wolf instincts to rebel and fight against the delay, but I was strangely content being here with Ryley. So it looked like we were staying here. With that decision made, I should get more comfortable. I moved my hand. Ryley whimpered and pushed into my touch.

My lust was about to spin out of control, but fuck. The sounds he was making were doing things to me.

"Let's get more comfortable, yeah?" I asked.

Ryley's eyelashes fluttered as he opened his eyes to look at me. I hadn't noticed how long his lashes were before. They looked so soft and made him look so innocent. But considering the bizarre and plentiful swear words he spewed and the other ways he behaved, I doubted he was as innocent as he appeared right now. But that look on his face? It inspired all kinds of wicked thoughts.

"You're trying to lull me to sleep so you can sneak out again." He frowned.

"I promise I won't go tonight," I said.

He narrowed his pretty hazel eyes as he studied me. Whatever he saw on my face convinced him of my sincerity. "Fine. I'll believe you. But can you keep doing whatever it is you're doing for a little longer? Right now, your touch has become one of my favorite things. It has even slipped ahead of my grandmother's black bean and chickpea salad, and that's saying something. You should see how much garlic she uses. It's one of the few things I miss about living with the herd."

My mouth twitched, and I was surprised that I wanted to smile. This man was doing strange things to me. That should concern me, but instead of picking him up and putting him back on the bed I'd made on the dining room table, I nodded at my bed. He needed sleep, and if my alpha power could do some good, he could have it. "Crawl up a little more. Get comfortable. I'll be right back."

I'd stay with him until he fell asleep, then I'd move over to the sleeping bags on the table.

First, though, I needed to know what Van discovered out there. I checked my phone and didn't see a damn thing.

I wished I could trust him to call me, but I couldn't. He liked to text, even when he knew I never checked my damn messages. Doc Roberts would have told him to let me rest, and Van wouldn't want to disobey the doctor, but he'd made a promise to me, too. So, yeah, he'd totally text and expect me to miss his message. That way, he could let himself believe he was listening to both of us.

But I wouldn't let him get away with that tonight.

I hated all the rings and beeps these irritating phones made, so I'd asked Buddy to turn them all to silent after I purchased this one. It was time to change that. Temporarily. Just so I didn't miss Van's text.

After an agonizing ten minutes, where I contemplated waking Ryley to help me, I finally found the volume settings for text notifications. In retrospect, I should have figured it out faster, but maybe it was time to admit, just to myself, that I was dead tired.

Ryley was curled on his side in the middle of my bed. His face was pressed into my pillow. I would say it was my favorite pillow, but that suggested I had more than one. My heart did a weird hiccup seeing this man in my bed for the second time in one night. He was cute, not handsome in a Hollywood way, or striking like those underwear models I used to admire when I was a teenager, but he was decidedly cute, with or without his glasses. Although, for some unknown reason, his spectacles made him even more appealing. Right now, though, he wasn't wearing them, and he was still… cute. Yes, I was overusing that word.

I just couldn't remember the last time I'd found someone attractive, and my brain wasn't used to thinking about shit like that. A lot of unusual things were happening tonight. Like me creeping on him while he was sleeping.

Since he was in the middle of the bed, it was tempting to crawl up next to him and wrap myself around him.

But, yeah...

Spooning a guy without his express consent was a terrible idea. I didn't want him to wake up and think I'd taken the opportunity to maul him while he'd been unaware and unable to stop me. I shook his foot to get his attention.

"Move over," I said.

He didn't move. Was he already sleeping again? I heaved out a sigh and eyed the makeshift bed on the converted dining room table. This was going to be a long night.

"Where are you going?" Ryley asked.

I turned back to find him sitting up. The hair on the side of his head was sticking up, and he was blinking sleepily at me.

"You said you'd work your alpha mojo some more. Or is it too much? Does it take a lot of magic?"

I thought about refusing him. I really did. It'd be easy to lie about the effort it took. But he looked so damn vulnerable. He plucked at every alpha instinct in me.

"Slide over," I whispered.

When he did, I turned out the light and joined him on the bed. He hummed happily and rolled toward me as soon as I stretched out beside him. My alpha power responded immediately, acting without me giving it any conscious thought. It wrapped around Ryley, who sighed and tucked himself tighter into my side. I tried my best to stay still. I didn't reach for him. I didn't hold him, although some strange wayward impulse inside me wanted to. Instead, I let my magic do all the touching it wanted. I just refused to let my arms get in on the action.

He was vulnerable right now. It would be too much like taking advantage of him. I wouldn't do that. Ever.

I stared at the seam in the ceiling above the bed so I wouldn't give in to temptation and stare at him some more. Instead, I listened to the steady hush of his breathing. I analyzed the nuances of his scent, identifying each distinct note and aroma. But what really captured my attention was counting how many places his body was touching mine.

Even when I sensed he'd finally fallen asleep, I didn't move. I stayed where I was, drawing his scent in, feeling the heat of his body against my side, listening to his breathing slow more and more as he sank deeper into his sleep.

Ever since I'd become an adult, I'd slept alone. I never stayed over at anyone's place. I never invited anyone to mine. This place was a dump, but it was my dump. My den. But it was unexpectedly calming to have a warm body pressed to my side. I didn't understand it, but the desire to protect and soothe this man was almost a physical thing.

It must have been because I was tired. I was letting my guard down. But I was done. Just for tonight, I'd take the comfort I found in holding him and let it wash over me. Through me. Let it sink into me. Just for tonight, I wouldn't have to be alone.

My eyelids drifted down, and sleep pulled me under.

A strange noise woke me. I jolted upright, sending Ryley, who'd been using my chest as a pillow, rolling away. Ryley's feet kicked out as he dropped over the edge of the mattress and whacked my knee.

We both cursed.

"Why are you always kicking me?" I rubbed my knee and peered at Ryley, who was crawling onto the bed.

"I was having such a good sleep," Ryley groaned.

The strange noise that had woken me pinged again.

What was that?

I looked at my phone and saw a light flashing. Right. The noise must mean I had a message. I got up and scooped up my phone from the counter. Sure enough, a text message notification popped up on the screen. I glanced at the time. It was already seven in the morning.

That couldn't be right. I never overslept. But now that I knew the time, I realized the trailer was brighter than it normally was when I got out of bed. The sun was definitely up. I tapped on the screen to open the message.

Van: Followed the trail as far as we could.
     Hit a dead end. Searched around to see
     if we could pick it up again. We didn't.
     Heading back now. Will come around to
     talk with you and the faun. Need to get
     his statement. Going to grab some
     sleep now.

I sat on the edge of the bed and stared at the screen. Damn it. I should have been out there. Van and the others were good, but I was the damn alpha. My wolf was inherently stronger than the others.

Wait. What the fuck?

I wasn't the damn alpha.

This shit was messing with my head. Maybe it was a good thing Van had texted instead of calling me. He'd have crowed like a rooster if he'd heard those words fall from my mouth.

"What's going on?" Ryley climbed onto the mattress and came up behind me to peer over my shoulder at my phone. I tilted it so he could see the message. After reading it, he flopped down on the mattress. "Well, fucker doodle do."

Yeah. I agreed completely.

Chapter Nine

RYLEY

After reading the message from Van, Hayden was as ornery as a wolf whose nose had been stung by a bee. I hopped into the bathroom to clean up before he did, because I knew the moment he was ready, he'd leave me behind if I wasn't ready at that exact moment, too.

I was still wearing the clothes and shoes I'd borrowed from Hayden last night. I wouldn't normally sleep fully dressed nor would I wear those same clothes the next day, but needs must. And speaking of needs, I also needed to check everything in my cloud, make sure my bank account was still secure, and find time to buy more clothes. None of that would be difficult. I just needed a computer.

Unfortunately, I doubted Hayden would stop long enough for me to sign in, let alone poke around and make sure everything was okay.

Although, wouldn't it be cool if when we found that asshole wolf, we found my stuff, too? It was wishful thinking, I know. But it *could* be in the bunker. I should have looked when I made my escape. That had been short-sighted of me.

Ha! Right! Like I would have wasted time wandering around down there. That would have just been begging to be caught again.

When we were in Hayden's truck, waiting for the electric gate to open so we could drive out of the secure parking lot, I chanced a glance in his direction. He looked a lot better than he had last night. His scar from my kick was almost gone, thank Magic. It was strange how long it'd taken. Was he ill? A spasm ran through my chest at the thought of him being sick. Despite having slept snuggled against him last night, I didn't know him, but my instincts told me the world would be worse off without him in it.

"What?" he asked gruffly, without looking at me.

"Can we stop for coffee? It can be to-go."

Hayden's mouth flattened in a line, but he didn't say no. When the gate was open wide enough for the truck to get through, he didn't waste time getting us out of there. I glanced over at the front of his shop, and I could see the *Open* sign lit up and the lights on inside.

"Do you have to work today?"

"Buddy can take care of things."

I frowned. Who was Buddy? His partner? I folded my arms over my chest as another weird ache shot through it. What was up with that? Maybe I was the one who was sick. Because what would it matter if Buddy was Hayden's partner, business or otherwise? I wasn't interested in having a relationship with Hayden, and nothing had happened between us. Except he shouldn't sleep in a bed with someone if he was involved with someone else.

Thankfully, nothing had happened between us. And nothing would, because I wasn't staying here long enough to get involved with him or anyone else. Sure, I'd thought about having a fling with him last night, but that was then. In the light of day, I knew better.

There were too many supes in this town for my comfort. It didn't matter that the ones I'd met so far seemed nice. I'd been around enough supes in my time to know better than to blindly trust them. As a hybrid faun, I didn't belong anywhere close to *real* supes. My herd had taught me that lesson well.

Hayden whipped the truck into an angled parking spot in front of a place called the Flying Rowan Café. He pointed at the place. "Coffee."

He was not a man of many words today.

I sighed. Why didn't this place have a drive-through lane? Hayden made no move to get out with me. So, it looked like this was where he planned to ditch me.

"Do you want anything?" I asked, as if I was unaware of his plan. I pushed the truck door open, then I paused. "Wait. I don't have any cash or cards."

I almost laughed as he grunted and yanked his keys from his ignition. He got out and slammed the door shut. Hayden marched to the door without saying a word. His body language, on the other hand, wasn't shy about letting the world know he was annoyed. Maybe some coffee would do him good, too. Put a little pep in his step. A jump in his rump. Some drive in his stride. Some gas in his ass.

What was I even saying right now? My brain was obviously dying from coffee withdrawal, because no one wanted gas in their ass, or a jump in their rump either, come to think of it. But it was excusable, right? It'd been ages since my last coffee, because Robbie and his asshole buddies hadn't come around with a coffee cart. They'd been terrible hosts.

"Alrighty then," I muttered. I hopped out and followed him into the diner.

Inside the exterior doors was a small entrance area with pictures of sunsets on the walls. Each featured a twisted rowan tree that appeared to have sprouted from pure rock. Considering the place was called the Flying Rowan, it made sense.

The diner itself was quirky. To the left was a dining area, with tables of different sizes in the middle and booths around the perimeter. The rowan theme continued here. A massive photo covered most of one wall. A sizeable bonsai version of the tree sat in one corner. It needed a trim; the branches and leaves were reaching out as if eager to poke someone's eyes out.

To the right was a counter where people clutching travel mugs queued for their morning fix of caffeine. I sensed at least half of them were supes. I didn't have the strongest senses in my human form, but the magic swirling around this place was almost a physical presence.

I fought the urge to turn around and run back to the truck. Too many supes in one place never boded well for me. But the decadent aroma of freshly brewed coffee kept me where I was. Damn it. My need for coffee was going to get me killed. I followed Hayden as closely as I could without tripping over his feet or bumping into his back, praying he'd shield me when, inevitably, someone decided the hybrid was an easy target.

When the people in the line saw Hayden, several ducked their heads and whispered, "Alpha." Each of the people who called him alpha waved to the space in front of them, offering their place in line to him. Hayden barely acknowledged them with a nod as he stomped to the back of the line. I followed. When Hayden pushed me in front of him, just like those other people had tried to do with him, a new energy filled the room. Everyone's attention was on us.

I edged back, closer to Hayden. I couldn't shake the feeling that if I stood close enough to him, I'd be safe. He didn't move away, thank Magic.

Suddenly, people were pulling their phones from wherever they'd stashed them—their pockets, their purses, their backpacks, and even their bras. And, just so you know, I hadn't needed to see a busty woman reach into her shirt and grope her boob until she finally pulled out a sweat-covered phone. Because eww...

I shuddered.

Suddenly, it was like we were celebrities being hunted down by paparazzi. Phones angled toward us. Flashes went off. Most of the people didn't even try to be sneaky as they snapped pictures of us.

This was not what I'd expected.

"Uh, Hayden?" I asked. "What's happening?"

"Ignore them," he muttered with a scowl.

Yeah. I didn't see how anyone could do that. I didn't want to give the rabid photographers a reason to turn on me, so I pushed down my apprehension. If I pretended everything was okay, I could trick them into believing it was true. At least until I had my coffee in my hand, and we could leave.

The vibe wasn't antagonistic, though. Nope. It was something else entirely. All these random people were happy to see Hayden with someone. If I showed them I was happy to be with him too, maybe that'd keep me in their good books.

I tilted my head at a jaunty angle and smiled. Everyone smiled back and encouraged me. Huh. Not the reaction I expected. I was tempted to test the waters by making a duck face. That's what celebrities always did, right? But I couldn't decide if I should keep facing the cameras or twist to look up at Hayden. If I did it right, made it look all lovey, they'd really lose their shit, including Hayden. The guy needed to loosen up. And would it hurt him to smile for the pictures? Just a little? I didn't want anyone to think I'd dragged him here under duress.

Hmm... Had I ever seen him smile? Sure, we hadn't met under the best circumstances, but I was certain I'd smiled since meeting him. And just like that, I had a new goal in life. I wanted to be responsible for Hayden smiling.

"Oh, for fuck's sake," Hayden muttered before I could make my duck face. Then, speaking louder, he said, "This is Ryley. He's new to town."

"He's wearing your shirt," someone from the front of the line said.

"He smells like you," someone else said.

"Is this a date? Or the morning after?" That person winked.

A large man in the middle of the line frowned.

Something about him screamed supernatural in a familiar way. My grandfather was buddies with a minotaur and this guy reminded me of him. Pops and his friend often got together to drink ouzo and reminisce about the old times. And by old times, I meant really old, like ancient. I was pretty sure my grandfather was already old when Homer walked the earth.

"Leave them alone," the minotaur barked out. The large man pointed at the two young cat shifters at the front of the line. "And Eli and Theo, pay attention. It's your turn. Get up to the counter or get out of the way."

"Oh, come on, Levi. You know Mama will want to know what's going on," one of them grumbled, but they still shuffled forward and placed their orders.

Hayden dipped his head in thanks to the large man after everyone spun to face the counter again.

When we climbed into the truck a few minutes later, I was drooling. The extra-large coffee with vanilla and hazelnut syrups and rich cream smelled amazing. The paper bag with my vegetarian breakfast burrito already had a greasy film seeping through from the melted cheese, and the icing on my cinnamon bun, which had its own little box, was so thick the box couldn't close. I didn't know what to devour first.

Hayden didn't have that problem. He'd finished his meat lover's breakfast bagel in the few steps it'd taken us to walk from the restaurant to the truck. That couldn't be good for his digestion. Then again, I doubted his plain, dark roast coffee—straight up, without any cream or flavoring, that coincidentally also smelled like misery— was good for his stomach either. Someone needed to invent a coffee syrup flavor called "raw meat" for predatory shifters everywhere. But now that I thought about it, there might be a bacon flavor, which could work in a pinch. I doubted Hayden was the only supe with a predatory alter ego in their shifted form, so maybe I'd suggest that to the barista when I was in there next.

If I ever went back, because I was leaving. Soon.

"Do you need anything else?" Hayden asked. I'd like to pretend he was being sweet, wanting to make sure I had everything I needed, but there was way too much attitude for that to be true.

"Nope," I said around a mouthful of my burrito. Holy Magic, was it good. The gooey, warm cheese was melted perfectly. I'd been too long without halfway decent food. The wolves kept me fed, but their idea of a meal had been mashed potatoes from a box. Weeks of exactly the same thing. If I never saw another mashed potato again, I'd be happy.

As soon as I was in the truck's cab, we were off again.

I expected Hayden to make for the outskirts of town, but he didn't. He turned a corner, then another, before he swung left into an angled parking stall in front of the police station. You wouldn't be able to do shit like that in the city. Crossing opposing traffic to park, even if there weren't any cars coming at us, wasn't really the done thing. Especially not in front of the place where police officers hung out.

I leaned forward and tucked a chunk of my sandwich in my mouth as I looked at the building. "What are we doing here?"

"*You* are making a statement about what happened to you."

"Hmm… And what about you?"

"That doesn't matter. Van needs your statement."

"Is Van even here now? Didn't his message say he was going to sleep?"

"So, talk to Dillon instead."

"Wasn't he out with Van all night too?"

"Ryley, get out of the truck."

I leaned back in my seat and took a sip of my sweet and milky elixir of life. "Nah. I'm good. Maybe later."

Hayden ground his teeth together. "Ryley…"

"We both know you're going out to hunt for that wolf. I'm not letting you go alone."

"I'm going to the garage."

Did he think I'd buy that lie? He could wear a neon sign over his head that said, "I'm lying," and be less obvious. Although his inability to lie was kind of sweet; it suggested he didn't do it much.

"Yeah. Of course you are," I said.

"Are you getting out?"

"Not yet. I need to finish my breakfast first. You know, since it's the most important meal of the day. You said you needed to go to work, so don't worry about me. I'll figure it out." I looked up and down the road for landmarks. "The garage is over there, right?"

"Right." Hayden's grip tightened on the steering wheel. He threw the truck into gear again and sped toward his garage. When he parked up, I made no move to get out. Hayden, on the other hand, tried to salvage his lie. "Well, I'll let you do your thing. I'll be inside if you need me."

"No worries." I waved him off.

He slowly climbed out of the truck and walked to the door. He looked over his shoulder at me, and I waved at him. You know, with how often the guy walked away from me, it was like he was trying to make sure I noticed his ass. And I had. It was a nice ass. I bet he did lots of squats to get a nice plump butt like that. Oh, the things I could do to it... I sighed as I watched him cross the sidewalk and open the door, because none of that was going to happen.

As soon as he was out of sight, I hopped out of the truck, which wasn't an easy task while balancing my hot coffee and my breakfast. I set everything in the back of the truck before climbing over the tailgate. I stretched out across the bed of the truck and wished I'd thought to grab a blanket to make it a little more comfortable.

Fauns had a reputation for not taking their responsibilities seriously, but I wasn't like most fauns. And I'd made a promise to the doctor to watch over the stubborn assed wolf. So that's what I was going to do.

It had nothing to do with the bizarre feeling I got when I was around Hayden. How could a stranger make someone feel warm and safe? I didn't know. But I couldn't shake the feeling that if I stuck close to him, nothing would happen to me, even in a town filled with supes. Nope. My decision to sneak into the bed of his truck had nothing to do with that at all.

A few minutes later, I heard the door to the garage open as I swallowed the last of my vegetarian sandwich. I stayed very still as footsteps neared the truck. Hayden muttered, "Thank fuck."

He climbed into the truck, then we were off again.

I needed to plan better if I was going to do this again. Drinking hot coffee while unable to sit up and being jostled around at the same time was awkward as hell. I should have picked up something with a straw.

And the dust. Ugh. Nope. I couldn't eat my cinnamon bun with all the dirt flying around. When was the last time Hayden washed this thing?

I frowned. He was such an ass, making me do this. I knew he hadn't told me to, and I knew he didn't know I was doing it, but this was all his fault.

I'd just finished the last of my coffee when he guided the truck to the side of the road. I sat up and pulled back the lid on my cinnamon bun. It would have been better if it was warmer, or if I could have taken my time, but it still tasted pretty good as I stuffed it in my face.

"No way. Seriously?" Hayden's window must have been open because I could hear him.

I turned around and, sure enough, there he was, twisted in his seat and staring at me. I grinned around a big bite and wiggled my fingers at him.

"What are you doing here?" A golden color flashed through his pale blue irises. That had to be his wolf pushing forward.

I held up my forefinger, in the universal sign of "give me a minute." I licked the last of the cream cheese icing from my fingers. Eating cinnamon buns was a messy business, but I refused to waste any of the yummy goodness. He watched me for a moment, before he cleared his throat and faced forward again, like he couldn't stand watching my tongue lap at my fingers.

"Parker put napkins in the bag," Hayden muttered.

"Sure, sure," I said. I turned my hand this way and that to make sure I got everything before I dug in the bag and pulled out a crumpled paper napkin. I wiped my hands and mouth quickly. "All done."

Hayden grunted, then he climbed out of the truck and slammed the door. Was he always this grumpy? Or was it something he saved for me?

Chapter Ten

HAYDEN

The image of Ryley sucking and licking his fingers was burned into my brain. It should have been disgusting, watching him take his tongue to his dirty hands. I should have told him to clean them on a napkin like an adult before his tongue had even touched his skin.

But I didn't, because…

I wiped my hands down my face.

He wasn't trying to be sexy. I knew that.

But, fuck.

I had to get control.

He'd pissed me off by tagging along, but then he'd gone and distracted me with all that *licking*. And now I couldn't think straight.

I needed to think about something else, like walking through the steps of rebuilding a V8. Instead, I gave my hard dick a squeeze through my jeans to get it under control. I jerked my hand away when I heard Ryley climb over the tailgate and jump down.

As soon as I saw him pop up in the back of my truck, I should have done a one-eighty and driven right back to Willow Lake, but I was so damn close to finding Robbie. I'd already put off coming out here for hours. I couldn't squander any more time.

I pinched my dick one last time and walked to the back of the truck where Ryley was standing. He smelled like sugar, cinnamon, and cream cheese. His lips looked sticky and wet, and he kept licking his tongue over them like he was determined to collect every insignificant speck of sugar.

Now my tongue wanted to slip out and see if he'd missed any.

I bit down on it instead.

Ryley pulled off his glasses and hung them from the collar of his shirt. I was about to ask what he was doing, but then his pupils changed into that weird square shape of his faun form. He didn't shift the rest of his body, just his eyes, and it was strange to see those eyes on a human face. But I'd done a little research last night when Ryley had been in with Doc, so I understood why he'd done it. Fauns were supposed to have excellent sight in their shifted form.

"The trail your friends followed is there." Ryley pointed at a patch of bent grass in the ditch.

I inhaled to confirm. "Yes."

"So, we're following it too? We'll go in there and see if we can pick up where they lost the scent."

"That's what I'm doing, but you're staying here," I said.

"Of course I'm not." He shook his head. "Don't you watch horror movies? You should never, ever separate from the people you're with."

"We aren't in a horror movie."

"No, this is worse."

I frowned. Because of course he was right. I couldn't leave him out here on his own. What if Robbie or one of Robbie's followers found him out here? He'd be vulnerable. We really should go back to town.

I stared longingly into the trees.

Robbie was out there somewhere. Right now. I was so damn close.

Ryley scanned the trees, too. "You told people we were coming out here, right?"

"Why?"

"Oh, for the love of Magic. You didn't, did you?" He rolled his eyes. Again. He did that a lot. "Robbie, or whatever his name is, comes out every day, first thing in the morning. Going out there with no backup plan is like delivering ourselves to him. We might as well put a red ribbon in my hair and call me a present."

And now I was imagining him as a present, waiting to be unwrapped.

What the fuck? I didn't lust after strangers. I didn't lust after anyone. I preferred it that way.

I also hated the idea of Ryley going anywhere near Robbie. But at least I understood *that* emotion; I was protective by nature. That was who I was. I'd feel the same about anyone from my pack—er, whatever.

"He won't touch you again. I promise." The words came out on a growl. "But I don't think it is safe for you to be out here, so just go back to town." I pushed my keys into his hand.

"No way," Ryley protested as he tossed the keys back at me. "I am coming with you. But you will also do the whole 'phone a friend' thing before we leave this road and lose cell service."

I scowled at him. Usually having an alpha scowl at a person was enough to make them cower and obey, but of course Ryley had to be different. He just stared right back at me. The seconds ticked by, becoming minutes. Why wouldn't he do as I wanted?

I didn't sense any discomfort from him, so maybe he wasn't uncomfortable about going into the woods with me. Besides, how much danger would he be in? I could take Robbie. I might not have sparred with him in over a decade, but Robbie had always been a lazy shit. From everything I'd heard from his former pack mates, he hadn't changed.

"Well?" Ryley said, challenging me.

I gritted my teeth but pulled out my phone. People rarely told me what to do. Most of them came to me, expecting me to tell *them* what to do, not the other way around. But here I was, texting—*texting*, for fuck's sake! —Van to let him know we were picking up where they'd left off last night, or earlier this morning, I guessed.

I sent the text and showed Ryley the screen, so he'd know I hadn't lied. When he nodded, I shoved my phone in my pocket.

"I'm shifting," I said. Without waiting for a reply, I transitioned into my wolf.

"I'm not." Ryley frowned at me. His pupils reverted to their human shape as he put his glasses on his face.

"Fine. Try to keep up."

I didn't have to look at him to know he was rolling his eyes at me again. I might be an ass, but it looked like we both knew I wouldn't leave him behind.

Chapter Eleven

HAYDEN

The trail Van and the others had followed was easy to find. Ryley's scent still lingered under the others. It'd been a long time since I'd gone for a run with someone else, not that we were running exactly. But having a bit of companionship while traipsing through the woods was surprisingly nice. Once upon a time, running with my pack had been one of my favorite things to do.

But I didn't have a pack anymore. By choice, *my* choice.

Van, the son of a bitch, always said I *did* have a pack, saying it included every damn supernatural in the town but that I was too stubborn to admit it. But that wasn't true, no matter what he believed, which he must have because hellhounds couldn't lie. So, that meant he was a deluded asshole. The bastard had even mangled a Shakespearian quote a few months back, saying, "The alpha 'doth protest too much.'"

But he was wrong.

I picked up the pace a little, eager to leave all those thoughts behind me. I was happy to proceed in silence, but then Ryley said, "So…"

He said nothing else, just the word "so." After a few minutes, when I didn't respond, he said it again. After a few more minutes, it happened again.

I spun around to look at him after the fourth time. "So what?"

His eyebrows rose. "I thought we should talk or something while we do this. But I didn't really know what to say."

"So you kept saying 'so'?"

He lifted his shoulders. "You could try being more approachable. And, besides, 'so' is a perfectly acceptable segue into conversation. Lots of people do it. It is a sign you want to talk."

"I am perfectly approachable. Ask anyone."

"Right. Sure. That whole growling thing you've got going on just screams 'talk to me'."

Gritting my teeth, I turned back to the trail. I was not biting back another growl. I didn't have a "whole growling thing", whatever that was.

"We did icebreakers at a conference I went to once. We could try that. Let me think." He adjusted his glasses. "Okay. Describe yourself in three words."

His question seemed simple enough, but it wasn't. It was something most people should be able to answer. But I didn't know where to begin. If other people were to describe me, they'd say leader, protector, and dutiful. Or something ridiculous like that. What else was there?

I could live with helpful. It seemed a bit like bragging, although I really did try to help the people in the community who were struggling. Knowledgeable about cars was more than one word, so Ryley would protest that. Same with reasonably priced. Which, now that I thought about it, was more about the garage than me.

What other word might work?

Lonely?

I shoved that one away. I wasn't lonely. I had tons of people around me, whenever I wanted, more than I wanted, honestly. Besides, that wasn't the type of thing you said to someone you just met.

That left me with only one word.

"No."

"Oh, come on. That's not an adjective. Although I could see how it is a reflection on your personality."

I circled around and nipped at the back of his calf.

"Hey! Be nice." Ryley laughed and swatted at my nose.

"*You* weren't being nice."

"How about this one? What are five things that make you happy?"

My first thought was Willow Lake: the people, the place, the everything. But that sounded too much like what an alpha would say. What else was there? "I like when my tools are organized."

Ryley let out a weird honking noise like a buzzer on a game show. "Nope. That's not happiness. That's being a perfectionist or someone with OCD or something. We're looking for pure happiness."

"Okay, then. What makes *you* happy?" If it was so easy, let *him* answer.

He waggled his finger at me. "I see what you're doing, but fine." He twisted his mouth around as he thought. "I always feel happy when I get a long sleep. You know the type of sleep where you wake up and look around like you don't have any idea where you are because you were so zonked out. I love that feeling. I am happy when I walk home through the park and the place is busy with people laughing and smiling and playing. The energy can be invigorating. I'm happy when I discover a new show, especially if there are a bunch of episodes I can binge. But I can re-watch my faves and be happy too. I love getting lost in a good storyline. I am happy when I'm in a wide-open field with a blue sky overhead and no one else around for miles. Some people like looking out from a hiding place in the woods, but not me. I need space. And let's see, what else?" He tapped his chin. "How many was that? I think I only have one left. I am happy when I climb into a freshly made bed with crisp clean bedding. There. That wasn't so hard. Oh, and I am thrilled when a client loves what I've done for them. Custom websites that are complicated are the best, but graphic design is fun too. That one is work-related, though, so I'll understand if you don't want to count it."

His answers didn't sound like real happiness to me. After all, could anyone feel pure, unmitigated joy binge-watching a show? But whatever. I also noticed he didn't talk about family or friends, and I wondered if one of his three words to describe himself would be "lonely" too. That thought sent a pang through my chest.

"Why work with computers?" I suspected Ryley was about my age, but most supes, regardless of age, shied away from technology. I wasn't even all that old by supe standards, and I hated the stuff. Technology was an aggravating tool, nothing more.

Ryley rolled his shoulder in a casual shrug. "It is decent money and there is always something new to learn."

The way he spoke suggested that was his easy answer, but not the complete one. But I didn't pry. If I pried, he might think I owed him reciprocal answers to whatever question he dreamed up. I'd gotten so used to people always knowing about me and my business, it was strange to realize I was a blank slate with Ryley.

Sure, he'd heard the others call me their alpha, but he didn't know the history. He didn't know how badly I'd fucked up in the past. It was oddly liberating. And I rather liked the anonymity. Ryley would only know what I shared with him. He'd only judge me on what information I gave him.

Although, admittedly, I hadn't tried to make a very good impression on him so far, so maybe that wasn't the best idea either. But if one person saw how unsuited I was to be the alpha, it could open other people's eyes, and they'd see the same thing.

"So..." Ryley said after a few minutes.

I huffed. Because, really? We were back to that?

"What about you?" Ryley asked.

Well, what do you know? He could actually follow the word "so" with other words. I should give him a prize.

"What about me what?"

"You know, what makes you happy? Besides your tools."

I wasn't sure what it said about me and the people I associated with, but the word *tools* triggered some kind of strange word association. If it'd been Isaac saying that to, well, anyone, he would have made the word *tools* sound like a dirty joke. Whereas Parker, if he was talking to Levi, would have said it suggestively too, but in such a way that you knew he was flirting with the big minotaur. I didn't detect any alternative meaning in Ryley's use of the word.

Maybe he wasn't good at flirting. Or maybe he wasn't interested in me.

Not that I wanted him to be. I didn't do relationships or one-night stands or anything, really.

"I'm happy when people don't ask me useless questions," I muttered.

"Ouch," he said. He was smiling, though, so I didn't think he was bothered by my answer. In fact, I thought he might be trying to stop himself from laughing at me.

I ignored him and sniffed the ground.

"What?"

"The scent trail ends here."

"Here?" Ryley looked around, as if suddenly remembering why we were taking this trek through the forest. "That's not right. This isn't the place."

Until now, Ryley's scent had been strong enough to follow, and I'd ignored the other scents in the area. Now, though, I inhaled deeply. Van, Adrian, and Dillon had separated here. They'd each gone in a different direction, presumably to find Ryley's scent again. I'd been with them on enough searches to know Van would have had them running along a grid-like pattern, but that hadn't worked.

So what had they missed?

Chapter Twelve

HAYDEN

Lifting my nose, I pulled as much of the peaty forest air into my lungs as I could. I didn't scent or hear moving water, so Ryley's old scent trail hadn't been swept away. What had happened? The answer was here. I just had to find it.

"What are you doing?"

"Shut up," I said. "I need to concentrate."

Ryley grunted but otherwise stayed silent. I drew in another breath. The rich scent of damp earth and dying vegetation was the strongest, so I pulled it away from the rest. I stripped away Van's scent, then Dillon's, then Adrian's.

Ryley's wasn't there, except it was?

My nose twitched. I sneezed. And again.

"There is magic here." I looked at Ryley. "Your magic and a hint of your blood, too."

"My what?" He lifted his eyebrows. "Did you say magic?"

Was his surprise real? Or was he mocking me? I couldn't detect falsehoods in what people said like the hellhounds could, but my wolf's instincts were pretty good at detecting lies all the same. I watched Ryley, looking for signs of deception. His skin didn't grow damp with sweat, and his gaze didn't dart around like he wanted to hide. And most importantly, he didn't smell like the cloying scent I always associated with deceit.

"You sound surprised," I said finally.

"You've been sniffing the ground for a while now. I think you've snorted something that's made you high." He glanced around the area, as if looking for the plant.

"I'm not drugged," I said. "I just don't get why you're surprised. You're a shifter. Of course you have magic."

"I change into a faun. Nothing more. That's it."

"Fauns are an ancient supernatural race. The older the race, the closer those shifters are to the Eternal Magic."

"Someone's been googling," he said.

"I may have looked up some stuff on Supenet when you were seeing Doc," I admitted. Supenet was a section of the internet dedicated to supernatural beings. I didn't know how they kept mundane humans out of it, but it seemed to work. Thankfully, it was easy to use, or I wouldn't know anything about his kind.

"Listen, I might look like a faun, but I don't have their magic, okay?" His cheeks darkened. He tugged off his glasses and started cleaning them on the hem of his shirt. "My dad was a mundane, so my genetic makeup is pretty watered down."

"Why would you think that? Supes mate with humans all the time."

"And magic is dying," Ryley said. "There are too many mundanes in the gene pool, it's getting diluted. I'm a prime example of everything that's wrong with the magical world."

It sounded like he'd heard that bullshit so many times he believed it. Someone had lied to him about his own magic. I hated how many bigots there were in the world. I wished supes weren't like that. We were so much stronger together. But even my asshole brother thought there was a hierarchy of supes with wolf shifters at the top. He was wrong for thinking that, but he'd have spread those same lies about bloodlines and gene pools.

I doubted I could change Ryley's mind in one conversation, but I had to try.

"That's a lie. As long as one parent is a supe, the child will be a supe too. Science has proven it."

Ryley crossed his arms over his chest. "Sure. But I'm weaker. My senses aren't as strong. I don't have magic."

"Being able to shift is magic."

He waved his hand through the air, as if to wipe away what I said. "You know what I mean."

I didn't, but what else could I say? "What type of magic do full-bred fauns have?"

"I know what you're doing." He frowned. "You're trying to find out what magics other fauns can do so you can attribute this, whatever this is, to my imaginary magic."

"Humor me."

He tapped his foot. I was still in my wolf form, so he

was taller than me. The perfect height for him to stare down at me. I wasn't intimidated. How could I be when he looked so…

I didn't need to think about him being cute or adorable. Nope. Those thoughts needed to shut the fuck up.

I waited.

"Ugh. Fine," he bit out.

His face was flushed, and I suspected he was angry about things that had nothing to do with me. Still, I hated how uncomfortable I'd made him. I had the urge to tell him it didn't matter. That I didn't need to know. That I could look it up on Supenet later.

Except it *did* matter.

If we were going to get any closer to Robbie today, I needed to know. Now. And it would be a hell of a lot faster if Ryley talked to me. It had nothing at all to do with me hating Supenet. Sure, the creators tried to make it foolproof since I wasn't the only technophobe in the supe world, but it still took me a ridiculous amount of time to unearth answers. I'd only found the most basic listing about fauns, which is why I didn't know much about their magic. I hadn't gotten that far.

"Fauns are musical. That whole flute playing thing? That's true for the purebreds, while I can't play a flute to save my life. But fauns are mostly known for their relationship with the natural world. Fauns can feel if the earth is damaged or thriving. My mother described it as a visceral sense of knowing, deep inside where their magic lives, whatever that means. They have a profound connection to nature in other ways too. You don't want to play hide and seek with other fauns in the forest, believe me. Those bastards can hide like no one else."

And there it was, the answer, even if Ryley didn't realize it. I also had an answer to my earlier unspoken question about his interest in technology. He'd turned his back on his magic and found a career in something as far away from nature as he could.

But for now, the important thing was that whole connection-to-nature bit he mentioned. I wanted to explore that a little more, but Ryley was still talking.

"When I was about six, the elders took me on a hike. It was just after my dad died from a sudden cardiac arrest, so I thought they were being nice, trying to cheer me up. Then they all just disappeared, and it was like the trail vanished right along with them. Later, they said it was a rite of passage that every faun had to go through at that age, but I was lost out there for days. Needless to say, I did not pass their test." He wrapped his arms around his stomach and slumped forward a little.

My wolf bristled at the thought of adults abandoning a grieving child in the woods. Who would pull shit like that? He could have died out there from exposure or an animal attack or so many other things. Those elders needed to be locked up. Then the SC needed to investigate the rest of them, expose their archaic traditions and narrow-minded beliefs, and drag them into the twenty-first century. Fewer and fewer supes were born each year and there was a group of assholes out there torturing the ones they were blessed with.

"Can we forget I said that last bit? But, yeah, that's what fauns do."

I wanted to ask more questions. I wanted details. I wanted names. But this wasn't the time or the place.

"So," I said.

Ryley pointed at me and shouted, "Ha!" He even managed a small smile. I regretted using that word, but making him smile, even a little after he'd seemed so dejected, did something to me. My stomach felt lighter. My skin felt warmer. I scrambled to finish my thoughts. "When a faun is in the forest and wants to hide, what happens?"

"How should I know? They just…" He lifted his hands and made a gesture that looked like something exploding. "Poof. Disappear. Vanish."

"Because the forest responds to their magic."

"Yeah. I guess."

I stared at him. He stared right back at me.

"No way." He waved to the forest. "I didn't do this."

"We can ask Van about your magic when we get back to Willow Lake, but bear with me for a minute."

Ryley's brow furrowed. "What's he got to do with anything?"

"Hellhounds can identify other people's magic. They can tell how strong it is."

He scoffed.

"In the meantime, humor me. Walk ahead of me a bit. Go that way." I pointed with my snout. It was a little further from where we'd stopped, but along the same trajectory as what we had been walking. I thought it would be good to move away from where so many people had been trampling through the underbrush. "Then shift. I want you to open your senses and see if you can detect anything useful."

He sighed like this was a huge inconvenience. He stomped a few feet ahead of me, muttering the whole way. He hooked his glasses on his shirt collar. A moment later, he was standing in front of me in his shifted form.

When I'd first seen him as a faun last night, we'd been in the shadows of a starlit forest. With my wolf's senses, I'd seen him well enough, but the darkness had obscured the subtle tones of his fur. I wasn't a poet, so I'd normally describe his fur as tan or beige, but there was so much more to it than that. It ranged from the color of sweet honey to the soft hue of sun-drenched sandstone.

Last night, I also hadn't seen him shift, so I hadn't noticed the smaller differences between his two forms. I saw everything this time as he transitioned right in front of me in the daylight. His torso was slim in both forms, but it appeared more toned when he was a faun. I wished I could stare at him longer to catalog all the minor differences, but he crossed his arms over his bare chest and gritted his teeth. He was uncomfortable and a touch angry with me. I doubted he'd just stand there and let me look at him.

"I don't feel anything. Are you satisfied now?"

Of course he didn't. He wouldn't feel a damn thing with that attitude. I approached him slowly. The last thing I needed was for him to kick me in the head again. I leaned against his side and sent out a wave of my alpha power to him. It took a moment for him to relax, but eventually, the tension eased from his body. His hand came to rest on my head. His fingers combed through my fur, like he was petting me. I didn't stop him because the action seemed to relax him.

Really.

That was the only reason.

"Now close your eyes."

His fingers tightened on my fur for a moment before they relaxed again.

I'd never tried to help someone connect with their magic like this before, but I remembered my dad doing this for me. Maybe every shifter had to be talked through this when they were first learning about magic and how to shift. Some of it was innate, which was how Ryley knew how to shift, but some connections to the Eternal Magic needed to be nurtured. If Ryley's parents had decided he wouldn't have a strong affinity for magic before he'd been given the chance to find out, they could have unwittingly stifled it.

It made me wonder how many other people were cheated out of their magic this way. Maybe magic wasn't fading from the earth, maybe people were just being trained to ignore it. Although that wasn't the full answer either, because look at Jake. He hadn't even known magic existed and yet his powers still pushed to be set free. Still, I couldn't help but think there was something there, but I didn't have time to think about it right now.

"Breathe in deeply. Now, let it out slowly." I spoke quietly. "And again. Deep breath in. Then out."

I didn't rush. That would defeat the purpose. So we stood in silence and simply breathed for a few minutes.

"Now, I want you to reach deep inside…" I almost said *where your magic lives* except that'd trigger him and make him tense up again. So instead, I focused on the magical part of himself he did acknowledge. "Go to the place that warms when you shift."

He swallowed hard, but he didn't protest or pull away.

"Now slowly brush against it with your mind. See how it responds? Feel how warm it is? How welcoming?"

His fingers spasmed against my fur again.

"Gently coax that feeling forward until it fills your chest." I paused to give him time to do as I suggested. "Let it spread down your legs, into your arms, and up the back of your neck." I spoke slowly, guiding him through each step. "Now your fingers and toes are getting tingly as it flows through them. Don't resist. Just let it happen. Let the feeling drip from your fingers into the forest. Feel it fan out from your toes. As the feeling expands, take another deep breath and let it go. Let it all go."

His breath hitched. I scented tears in the air. He was gripping my fur hard now.

Something was happening.

Chapter Thirteen

HAYDEN

"Do you feel it? Do you feel the forest? Do you feel how familiar it is?" I whispered, needing to keep him focused.

Ryley let out a shuddering exhale. His eyes fluttered open. He swayed, and I leaned in closer to steady him.

"Fuck me," he said in wonder. "That's… I'm… But…"

"Do you feel your magic in the forest now?"

"Yes, but I don't understand."

"Can you sense where you walked? Can you follow the trail?"

"I think I can," Ryley said with a shaky voice. "But how is this possible?"

If he started asking those questions, he was going to lose the fragile connection he'd made.

"Point in the direction," I said.

Thankfully, he didn't argue with me. He pointed toward the northwest.

"Good," I said. "Do you think you can hold on to that feeling?"

"I don't know. I don't know how I'm doing this to begin with."

"That's fine. Just try it. If it doesn't work, we'll try something else."

He scanned the forest like he was seeing trees for the first time in his life. "This is so messed up. It's like I can see things I've never seen before."

"I think you could always see them," I said. "You were just taught to ignore them."

Ryley pressed his lips together but didn't disagree.

"Let's see what we find over here, shall we?"

We walked in silence for a bit, then Ryley stopped abruptly. He clenched his hand into a fist. "I lost it. I knew it wouldn't last."

And that was why it hadn't lasted. The brain was a powerful thing. I sighed. "Let's try again."

He shook his head. "I'm done. My head is swimming."

I wanted to demand he try again, but if I pushed him, I suspected he'd just dig in his hooves. So I lifted my head and inhaled, looking for new clues while he calmed down. Ryley's scent was still masked, but there was something more. Robbie. My brother had been through here recently. He might even be here right now.

My heart thundered in my chest. This was it. I'd finally put an end to all the problems my brother had caused. I'd finally confront him. Stop him. Turn him in to the Supernatural Council.

"Stay here," I whispered. "Hide. Better yet, go back to the truck. Call Van."

I tacked on that last bit about Van because I figured that was the only way I'd get Ryley to leave without me. His gaze snapped to me.

"Is he here?" Ryley asked, way too loudly. So much for the element of surprise.

"Be quiet!"

He clamped his hand over his mouth. His gaze darted over the woods, jumping from one shadow to the next. His chest rose and fell rapidly as his breathing quickened. At this rate, he'd pass out from panic before he escaped.

Fauns were similar to goats. So, were fainting fauns a thing? Buddy loved watching those fainting goat videos on his breaks. They made him laugh his ass off. I'd even chuckled at a few too, but I wasn't laughing right now.

"Ryley, you're safe. I won't let him touch you." I imbued as much conviction as I could into my voice. My alpha energy surged, and I didn't shy away from it. He needed to know I was serious. Confident. If Ryley was part of my pack, it would have been enough. But I wasn't sure if it would work on him.

He whimpered and crouched beside me. His head was still whipping around as he scanned the area for Robbie. His fingers clutched at my fur, pinching and pulling it. I could have done without that, but the sting of pain heightened my alertness.

I strained my ears to pick up any new sounds. Given how Ryley was panting beside me, it wasn't easy.

"Stay here. I'll check things out."

"Fuck no," Ryley whispered frantically. "I knew we should have waited, but oh no, Mr. Lonewolf had to—"

"Ryley?"

"Hmm?"

"Shut up."

He scowled at me, but at least the first blush of his panic was fading. As I stepped forward, I expected Ryley to let go of me. He didn't. He crept along beside me with his fingers tangled in my fur.

Every few steps, I stopped to listen and sniff the air. Robbie's scent was fresh. He'd been through here this morning, but not within the last half hour. He must have discovered Ryley was missing and tried to find him. The question now was: Was he still here?

I fucking hoped so.

We made slow but steady progress. Ryley's panic was still riding him hard, but he had it under control. So, when he tugged at my fur, I stopped and assessed the area again. What had he seen?

As if hearing my unspoken question, he lifted a shaking hand and pointed at a dip in the forest floor where the fallen leaves were disturbed. I inched forward.

There was a trapdoor. In the forest. That didn't belong out here. The disturbed ground suggested a screen of broken twigs, dirt, and pine cones usually concealed the trapdoor. The door would likely have remained hidden if the area around it hadn't been cleared.

Why was I surprised? I'd known there wasn't another building out here and I couldn't imagine Robbie roughing it in the trees. An underground den made sense.

The bigger question was: How the hell had I missed it before now?

My heartbeat ticked up to a faster tempo. I tried to shake Ryley's hand off, but he refused to let go. Fine. It looked like we were doing this together. I crept around the door in a wide circle, hunting for signs of booby traps. The concentration of Robbie's scent led away from the door.

I wanted to follow it. Desperately.

Except, what if more people were trapped in there?

Damn it.

I circled the door again, this time drawing closer. I didn't find any traps. Either he was arrogant enough to think he didn't need any, or I'd find something under that door. I sniffed and listened for a long time before I finally shifted into my human form, bringing with it my clothing, and more importantly my phone.

"I don't sense any other wolves close. Robbie was here, but he isn't now."

"Are you sure?" Ryley's gaze darted around the area.

"I'm sure."

Surprisingly, my phone showed a signal. Sure, it was weak, but it was still there. I motioned Ryley over and handed him my phone.

"Can you do another tack on a map thing for Van?" I whispered.

"A pin?"

"Whatever. It looks like a tack." Then I remembered his request from last night. "Shit. You wanted to borrow my phone this morning. I forgot."

"It's fine. I'll do it later." Ryley did something on my phone and handed it back. I tucked it into my pocket again. I looked at him. He was eyeing the door warily.

"You don't have to come." I reached for my phone again, then held it out for him. "Take this."

He shook his head. "We're a team. Besides, I got out once. I can do it again if I have to."

I didn't want to waste time arguing with him, but everything in me was protesting the idea of him going back to the place where he'd been imprisoned. Yes, he was an adult. He could decide. But, man, I wished I could convince him to do what I wanted. It'd be for his own good. He'd be safer up here. He had the forest all around him if he needed to escape. Now that he knew how to access his magic, he could hide if he needed to.

But I wasn't surprised when he wouldn't listen to me.

I shoved my phone in my pocket again, then I wrapped my hand around the cool metal handle. I expected a lock, or at the very least, a latch. There was nothing. The door lifted easily and silently. I peered into the cylindrical hole. It reminded me of a root cellar we used to have at the old pack house years ago. I bet that was where Robbie had gotten the idea.

A large, corrugated metal culvert had been stuck in the ground vertically with a ladder fixed to the side. The hole was deeper than the average basement, so I couldn't see much at the bottom. This bunker must have been out here for years, because the land showed no signs of construction.

Ryley stood at my side and peered into the hole too.

"Yep. That's the place." He shuddered. "That's where I was held."

I wanted to hold him close. I wanted to pick him up and carry him away from here. I wanted to protect him from whatever was down there.

Instead, I asked, "What can you tell me about it?"

"I didn't spend time sightseeing. I looked for a way out and took it."

"So more than just the one room?"

He nodded. "Yeah. There are a bunch of tunnels. Only an ant or a gopher could make sense of the place."

Great. Well, there was no time like the present to go get lost in a maze. "Shall we?"

Ryley blinked at me. "Shouldn't we wait for the others?"

"I'm going in."

"I knew you were going to say that." He heaved out what sounded like an aggrieved sigh and let his shift wash over him.

I lifted an eyebrow. Most supes preferred to stay in their shifted forms if they were scared.

"It's easier to go down a ladder when you don't have hooves."

Right. That made sense. "I'll go first."

Ryley grabbed my forearm. His fingers dug into my skin. I looked at him, surprised.

"Just... Just be careful."

I nodded. "You too."

I wanted to comfort him. Offer him anything I could to show him I'd do anything to keep him safe. The best way to do that was to use my alpha power. Again. It'd be for a good cause.

It was weird how the one thing I'd wanted to get rid of for most of my life was the one thing I wanted to give Ryley over and over again.

Chapter Fourteen

RYLEY

Hayden went to put his hand on my neck again, but I swatted it away. I didn't want to be lulled into a feeling of safety and security. I was *not* safe or secure, and I needed all my senses so I could protect myself.

He pressed his lips together but dropped his hand.

My heart was pounding a bazillion times a minute. The last time I'd been in this tunnel system, I swore I'd never go back, that I'd die fighting anyone who tried to make me. And yet, here I was, less than twenty-four hours later, traipsing through the door like I was an eager guest with an embossed invitation.

Reckless. That was the only word for it.

Still, I followed Hayden into the hole in the ground like I wasn't living through my worst nightmare. I left the hatch open. It was our means of escape, and I didn't want anything blocking it. Lights flickered on as we neared the bottom of the ladder, and I figured they were motion-activated because they'd done the same thing when I broke free of my cage last night.

As soon as my feet were on the ground and the tunnel walls were pressing in all around me, I regretted all my life choices that'd led to this moment. Okay. Maybe not *all* my decisions. I didn't regret leaving my herd. But I absolutely regretted not rolling over in Hayden's bed this morning and letting him come out here on his own.

What had I been thinking? I was a faun. We weren't known for our heroics. My kind also weren't meant to live underground. We were a one-hundred-percent above-ground kind of being.

I shifted into my faun form to give myself a little more strength, but even that didn't give me a lot of comfort. My shifted form didn't come with armor. My bare-assed chest was very vulnerable to bullets and bites and knives of all kinds.

I eyed the ladder going up to the surface. I could be up those rungs in a matter of minutes and run back to the truck, like Hayden had suggested. From there, I could call Van and let him deal with Hayden's single-minded and foolish quest to confront Robbie.

Yeah. But I wouldn't do that, would I? Because that'd mean going out there into the woods. Alone. Again.

Van could already be on his way. He seemed like the guy who'd come running as soon as he opened the text I'd sent him marking our location. Of course he would, and he'd bring the rest of his merry little gang, too. Because, unlike me, Hayden had people who seemed to care where he was and what he was doing. I just had to stick close to him until they arrived. So, I crossed my fingers and hoped for the best. Out of the corner of my eye, a shadow flickered up by the ceiling. I scanned the tunnel, but everything was quiet and still.

"What?" Hayden asked.

"Did you see that? Something moved?"

Hayden shook his head and scanned the ceiling. "What did it look like?"

Great. Now I was imagining things. This place was messing with my head. "I guess it was nothing."

"But it might not be," Hayden said, looking around for threats again. Nothing appeared. "I smell..." He hesitated, like he wasn't sure if he should finish his thought. "Death."

Yeah. That wasn't a troubling thought at all. And, obviously, that wasn't the source of the movement I saw because dead things didn't move. "Let's go. I think it might have been a moth."

"If you're sure..."

"I'm sure," I lied, because saying that I was seeing shit that wasn't there wasn't a comfort to anyone.

He nodded, but I could tell he didn't believe me. He spun in a circle, taking in the less-than-luxurious accommodations. We were in a room of sorts with tunnels leading away from it. The wall sconces were the cheapest motion-activated outdoor lights you could buy at the hardware store. The light was bright white and made my eyes water. Two-by-fours and plywood crudely supported both the walls and the ceiling, though the earth floor remained bare. Based on the haphazard spacing of the posts, I doubted they complied with any kind of structural engineering standards. None of those observations eased the impending sense of doom clinging to me like burrs on my faun's furry ankles.

Dark tunnels led away from the room. I couldn't remember which one I'd used, but Hayden sniffed the air and chose one. I shuddered and tried to peer down the ones we weren't taking. If only they led to something interesting, like a stash of gold or a wine cellar or... What else did people store in creepy underground bunkers?

"You sure this isn't a trap?" I whispered.

"Nope. But I can't sense wolves in here. There are other scents though, so stay close. I can't tell if they are new or not. The lack of fresh air is messing with my nose."

"Great, just great," I mumbled, but I followed him anyway.

No way was I letting him out of my sight; splitting up was how people died in slasher movies. Statistics showed that more women than men survived horror movies. Yes, yes, I knew this was my real life, but it *felt* like one of those fictional movie sets, and I was determined to be the exception to the survival statistics. I also wanted Hayden to survive too, because I was generous like that.

As we walked into the tunnel, more lights came on. Our footsteps scuffed against the bare ground loudly enough I could hear them over my thundering heartbeat.

Nothing in the hall was straight. The walls tilted a few degrees this way or that. The ceiling wasn't level either. Whoever installed them clearly didn't understand how to use a plumb bob, a level or, you know, just their eyes. The only other explanation was they really liked those creepy human fun houses, except this one didn't have mirrors or the weird circus music. And if we were lucky, nothing lurked behind corners waiting to lunge for us, either.

We got to the first door. It was ajar. I hadn't thought my heart could beat any faster, but it tried anyway.

"Wait a minute," Hayden whispered. Then he shifted, not fully, but enough that his face changed into a wolfish configuration, and he grew bigger. He sniffed at the gap. When he didn't stiffen or shout at me to flee, I figured we were safe.

"I don't scent anyone," he said, confirming my brilliant deduction.

He nudged the door open to reveal a small room of shelves filled with garbage. Upended, empty boxes and plastic food wrappers were strewn across the surfaces.

"This must be how they hid from us for so long," Hayden said. "They had food stockpiled. Looks like they are getting to the end of their supplies, though."

Then he peered into the hallway, one way, then the other. He motioned for me to follow him, as if I needed the reminder. We explored room after room. We didn't find anything, and I can't say I was disappointed, especially when Hayden had talked about smelling death earlier.

At the first fork in the tunnel, we turned right. If we continued to turn right each time, we should make it out again. Wasn't that the trick for mazes and labyrinths? I hoped it was. I'd never been in one before. The next door we found was closed, but the doorknob turned easily under Hayden's hand. As soon as it opened, Hayden froze. He looked at me.

"You don't have to come in here," he whispered, and I knew we'd found the place where I'd been kept. I shoved him aside and walked in. When was he going to figure out I wasn't letting him leave me behind anywhere? Not even in the hallway.

I ground my teeth together so I wouldn't gasp or curse or scream.

The room, with its cage, looked the same as when I'd left it. The pot I'd been given to piss in was still in the corner. The water bottles I'd rationed were in the other corner. The bars protruding from the ground and the ceiling should have made it impossible for a faun like me to break out. Except, luckily for me, they hadn't given nearly enough thought to the locking mechanism, which hadn't survived being kicked repeatedly by a hoof.

"You see that? I did that. I broke out of there. Ha! Fuck them and the turtle they rode in on!" I pointed at the broken bits of lock scattered across the ground. In amongst the debris were chunks of my hooves and a few splatters of blood too. My gaze skittered away from those.

"Good job." Hayden nodded.

I didn't need his approval, but I still liked the acknowledgement that for once in my life I'd been badass enough to break out of a cage, all on my own. I'd rescued myself. I wasn't a weak-assed dimwit in distress who needed someone to save him. I'd saved my own damn self. Fucking A. Oorah, or whatever it was that marine dudes said in movies. Was I saying that right? I'd never enlisted, so what did I know about those things? Fuck it. I was going to say it anyway. Oo-fucking-rah.

"I'm glad my head is tougher than that lock." He laughed, so I knew he was teasing me. "You did some pretty good damage in here."

I grinned back at him, feeling better about this whole situation than I had just seconds earlier. We left the room, and I didn't look back.

Behind the next door, we found my backpack. I couldn't believe it. I ignored everything else and ran for it. A quick search confirmed everything was exactly as I'd packed it. Even my laptop was still in there. Fucking awesome with coconut on top. My phone and my shoes were beside my bag like they'd been tossed there and never looked at again.

When we got back to town, I was buying a lottery ticket.

I shoved my phone in my pocket, and I tied my shoes to my bag. If I hadn't been wearing my hooves, I would have switched shoes right then and there. I tugged the backpack over my shoulders, and everything seemed right with the world.

Except... My backpack wasn't the only one in the room.

There had to be at least another six or seven sets of belongings in here. Son of a corn-filled turd. This was bad.

"Let's finish our search," Hayden said. "If we don't find anyone else, we'll come back and search for IDs."

I nodded. I had no desire to rifle through someone's belongings. If they were caged like I had been, they'd been violated enough already.

After finding the next several rooms empty, I wasn't holding out much hope of finding survivors. Our luck didn't improve. When we arrived back at the place we'd started from—only making right-hand turns had worked— we decided we'd found all we would. The cages had all been empty. There were no survivors, but thankfully there weren't any bodies either. At least I hoped that was good news.

Then we doubled back to the room where we'd found my backpack.

I eyed the heaps of other bags.

"I guess we need to look through them." I swallowed.

We couldn't carry everything back, but we couldn't leave it here either. What if Robbie came back and found his brother's scent in the tunnels? I wouldn't put it past him to destroy everything.

Hayden nodded. "You can stay outside if you want. You don't have to do this."

I appreciated the offer, but I wasn't standing out in the hallway by myself. I didn't care if the tunnel complex was empty; the place gave me the creeps. The sooner we got out, the better. If we went through the bags together, we could leave faster.

I took my bag off my back and set it beside the door, then I got to work. Hayden started at one side of the room, and I took the other.

"Look for wallets, identification, phones, that sort of thing. Anything we can use to identify who this stuff belongs to," Hayden said.

"It feels wrong to go through their stuff," I said as I dumped out a bag.

"I know." Hayden grimaced. "We can come back and collect it later, when we have more people, but I don't want to risk having this stuff go missing before we can return."

"So, we're leaving after this?" That was even better

news than finding cinnamon buns on the menu this morning.

"Yeah," Hayden agreed as he shook everything out of a toiletry bag. "Let's put the stuff in here to carry out."

I tossed the two wallets to him, and he shoved them into the bag beside a phone and a wallet he'd found.

Three wallets. So, that was at least three people so far. My hands shook as I grabbed the next bag. From the corner of my eye, I saw Hayden scoop up another too.

There was a click.

It must have been loud if I could hear it over the pounding of my heart.

Hayden was closer to the door, but he spun toward me faster than I could register with my eyes. He grabbed me and hurled me toward the door. I went flying into the hallway as a loud clang resounded behind me. I rolled over to see what'd happened.

Oh, fuck a puck.

Where in the Magic had those bars come from? We must have triggered some kind of booby trap. What was worse? Hayden lay sprawled across the floor on the other side of the bars. Trapped. He wasn't moving.

"Hayden!" I ran over and grabbed the bars. They didn't even wiggle. "You better be alive. You hear me? You are not allowed to die in this place."

He groaned.

"Thank fuck." I should probably thank the Eternal Magic too, but right now she didn't seem to be on my side, so she could damn well wait.

Hayden rolled to his side and gingerly probed the top of his head. "Why'd you kick me again, Ry?"

"I didn't kick you." I crossed my arms over my chest.

"You sure? Because…" he slurred.

"I think the bars conked you on the head when they dropped out of the ceiling. Why did you do that? You were closer to the door. If you hadn't tried to save me…" Tears welled in my eyes.

"Bars?" He blinked like he was having trouble focusing. He rubbed his unusually pale face in an uncoordinated way like he was drunk. "Where did they come from?"

"You look like shit. If you're going to throw up, aim away from me, okay?" I wouldn't win any awards for my bedside manner, but if he was concussed enough to toss up his breakfast, I'd really lose it. I didn't do well with sick people. And it should have been me in there. He was the big, huff-and-puff-and-I'll-blow-your-house-down were-wolf dude. He should be out on this side so he could figure out how to get me out. Instead, everything was all wrong, and I had to save him. I was not meant to be a hero.

"Think, Ryley, think." I scrubbed my fingers over my scalp.

Where was the lock? I scanned each bar. No fucking lock. Son of a turd-filled twit.

So there had to be a lever. Something to make the bars pop back to where they'd come from. We hadn't found a control room. Had we missed something? I hated the idea of leaving Hayden to go looking for one, but what else could I do?

I tugged at the bars again. They didn't even rattle. Criminy, we were lucky the bars hadn't landed on either of us. That would have been messy. Skewered by a boobie-trap wasn't how anyone would want to go.

Nope. Don't think about skewering. I needed to twist this narrative around. Embrace the power of positive thinking. Wasn't that the trick Hayden had pulled on me in the woods earlier? And how did I do that exactly?

Think, Ryley.

"We aren't as bad off as we could be. No one is a shish kabob. Yay, us!" I flashed two thumbs up toward Hayden, who still looked dazed. "I can do this. I can get you out. I got myself out, so this will be so much easier because there are two of us."

In other news, I was also brilliant at lying to myself.

Chapter Fifteen

HAYDEN

My head hurt. Again.

The doc was going to weld a helmet to my head if he found out about this.

I would have to make sure he never did. Of course, I might not get out of here. It'd be difficult for him to scold me if I was dead.

I touched the bump on my head and pulled my hand away to look. No blood. That was good.

All I needed to do was shift, and everything would be fine. I reached deep inside myself and pulled on my magic. I waited for the shift to come.

It didn't.

My chest tightened like a vise was squeezing it... And squeezing... Tighter and tighter.

Fuck.

This couldn't be happening. I tried again. And again, my magic fizzled away. A few coarse hairs sprouted along my forearms and on the back of my neck before disappearing again.

And then nothing.

Yes, I'd used a lot of magic today already and last night too, but what was it Xander had said about my magic being out of whack? His words sounded more and more like a premonition now. It looked like he hadn't been exaggerating. Too bad I didn't know that earlier, I would have ordered steak and eggs for breakfast. And, you know, not gone to the woods with Ryley today.

I struggled to sit up. I couldn't make it to my feet. Not yet. So I leaned against the wall. Ryley was pacing on the other side of the bars. He was pulling at his hair and muttering to himself.

"Hey," I said. "It's going to be okay. Why don't you get out of here?" I pulled out my phone and the keys to my truck. I pushed both through the bars. "Drive into town. Van should be at the police station by now."

Ryley's face contorted in disbelief at my suggestion. "I'm not leaving you here. Not like this."

He flapped his hand at me. Could he tell how fucked up I was? Was that what was holding him back? Yeah. I could see it. He'd never leave if he thought I was vulnerable. Which meant I needed to stand and show him I was fine. Wrapping my hands around the bars, I hauled myself up. I was more unsteady on my feet than I would ever admit out loud. I hoped he didn't notice.

"Come here, Ry," I said softly.

As soon as he was close, I pressed my head against the bars to get closer yet. Our foreheads touched. His fingers wrapped around mine where I still gripped the bar.

"Breathe with me," I said. I inhaled slowly and released it just as slowly.

"I don't need a meditation coach," Ryley grumbled.

"Quit talking and do as I say. In and out." I lifted my hand and rested it on his shoulder. When he didn't bat it away like he had earlier, I slid it over his body at a languid pace until I had the back of his head cupped in my palm. With anyone from my pack, I wouldn't have taken so much time, but Ryley wasn't in my pack. Or, uh… I guess no one was because I didn't have a pack.

My head hurt too much to go down that path.

My magic wasn't responding to my desire to shift, but apparently I could still feel the stir of my alpha energy. It was fainter than normal, but it was still there, intuitively responding to Ryley's fear. I needed to calm him, and my magic was determined to help, at any cost.

Easing his panic was the least I could do since I was the one who'd gotten us into this mess.

This was just one more shitty decision to heap on a lifetime of shitty decisions. Why anyone would think I'd be a good alpha was beyond me. I was a sorry excuse for a wolf.

I'd put Ryley in danger. Me. I'd done that. Just like I let someone get away with destroying my dad's pack. And if Van was right, my parents' murderer had escaped justice too.

A true alpha kept people safe. A true alpha didn't hide from difficult confrontations. A true alpha stood up for their pack and sought justice.

I wasn't an alpha. I never had been. And I would never be worthy of that title.

Nothing would change that, but my parents and the remnants of their pack deserved better. I'd let them all down for too long. And now I'd let Ryley down too.

All those years ago when my life went to shit, I hadn't wanted to believe Robbie capable of instigating so much destruction, but this past summer had shattered any lingering delusions I had about him. And now, having searched his hidden bunker, I had more evidence of how messed up he was.

Fucking Robbie.

I hated him. I loved him. Still. Somehow. I wanted to blame him for everything that'd happened, but that wasn't fair. Since the Eternal Magic had gifted me with alpha power as a child, everyone had treated me as the next leader of the pack. I should have realized Robbie's childhood jealousy wasn't something he would grow out of. I should have paid attention and stopped him before it was too late.

If we'd formed a closer relationship, would things have been different?

Watching a few more after-school specials together or taking him for runs in the woods wouldn't have solved all our problems, but I might not have been so damn oblivious. How had I missed the signs he was a murderous, power-hungry asshole?

My eyes were open now, though, and I *would* stop him before he did anything more.

But first, I needed to get out of here.

"Better?" I whispered when Ryley's energy felt calmer.

Ryley tilted his head to look up at me. He blinked. His hazel eyes stared straight into mine. The intensity of the look made me freeze. I didn't know whether to pull away or try to get closer. As close as the bars would let us, anyway. He licked his lips, and I knew I wouldn't be letting go of him. Not yet.

His mouth brushed against mine and my fingers tightened at the nape of his neck. He tasted as sweet as I'd imagined, with a hint of cinnamon. My eyes closed as I savored the feel of his lips and his mouth and his tongue... Fuck, his tongue. It danced against mine in the most erotic way. I couldn't remember the last time I'd let myself get lost in something as simple as a damn kiss.

When the kiss ended, we stood looking at one another through the bars of the cage. I cleared my throat and let my hands drop to my side.

"You should get out of here," I said.

"You have the worst ideas," he said, but his words didn't carry any heat.

A screech, like feedback on a microphone, shot through the room.

"Well, look at the rat caught in my trap," someone said.

I froze, because I recognized that voice. Sure, I hadn't spoken to Robbie in a dozen years, but I'd never forget what he sounded like.

Ryley turned to face the door with his fists raised, but no one was there. I strained my ears and caught the crackle of static.

"He isn't here. It's a speaker," I told Ryley.

"Did you set my other pets free too? That's not nice, brother. I don't play with your things. You shouldn't play with mine."

"Come here, turd wrinkle," Ryley shouted as he

pranced on his hooves. "Call me a pet to my face, I dare you." Then he whipped around and frowned at me. "And did he just call you his brother? Is that true?"

Before I could answer, Robbie's laughter filled the room. The sound made my hair stand on end. I tried to shift again. I begged my magic to listen, to obey. It didn't.

"Yes," I reluctantly admitted. Thankfully, Ryley didn't threaten me with his hooves again. "Let me out, Robbie. This has gone on long enough."

"I've lost everything because of you," Robbie said. "But I'm not giving up. When you're gone, I'll finally be the alpha I was supposed to be. Your magic will pass to me, like Dad's passed to you."

Ryley glanced over his shoulder at me. "Did he have a Darth Vader poster on his wall when he was a kid? Because I feel like there had to have been signs. Did he have a teddy bear? Someone should have given him a teddy bear. And a vintage poster of the original *Star Trek* officers. Just sayin'"

"It doesn't work that way, Robbie," I said, ignoring Ryley's commentary. "You know that."

"Of course it does," Robbie scoffed. "Dad lied. Mom lied. *Everyone* lied to keep the power to themselves. But it doesn't matter now. This isn't how I'd planned this, but…" It almost sounded like he was sniffling. Was he crying? No way. My brother didn't succumb to feelings like that. He never had. But he'd always excelled at mimicking them. "You took my pack, Hayden. Why did you do that? Everything is gone. My pack and my house and my property and my pets…"

"Enough with the *pets* shit already, you fruit fart,"

Ryley said, waving his fist toward the part of the wall from where the sound was emanating.

Sharp pain reverberated through my chest as I remembered exactly what it was like to lose everything. Only, in my case, my life had been upended because of my brother, whereas Robbie had lost his through poor choices and greed.

"I still love you, Hayden," Robbie said. "You're my big brother. You were supposed to protect me."

"I love you too, Robbie. I'll help you. You know I will." My voice sounded clogged with more emotion than I'd expected. I rubbed my chest. I hadn't expected talking to him to hurt this much.

"Help. Yeah, right," Robbie scoffed. "I think I'll pass. I don't need your kind of help."

The static-filled background noise ended abruptly.

"And I thought the fauns were bad," Ryley whispered to himself. "You must have had some fucked-up family dinners."

"Let me out," I shouted, ignoring Ryley's mutterings. "Robbie?"

"I think he's gone," Ryley said.

"He might still be listening. Are you listening, Robbie? Let me out. You know you want to. We're family. Remember what Mom and Dad said? Family sticks together. We're a unit."

No response.

I shouldn't have expected him to free me, except I think I had. Deep inside, I still considered him family. Yes, I wanted to stop him. Not just to help his victims, but to help him too—even after all the terrible, horrible things he'd done. It felt foreign and strange to believe he wouldn't or couldn't feel the same way.

"Fuck twit thinks you're going to die in here," Ryley said.

I knew Ryley was right. Except Ryley was on the other side of the bars, so why would Robbie think that? I wouldn't die in the time Ryley took to walk out of here and get help unless...

What if this cage wasn't the only thing that'd changed when I hit that trigger? What if the entrance was sealed now, too?

"Ryley, go. Check the exit. See if it's locked."

Ryley's eyes widened, understanding my worries immediately. "I'll be right back."

"I'll be here."

It wasn't like I had any other choice. Son of fuck. I couldn't believe I'd let us get trapped in here.

Chapter Sixteen

RYLEY

I rushed through the tunnels, keenly aware that something besides mystery speakers and metal bars could be hiding behind the walls. If something sprang out at me right now, I'd have a heart attack, hit the dirt floor, and die before they even touched me.

I never should have compared this place to a fun house, because now that the thought was in my head, it was haunting me. When I'd first left my herd, I'd wanted to experience everything the mundane human world had to offer. Going to a fun house had seemed like it'd be, well, fun. It wasn't. There were creepy clowns, eerie laughter, nothing being what it seemed, and people jumping out at you to make you scream. Why did humans like to be piss-your-pants scared? They were almost as messed up as Robbie was.

I skidded to a halt on my hoofed feet when I reached the ladder to freedom. I looked up. The damn hatch was covering the exit. Without giving myself time to panic any more than I already was, I shifted into my human form and scrambled up the rungs. The hatch, which had opened easily for me last night, refused to budge. There was no latch or handle, but the thing wouldn't move. I put on my glasses to see if I'd missed something, but nothing stood out. It would have been better to do a partial shift and look through my faun's eyes, but my nerves were too frayed. I was scared I would lose control and my whole body would change. The last thing I needed was to suddenly have hooves while trying to balance at the top of a metal ladder. I pushed up against the lid. I beat it with my fist. Nothing worked.

Son of an ass-zit. This was bad.

I reluctantly climbed down the ladder again. My brain scrambled to come up with a new plan. There had to be a way out of here. Every building needed at least two exits. There were regulations.

Right. Because people who built illegal bunkers on their land cared about building codes. But there had to be vents for air or, if we were really lucky, a hidden escape hatch. We had searched the tunnels and found nothing like that, but that didn't mean they weren't there, just like that speaker.

I pushed myself to shift again as soon as I stepped off the last rung. My transition was sluggish. My muscles quivered with the effort. I wouldn't be able to shift many more times without food to balance my magic. But I felt a hell of a lot better being in my shifted form, even if I'd never be as powerful as a wolf shifter or a hellhound. I trudged back to the cell where Hayden was trapped.

He took one look at me and cursed. "No luck?"

"No luck," I confirmed. "I have a new plan. There is a speaker behind this plywood, right? And every wall and ceiling has plywood just like this. I bet we'll find other things if we rip it down." *Like hopefully a way out.*

Hayden eyed the haphazard supports. "Sounds like a good way to have the whole place collapse on us."

I ignored him. No one appreciated a Negative Nelly. "But first, we'll get you out of the cage."

"Good idea, Sherlock. And how are we going to do that?"

"I had a lot of time to plan my escape. I went for the lock because it was the easiest thing to do, but we don't have that option here," I said, absently waving toward the lock-free bars. "But I saw a documentary once about how when people were locked in a room, they always focused on the door and the lock, but the weak spots are often the walls."

"It is a place to start, I suppose." Hayden eyed the walls skeptically. "But I don't think this will be as easy as kicking through sheetrock."

"We won't know until we try. Can you shift?" I asked. "Maybe you could claw at the plywood. I once saw a video of someone's dog ripping through a door like they were digging a hole." I tapped my foot on the ground. "What if you dug under the bars? These bars can't be embedded too deeply."

"I…" Hayden swallowed and averted his eyes. Color rose on his cheeks. "I tried shifting, but…"

Shit. This was worse than I'd thought, but I wouldn't get on his case about it. I knew how fickle magic could be.

"Hey. No worries at all," I said quickly and with false cheer. "It was just a thought. We can absolutely do this without you shifting. One hundred percent. No problem. We've got this."

The color on his cheeks darkened even more, but I pretended I didn't see. I made a production of taking off my backpack and setting it aside. I studied and poked at the walls on one side of the room, before doing the same to the other. One panel moved more than the other. Hopefully, that meant it was a weak spot with nothing behind it. I thought about going through the tunnels to hunt for something to use as a pry bar, but I couldn't bear the idea of going out there alone again. If this didn't work, I would do that next. Everyone needed a Plan B.

"So, um, I'm just going to, you know, kick the shit out of the wall over here."

As soon as my ass hit the ground, I flopped onto my back. I scooted over so my ass was closer to the wall and my feet were resting at a comfortable angle against the plywood. The bars to the cage were pressed against my right side. I really hoped this worked.

"Here goes."

Quite a few years ago, when I still lived with the herd, my brother Conny—man, he'd hated when I called him that, but he'd been too small for a name like Constantine—discovered a stash of old VHS tapes when he was about nine. Amongst them was a recording of a *Riverdance* show. It'd been love at first tap. He came up with his own routines, determined to be the next big name. I knew that would never happen. Fauns couldn't be in human shows. But I didn't see the problem with him having an interest outside all that damn flute playing fauns were *supposed* to enjoy. Because *anything* was better than having another flute player in the family.

He was the youngest in the herd, so everyone spoiled him. But I was the only one who'd encouraged his love of dance. I was already in my twenties at the time, but I'd been right there beside him. I let him teach me his choreography, which was impressive for a kid under ten. Unfortunately, the other fauns, including my parents and their siblings, were assholes and didn't like his too-human hobby. His obsession lasted for three years before he succumbed to the pressure to stop. It'd broken my heart when he tossed all his CDs and videos.

CDs and videos. Did anyone have those anymore? Well, besides me? I still had every bit of electronics I'd ever purchased. My apartment was full of gadgets and machines. My herd would flip if they saw it. If I hadn't already left them, they would have banned me for sure.

But before that, when Conny and I had been dancing, I'd learned a lot about hoof health and how to stomp for hours without hurting your hooves. Although I never imagined how important good strong hooves would be in my life until now. Yesterday, I'd been relieved to escape with only a couple of nicks in my hooves when I'd broken the lock. My left hoof was also smaller after they'd taken samples of it to test them for residual magic, so it wouldn't be able to take as much abuse. But an injured foot was better than the alternative.

Today would test my hoof strength. When we got out of here, I really needed to look up the manicurist the scary dragon mentioned last night. You know, if this worked, and we got out of this place before we died.

"It's working," Hayden said.

I glanced down at my feet to see the wood splintering and breaking away, but I wasn't through to the other side yet. Emboldened by this modest success, Hayden sifted through the stuff we'd dumped out of people's bags earlier. When he found a small camera tripod, he lifted it like it was Excalibur. Then he used it to chip away at the plywood on his side of the bars, too.

When the first hole appeared, we both crowed in victory. I tried to peer through the splintered wood to the space behind it, but I couldn't see anything in the shadowy gap. The hole was big enough for my finger.

I swallowed. I had a thing about not sticking my hands or anything else through mysterious holes. All those glory hole clips on porn sites made me cringe and want to cover my junk. But it couldn't be helped in this situation. At least it would only be my finger at risk. It also helped that I didn't expect there to be anyone waiting on the other side with pruning shears. I shuddered. Nope. I shouldn't have thought about that.

I'd definitely watched too many slasher movies when I'd first joined the human world.

Damn it. Why couldn't the first hole have appeared on Hayden's side?

With clenched teeth, I eased my finger into the hole. I was tense, ready to whip my hand away if anything—any tiny little thing—brushed against it. I got to the first knuckle. Everything was okay. I still had my finger.

Second knuckle. My finger was still attached. I pushed my finger all the way in.

"Huh," I said, wiggling my finger.

"What?"

I pulled my finger out and tried to look inside the hole again. I still couldn't see anything. "I can't feel anything on the other side."

"Really?" There was a whisper of hope in his question.

I glanced at him. "Really."

"This might actually work." He sounded surprised. His reaction didn't offend me. I couldn't believe my idea was working either.

With renewed energy, we beat at the wall some more. The hole grew larger and larger. This time when I looked through it, I could see the chiseled earth several inches behind it. The gap wasn't a lot, but if we could get the plywood out of the way, Hayden might be able to squeeze through it.

Hayden grinned at me.

I didn't think he'd ever smiled at me before. I hadn't known him all that long, but I would have remembered something like that, because he was…

I swallowed. Was it hot in here?

"What?" Hayden was watching me carefully.

"Uh…" I blinked.

"Ryley?"

I shook my head. "Nothing. I just…" Just what? Nothing. At least nothing I'd say aloud. "Let's, uh, let's get this out of the way."

His forehead crinkled like I'd confused him, but he nodded, and we got to work again. My fingers were bleeding. My feet hurt. I had splinters in weird places, like the webbing between my fingers. But after a while, we finally had the plywood removed from floor to ceiling. The gap extended about a foot or so on either side of the bars.

Hayden hurriedly went through the remaining bags for people's identification, then he shoved the small bag with the few wallets and phones through the bars to me. Then we both stared at the hole we'd created. This was it, the moment we'd find out if it worked. If I'd been stuck on the other side instead of him, I wouldn't have been as apprehensive, but Hayden was a big, muscular guy.

He cracked his knuckles and twisted his body one way and then the other, like he was preparing for a marathon. I didn't know what good that would do, but whatever. He put his back against the wall and pressed up to the hole we'd made.

Fuck. I couldn't watch.

Fuck. I couldn't *not* watch.

This was so not going to work.

I held my breath and squeezed in my stomach like I was the one trying to fit through the gap.

"Come on, come on, come on," I muttered quietly. I hadn't been this stressed since… Well, since I broke myself out of a similar cage yesterday. I swear I didn't know how my life had become so messed up.

Then he was through.

Holy fuck a doodle. It worked. I crashed into him, and he hugged me tight.

Now we just had to open the hatch, and we were golden. Hell fucking yeah.

Chapter Seventeen

HAYDEN

"I thought for sure you'd get stuck trying to squeeze through there," Ryley said with a wide grin. His relief was so immense it felt tangible.

I could have kissed him again, but I held back.

The last time we'd kissed, it felt like we were trying to conquer our resignation, worry, and fear in one comforting moment. But if we kissed now, I wasn't sure what it'd mean. Not that a kiss needed to mean anything, but with Ryley it seemed like it should. And, if we kissed, I wouldn't want to stop. I didn't know what to think about that either.

"Me too," I agreed.

I couldn't believe Ryley's idea worked. We were one step closer to freedom. Now we just needed to get out of the bunker.

I eyed the bars and shuddered, thankful to be on this side of them. I never wanted to experience that again.

Ever. I couldn't imagine what those poor people like Ogden, Brodie, Dakota, and Ryley had gone through, locked up for days or weeks or longer. And those were just the people I knew. There were so many others I had never met. Van said some people in Babette's warehouse had been imprisoned for months or more.

My wolf bristled under my skin at the thought. Hallelujah. My magic was coming back. Had my wolf just been saving its energy?

Yeah. I doubted that was it, but I could pretend.

On the upside, I'd escaped the cage, so that had to mean the Eternal Magic was helping me. She hated seeing her children contained, and we were her creations, an extension of her own magic. At least that's what my parents had taught us.

Had Robbie forgotten you couldn't cage magic? What would the Eternal Magic do if someone abused her gifts like that? Could she be driving him mad because of that? What other explanation could there be?

Would I be in the same shape if I kept ignoring the Eternal Magic's role in my life? I wasn't sure I wanted to test it. I'd begged the Eternal Magic to strip me of my alpha powers for years, but what if she took it all? What if she killed my wolf? Sharp pain ripped through my chest. I would never survive without my wolf.

Had this been a wake-up call?

Either way, my wolf was back for now. I was ready for whatever came next.

Even if we couldn't open the hatch to the surface right away, it'd be okay. I had faith that the Eternal Magic wouldn't abandon Ryley and me. She wasn't done with us yet. I knew it in my bones. We had both ignored her gifts, which earned us her ire, but Ryley had done it unknowingly. He was the victim of his herd's abuse. He deserved to be saved. She wouldn't abandon him too.

Of course, I'd rather not sit back and wait for her to save us. Just in case.

"Let's get out of here," I said.

After Ryley shoved the toiletry bag containing all the phones and wallets we'd found in his backpack, we left the room. I shivered as I passed into the hallway; there'd been a moment there when I'd wondered if I would be stuck in that little room for the rest of my life.

I listened for a sign that we had company, but I didn't detect anything. Did Robbie know we'd escaped? He must. He'd known when I was trapped, so he must know I'd escaped. I hoped he had no more surprises rigged in here, waiting for us to trigger them.

Ryley and I hurried through the tunnel. I stayed as close as I could to him. I didn't want another set of bars to crash down and separate us again. At least if we were on the same side of the barrier, I could protect Ryley if Robbie returned.

We reached the exit without incident.

"Go ahead," Ryley said, motioning to the ladder. "I tried and couldn't budge it."

"Don't go anywhere. Stay right there." I wasn't going far, but I needed to know he was close, so that I could look down and see him.

He nodded. "You and me, we're stuck like glue."

I hauled myself up the ladder. As soon as I got to the top, I reached for the hatch. It wiggled before I touched it.

Robbie was here. I let go of the ladder and let myself fall to the ground. Pain shot through my legs at the impact, but I was still standing. Ryley gasped, but I put my hand over his mouth before he could demand answers. I dragged him over to the wall where we'd be out of sight of anyone descending the ladder until they got to the bottom. I shoved him behind me.

I reached into the place where my magic lived, because now would be a fine fucking time for my shift to come back to me. Magic fluttered inside me, before slipping away. Nothing happened. Damn it. Again? I thought we were past all that.

Footsteps clanged on the ladder rungs.

Then, in a blur, someone landed in front of us.

I was out of time. It didn't matter if I didn't have my magic; I had to fight. I had to save Ryley. This was going to hurt, but I had to take Robbie out before he shifted. I was about to throw myself at him when the intruder's scent hit me. Relief swept through me. The cavalry had arrived for the second time in two days.

"Adrian," I said. "Fuck, it's good to see you."

"What the hell, Adrian?" Jeremy complained. "You weren't supposed to do that. You were going to wait for me." He chattered the entire way down the ladder. "Operation: Save The Alpha So We Can Kick His Ass isn't a solo mission, damn it."

Ryley snorted behind me. Right. Now that I knew we weren't about to be attacked, I didn't need to have him pressed up against the wall. It was harder than it should have been to step away and stop shielding him with my body.

When Jeremy was almost at the bottom rung, he looked over his shoulder, assessing the situation.

"Oh, hello, Alpha," Jeremy said. "I was just talking about you."

"Is he here? Did we find him?" Ash called down from the top.

"We got him!" Jeremy called up.

More footsteps clattered down the steps.

"And damn it, Jeremy." Ash talked almost as much as Jeremy had as he climbed down. "You weren't supposed to go down next. I can't believe you shoved Dillon so hard he fell on his ass."

"He took me by surprise," Dillon mumbled. "And I wasn't about to manhandle him out of the way. Adrian would have gone for my throat if I'd done that."

Then Dillon was coming down the ladder too.

"How many people are here?" I asked.

"Pretty much everyone from last night again." Jeremy grinned. "Except Van. But he is expecting you to go straight to the station as soon as we get back to town. He said something about making sure you knew how much of a pain in the ass you were."

I smothered the groan threatening to break free. I'd deal with Van when I saw him. But first, I had other priorities. "Make sure someone stays topside. We were locked in here until you opened that hatch."

"Stay up there, Isaac. Watch for wolves," Adrian shouted.

"Yeah, we had to move a monster-sized boulder to get you out." Jeremy gestured, holding his hands far apart to show the size.

"A boulder?" I reiterated in disbelief.

Damn it. Someone had been watching when we'd gone into the tunnel. How had I missed them? I rubbed my forehead. Was my magic fading? Could it do that?

"It reeks of an unfamiliar wolf," Dillon said.

"Was it Robbie?" I asked. No one answered. Right. None of these people had met him. "I'll check when I go up."

"We found some wallets and phones in one room," Ryley said as he held out the toiletry bag to Dillon, who was dressed in his police uniform. Dillon opened the bag and flipped through what we'd gathered. "We think they belong to other people the wolves held here."

"Are there more people to help?" Adrian looked around. "Where are they? Are they stuck in cages?"

I shook my head. "I think they escaped last night too. Like Ryley. We didn't find anyone."

"Except there might be other hidden rooms down here. We know there are speakers and mics behind some walls," Ryley said.

Adrian stilled and lifted his nose to sniff the air.

Dillon peered down the tunnels. "It could take ages to search this place safely. That bit of wood might be all that's preventing the tunnel from caving in."

"We need to call my brother," Ash said. Dillon nodded.

Ash's brother Birch had helped seal a hidden tunnel at the inn a few months ago. He was an earth mage and a good guy. He could at least make sure we didn't do something that would have the whole place falling in on us.

"Good idea," I said. "I don't think we should stay

down here." I wouldn't know how to deal with the guilt if anyone got hurt. I couldn't take that risk.

"Until then we'll set up a schedule to guard the place," Dillon said.

I shook my head. "We don't know how many people Robbie has with him. They are adept at kidnapping supes. No one is staying out here, not even in pairs."

Dillon looked like he wanted to argue, but Ash caught his hand and gave it a squeeze.

"Alpha is right," Ash said.

"Fine. We'll head back together and come up with a safe plan," Dillon said after a moment.

The tender look Dillon shared with Ash made my insides clench. I'd seen them go all gooey for one another many times over the last few months, but I'd never thought much of it. I'd been happy for them, but my reaction felt different this time. Envy? Longing?

What would it be like to share that gentle understanding with someone? I glanced at Ryley. His gaze caught on mine, and my stomach did that same weird swoopy thing.

I hoped I wasn't coming down with something.

"Let's get out of here," I said.

Chapter Eighteen

RYLEY

As we walked back to the vehicles, Dillon tried to convince Hayden to go straight to the police station when we returned to Willow Lake, while Jeremy argued we should go to the doctor's place first because of Hayden's latest head injury. Hayden refused to commit to either destination. When we got to the vehicles and I climbed into Hayden's truck with him while the others got into their own vehicles, I doubted we'd be going anywhere but the garage.

I was right.

Dillon stopped right beside us when Hayden parked outside his business. He did his best to coax Hayden to the police station, but Hayden just turned and walked toward the garage as he said, "Van knows where to find us."

He only looked back once, when he got to the door. He frowned at me, like he couldn't figure out why I wasn't following right behind him. "Are you coming?"

As I trotted after the moody werewolf, who was holding the door open for me like a gentleman, I shot Dillon an apologetic smile. I thought I'd outgrown my need to follow people around when I left the herd, but apparently I hadn't. The almost alpha made me feel safe, and I wasn't ready to turn my back on that feeling quite yet. It'd been so long since I'd felt it. It was nice.

Of course, it may have also helped that I couldn't get that impulsive kiss out of my head. I wouldn't mind doing that again, so I was sticking close. You know, just in case the opportunity to smash our mouths together again presented itself.

I adjusted my glasses as I entered Hayden's business. The waiting room inside the place was clean but not pristine. The worn-out furniture, the cracked lino, and the dreary fluorescent lights matched how I'd always imagined an old mechanic's shop waiting room would look. Even the air helped set the atmosphere with scents of all things mechanical. I couldn't tell you if I was smelling oil or grease or some other mechanical fluid, but it suited the place.

A vending machine with pop, candy, and chips sat in one corner, and a large metal statue sat in another. The statue was unexpected, but I didn't stop to study it because I didn't want to lose track of Hayden. He passed a windowed door that led to the left, which, based on the sounds of machinery and clanking metal, must lead to the bays where they worked on vehicles. He also marched by the door marked with a washroom sign and didn't stop until he got to the unmarked door behind the desk.

I followed. Because apparently that's what I did now.

Hayden's office was a mess. It was dusty and grimy and covered with all kinds of administrative clutter. But the most horrifying thing was the desktop computer perched on one end of the paper-strewn desk. It belonged in a museum or, even better, in my collection of electronics. I had every piece of electronics I'd ever owned since leaving the herd, but I didn't have something like this. I'd love to pull it apart and study it. When had he bought that thing? Had there still been glaciers covering the continent? He grabbed a couple of coins from his top drawer and looked at me.

"What do you want from the vending machine?"

"Ginger ale?"

He nodded, then disappeared through the door again. I heard the clunk of the vending machine spitting out a can. He returned and thrust my drink at me.

"I need to check on the guys," he said. "I'll be right back. Have a seat."

The chair behind the desk looked like it'd been manufactured in the 70s, and another newer one, which was covered in boxes, sat on this side of the desk. By newer, I meant it was from the 90s. Neither chair was in great condition. They both had holes in the seats and grime caked into the crevices.

I moved the boxes off the chair in front of the desk and set them on the floor. I dropped my backpack beside them and sat down. Now what? My gaze strayed to the desk and all those papers. Client invoices, supplier invoices, order forms, and Magic only knew what else was all mixed up together. I itched to go back there and straighten shit, but people got pissy when you re-organized their space.

Instead, I dug into my backpack and found my phone. Of course the phone was dead, so I went hunting for my charger. After that was sorted, I pulled out my laptop and plugged it in too. Just having it in my hands again sent a wave of joy through me. I'd thought I'd lost it forever. Sure, I backed up everything on the cloud, but it always took so long to set up a new computer, organize my apps, get the screensavers right, adjust short cuts, and everything else. And until that was all done, it always felt like I was wearing someone else's shoes.

I looked down.

Actually, I was still wearing someone else's shoes, literally. I should change those. But first, I needed to get into my files and make sure everything was okay.

My laptop fired up like usual. So far, so good. At least it didn't appear to have suffered any damage. I bit my tongue as I typed in my password and scanned my finger-print. As soon as the familiar home screen came up, I reviewed all my security protections. Everything looked normal; there'd been no activity since the last time I'd logged in.

Thank Magic. Tension ebbed from my body.

My projects didn't deal with classified information that needed to be protected under layers of encryption, nor did I have heaps of money to steal. But cyber security was important. It kept people out of places they didn't belong.

And, yes, my paranoia came from living in a herd for so long. Those bastards were snoopy, constantly sticking their hooves into everyone else's business. "What's yours is ours" was one of their favorite mottos. Sometimes, even after all these years, I still missed a few things about living with the herd—my brother especially—but herd mentality definitely wasn't one of them.

I signed into my socials next. My friendship circle IRL was pretty much non-existent, but I had a few online groups I loved. I found a few DMs wishing me a good holiday, so I guessed someone may have missed me if I'd never returned.

My work email was next. A few calls for proposals had come and gone, but the rest of my emails were pertaining to simple maintenance work on websites for existing clients. Those took no time to deal with at all.

By the time Hayden returned, I was finishing the last change.

Right on his heels was Van.

"You think because you're the alpha that you get VIP treatment? Making me come to you?" Despite his words, the hellhound didn't sound angry, more annoyed than anything.

"I'm not the alpha," Hayden said.

As soon as the words left his mouth, a strange look passed over his face, like he wasn't sure if he believed what he was saying. He rubbed his chest, right over the spot I'd always been told our magic lived inside us.

Van's gaze snapped to Hayden. "Hayden?"

"Not now, Van." Hayden shook his head. "You're here to talk to Ryley. Can we go over what we found in those tunnels? Unless Dillon discovered something from those wallets or phones."

Van looked like he wanted to argue, to press the issue. Instead, he said, "I'm here if you want to talk. You know that, right?"

"Yeah. Sure," Hayden said, but he didn't meet Van's eyes. "About those wallets?"

"We're still following up."

Hayden frowned, but there wasn't much he could do. "I'll go grab another chair. Unless you want to talk alone? I can always go help the guys in the back."

"Can he stay?" I asked Van as I closed out of what I was doing and secured my laptop.

"I'll get a chair," Hayden said, without waiting for Van's response. He looked relieved that I wasn't sending him away.

I thought Van would go sit in Hayden's chair behind the desk, but he didn't. It was probably a territorial thing. My kind were less territorial than other supernatural beings. Our isolationist tendencies stemmed more from a false sense of superiority than a need to defend our property, so I had to remind myself wolves and hellhounds were different.

Hayden set a chair beside mine and shut the door. Van dropped onto it as Hayden made his way around to his desk chair. As soon as he was seated, they both turned their attention to me. Having a werewolf and a hellhound stare at me was unsettling. I knew they weren't trying to intimidate me, but my racing heart wasn't getting the message.

I wished Hayden wasn't so far away. What was wrong with me that I was both unsettled by his eyes on me but wanting him close to comfort me, all at the same time? It made no sense.

I usually prided myself on my common sense, mostly because people didn't consider fauns very logical. I'd always thought I'd inherited common sense from my dad's side, but maybe my faun genes were more powerful than I'd guessed.

"What do you want to know?"

"Why don't you start at the beginning? Describe what led you to meeting Robbie and go from there."

I wished we could skip this part. Except, what if those asshole wolves abducted someone else? I sighed. Yeah. I had to talk about all that stuff. Damn it.

Chapter Nineteen

HAYDEN

Ryley was distressed. Every part of me ached to comfort him, and he hadn't even started talking yet.

I jumped up from my chair behind the desk.

"Van, come sit over here," I said, yanking him out of the chair I'd brought in for him.

He didn't fight me, but I could see he had questions. As soon as he was out of the way, I sat in the chair he'd vacated and scooted it closer to Ryley's. I didn't relax until my leg touched his.

"You gonna do that thing with my neck again?" Ryley asked. It sounded like he was teasing, but the look in his eyes told me he was serious.

"Of course," I said, and slipped my hand around the back of his neck, just like I'd do with someone from my pack. The tension in his shoulders eased almost immediately. He still didn't talk.

"Hey," I said. "Would it help if I started?"

Ryley's forehead crinkled. "What do you mean?"

"I'll tell Van what happened today. What we found. Then you can fill him in on everything else."

"Yeah, um, okay." Ryley nodded.

I told Van about how we picked up the trail they'd lost last night, how we found the tunnel, what we'd discovered down there, how Robbie had talked to me, and then about Ryley's plan to get me out of the cage. Van scribbled notes as I spoke. He asked a few questions, but I'd been with him in interviews enough times that I'd started off by giving him as many details as I could think of as I walked through what'd happened.

Then it was Ryley's turn.

I thought Van might poke at him to get him to talk, but he waited until the faun was ready. I pushed more of my alpha energy into Ryley, thankful at least that part of my magic was still working.

"What's your last name, Ryley?"

"Bell. My name is Ryley Bell." Then he rattled off his address and a bunch of other random details, as if happy to recite all the boring facts of his life if it meant he didn't have to talk about being captured.

When his words petered out, Van nodded. "Okay. Why don't we talk about what you were doing before Robbie found you?"

Ryley sighed, then he swallowed hard. "It was around the end of July, when I decided I needed a vacation." He glanced at the old school calendar I had pinned to the wall. "That was over a month and a half ago. Almost two."

"When did you leave your home?"

Ryley checked his phone. Although I didn't think he

really needed to, I could see it gave him something to do with his hands. Something to look at other than Van and me. He gave us a date and continued his story again. "I've never really had a vacation since I started my business about eight years ago, but suddenly I just…" He shook his head. "That part isn't important. So, anyway, I decided to tour around for a bit. I thought I'd go home when the snow started to fly. Or maybe not. I've never tried skiing, so…" He shook his head again. "Yeah. You don't really care about that either."

"There is no right or wrong way to do this," Van said softly. "Just talk to us. At your own pace. Say whatever you want to say. If I want to know more about something, I'll ask you some questions. Relax and take your time."

Ryley reached for his ginger ale with a shaky hand and took a large gulp of it. When he finished, he wiped his mouth with the back of his hand. He sucked in a deep breath and let it out slowly. He did it again, just how I'd instructed him when we'd been in the woods earlier. Then he closed his eyes. I gripped his neck a little tighter, to remind him he wasn't alone. Another deep breath in, then out.

"I don't know why I'm—" he waved his hand through the air, "—being so weird about this or whatever."

"You're doing great," I said. "This is the first time you're talking about it. The first time you've let yourself really think about it, since you escaped. It is going to be raw. And what happened today wouldn't have helped."

Ryley leaned into my touch a little more and let out a shuddering breath. "So, like I was saying, I went on a holiday. I'm self-employed and can pretty much work from anywhere, so I'm not sure it was really a holiday."

"What do you do?" Van asked.

"I design websites for people and do some graphic design work." He patted his laptop, which he was holding against his chest like a security blanket. "This is all I need. Anyway, I bought a twenty-year-old convertible on a whim, thinking it'd be cool to drive through the mountains with the top down. I threw what I needed in my backpack, and I hit the road. On my first night, I grabbed a room at a motel off the highway. Nothing special, but it didn't look like a dive, either."

"What was the name of it? Was it close to a town?"

Ryley pushed up his glasses. "I wasn't really paying attention. It might have been something like Sleepy Hills Motel."

"You didn't plan your route on one of those, what do they call them…? Apps or whatever?" I asked. He seemed way too techy not to have used a program to plot his route.

His cheeks darkened. "Normally I would have, yes. But I'd had the bizarre impulse to see where I ended up. I took it as a sign the Eternal Magic was trying to tell me something, like she had when I left my herd. But then, when I was jumped leaving my room to get ice my first night, I wondered if some other magic was messing with me. That's a ridiculous idea, isn't it? Bad things happen to people all the time. It doesn't mean magic is involved. But that compulsion to get in my car and drive right to the spot where someone was waiting to abduct me, I wondered if something else was at work, you know?"

Van and I exchanged a look. That didn't sound good. I

didn't know of a magic that could do that, but magic could be twisted to do a lot of things. What happened between Simon and Ogden was just one example. But how would Robbie get his hands on something like that?

"You know what? Never mind about that whole magic thing. I'm being paranoid or letting my brain think it was a big conspiracy because I'm horrified at how unprepared I was."

"We've seen magic twisted and manipulated into doing a lot of strange things this summer. Anything is possible," I told him.

"And you've been with those wolves ever since?" Van asked, steering Ryley back on topic.

"Yeah." He shivered, and I wished I could pull him into my lap and hold him. "My mind is blank from the point when I stepped into the hallway to waking up in a cage in that bunker."

A low growl rumbled through me. I couldn't stop it. I didn't try. Thinking about Robbie and his pals attacking random supes—no, not any random supe, but *this* supe in particular—made me want to stop them. Permanently.

I'd been hunting Robbie all summer, but I'd never considered killing him before. I always imagined turning him over to Van. Getting him help. But suddenly my plans turned a hell of a lot darker. But could I do that? Kill my own brother? The last family I had?

Yes. I thought I could. For Ryley.

How fucked up was that? I'd known the guy for less than twenty-four hours and I was thinking of killing for him. What was going on with me? First, my magic was acting up and now this?

The chair creaked when Van leaned forward in it. "Did you see who grabbed you?"

"I think they must have drugged me. I didn't see a thing." Ryley shook his head, and his shoulders drooped.

"That's okay. From what we understand, they've been doing this for several months at least. Enough times to get good at it. Once they targeted you, there probably wasn't much you could have done," Van said. "Now, how about when you were in the bunker? Did you see anyone while you were down there? Any guards? Any other prisoners?"

"Three wolves. All of them were guards, I guess. No one else." He pushed up his glasses again. "Wait. I think I heard someone crying one night. The wolves always talked about leaving the bunker at night and sleeping in a bed, so I don't think it was one of them I heard. I might have imagined it. It got spookily quiet down there. It made you hear things that weren't there. Anyway, Hayden and I didn't find any beds when we looked through the tunnels today, so Robbie and his guys must have been living somewhere else."

That was important. Because if Robbie and the others weren't sleeping in that tunnel, where did they go? And where was that other prisoner who'd been crying? Robbie had said something about other pets too, hadn't he? Were those the shadows Ryley mentioned when we'd first stepped into the tunnel? Where had they gone? Van and I shared a look that told me he was thinking the same thing.

"Okay, Ryley," Van said. "That's good."

Van asked a bunch more questions. A lot of them were variations of the same thing, trying to get as many details from Ryley as he could, including Ryley's observations about what'd happened when he'd gone back down in those tunnels with me. When their interview finally ended, I decided I had a few of my own questions.

I turned to Van. "We need to get back to that tunnel. Have you called Birch Avery yet? When can we get out there?"

"Birch will be here in a few days." Van held up his hand when I opened my mouth to protest about the delay. "He knows this is important, but the SC has him checking the Fardale Prison. A team of independent mages go through the place every six months to make sure the Eternal Magic isn't undermining our efforts to keep all those bastards off the streets. Birch is on the team this time around."

Van made it sound like the Eternal Magic herself was breaking criminals out of prison, like a scene from an action and adventure movie, but we both knew it wasn't like that.

A supe was blessed with magic when they were born. I'd heard of occasions when the Eternal Magic would bestow additional blessings as a person aged, but I'd never heard of her removing magic from someone. Once a supe, always a supe. And that made it tricky for prisons, because magic didn't like to be trapped. It had nothing to do with the Eternal Magic going out of her way to help criminals; it was just a fact of supernatural life.

So, it took a tremendous effort to keep supes imprisoned. That's why, in the past, hellhounds were tasked with executing the worst criminals. It made things simpler. And I was beginning to see the benefits of the old system.

And once an alpha, always an alpha, a little voice

inside me whispered. I ignored it, because it wasn't the same. It just... It wasn't.

I clenched my teeth. "Fine. So when can he get here?"

"Two days at the earliest. If they find a problem, it could take longer."

That was too damn long.

"I know," Van said, agreeing with me even though I hadn't said a word. My growling, which had grown louder, must have clued him in on what I was thinking. "But I haven't found another available earth mage who can come any faster."

I didn't like it, but what could I do? "Let me know when he's here."

"Yeah. Whatever. You can talk to him when he gets here. He'll be staying at the Willow Lake Inn. Jake's offered him a free room, as a thank you for what he did with that tunnel at the beginning of summer."

"They already have rooms ready?" After Robbie and his asshole buddies had detonated bombs at the inn during the summer, Jake and Gage had been renovating and fixing the place up with plans of it becoming a sanctuary, but I hadn't heard they'd finished already. "I thought they were still working on the dining room."

"They are." Van nodded. "But Jake also wanted to get a few rooms done, at least the ones that needed less work. After replacing the windows, Gage said most of the second-floor rooms only needed cosmetic upgrades. You'd know this if you'd been to the inn recently. Anyway, Gage said there are a few rooms that are ready. At least three, I guess, since he said there were rooms for Ash's brother, one for Ryley, and one for you too."

"I don't need a room." I'd almost said, "*We* don't need a room," but Ryley would probably benefit from being somewhere with a decent shower and a bed that wasn't created from a table, lumpy cushions, and a couple of musty sleeping bags.

"Yes," Van said. "You do. Because the doc said you need a keeper. You should have heard him when I told him you'd gone out to the hills today."

I rubbed my eyes. "Why did you have to tell him that?"

"I didn't go tattling on you. He came to the office this morning after discovering you hadn't gone to work. He was at the garage to check up on you. When you weren't there, he wanted me to do a damn wellness check. He thought you might have dropped into a coma."

"Oh." That was unfortunate.

"He came with me to your place in case you needed medical assistance."

I guessed that answered one of my questions. Van knew where I lived, and now Xander did too.

"Here. I can tell you exactly what he said because he made me write it down." Van flipped back a couple of pages in his notebook before glancing at me to make sure I was paying attention. "He said, and I quote, 'If he refuses to stay with me, he is going to stay at the Willow Lake Inn where there will be lots of people around to make sure his stubborn ass'—his words, not mine—'doesn't sneak out again like an impulsive teenager with an underdeveloped prefrontal cortex.' He also said, 'If he refuses, lock his stubborn alpha ass'—once again, these are his words not mine—'in a cell at the police station, for his own damn health.'" Van looked at me. "Listen, I don't know what all is going on with you, but the doctor has the authority to intervene if he feels someone's health is at risk. You know that as well as I do. Supes don't normally get sick, but if they do, they need to be monitored because of the weird way magic affects an ailing body. You could become a danger to yourself or others. So don't doubt me when I say I will lock you up if he tells me to. Is that what you want?"

I shuddered. If Xander told Van to lock me up, the bastard would do it too. I wasn't going back in another cage.

"Ryley can stay with me."

Van snorted and looked at Ryley. "Right. Like that worked out so well this morning."

"Well, I stopped him from going out in the middle of the night," Ryley said. "But, yeah, after he slept and stuff, I didn't think it'd be a problem. I didn't know I was supposed to keep him home indefinitely."

"Well, Xander says you need two days of nothing but rest and lots of protein." Van's gaze held mine. "After that, he'll reassess and see how you are."

"So, it looks like we're going to the inn," Ryley said.

"Yep," Van said.

After the scare with my shift to my wolf not working earlier today, I couldn't even argue. If I tried to convince them I was fine, Van would hear the lie. So I said the only thing that came to mind. "Fuck."

Chapter Twenty

RYLEY

Hayden grumbled when he shoved clothes into a plastic shopping bag. He grumbled when he threw his bag into his truck. He grumbled when he drove us the short distance to the inn.

None of that surprised me. But what *was* surprising? For as much as he grumbled, he was obeying the doctor's instructions.

Not being able to shift into his wolf earlier must have really rattled him.

When we pulled up to an old three-story brick building, Hayden frowned at the six people and the fat calico cat standing in a line outside the doors to the inn. It almost looked like they were there to welcome us in the driveway, like we were walking into a Downton Abbey spin off. People didn't normally stand around like that. It was weird. Unless they thought Hayden was going to dump me on their doorstep and run.

Actually, yeah. I could see why they might think that.

At the far end of the building was a one-story extension that had a pub sign over the door. I hoped they served food there because, with everything that'd happened today, we'd forgotten to eat lunch. I was starving. Although I often forgot to eat when I was working on a project, today had been an exhausting day and I was ready to devour something big and greasy. I hoped they had more vegetarian options than just French fries.

Hayden hopped out of his truck and grabbed the plastic bag with his clothes and other necessities. I grabbed my backpack and followed him. Everyone smiled and looked relieved when we approached. I recognized a few people: Jeremy, Adrian, and Isaac. But there were others I didn't know too. Two of them, a demon and the man standing next to him, looked surprised when they saw me. They exchanged a look that I wished I could interpret.

"What are you all doing out here?" Hayden asked, glaring at each of them one at a time, including the cat.

"Waiting for you," Jeremy said with a wide smile. "We had the whole thing worked out for what we'd do if you tried to drive away. I named it Operation: Stop the Alpha Before He Does Something Stupid Again."

"It's like they know you," I said to Hayden.

That earned me a glare of my own. I laughed. Then Jeremy motioned me closer.

"You've met some of us but let me introduce the others." Jeremy motioned to the demon. I hadn't met many of his kind in my life, but after you've met one demon, you never forgot what they looked like. "This is Gage, also known as Mr. Dimples. Don't worry, he's bonded to Willow Lake, so he won't murder you."

"For Magic's sake, Jeremy," Adrian muttered.

"Well, it's true," Jeremy said with a little shrug.

Gage's dark horns glinted in the sun as he reached out to shake my hand. His horns were way more impressive than mine, although at least mine disappeared when I was in my human form. It was one of the quirks of demons that their horns were just always there, no matter what form they took. The only people who didn't see them were humans who hadn't seen under the Eternal Magic's glamour yet.

"I'm Gage Stewart. You can call me Gage," he said. "Welcome."

"So, Mr. Dimples isn't your formal name. Good to know," I said, making the demon grimace.

Jeremy snickered. Next, he gestured to the young man with curly brown hair standing beside the demon. "And this is his mate, Jake. Jake owns the place. He's also an oracle and a painter. He kind of does it all."

"Well, now that we're bonded, Gage and I both own the place," Jake amended as he shook my hand next. "And please don't ask for a reading or whatever. I can't do it on command. But I'm glad you are here. Probably happier than you could know." His gaze darted over to Hayden, then back to me.

"Over there is Teague," Jeremy said, pointing to a young-ish looking guy with reddish-brown hair. He had an average boy-next-door look about him. "He is our death mage, but don't worry about that. He's one of the good guys."

Teague looked confused at Jeremy's implication that he might not be a good person because of his magic. But he shook my hand. Then the cat, who was standing beside Jake, shook out its tri-colored fur and seemed to clear its throat.

"Don't worry, Paws, I didn't forget you." Jeremy pointed at the cat. "And this is Paws, also known as Pawington the Third."

"A pleasure, I'm sure. Yours, not mine," the cat said, tilting its head up regally.

"As he likes to remind us," Jeremy continued, "his pronouns are he and him. He insists we tell everyone from the start, so no one stares at his you know…" He gestured to his crotch.

"Um, okay. Hello." I waved at the cat. I didn't think you shook hands or paws or whatever with cats. I was pretty sure that was exclusively a dog thing. But I also knew this was no mere cat. I didn't know what he was, but magic clung to him.

"I think you met everyone else last night," Jeremy said, motioning to Isaac and Adrian. "But we might see some others inside."

"Can we go in now?" Hayden said. "Or do you want to introduce him to all the trees and shrubs too?"

"I'll grab your keys and show you where your rooms are," Jake said, ducking inside the door.

We followed him.

The doors opened into a large room with a reception desk to the right. Between the outside wall and the desk was a hallway. My stomach rumbled at the sight of the sign that said it led to the pub. I hoped we'd be going down that corridor soon.

The rest of the space was big and empty. There wasn't a bit of furniture in there and the walls were bare. On the far side of the room was a wide opening that led into another large room with a bunch of mismatched tables that looked like they'd been sourced from the side of the road on garbage day. The dining room, perhaps?

"Sorry," Jake said, catching my assessing gaze. "We're in the middle of doing some renovations, so things are a little unfinished at the moment. The tables are temporary until we can all agree on what we want. Although, between you and me, we'll probably just go with whatever Isaac suggests."

I shook my head. I didn't want the guy to feel bad about the place. "It looks great and I bet it'll be fantastic when you're finished."

Jake nodded. "Isaac has been amazing. He's over-seeing most of the renos. We're just doing what he says. Anyway, here we go, your rooms are on the second floor. They should be stocked with all the various common toiletries from shampoo in the shower to lube in the night-stand, but if you are looking for something you don't see, let me know. Do you want help with your bags?"

I glanced at my backpack and Hayden's plastic bag and shook my head.

"We're fine, Jake. Thanks for letting us stay here," Hayden said. "I appreciate it. And don't worry. We can find our own way."

Considering how gruff he'd been with Van and some of others, he was surprisingly gentle with Jake. I wondered what that meant, but before I could figure it out, Hayden scooped up the keys from the counter and turned to the stairs by the desk. He seemed to know where to go, so I followed behind him.

The stairs dumped us into a wide hallway. Another set of stairs continued up, but Hayden ignored them and marched all the way down the hallway like he owned the place. His hand clenched around the old-fashioned keys as he turned to the last door on the right.

It was only then that he glanced at the numbers on the keys. He swallowed and checked the sign on the door.

"Right." His voice cracked. "I'll stay in this one."

He offered the other key to me. I took it, but I didn't retreat down the hall to find my own room. I stayed at Hayden's side. He didn't seem to notice as he pushed the key into the lock and opened the door. He swallowed hard as he looked inside the room without entering it.

"Something wrong?" I asked.

He jolted like he'd forgotten I was standing there.

"Huh?"

"Is something wrong with the room?" I studied his face. "You look like you saw a ghost or something." Given the age of the place, I suspected more than a few ghosts lingered around the place, but I didn't think werewolves could see them.

He shook his head, then his gaze darted back to the room. "Nothing's wrong. This used to be my room. Years ago."

"Your room? You lived at an inn?" Had he been homeless?

"This used to be the pack house," he said. "My dad was the alpha."

Oh. That was good to know. People's deference to him made so much sense now.

I peered into the room. Everything was new, from the paint to the sturdy furnishings to the fluffy cream-colored blankets and crisp white sheets on the bed. If Isaac had really made all the decisions, he had a good eye. The place was cozy and comfortable, but still elegant.

Compared to the hallway and the staircase, which showed decades of wear, the room looked brand new. I doubted the space had looked like this when Hayden had lived here but, based on the way Hayden was staring at it, I wondered if he was even seeing what was here or if he was caught up in his memories.

"Come on, let's get settled," I said.

"Your room is next door, I think." His face contorted with pained emotion as he glanced down the hallway. He covered his emotions quickly, but I figured his memories were still getting the better of him.

I slipped his hand in mine and guided him into the room. Once we were inside, I shut the door and dropped my backpack on a luggage stand. When he did nothing but stand frozen where I'd left him, I pulled the plastic bag that held his clothing from his clenched hand and set it on a little table by a window. Then I approached him cautiously, making sure he could see me coming, not stopping until I was standing right in front of him. I pushed my glasses up and tilted my head back to look at him.

"Are you okay?"

His Adam's apple bobbed as he worked his throat. He

opened his mouth like he was going to speak, but he nodded instead. Except it was obvious he wasn't fine, and he was shit at hiding it.

"Do you want me to show you where your room is?" he asked.

"Nah. I'm good staying here with you." I probably should have asked him if he was comfortable with that before making my decision, but I wasn't leaving him alone right now, no matter how he might have answered.

His forehead furrowed. "They gave you your own room."

"Meh." I shrugged. "I've decided I'm staying with you."

"Why?" His confusion was turning into suspicion. At least he wasn't frozen in place anymore.

"Do you want a list?"

"Is this about the kiss?" He licked his bottom lip.

"Do you want it to be about the kiss?" I waggled my eyebrows.

He stepped back and rubbed his forehead. "Why do you keep answering my questions with more questions?"

The guy had been through a lot today, what with his shift not working and his brother trying to kill him. I shouldn't have teased him.

There were several ways I could answer him, and all of them would be the truth. I opted for the one that would tug on his alpha instincts, since those seemed to drive a lot of what he did. Maybe thinking about someone other than himself would jolt him out of the past.

"I don't think I can sleep in a strange room by myself

tonight." I shivered. "The last time that happened, I was abducted."

"Robbie wouldn't dare attack you here."

"I know you're right, but is everything you feel and think logical?"

"Fair." He eyed me more closely. "What else? What aren't you telling me?"

I met his gaze steadily. "I don't trust you to stay put. The doctor trusted me to keep you safe and I failed. I won't mess up again."

Hayden scowled and turned away from me. He stalked to the window and yanked open the curtains to peer out at the trees. I could still see his face reflected in the window.

"Why are you squishing up your face like that? You know it is true."

"I'm responsible for my own actions," he said.

"Sure. But that doesn't change how I feel."

"How you feel? Right. You think I'm no better than a young pup who needs to be babysat." He was all bristly and sharp. His back was rigid. His hands clenched into fists. His jaw was tight.

I sidled up to him, pressing my front to his back, and wrapped my arms around his tense body, pleased when he didn't pull away. He was taller than me, so I rested my head against his back, right between his shoulder blades. He was warm and solid, and I kind of wanted to melt into him.

"Well, that's not all that I feel," I whispered. "We should talk about the kiss."

He inhaled sharply.

"I want to try it again. You know, when we don't think we're going to die."

With my ear pressed to his back, I could hear the tempo of his heart pick up.

"This is a terrible time to do this," he said. "You just escaped from that tunnel. I had no business putting you in danger again. You aren't—"

I smacked his chest, not enough to hurt him, but enough to get his attention. He stopped talking. "If you are going to say I'm not capable of making decisions right now or I'm suffering from some kind of white knight syndrome or I've imprinted on you like a baby duck, you can stop. I'm old enough to know my mind. I'm old enough to know what I want. I've been on my own for over a decade. I created a life and a business all on my own with no support."

"I hate that no one was there to support you. That's so fucking wrong. What a bunch of assholes."

Yeah, it had sucked, but I'd survived. I didn't regret what'd happened. But Hayden's unequivocal belief that my herd was in the wrong made me smile. This guy. I snuggled closer.

"Thank you, but that's not the point I'm trying to make," I said. "Just because I'm smaller than you, and my supernatural form doesn't lend itself to fighting, doesn't mean I'm weak or weak-minded. So, fuck off with all those thoughts. The only thing you need to be thinking about is if you want to kiss me again too."

He didn't answer for several long minutes. Then he brought his hands up and covered mine with his where they were pressed against his torso.

"And if I do?" he whispered.

"Then we have a plan. I'll stay in this room with you. But we'll go downstairs and get something to eat because I'm starving, and I know you could stand to eat something too. After that, we'll come back up here and kiss again. We don't have to sleep together—as in the naked, sweaty kind of sleeping together—I'm sure they have a cot kicking around somewhere. But we're going to stay in this room together. I think both of us will feel better that way."

His chest was rising and falling quickly. "You are sure you don't want your own room?"

"Do you not want me in here? I don't want to make you uncomfortable. I won't force myself on you," I said, even as I kept my arms wrapped around Hayden. "If you don't want me here, I'll go."

His hands tightened on mine, and he shook his head. "I want you to stay."

I closed my eyes and hugged him tighter. "Good."

Chapter Twenty-One

HAYDEN

I couldn't figure Ryley out. He wasn't like anyone else I knew.

Only a few people in Willow Lake didn't automatically defer to me—Van, Gage, Xander, occasionally Buddy, and I supposed Paws should be on that list too. But, even with them, there was a subtle recognition that I was the alpha here, no matter how many times I corrected them. Being an alpha was a position that demanded respect. Sure, I could laugh with them and the others, chat with them, maybe joke around once in a while, but in the end, everyone deferred to me.

So having Ryley stand up to me, confidently, I might add, and tell me what he wanted without being coy or averting his eyes or any of the usual shit... Well, it was confusing. But that was nothing new. He'd been confusing me right from the start.

I didn't want to wait to kiss him, but when his stomach

growled again, almost as loud as my wolf did when he was feeling moody, I figured I'd better get him fed. It wouldn't hurt me any to grab a bite too, I supposed. Because, fuck, it'd been a long day. Since I worked a physical job, I rarely tired so easily, but the last couple of days—or maybe the last couple of months—were finally catching up with me.

When was the last time I had a decent meal? I couldn't remember.

Lately, I'd been skipping nights out at the pub to chase down Robbie. But my wolf's usual desire to hunt my brother was abnormally quiet, even with this new lead. Damn it. I had to figure out what was wrong with my magic. I couldn't stay benched. Not now.

And if my wolf never responded again?

My heartbeats stuttered at the thought. Was that possible?

If it was, I'd have to figure out a different way to confront Robbie. But one way or the other, he had to be stopped. And I had to be the one to do it. This whole situation was my failure to correct, my responsibility.

"Hey, you." Ryley snapped his fingers, jolting me out of my thoughts. "I don't know what you are thinking about, but that's enough."

"I didn't mean to ignore you."

He shook his head. "Don't say shit like that. I'm not high maintenance. I don't need your attention on me twenty-four seven. But whatever you were thinking wasn't good, and no one needs that."

I supposed he might be right.

"So, tell me about this place," he said. "It might help you relax a bit to talk through whatever is bothering you."

"Do you always use the word 'so' so much, or are you still trying to make a point?"

"Fuck off," he said with a laugh. "I keep telling you it is an amazing word to start a conversation with. Just roll with it."

"Why don't we get cleaned up and then head down to the pub? It'll be easier to just show you around."

I let Ryley take the bathroom first. He seemed eager to change out of the clothing he'd been wearing, and now that he had his backpack, he had options.

As I waited, I looked around the room. It'd changed a lot, at least on the surface. But I could still envision it as it had been when I'd moved out. For a moment, I couldn't quite take a full breath. My chest was so damn constricted with emotions and guilt and other shit I didn't want to deal with right now. Why did Ryley want to talk about this place? What would I even say?

The last thing I wanted was to talk about the pack house and why it was no longer a pack house and all the stuff that happened twelve years ago. If I didn't tell him, though, someone else would, because they always did. It didn't take long before newbies called me alpha, like the rest of the assholes around here. But I didn't want Ryley getting filled in by someone else either…

I rather liked how things were between us now. And, okay, I might have been thinking about the possibility of more kisses. Although why, I didn't know. The idea of hooking up had never influenced me before. Would that change when he found out about my past? Would he look at me the same way other potential lovers had looked at me? I didn't want that.

As bizarre as it was, I liked how Ryley saw me as a flawed guy. He already knew I lived in a rundown travel trailer behind the garage, so he didn't have any illusions about me. And yet he still wanted to kiss me.

Was something wrong with him that none of that had scared him away yet?

Did I want to scare him away? When would I have another opportunity to be with someone who saw me, Hayden, as I was right now? Not as I had been before the pack dissolved and not as I could be if I became alpha.

Ryley opened the bathroom door. Warm humid air from his shower followed him out. His wet hair glistened under the light. I was disappointed he wasn't wearing my shirt anymore, but his clean clothes, wrinkled from having been bundled in his backpack for weeks, molded to his slim body in a way that made me want to explore him. But the best part was how refreshed and happy he looked.

"Your turn," Ryley said with a grin. "Do you need help cleaning any hard-to-reach places? I just put these clothes on, but I could take them off again."

"I think I can manage." I laughed as I stepped around him to get to the bathroom.

I closed the door and glanced at the mirror over the sink to see I was still smiling. He was so damn easy to be around. I liked it. I kept grinning as I stripped off my clothes. Yeah. I definitely wanted to kiss him again. And maybe, probably, absolutely do more. At least for a few nights.

And just like that, my smile faded.

Right.

Ryley would leave soon.

Why did that thought make my chest ache?

I stepped into the tiled shower stall and turned on the water. As the water washed over me, my muscles refused to relax. My heart raced. I didn't want him to leave.

Wait. He couldn't be my mate, could he?

Shit, shit, shit.

My heart galloped as I stood frozen under the pounding water. All the signs were there, weren't they? First, Ryley was drawn to the area. Then my compulsion to be close to him was strange, to say the least. And the icing on top was my unusual desire to kiss him when I hadn't wanted to kiss anyone for years.

What the ever-loving fuck was I going to do about that?

The last thing anyone needed was to be saddled with a dud of a mate like me. Assuming Ryley even wanted a mate, he wouldn't want me if he knew more about me. I made bad decisions. I hurt the people who counted on me. I wasn't fit to be an alpha, and I definitely wasn't fit to be Ryley's mate.

Then there was the fact that Ryley didn't feel comfortable being around supes. He'd been anxious every time he met someone, and I knew that wasn't because he was shy. Ryley was not a shy guy by nature, but his herd had really fucked him over. So how would that work when I couldn't leave Willow Lake, and he wouldn't want to stay? I wasn't the alpha, but I could never leave, not until a new alpha was here to take care of everyone.

What was it that Ryley had said when I'd first found him in the woods? Son of a fucking, cloven-hoofed dick weasel. Yep, that sounded about right.

Chapter Twenty-Two

RYLEY

Hayden was quiet when he came out of the bathroom. He remained quiet the whole way down to the pub. I wasn't sure what'd happened between him going into the bathroom and now, but I doubted it involved any masturbatory fun. No. He looked queasy. And whenever I caught his eye on me, he looked away.

Shit. I'd come on too strong.

Oh well. If he wasn't interested, I could take a hint. I hadn't surrendered the key to the other room to Jake yet, just in case, so I'd still have a place to sleep tonight. It was a letdown, though. I thought he was as keen to kiss, and possibly do more, as I was.

My brain scrambled for some other explanation. Like, what if he was hungry? That could make him queasy, right? Wolves had enormous appetites and all he'd eaten today was that breakfast bagel.

So, before I got worried that I'd be sleeping alone

tonight, I'd get him to eat a big supper to get his blood sugar up and his magic replenished. I hadn't lived with supes for a long time, and I didn't use my magic often, but I knew the supe equivalent of being hangry was not something to mess with.

When we stepped into the pub, the amount of magic in the place overwhelmed me. My skin tingled, and the hairs on the back of my neck quivered. I grabbed Hayden's hand.

"Holy fuckeroo."

"What?" Hayden cast his gaze around the room, as if looking for a threat. "What's the matter?"

"There are a lot of supes in here," I whispered into his ear. "Is it safe? Should I order and take it back to my room?"

I should have expected this, especially when I'd met so many supes in Willow Lake already. But somehow none of that had prepared me for seeing all these beings gathered in one place.

Was that a troll in the corner? And over by the pool table, the minotaur we'd seen at the café that morning was leaning over to take a shot. Plus there was the incubus and the merman and the bear shifter... The list kept going on and on.

Hayden's forehead furrowed. "We can eat upstairs if you want, but why?"

I'd told him this already. Had he forgotten? I leaned in close until my lips brushed his ear. He shivered as my breath washed over his skin. "I'm only half-supe, remember? My dad was mundane. Most supes don't like my kind."

"That's bullshit," Hayden said, way louder than I was comfortable with.

People all around the bar swung their gazes in our direction. I cringed and tried to hide behind Hayden. If I had to butt heads with someone, I would, but I'd prefer not to. Not that it usually got that far when I shifted. Most people thought twice about banging heads with someone who had horns, even when said horns were on the diminutive end of the horn spectrum.

"Shut up," I whisper-shouted to him out of the side of my mouth. The last thing I needed was for Hayden to draw more attention to us.

He dragged me back through the doors leading to the inn. Damn it. I guessed we wouldn't be eating. Maybe they had room service. But Hayden didn't pull me all the way back to our rooms. He stopped in the hallway and spun me to look at him.

"I swear on the Eternal Magic that not a single person in Willow Lake will care about your lineage. And they'd never know you had a human for a father anyway. Not if you didn't tell anyone. No one can tell something like that, because it doesn't matter. Magic wins, remember? The supernatural side of your genes trumps everything else. But if you don't feel comfortable, we won't go in there."

"I'm pretty sure they can tell," I said, pushing my glasses up my nose. It was a nervous habit that gave me something to do with my hands other than wringing them like a dishrag. "I've been roughed up enough to know that hybrids aren't welcome in supe towns."

"Has anyone made you feel uncomfortable while

you've been here?" A deep growl punctuated his question. His eyes flashed with the gold of his wolf.

"Hey, your wolf…" I pointed at him. "I saw it in your eyes. That's a good sign, right? Is it back?"

"Ryley," he said, in a tone that suggested I was being difficult. "Answer my question. You've met a lot of supes since I found you in the woods last night. Have any of them been less than welcoming?"

He was right. None of them had called me anything nasty or made me feel uncomfortable. Well, except for the dragon. But I thought his behavior was because he wanted to protect Hayden, not because of who or what I was.

"We were talking about other things then. I was useful to them. But I'm not useful to all those other people in there." I glanced toward the door. "A dozen supes are in there. Maybe more."

Hayden cleared his throat, as if trying to tamp down on his growling. "So I don't have to kick anyone's ass?"

"You said 'so,'" I said, forcing a grin. I said it to distract him from whatever hell he was thinking about unleashing on his friends and neighbors. He didn't need to burn any bridges because of me. I was used to being the odd guy out, but I'd prefer to skip the part where people were assholes to me. It was easier to avoid them. "I should go to the room."

"Is that a 'No'?" Hayden pressed.

"Fine. No. Everyone so far has been nice. But I don't want to tempt fate."

"Good. That's good." He nodded. His gaze caught on mine and held. "I swear, Ryley, we would have gone somewhere else if I didn't think it would be safe here. I've known most of these people for years. They are good people." He rubbed the back of his neck. "I didn't want to talk about this, but it might help." He met my eyes again. He sighed, and I didn't like the dejected way it sounded. Hayden should never sound defeated or sad. "About twelve years ago, my parents died."

I opened my mouth to say something, but sorry didn't seem like enough.

"Don't," he said. "Don't say anything yet. Let me finish saying this."

I nodded.

"My brother seized the opportunity to splinter the pack. The ones who left, they were assholes who might have believed in all that hybrid shit. They only wanted wolves in Willow Lake. They didn't want any other supes here. Just wolves. They were assholes, the whole lot of them." He shook his head like he couldn't make sense of their bigotry. "But the ones who stayed? They are the ones who are in that pub right now or the ones who moved here since that happened and have been welcomed."

I glanced toward the pub doors. It was strange to see so many types of supes in one place. *Was* there something different about Willow Lake?

"Think about it," Hayden continued. "Think about all the supes you've already met here. We don't tolerate bigots. Jerks who think they are better than everyone else because of their narrow-minded opinions, or their cultish ideas about the Eternal Magic, or their incorrect views about supernatural hierarchy aren't welcome here." Emotion laced Hayden's passionate words.

I was starting to see why people called him Alpha. His

love for this place and these people was as much a part of him as his wolf or the color of his hair.

"That's what makes Willow Lake so special," he said softly. "It's become everything my parents dreamed about. They believed in inclusivity and helping others and the joy in discovering all the things that bring us together rather than the things that pull people apart. Hateful rhetoric like what you're talking about, that shit doesn't fly here. I swear. Those people in that pub, they won't judge you based on the type of supe you are or that your father was human. People like that aren't welcome in Willow Lake. In fact, I sometimes wonder if the Eternal Magic herself encourages them to leave. The ones who stay save their judgments for things that matter, like how you treat people."

I swallowed hard. I wiped my eyes because they were burning and blurring a bit.

"I think the Eternal Magic brought you here, Ryley." Hayden bit his lip, but it wasn't a sexy move. He looked nervous. "I think she wanted you here because you fit here, with me... I mean, with us."

I couldn't deny that I'd felt like she had been steering me in this direction ever since I'd set out on the road, but what Hayden was saying? That sounded too good to be true.

"I thought you changed your mind about me."

"Why do you say that?"

"You've been acting weird since you had your shower."

Hayden frowned. "That's on me. Not you." He rubbed his neck. "I have some shit I need to figure out. Van says I overthink things and get stuck in my thoughts, but I don't know how to stop doing that. I didn't mean to make you think I'd changed my mind about you."

I didn't think he was lying to me. "Do you really think they won't know my dad was mundane?"

"They might judge you for your T-shirts," Hayden said, "but they won't care about your parentage."

I glanced down at what I was wearing. It featured a cup of coffee with squiggly lines coming up from it like steam and the word *Energize*.

"Hey, my T-shirt is amazing." I swatted at him. And after being joyously reunited with coffee this morning, I thought it was appropriate.

He grinned.

Some of my anxiety eased while I was talking with him, but it spiked again when I glanced toward the pub. There were a lot of supes on the other side of that door. "Are you really sure? I don't want to cause problems."

"I'm sure. But if you feel uncomfortable, we can leave."

"I wouldn't want to drag you away from your friends," I blurted. "I'll go if it gets weird."

"Ryley," he said, shaking his head.

"What?"

"We'll do this together." His gaze held mine, as if he was willing me to see his sincerity.

And I did. It was like a warm hug. He trusted his friends, but if things went sideways, he would have my back. He wouldn't abandon me. I sucked in a shaky breath. Had anyone else in my life done that for me? I couldn't remember a time when that'd happened. Not one instance where someone said they'd stand with me. The burning sensation in my eyes grew more intense, so I looked away and blinked rapidly. Regular people didn't get emotional going to a pub and I shouldn't either.

"If you want to leave, let me know," Hayden said quietly. "I'll go with you."

Any other protests or worries faded. They didn't go away completely, but I straightened my shoulders and nodded. "Okay. Let's try this again."

Hayden slipped his hand in mine and gave it a gentle squeeze. "I'm going to be right beside you."

And that made it easier to step through those doors again.

Chapter Twenty-Three

HAYDEN

The pub was surprisingly busy for a weeknight. And, given the way most of the people stared at Ryley and me when we walked through the pub doors that second time, I had a pretty good idea what had drawn them all out tonight.

Nosy bastards. The whole lot of them.

Even Daphne Rivers was here, sitting with a bunch of other well-seasoned gossips. I should have expected as much when I'd seen two of her sons in line at the Flying Rowan this morning.

Normally, that would make me growl, but today it didn't. What I said to Ryley was true. None of these people were malicious. They cared about each other, and, for some reason, even after I'd messed up so badly, they still cared about me, too.

The deeper we walked into the pub, the more the feeling of rightness settled over me. How had I never realized how calming it was to be surrounded by these people? Talking to Ryley about these people had cracked something inside me and now everything was just... More? Different? Better? I squeezed Ryley's hand, hoping he sensed it too.

My eyes were getting watery. I swallowed hard and hoped no one noticed. Not that I cared if they saw me cry, but because I wasn't ready to talk about *why* I was crying, not until I understood what all of this meant.

And who knows? Maybe I was just feeling this way because I was tired. Yeah, okay, I didn't think that was the real reason.

A surge of energy rushed through me as if people's affection for me was a tangible thing. I didn't deserve their caring and goodwill, but I needed to quit fighting it. If I worked hard, someday I might be able to redeem myself and be worthy of it.

I nodded to several of the regulars as I led us across the room to where the guys Ryley had already met were sitting. They'd pushed a couple of tables together, so I suspected more people would be coming. I hoped it wouldn't be too overwhelming for him. Like always, Jeremy was sitting in the middle of the group, scribbling madly in one of his many, many notebooks. Adrian was at his side, watching Jeremy like he was the center of his world, which I guessed he was.

Dillon was looking at Ash the same way. The big hellhound had his mate tucked under his arm. Ash was in another of his pink sweaters. He must wear nothing else. Just pink sweaters. Every pink under the sun. Although, I mostly wore T-shirts in various shades of gray, so maybe it wasn't all that different.

Surprisingly, Ogden and Simon were there too. Simon had changed a lot since he'd met his mate, grown more confident and settled, but right now he looked ready to shift and hide. His mate whispered that he didn't need to do anything he wasn't comfortable with.

It was the same type of thing I'd said to Ryley. Shit. Was that another sign he was my mate? Maybe it was better not to think about that too much right now. If Jeremy sensed something, he'd start asking ten thousand questions about it.

Isaac and Teague were at the other end. They nodded at us in greeting.

"Wait," Jeremy said, not looking up from what he was writing. "Slow down. One idea at a time."

Paws sat on the table beside Jeremy, leaning over to watch Jeremy's pen move over the paper. He swatted at the end of the pen, like a house cat.

"Stop that, Paws," Jeremy muttered. "Adrian, can you get one of my pens from my bag and give it to Paws to play with? I'll have to remember to grab one of Clawie's toys and stick it in my bag for next time."

Paws froze. "I never… I wouldn't… I wasn't…"

"I hope I'm here when Jeremy gives a cat toy to Paws so I can record it. My parents would love to see that," Ogden whispered to Simon with a grin as he watched the confused cat-like creature try to deny what he'd been doing.

"I don't know what you're talking about." Paws flicked

his tail and started cleaning his face with his paw, like that had been his intention all along.

When I let go of Ryley's hand to pull a couple more chairs over, I missed his warm touch immediately. It must just be that my magic, even in its weakened state, was still encouraging me to comfort him. The others shuffled their chairs around to make room for us.

"Do you know everyone?" I asked Ryley once we were seated. I slipped my hand into his again under the table, just to comfort him. Remind him he wasn't alone. Really.

Ryley's gaze darted around the table, like he was apprehensive about making eye contact with anyone. I hadn't known Ryley for long, but it was strange to see him so uncertain. Where had the guy gone who'd kicked me in the face? Or demanded I get my ass back inside when I'd tried to leave last night? Or snuck into the back of my truck when I'd tried to go out to hunt Robbie this morning?

"Yeah, I think so," he said with a quick nod.

"So, the other day we were talking about human sports," Ash said to us. "And you can imagine what happened next."

I lifted an eyebrow. "What?"

"They want to have a Willow Lake Olympics for supes," Ash said.

"Of course they do," I muttered.

Jeremy looked down at his notebook. "I still don't see how this is going to work. Let's say we have a swimming competition. Is it fair to put all these different supes in the same race? Kelpies, mermen, and octopus shifters don't really have anything in common except that they all like water. Have we missed anyone? Are there any other supes in town who like water?"

"Who is in charge of the betting?" someone from another table asked.

"Isn't it illegal to gamble on things like that?" Ryley asked.

I shrugged. "As long as the wagers are small, Van turns a blind eye to that kind of thing."

"There will be betting?" Paws perked up and started purring. "Perfect. Ash, get a piece of paper and a pen from Jeremy. You can record the bets." He cleared his throat. "Listen up, everyone. The first competition is open for bets now. Brodie, Weston, Henrietta, and Gary are competing in the swimming competition."

Brodie, who'd been delivering a big plate of nachos, froze when he heard his name.

"Bets for each sport will be kept separate," Paws continued. "All bets are final. Doesn't matter if new competitors are introduced later. Place your bets with Ash now. Two dollars a bet, maximum five bets per person per competition."

"Shouldn't we ask everyone if they want to compete first?" Ash asked, but he was already grabbing a pen from Jeremy's bag.

"My money is on Weston," someone yelled over to Ash. "That merman's been swimming in that lake every day for years. He knows that lake better than anyone, and have you seen the size of his tail? That thing is massive."

"That's not all he's got that's massive," another man said, rather loudly. "It's true what they say about the size of a merman's fins being proportional, if you know what I mean."

A few people chuckled.

Brodie's nostrils flared. He glared at the man who'd spoken. He marched over with the nachos and appeared to trip as he approached the table. The nachos went flying, right onto the guy who'd more or less announced he'd slept with Weston. Shouts of surprise shot up from the man and his friends.

"I'm so sorry," Brodie said with false sincerity. "Are you okay?"

They brushed away his apology, even the guy covered in chips, salsa, and sour cream. Everyone in town knew Brodie's unfortunate history, which gave him a lot of leeway. No one wanted to be the asshole who yelled at the kid who'd been rescued from a cage.

I caught Brodie's eye when he rushed by. His eyes widened and his cheeks darkened when he realized I'd seen what he'd done. He ducked his head and rushed across the room. I was going to have to monitor him. If his crush on Weston started interfering with his work or the pack dynamics, I'd have to talk to him. As it was, no one else seemed to realize Brodie's accident was anything but accidental.

"I don't know, man," someone else, from yet another table, said as they watched Brodie disappear into the kitchen. "That Brodie is a kelpie, so yeah, more horse than fish, but he's young and that gives him the advantage."

"So, no one's betting on Henrietta or Gary?" Ash asked.

Silence. Sure, they were octopus shifters, but they were

also the local bakers and liked to sample their own goods. Looked like no one thought racing would be their forte.

"I will," Sally shouted from the bar. The incubus had been in a casual relationship with them for years. They'd finally made things a little less casual this summer. "You'd never know it, but they have a lot of stamina." She waggled her eyebrows. "If anyone wants details so they can make an educated bet, I'll tell you all about it."

Yeah. I didn't think any of us needed to know those details.

"Next we have long distance running," Jeremy said. "So, mostly shifters, I guess?"

"Dillon will compete," Ash volunteered.

Jeremy turned his head to his own mate.

"Fine," Adrian said. "I will too."

"Then there is Hayden. Oh, and Van too," Jeremy said, making more marks in his notebook.

Adrian groaned. "I'll never win against the alpha."

"Wait a minute," I said. "When did I say I'd compete?"

Everyone turned to look at me with varying degrees of exasperation.

"Don't bother protesting," Paws said. "We all know you'll do it in the end, so let's skip to that part."

"Fine," I said, sitting back in my chair. The damn cat was probably right.

"It doesn't matter anyway," Isaac said from the other end of the table. "I'm going to win."

"No way," Teague said. "Nelson will win, hands down."

Isaac's jaw dropped in disbelief. "Nelson can't compete in a race like that. He doesn't run; he just pops from one shadow to another. Is there a flying competition? Stick him in that instead."

"But is he really flying?" Jeremy stroked his chin. "I should make a note of that for my *Amazing Book of Super Supes*. But it brings us back around to the concern I had right from the start. I don't see how this can work."

"We don't have to figure it all out tonight," Adrian said, rubbing Jeremy's back.

Ryley leaned close to me. "Is it always like this?"

I glanced around. Jeremy and the others were still arguing over competition categories and who should compete in what. People were shouting out bets to Ash for categories that hadn't even been discussed yet. Levi and Carter were over at the pool table, trying to distract Parker from noticing what everyone else was saying. He was the only human in the place who didn't know about supes. Jake was busy behind the bar. Buddy and Alice were feeding one another fries in a back corner of the pub. Old Thom was tucked away in another corner with a honey-colored beer, grumbling about how it wasn't as good as Witch's Milk. Paws was sitting in the middle of our table with his head tilted at an imperious angle, as if we were all his minions.

"Yeah. Pretty much," I said.

"Huh," was all he said, as he went back to studying everyone in the pub.

Jake finished up with a patron at the bar and came over to us with a couple of food menus. I didn't need one, but I took it anyway.

"Sorry it took me so long to get over here. But, holy O'Keeffe, is it busy in here tonight," Jake said, glancing around with a bemused look on his face. "What can I get you to drink?"

"You didn't have to bring these over. I would have come to the bar," I said, realizing I should have done that as soon as we walked in. But I hadn't wanted to leave Ryley alone.

"No worries," Jake said. "You want your usual, Hayden?"

That was the thing I'd always liked about Jake. He usually called me by my name. None of that alpha crap with him. "Yeah. That'd be good."

Ryley read the list of what was on tap. "And I'll have a wheat ale."

"Yes," Jeremy said as he grinned at us, like he'd been listening to see what Ryley would order. Then he made a note in his book. "I totally called that. Wheat ale for the faun, just like Isaac and Levi."

"If you want food, I'll grab your order when I get back with your drinks."

After we had our drinks and had ordered our food, Ryley and I sipped our drinks and watched everyone organize a mini Supernatural Olympics. That was entertainment enough. Being surrounded by people I considered friends while holding Ryley's hand was surprisingly comfortable. I could see the speculative looks on people's faces, but no one bombarded us with intrusive questions. Not even Jeremy.

That was also surprising, because my pack rarely held back their curiosity or their opinions.

My pack.

That wasn't the first time tonight that I'd thought of

these people as my pack and hadn't cringed. And if I was being completely honest, that'd started before tonight.

Did that mean I wanted to be alpha?

For the first time, that question didn't make me nauseous. I looked around the room again, letting my gaze drift over all these people. Warmth filled me. A tingling sensation that started deep in my core fluttered to life. It felt like magic. Then, as if that thought triggered a gateway to the alpha magic I'd always tried to shun, the little fluttering sensation grew. Streams of light flickered to life. They seemed to come from me.

What the—?

More threads than I could count wove through the air like beautiful, shimmering streams of magic. I gaped at them. What was happening? My heart pounded, but I wasn't scared.

Ryley turned to me. "Is something the matter? Is your beer off?"

He couldn't see the thread. Was I imagining this? At the other end of the table, Teague bolted out of his chair and stared at me in shock.

"What?" Isaac, Adrian, and Dillon said in unison as soon as Teague reacted, and they jumped to their feet. They were poised to attack as they looked around for a threat, but they didn't seem to notice the dazzling light show any more than Ryley had.

Teague's expression turned into a smile. A wide, exuberant smile.

"Alpha," he said in an awed tone, as he tilted his head to the side.

The threads undulated as they stretched out from me.

The first one, the strongest one, reached for Ryley. As soon as it touched him, he gasped. A sweet smile crossed his face. He rubbed his chest. Immediately, a soft wave of acknowledgment and acceptance rolled back to me along the thread that connected us. Was he aware he'd done that? Agreed to be in my pack? Because that's what that was, right?

I gulped.

My pack…

I had a fucking pack.

"What was that?" he asked.

But I didn't have time to answer, because more threads were reaching out. Some stopped at the people in the room, but others shot through the walls to places beyond the room, extending way beyond the building.

A ripple of awareness and joy bubbled up around me, through me. Those golden threads vibrated and pulsed with warmth and happiness. All except one. But a tsunami of joy swept away that shock of pain. These people—I let out a bark of laughter even as my damn eyes were stinging again—were my pack.

These people were my pack.

Everyone turned to face me and a wave of soft, reverent whispers of "Alpha" swept through the room.

I rubbed my chest, feeling the magic inside me grow stronger and stronger as it reached out to each person in the pack, and they wordlessly accepted me as their alpha.

Fuck.

I had a pack.

Maybe I always had.

I could admit to myself this much, at least: I didn't hate

the way it felt, this nearly tangible connection to the people in Willow Lake. I'd denied it for so long, so many times, that the idea of it still made me squirm, even if the reality of it was… nice.

But was it normal to hate it too? Because, now what? How could I live up to this important duty? I was a disaster. The decisions I'd made in the past had injured the pack. How could I ever make all this right?

I couldn't figure this out tonight. I knew that. And suddenly I wondered if Jake had anything behind the counter that'd calm my rising—I should call it what it was —panic. Sweat beaded along my hairline. My hand squeezed Ryley's. I fought the urge to run out of the pub and find a place to hide like Simon used to do.

In retrospect, I should have known that the Eternal Magic would figure out a way to get what she wanted in the end. And now, in less than twenty-four hours, I suddenly had both a pack and a potential mate.

Fuck my life.

Chapter Twenty-Four

HAYDEN

"Hayden? What's the matter?" Ryley's soft question jolted me out of my spiraling panic. "You look a little flushed."

"Uh, yeah…" I cleared my throat.

The blazing brightness of the shimmering golden threads softened and dimmed. They weren't gone, I could still feel them in the core where my magic lived, but they started to fade from sight.

As one, the people in the pub moved closer to me. Ryley's eyes widened, and he leaned closer to me.

"Sit the fuck down," Paws shouted. His words vibrated through the room. "Give the alpha some damn space. We all knew he was our alpha, nothing's changed, so sit your asses down."

People grumbled, but they did as the cat said. I let out a shaky breath.

"Ash," Paws said, "go check the board. Who won?"

Ryley's forehead crinkled, and his eyes narrowed behind his glasses. "What's going on?"

I wiped my hand down my face. "I, uh, may have acknowledged the people in Willow Lake as my pack in my head, and the Eternal Magic jumped on it and let everyone know I was now their alpha. It bothered me for a minute there, but I'll figure it out. I don't have any other choice."

"Was that what I felt?" Ryley rubbed his chest.

I nodded. "I don't think most people could see it, but there were these magical thread things connecting me to the pack. There was one going to you too."

"But I'm not your pack," Ryley said, blinking at me like he didn't understand, his forehead furrowing even deeper in his confusion.

My chest spasmed at his words. He didn't mean to hurt me; I knew that. It wasn't his fault that he didn't understand, and I didn't blame him. But it still stung.

"You could be," I said. "I would like you to stay."

"You would? But I'm..." He glanced around, as if suddenly remembering the room was full of supes. He was worried about having a mundane human as a father again. As if any of these people would care about something like that, but he'd figure that out, eventually.

I'd love to track down his damn herd and hurt them as much as they'd hurt Ryley. An angry alpha wolf shifter set loose in a herd of fauns could do a bit of damage, especially with the Eternal Magic as my sidekick. Because she would have my back in this case, I just knew it.

"Of course I would. I think you belong here, if you want to stay."

His eyes were glossy, but he didn't look away. "I might like that, for a little while. We could try it for a bit. See if it works."

On impulse, I raised his hand to my lips and kissed it softly. "I think this will work."

People hooted. Shit, I'd forgotten we were in the pub.

A few tables over, Daphne Rivers said, "I told you we needed to be here tonight, and I was right, wasn't I?"

A series of curses cut across the room of hushed whispers. I glanced over to see Ash struggling to get a vintage sign down. The bets were usually taped to the side that faced the wall. I supposed it was a good hiding spot, but I was a little disappointed that they hadn't found a different place for this last bet. Jake, who owned the place, had been the subject of a betting pool for almost a year and had never known it was there, but I had.

"Dillon," Paws said, "go help your mate get the board off the wall. He's too short to unhook it."

"Fuck off, Paws," Ash shouted back. "I'm not short. The damned wire is caught on the hook. I just need to..." His words tapered off as he wiggled the sign to get it loose.

Flames flared in Dillon's eyes with the fire of his hellhound as he watched his mate stretch and twist. He jumped up from his seat, his gaze never leaving his mate's body, and stalked over to Ash. When he got there, he wrapped his hands over Ash's hips and kissed his neck.

"Dillon, quit kissing your mate and bring the board over here," Paws ordered.

"I think I'm missing something," Ryley said.

"They have a bet going on. They wagered when I would accept that I was their alpha," I explained.

"You knew?" Jeremy asked.

"Of course I knew. There is always a bet. So, when no one asked me to place a wager on something after Jake's bet ended, it was obvious the new bet was about me."

"Whatever," Paws muttered. "Just because he figured it out doesn't invalidate the wager."

Dillon and Ash returned to the table, smelling of arousal. I rubbed my nose. I hadn't needed to scent that. Dillon set the board on the table in front of us and circled today's date on the calendar that showed everyone's guesses. He frowned at Paws. "You're just saying that because you had today as your guess."

"Oh? Did I win?" Paws' fake surprise wasn't fooling anyone. I knew from experience that the cat knew perfectly well what days he had picked. He probably had everyone else's wagers memorized too.

"Why does he get to bet?" someone moaned from a nearby table. "It isn't like he needs money. Jake feeds him and houses him. Can he even spend money anywhere? I bet he doesn't even have a bank account or a wallet. Where would he put his winnings?"

"Come here and say that to my face, asshole," Paws said. "Because the last I heard, what I do with my money isn't any of your business. But, please, keep talking if you don't want to bet on anything in the future."

The complainer didn't say anything more, but I could tell he was wondering who appointed Paws the one who controlled the pub's betting. I'd pay to watch someone try to wrestle control from the cat. My money would be on Paws. I didn't know what he was, but he was no mere cat shifter.

The more attention Paws drew to himself, the less panicky I felt. The cat, as if sensing I was thinking about him, winked at me like I was in on a joke, then shouted out more insults and commands. Slowly, people quit staring at me like I was a novelty. I sat back in my seat and watched everyone carry on around me. Except for the lingering warmth in my chest, I could almost pretend it was a normal night at the pub. Almost.

Then Gage and Van rushed into the pub, followed by a whole mob of townsfolk.

I groaned.

Gage and Van pushed through the pub to get to our table. When they arrived, Van stared at me for a long moment, before nodding sharply. "It's about time."

I shook my head. "Fuck off."

"I'm glad to see nothing else has changed," he said. "I told you it wouldn't. You've always been Willow Lake's alpha."

"Yeah, yeah, yeah," I muttered. "Grab a drink and sit down. I don't need you towering over me." I glanced at Gage. "You should do the same."

Van glanced around the room.

"I need to sort out this crowd first." He went to the bar, where Jake was staring at the massive crowd with a panicked look on his face. Jeremy and Alice had already gone behind the bar to help him. Van said a few words to Jeremy, who nodded and looked relieved. Then they propped open the doors that led to the parking lot, where a bunch of people were waiting to get in.

It was like all of Willow Lake had come. It was almost as if I'd called them here.

But I hadn't, had I?

Van whistled, getting everyone's attention.

"Anyone parked in the parking lot, get out there and move your vehicle to the road. We're closing the gate. After that, you can take your drinks outside if you want. No drinking and driving. And this is for tonight only."

I'd expected Gage to go help his mate behind the bar, but he was studying me with a speculative gleam in his eyes.

"Stay out of my head." I pointed my finger at him.

His eyes weren't changing to red like they did when he used his demon magic, but the way he was looking at me was still weird.

"I don't need to read your mind—" Gage paused, obviously for dramatic effect, "—*Alpha*." He emphasized the word with a tiny waggle of his eyebrows. He'd clearly been spending too much time with Jeremy and Ogden.

I flipped the demon the bird, earning a smile that flashed the dimples Jeremy was always talking about.

"Why are you in such a good mood?" I asked when he kept grinning at me. It was unsettling to see the usually grumpy man smiling so much.

He shrugged. "Willow Lake is happy." He rubbed his chest and that little smile on his face became a little dopey-looking. "It's intoxicating. Literally. I haven't felt this drunk since I was a wee lad and discovered my grandfather's stash of magic-infused whisky."

"You mean because of the pack?"

He nodded, making light shimmer over the surface of his dark horns. "The pack, the magic, everything."

I guessed he would know. As our demon guardian, the

guy had bonded to the place. I considered asking if Willow Lake had been unhappy before, but I wasn't sure I wanted to know.

"Enjoy your night, Alpha," he said. Then he wandered off toward the bar to help Jake, or at least offer him moral support.

I glanced around the pub. People were everywhere. The place had to be overcapacity, but neither Van, the Chief of Police, nor Carter, the Fire Chief, were sending anyone away. And, despite the crowd having been drawn here because of me, no one was getting into my space. Everyone just seemed to be happy to be here, mingling with their family and friends. Their pack.

And, damn it, Van was right. We'd always been in a pack, but now that I'd acknowledged it, something had changed. I closed my eyes, and I knew Gage was right, too. Happiness was zinging through the air.

The assholes were going to be insufferable after this.

Because Willow Lake—the people, the place, the pack —was happy. That feeling of joy was a physical presence both in the room and inside me.

I rubbed my chest where the warm pack magic hummed.

Would it feel like this all the time? I doubted it. Sensations like this always went away. The world felt wonderful and full of opportunity when you were a child, but then you grew up. Orgasms felt amazing in the moment, but then they were gone. My family and my pack had once filled me with a sense of belonging, but then so many of them had abandoned me.

As soon as I had the thought, the dazzling streams of light disappeared completely.

Ryley's fingers twitched against my palm where our hands were clasped under the table, drawing my attention back to him. Holding hands with him, that felt good too. And, if we kissed tonight, I expected that would feel damn spectacular. But those things wouldn't last either. Even if he was my mate.

Nothing good stayed for long.

I needed to remember that. But, for tonight at least, all I wanted to do was jump into that feeling. Cling to it. Savor it. Memorize it. That way, when I was alone again, I would have something amazing to remember during those long winter nights in my trailer behind the shop.

Chapter Twenty-Five

RYLEY

No one knew Hayden and I were staying together tonight.

So, as we snuck back to the room around midnight, leaving the others laughing and chatting in the pub and the grounds around the inn, it felt like we were doing something illicit, even though everyone had seen us holding hands all night. I didn't think anyone would be surprised when we ended up in the same room.

The mood in the pub had been joyful, but in a contented, let-out-a-deep-breath-at-the-end-of-a-long-day sort of way. They were happy to have Hayden accept he was their alpha, but it hadn't been a surprise. They'd known. It must be some kind of innate connection. And, when I'd watched him make his rounds through the people who'd gathered here tonight, I knew he was well-loved and respected. How had he avoided being alpha before now? Because it was obvious that he'd been the leader here for a long time.

I wasn't sure what to think about Hayden saying I was a part of his pack, but his words didn't feel wrong. Maybe some innate connection had formed between Hayden and me now too.

Could I be in a pack led by a wolf when I was half-human and half-faun? Hayden seemed to think so. So, that brought me to the next question: Did I even want to be in a pack?

When I'd left my herd, I swore never to live with supes again. But being surrounded by mundane humans all the time hadn't been an easy way to live either. Fauns were herd animals. And supes were supposed to use their magic, even if they didn't have much.

If I stayed in this pack, what would that mean? I found Hayden attractive, but what happened after we sated our lust and reality set in? Hayden would realize that as the alpha he'd need to have an appropriate mate. Someone who was strong and full of magic and who people looked up to and respected. A half-human, half-faun guy with wonky magic wouldn't be appropriate. My birth pack hadn't wanted me, so I couldn't see a powerful pack like Hayden's wanting someone like me in a position of influence. They had hellhounds, a demon guardian, a damn oracle, and Magic knew who else living here. Hayden could do so much better than me.

Could I stomach hanging around in Willow Lake if Hayden and I weren't together? A sharp pang shot through my chest at the thought of Hayden's future rejection. And that was just from me thinking about the possibility. If I had to live through it, it would be so much worse.

But I couldn't answer any of those questions tonight.

Tonight, I wanted to kiss and be kissed. I wanted us to hold one another. And if we went further than kissing and embracing, it would be even better.

As soon as we were in the room, Hayden shut and locked the door. He grabbed me and spun me around. He grinned down at me as he crowded me against the door. His body pressed against me as his mouth smashed mine in the hottest kiss I'd ever experienced.

Holy Mother of Magic.

His hand cupped my face as his tongue swept over mine. He tasted like the lager he'd drunk at the pub.

Oh no, I hoped the taste of what I'd eaten for supper wouldn't turn him off.

What had I been thinking ordering the veggie lasagna and garlic toast? I'd been so happy to see the vegetarian options on the menu I'd ordered with my stomach and not my head. Because I'd known we were going to kiss, and I never should have eaten something with garlic in it.

Hayden didn't pull away, though. He didn't demand I brush my teeth either. So, maybe it was okay.

He reached down and wrapped his arms around me, and I forgot to be worried about what I tasted like. Our bodies pressed together, without even a sliver of space between us, but I still arched into his solid, muscular body, needing to feel more of him. I wanted to wrap my legs around his hips and grind against him. I really wanted to lose our clothes.

So much for this being a simple, pleasant, and exploratory kiss to see if we wanted to do anything more. I was being devoured, and I was here for it.

"Ryley," Hayden whispered against my mouth. Then

he raised his head just enough to look into my eyes. His lips were red and wet, and I wanted them on mine again. Now. "I don't usually like kissing, but it's like I *need* to kiss you. Taste you. My wolf is still a royal bastard right now. I can feel him there under my skin, but I don't think I can shift yet, even after tonight." He cleared his throat, obviously not wanting to talk about the whole alpha thing. "But I can feel my magic writhing inside. It wants to be close to you too."

"We can stop," I offered. "I don't want you to feel like we have to do this now, tonight. If your wolf still isn't—"

"Do you want to stop?" Hayden interrupted me. His gaze locked on mine. I knew he'd stop if I said we should. But fuck that. I was only offering because I didn't want him to feel pressured into anything when so much had happened already tonight. No, I didn't want to stop. Not now. If this kiss was a glimpse of how sex was going to be between us, sign me up.

"No," I confessed.

"Me neither." Then his mouth was on mine again.

I reached for his shirt as he reached for mine. Then we were shedding clothing and stumbling toward the king-sized bed. I remembered Jake helpfully listing all the toiletries they'd placed in the rooms. Yeah. Had he known we'd end up in bed together tonight? Was that why he mentioned it? He was the town's oracle, so it was possible.

Then again, those people in the pub would have picked up on our attraction, even if we hadn't held hands all night, which we had. That was the problem with hanging out with supes instead of mundane humans. There were too many of them who could pick up on our interest in one another.

Yeah. Okay. I didn't want to think about those guys smelling how aroused I was around Hayden. I had much better things to think about right now.

"There is lube in the bedside table," I said.

Hayden paused. His gaze darted to the table. "Right. It's been a while. I forgot…"

"It doesn't matter, since it is here." And we didn't need condoms. That was the benefit of having sex with other supes, no sex-related infections. It'd been a long time since I'd had sex with another supe. I'd surrounded myself with humans and lived as one for so long that I'd almost asked Jake about condoms, too, when he'd mentioned the lube. But nope. We didn't need those. I would be inside Hayden. Bare. Skin to skin.

Unless he wanted to top. I could work with that too, but I preferred topping. Especially tonight. I wanted Hayden to have the best sex of his life. I wanted him to lose himself under my touch. I wanted to unravel his control. But mostly, I wanted to take care of him.

Yes, I could do that in either position, but when I'd imagined this moment, I envisioned having him under me.

"Do you bottom?"

Hayden blinked, as if he couldn't process my question. "No one has ever asked me that before. I've never done it. Everyone makes assumptions." His cheeks darkened as his words trailed off.

"Do you want to try it?" Shit. Did that sound like I was pressuring him? "If you don't, that's fine."

His Adam's apple bobbed as he swallowed, and I

wanted to lick it, just because it was there. I wanted to do everything with this man. But I wanted to wrap him up in my arms and give him the world more than anything else. Ever since I'd met him, I'd watched how people were with him. When was the last time he wasn't expected to be in charge? Not since his parents' deaths, I bet. Even when his friends were corralling him into going to the doctor, there was an unspoken understanding that he still maintained a position of power.

I didn't want him to feel like he always had to be in charge with me too. Yes, I liked how he'd backed me up against the door—that shit was something straight out of a movie—but I didn't need that all the time. And something inside me demanded that I take care of him, cherish him, prove to him I cared about him, not as the alpha, but as a man.

I hadn't realized I wanted that until this very moment. But now that I'd had that thought, it felt right.

"You'd want that?" Hayden swallowed hard. His cheeks had darkened. Yeah. I thought he rather liked that idea. "With me?"

"Hell yeah," I said. "Come on, let's get these clothes off and I'll blow your mind."

He stared at me for a long moment before nodding.

I tugged off the rest of my clothes, not caring where they landed. I crossed to the bedside table and found the lube. It wasn't the biggest container I'd ever seen, but it'd work for tonight. Then I flicked back the top blankets and sat down.

Hayden was still standing there, looking so damn

vulnerable. He hadn't removed the rest of his clothes yet. Hell, he hadn't even moved.

"Hey. If you change your mind or don't like what I'm doing or whatever, we'll stop. We can do something else or stop everything completely."

He licked his lips. "Yeah. Okay."

"Now, come over here and I'll help you get undressed." My fingers itched to slip over his skin and trace all the dips and hollows on his body. I wanted to watch how his chest rose and fell when he was on the brink of coming. I wanted to slide my tongue along the seam where his leg met his body and taste him there before dipping lower and lapping at his entrance. I wanted to do *everything*.

He closed the distance between us and stood between my legs. I looked up at him and rested my hand against his stomach. As soon as our skin connected, he let out a shaky exhale. Then he smiled down at me and pushed my glasses up.

"Oh, right, I should…" I reached for my glasses.

"Leave them," he said.

"I can do that." I grinned at him as I reached for the button on his jeans.

He rested his hand on my shoulder. A solid, warm weight. He didn't move me or change what I was doing; the touch was about connection. He watched as I slid the zipper down. He wasn't wearing underwear. Oh. Now *that* was fun. His stomach quivered as I leaned forward and pressed my nose against the triangle of skin I'd exposed. His cock was hard, leaning to the right, so I nuzzled it until it jerked.

"Ryley," Hayden groaned. His fingers grasped my hair as he rocked his hips closer to my face. I didn't know when he'd pushed his hand into my hair, but I loved that he had.

I smiled against his warm, musky skin as I peeled his jeans down a little more, revealing more of his length. It was big, beautiful, and so fucking tempting. Tonight, I wanted to spoil him. Take my time with him. I definitely didn't want him to come yet. Eventually, yes... but not yet.

Chapter Twenty-Six

HAYDEN

Ryley was gorgeous.

I was standing over him, so you'd think I would feel in control, but I was at his mercy. It was an unfamiliar feeling, but I didn't hate it. He peered up at me over the top of his cute little glasses. His gaze held mine as he extended his wet tongue and tapped it against the tip of my cock. I shuddered at the soft, warm touch. My fingers tightened in his hair, but I didn't tug him closer.

He grinned up at me as he pulled away. My cock throbbed and strained toward him, eager for more. Anything. A touch, a lick, the heat of his breath. I didn't care what. I just needed *something*.

"Let's get you naked," he said.

I stepped back, so I had room to stoop and take off my shoes and socks before pushing off my jeans. I straightened with the intention of diving straight into bed with him, but then I saw him. He was sitting on the edge of the bed, watching me. He was still wearing his glasses, as I'd requested. I didn't know why those glasses were such a turn on, but they were.

His legs were still open from where I'd stood between them a moment ago. His ruddy cock jutted out from his hips. He was as hard as I was. I licked my lips. Yes. That's what I wanted. I dropped to my knees between his legs.

"Hayden." My name fell like a whispered prayer from his tongue, full of awe and wonder and hope.

"I want to taste you." Normally I'd have sucked him down—because, seriously, who didn't love a blow job—but something held me back. I wanted his permission. Not because I didn't think he'd like it, but because…

Fuck. I didn't know why.

That was a lie. I wanted his permission because some part of me thought he wanted that control, and I wanted to give it to him. My stomach clenched at the realization. Because I was always in control of things, even when I didn't want to be. It'd only get worse now that I was the Alpha of Willow Lake, all in caps.

"Hey," he whispered, reaching out to cup my face in his hand. "I don't know where you went just now, but nothing will happen in here that you don't want. I want to make you feel good."

I nodded.

"Good. Now, you have a choice. You can taste me, like you asked. Or you can crawl up on the bed and let me get to know you." He waggled his eyebrows.

"I want to taste you," I repeated. I wanted it so badly I was salivating. I didn't know if it was a wolf thing or a me thing, but I needed to coat myself in his scent both inside and out. I needed to press my nose against those most intimate places on his body and breathe him in.

His eyes, with their pupils already blown wide with lust, held mine for a moment. Then he nodded. "Whatever you want."

He widened his legs and leaned back, giving me more access to his cock. It was beautiful. *He* was beautiful. I licked my lips again. Everything about his scent was intoxicating, from his arousal to his pre-cum to his sweat. And under all those, his own unique aroma was there, reminding me of the wild prairie lands along the east side of town. Grasses, sage, and clover all mixed together with the musky perfume of his arousal had become my very own aphrodisiac.

My pulse raced as I leaned forward and pressed my face to his chest. I'd wanted to start right at the apex of his legs with my nose against his sac until we both groaned, which I doubted would take much, but I also didn't want to rush this. I'd get to his cock soon, just not yet.

I couldn't count on this lasting, whatever it was that was between us, so I wanted to savor it, savor Ryley, while he was here.

My lips brushed against his nipple, and his breath caught. My tongue lapped at his throat, and his pulse jumped. My hand gripped his hips, and he wrapped his legs around me. Without clothes to hide or obscure, the perfume of our arousal and pre-cum blossomed and exploded between us. I wanted to bathe in the scent of his want for me.

"Hayden." He said my name like a plea as he sat up on his elbows.

"Hmm?"

"Come join me on the bed."

"Not yet," I whispered in his ear. I pushed him, urging him to his back again. He resisted for a moment before surrendering. I looked down at him, sprawled across the crisp white linen. His dark hair was a mess from when I'd gripped it earlier. His glasses skewed and fogged up. He was panting, flushed, and sexy as fuck. I wanted to devour him, worship him, do anything he asked. But mostly, I wanted to leave no doubt in his mind that I desired him, that I wanted him in my life, that all those other people before me were wrong to have let him go, because he was everything and more.

Instead, I did what I'd been dreaming about since I saw him naked on the bed. I leaned forward and nuzzled his balls. This stretch of heated skin was intoxicating, heavy with his scent. His cock bobbed up and nudged my forehead.

"Do it," he said. "Suck me."

He wasn't begging. Not exactly, anyway. His words sounded more like a command. A delicious shiver rolled over me. I'd do anything he asked. Anything at all.

I glanced up and found him watching me.

"Whatever you wish," I whispered.

It was a promise, although he probably didn't know that. But I instinctively knew that of anyone in my life—and I had a lot of good people in my life somehow—this man would never abuse my trust. Not intentionally.

"Hayden." This time, he spoke my name like his own promises to me: *I'll never let you go, I'll never leave, I'll never abandon you.*

It had to be because of the intimacy of this moment. Promises made in bed weren't to be trusted, I knew that, but my eyes still burned anyway, for what felt like the billionth time tonight. I swallowed and nodded, then I pulled my gaze away from his, unable to hold it a second longer. I was too raw. Too vulnerable. I wasn't ready for all of that. Not yet.

I wondered if I ever would be. I was too damaged.

"Hayden?"

I didn't answer. Not with words. I took his length in my mouth, needing to taste him and pleasure him and show him everything I couldn't say aloud.

He groaned. His hips tried to buck, but I held him in place.

I licked him, sucked him, and stroked him until his pleasure burst across my tongue. He collapsed against the bed.

He groaned again. "That wasn't supposed to happen like that."

"You didn't want it?"

"That's not what I meant," he said. "But I wanted to make you come to pieces, and then you did it to me instead."

I grinned against his leg. "We don't have to end things here."

He raised his head to look at me. He was grinning as he adjusted his glasses. "I like the way you think."

Chapter Twenty-Seven

RYLEY

I didn't think getting my dick sucked could be a transcendent experience, but I didn't know how else to describe it. I felt like I'd just survived an out-of-body episode. Sex with Hayden was unlike anything I'd ever experienced. It wasn't a mere sexual release; it was an emotional connection.

"Come here," I said. "Let me help you get off, first. Then we'll see what we feel like doing next." I hoped it'd involve buckets of lube and Hayden losing control on my dick, but I was ready to be open-minded. If a blow job could rock my world that much, I was pretty sure anything else we did would be equally spine-tingling.

I scooted back on the bed so he could crawl up beside me. His hard, thick dick swung between his legs. It was an impressive sight.

"It won't take long," he said. "Lie back and let me look at you."

"Straddle me. Come on my chest," I said. Where the fuck had those words come from? I wasn't a prude, but I rarely got off on someone marking me with their load. Yet, here I was, begging for it.

Hayden sucked in a quick breath and nodded, and in the next beat of my heart, he was straddling my hips. Oh, my alpha liked that idea. I reached for him, but he swatted my hands away.

"Fuck, Ry," he moaned as he stroked his cock hard and fast. "You are so fucking beautiful. You're going to look even better covered in my cum."

I licked my lips, drawing his attention to my mouth. I opened wide, offering my mouth to him. He grunted. His hand jerked faster. His gaze collided with mine and, in that moment, his muscles tightened as he came on a low, deep groan. His gaze locked on mine as his release spurted across my skin.

"That was so hot," I whispered, drawing my finger through his warm release.

His eyes locked on my movement. The bright light of his wolf shone in his eyes. I grinned and brought it to my mouth to taste. I lapped at it and moaned. I pushed my finger all the way into my mouth before closing my lips around it and pulling it out slowly.

"If I hadn't come already..." Hayden murmured, then he was leaning forward and kissing me. Hard. Thoroughly.

I was a shifter—at least half of my genetic coding was —and that was enough to ensure my recovery time was faster than a human's. It looked like Hayden's matched mine, because it didn't take long for either of us to be ready for another round.

"I want you inside me this time," Hayden said.

"Fuck, yes," I agreed. I patted the mattress to find the lube. I just had it. "Where is it?"

"What?"

"The lube."

It couldn't have gotten far. But what if we'd lost it? Jake had said we could ask for anything we needed, but did I have the balls to phone and ask for a lube delivery to the room? That would be awkward. Where would they store things like that? Would Hayden know where it was? We could sneak in and raid the supply cupboard.

Visions of Hayden and me, reeking of sex and tiptoeing through the inn in search of lube, filled my mind. What were the odds of us getting caught? We could do it, right? And if we found their stash of supplies, we should grab several because our complimentary container was too small to last the night. Oh, wait… There would be more lube in the other room. Aha! Excellent plan!

I got halfway to the door when Hayden growled. "Where are you going?"

"To the other room to grab the other lube," I said.

"Naked?"

I glanced down. Right. Clothes. And I should probably wipe off the drying cum too. Although I wasn't sure I wanted to, not quite yet.

"Get back in bed. The lube can't be that far," Hayden said.

I bleated, which startled me. I sounded like a kid impatient for their supper. I couldn't remember the last time I bleated.

Hayden chuckled and shook his head. "We'll find it. It

couldn't have gone far." He climbed off the bed and checked the floor. "Here it is."

"Thank fuck," I muttered and jumped on the bed again. Still, if we planned on doing more tonight, we might still need to raid the other room later. It was a good contingency plan.

Hayden tossed the lube to me. "Here. You take it. Get me ready."

He climbed on the bed and propped himself on his hands and knees.

"Gorgeous," I whispered as I took in the way he'd presented himself to me: his strong muscular back on display, his firm ass lifted toward me, his thick legs with their light dusting of hair, holding himself up for me. I almost came, and I hadn't even touched him yet.

I squeezed the base of my dick to get it to calm down. He hadn't done this before, so prepping him was important. Imperative. My number one priority. I took my time with him and used as much lube as I thought I could spare while still leaving enough to coat my dick later. It was more lube than I usually used, but this was Hayden's first experience bottoming. I needed him to feel good. It'd kill me if he trusted me with his first time and I botched it.

"Come on, Ry," Hayden muttered. "I'm ready. Fuck me already."

As soon as the words were out, both Hayden and I stilled, because this didn't feel like fucking. The word sat awkwardly between us. But what else could it be?

"I don't want to hurt you," I said.

"I trust you." He wiggled his ass with my fingers still inside. "And I feel at least, what? Two fingers?"

"Three," I confided.

"Yeah. If you have three fingers in my ass, I'm ready."

I blew out my breath. He was right. Why was I so anxious about this? No one had ever complained I was a terrible lover in my past. Sure, some of us had more chemistry than others, but—

Why was I thinking about past lovers when I had the sexiest man I'd ever met waiting for me? I looked down at him and dragged my hands over his back. My cock was hard and so ready to do this, but something wasn't right. This was my favorite position, entering a man from behind, feeling his muscles tense as he braced for my thrusts, but that wasn't what I wanted this time. This position was too impersonal. I needed to see Hayden's face. I needed to kiss him.

"Get on your back," I said as I swatted his ass lightly.

He hesitated a moment before flipping over. Hayden watched me as I grabbed a pillow and tucked it under his ass. I moved between his spread legs. He looked so damn turned on and vulnerable all at once that it nearly undid me. I leaned forward and pressed a soft kiss to his lips.

"Are you sure you want this?" I asked.

"Yes." The single syllable word said so much more than yes. It said, *more than anything, I want you, you are more than I could have imagined.*

Or those might just have been my own thoughts.

I positioned the crown of my cock against him. Hayden held his legs open wider. I pressed forward, slowly, steadily. Our gazes locked as our bodies joined.

"Hayden." I whispered his name reverently, because there was something magical and beautiful and so fucking tender growing between us. I needed to acknowledge it. I needed to know he was there with me, not only in body, but in spirit, too.

We simply stared at one another for a long moment. He reached for me, pulling me down until our mouths met in an exquisite and oh so fucking gentle kiss that seemed to convey all the things I was too overwhelmed to put into words. The place where my magic lived burst to life, and I swore I could feel it rush through me, filling me, until it was too much to contain.

As we moved together, I was sure my heightened emotions were playing tricks on me because I swore lights sparkled to life around us. I blinked. No, it wasn't lights, it was magic. And something deep inside me told me this wasn't just *any* magic, but *our* magic—mine and Hayden's. It burst free from our bodies to dance and spiral around us. The vivid, rich green of his wolf shifter magic and the pale yellowy-green of my own shimmered as they wove together until they merged into something that wasn't his or mine, but ours.

I'd never seen anything like it. I would never have thought a half-supe like myself could experience it. How did I have enough magic to manifest it like this? But here it was. Beautiful seemed an inadequate word to describe it.

The swirling magic pulsed in time to the rhythm of our bodies, faster and brighter. I sank deep inside him with each thrust, needing to be as close as possible to him, and Hayden's hips rocked against mine as if feeling the same need. His wolf shone through his eyes, and when his mouth dropped open, I saw the sharp edges of his elongated canines.

Yes. I wanted that. I wanted him to bite me and taste my blood. I wanted everything with this man. I wanted him forever. I never wanted to be without him.

"My mate," I choked out.

"My mate," he agreed. Then Hayden's eyes widened, as if he was surprised by his own words. His grip tightened on me.

Something in the air changed. At first, I thought we were on the precipice of our release, but it was more than that. Love and joy and such an immense feeling of home surged through me.

Strange words in a language I didn't know started falling from my lips. I'd never heard them before, but I wasn't scared. Instinctively, I recognized the ancient incantation as a magic-filled blessing from the Eternal Magic herself.

"Ryley, no." Hayden's fingers bit into my hips. "You deserve so much better."

The words poured from my mouth. I couldn't stop them to soothe him, so I did what I could with my body. I held him tight, willing him to understand that I was choosing this. Choosing *him*.

He relaxed in my arms. Then he shuddered and moaned, succumbing to the power of this moment like I had. As soon as his mouth opened again, the same magic-laden words burst from his lips too.

As our voices joined as intimately as our bodies, our magic became brighter and more radiant. It pulsed like it had a heartbeat of its own, as if to suggest we were no longer two separate individuals but one. Somehow, the magic from my core kept feeding it, nurturing it. I'd thought I barely had enough magic to shift, but here it was, streaming from me strong and full like it had no end, and Hayden's was right there with it.

When the words faded, I slammed my mouth onto Hayden's. Then our bodies raced toward completion. I was so damn close, but I needed Hayden to be there with me. I reached between us and stroked his hard length. He grunted and bucked into my grip. On a low groan, he shuddered. As soon as his release sprayed across my stomach, my own climax had me shuddering and shooting deep inside him. Marking him as mine.

All around us, our merged magic, that beautiful green with a hint of yellow that reminded me of pine needles, erupted in a dazzling explosion. The shimmering sparkles of magic floated down to us, coating us, until they faded into our sweat-soaked skin.

I lifted up to look into Hayden's eyes, scared of what I'd find there. He'd tried to stop me from speaking the Eternal Magic's words. Had he not wanted this? Not wanted me?

Hayden swallowed and looked away.

"Hayden?"

"I'm sorry," he whispered.

My first reaction was one of anger, but I knew that anger was born out of fear. Fearing this man the Eternal Magic had given me was about to reject me was easy. And I didn't think he *was* rejecting *me*. I suspected he was rejecting himself, if that made sense.

I brushed the sweat-damp hair from his forehead. A

wide streak of that pine needle green marked his hair. It was the color of our combined magic. I caressed the strands with my fingers, but I didn't mention it. Not yet. He wasn't ready yet, even though he could probably see a matching patch of green in my own hair. I wanted to keep combing my fingers through it, this manifestation of what'd happened. Instead, I forced myself to pull my hand back. I adjusted my glasses, which had miraculously survived what we'd done, but I didn't climb off him. If I did, I was sure he'd bolt.

"Hayden, I don't regret this. I could never regret you."

He sucked in a shuddering breath. I wrapped my arms around him, and he pulled me tight and pressed his face into my neck.

"The Eternal Magic is a bitch," he muttered.

"Why?" I asked, trying not to be offended that he was cursing the entity that'd just joined our lives together.

"You deserve so much better," he whispered. "When the others mated, the Eternal Magic had given them time. They weren't joined their first time together. They had time to decide if that's what they wanted. But not me. Oh no. She had to do this now, like she was determined to trap you with me before you knew enough to make your escape. She's been trying to control my life for years and now she's fucking with yours too."

"There is a lot to unpack in what you just said, but I'm not trapped," I said. "I'm where I want to be."

He rolled us to our sides, and I shivered as I slipped free of his body. I rested my hand on his hip, determined to hold him in this bed so we could talk through whatever was going on in his head. He finally met my gaze.

"How could it be? You were hesitant to join the pack, but being my mate, that's more. That's permanent." His forehead crinkled. "Although Teague might be able to sever—"

I froze. It was either that or double over in pain. "Are you… Are you rejecting me?"

"What? No!" He looked surprised.

"Then why are you talking about severing our brand-new mate bond?"

"I want you to have a choice," he said.

"I had a choice. I chose you." I shoved aside the magic-deep pain I felt at the talk of removing our bond and held his gaze. I needed him to understand this. I needed him to pay attention to what I was about to say. "I may not be as old as you, but I know it takes two people to decide that they are mates and accept that before the bond will form. You and I might not know everything about each other, but we don't have any important secrets between us. If we did, the Eternal Magic would not have given us her blessing. I understand why you don't know if you can trust this but believe me when I say I wanted this. And I think you did too."

My heart pounded as I waited for his answer. *Please let me be right.*

"I'll always want you, Ryley. I suspected we might be mates before we got into bed tonight. I knew it was a possibility and I…" He swallowed. "I chose you too."

"Oh, thank Magic," I said. The breath I'd been holding while I waited for his answer blasted out of me.

Hayden pulled me close again. "I'm sorry if my reaction hurt you. That wasn't my intention. But it's all happened so fast. I can't help but think the Eternal Magic has rushed us. First the whole alpha thing happened, and now this?" He shuddered. "I know you picked up on enough of the conversation tonight to know that I've denied my role as alpha for a long time. Twelve years. Ever since my parents died. I let all those people down. I let down my pack."

I doubted that was true. "Tell me about it."

"I froze. I couldn't cope. All those people were depending on me and I just walked away. I disbanded the pack. I sold the pack house right away and gave whoever hadn't left with Robbie a share of the money I got for it. I couldn't stand to be here. I couldn't handle all the memories."

He paused and sucked in a shaky breath.

"The whole pack lived here?" I asked, because that just didn't sound possible.

"Back then, the official pack was just made up of wolves. My parents had wanted to change that. Having a whole bunch of different kinds of supes living in Willow Lake was their dream. But, no, not even all the wolves lived here, but a lot of them did. So, all those people lost not only their pack but their homes too." Tears shimmered in his eyes.

I wished I could ease his pain, but all I could do was listen and be there for him.

"But the worst part was that I let my brother get away with doing all that. Van was sure he killed my parents, but there wasn't enough evidence."

I gaped. Robbie had killed his own parents? Even in my darkest moments in my old herd, I'd never wanted to do that. What kind of person would? But why was I even surprised? Robbie had tried to kill Hayden too, hadn't he? "Do you think he did it?"

"I didn't want to. I couldn't wrap my head around it. It was just so... so..." He swallowed hard. "But if I'd stopped him then, he wouldn't have been able to hurt anyone else. I don't know why they would ever want me to be their alpha. I've been hiding for twelve years. Alphas shouldn't hide. Pack should always come first."

"I think you're too hard on yourself." I wiped away the tears rolling down his cheeks. "You were young and going through a traumatic experience. No one should have expected you to take care of the pack when you were grieving, both for your parents and for your brother's betrayal. It wasn't fair to thrust you into that."

"I wasn't that young," he argued. Because of course he did.

"In shifter years, yes, you were," I said. "In my herd, kids weren't considered adults until they were at least a hundred." Well, except for me. I was deemed to be too human, so I'd been labeled an adult at eighteen and encouraged to move out of my mother's house. She allowed me to stay until I was in my mid-twenties, but by then it'd become too much. I not only left the house, I left the whole herd. In all honesty, I hadn't been ready. The herd hadn't prepared me to live on my own. It'd been damn tough in the beginning.

But my brother, a purebred faun, was still considered a kid at that same age. He would have only turned twenty-five this past spring. Maybe when he was an adult, we could meet up. Would he remember who I was in another seventy-five years? Would I recognize him? How long would I even live? My mother had always told me my life would be short, like my father's.

"Wolves don't live as long as other supernatural beings like fauns. We aren't considered pups past the age of twenty," Hayden said.

I sighed, because of course he was still arguing. "But you'll still live longer than a mundane human." I paused as something occurred to me. "Wait. You think I have all the same magic as a full faun, right? Do you think I'll live as long as they do?"

"Huh. I hadn't thought of that, but yeah. You are a faun. Full stop."

"We'll have a long life ahead of us, if that's the case." I grinned. "Now that we're mated and blessed by the Eternal Magic, your life span will have extended to match mine."

That little gift from the Eternal Magic was one of the biggest perks of being a fated mate. It didn't make us immortal—anyone could be killed—but, if we lived to the end of our natural lifespan, we would never be without one another. I liked the idea of him being at my side for the rest of my life. My grin widened.

"I'm being an ass, aren't I?" He finally met my gaze. "I'm surprised you're accepting this so easily."

I thought about it. "I guess I am. I will admit that earlier I hadn't planned on staying in Willow Lake."

Hayden whined a little, and his eyes flashed with the golden light of his wolf. I rubbed his hip to soothe him.

"But I didn't realize you were my mate then." I swallowed. "I am still apprehensive about what will happen when your pack realizes I am your mate. Not only am I not a wolf, but I'm only half-supe. Don't say your pack won't care, because you can't know that. Not yet. I will admit they're more welcoming than any other pack or group of supes I've known, but we can't predict what'll happen."

"Actually, we probably can," Hayden said. "I think Jake's had a vision of us."

"Really? What did the vision show?"

"I don't know, but I saw the way he reacted the first time he saw you. He recognized you. The only way that'd happen is if he'd already seen you." Then Hayden frowned. "And the assholes kept it from me."

"Would it have changed anything?"

"No," he admitted. "But it makes me wonder what other secrets they've been keeping from me."

He looked at me, really looked at me. Something pulsed in the air between us.

"I will do everything I can to be a worthy mate to you," he promised. "I will undoubtedly make mistakes and say shit I shouldn't. Let's face it, I already did within the first few minutes of receiving our mate bond. That must be some kind of record. Sometimes I feel like that is all I do, make one mistake after another. But I will never hurt you intentionally. I didn't mean to make you think I didn't want you. Because I do. Despite what happened tonight, I'm not cut out to be an alpha. And I'm scared I won't be a good mate either."

I could have said something like "you are the perfect mate for me", but I doubted that'd help ease his worries.

"No one is perfect," I said instead. "I can promise you I'm not perfect either. We'll have to learn to be good mates for one another. The Eternal Magic provides her blessing, but that doesn't mean that everything will be easy from here on out. We still have a lot to learn about one another. But the important thing is that we both want to try. You do, right? Want to try?"

He swallowed hard. "Yes. I do."

"Phew," I said with a laugh. I pretended to brush sweat off my brow.

A tiny smile played over his lips, and I took that as a victory.

"Hi, mate," I whispered.

"Hi, mate," he whispered back.

We grinned at one another and any lingering tension faded away. Yeah. That was better. We'd be okay. I hoped.

Chapter Twenty-Eight

RYLEY

"Are there any bird shifters in town?" I asked as I stared out the window at the woods behind Willow Lake Inn. The room had windows on two walls, north and west. I was standing at the west facing one, so I couldn't see the sun inching above the horizon from here, but there was a beautiful yellow glow hitting the tops of the dark green pines. The resulting color was a lot like the mating marks we shared.

We weren't high enough to see the western mountains over the trees, but I bet they would look stunning in this light. We should go up to the next floor and see.

Okay. I might, possibly, maybe have been trying to think of any reason to avoid going downstairs.

"Yeah. Why?" Hayden asked warily, looking over my shoulder like he expected to see a flock of peeping sparrow shifters looking in at us.

"Do you think they'd deliver food up here to our window?"

"Doubtful." He wrapped his arms around my waist. His chest pressed against my back, and he rubbed his cheek against my neck. I tilted my head to the side because I loved the feel of his skin against mine. I wanted more. "What's going on?"

"It's nice up here. With you. Alone." For all my brave talk in the middle of the night about wanting to be Hayden's mate, I still felt nauseous about seeing his pack today. The patch of green in my dark hair wasn't notice-able, but Hayden's hair was a lot lighter and a striking contrast to the mark. Everyone would know what'd happened as soon as they saw him.

What if they turned their backs on him because of me?

He kissed the side of my neck, making me shiver and press closer to him. My idea for food delivery by winged courier sounded better by the minute. Or we could return to bed and forget about food and the rest of the world. There was water in the bathroom. We'd survive.

"What else?" For a guy who kept asking questions, he was doing everything in his power to make me forget how to talk. I closed my eyes and savored the feel of his lips on my skin. "Because I don't think that's everything," he said softly.

"Probably not." I sighed. "Although I do like the idea of staying in bed with you all day."

"I like that idea too, but not today," Hayden said.

I turned to face him. "Why? What's going on today?"

"I want to meet with Doc. With everything that

happened yesterday, I want him to check my magic. I feel stronger than I have in a long time."

"You think he'll let you go looking for Robbie."

He shrugged and looked out the window at the woods. "He's out there. I need to find him."

"Don't go alone. And don't go until the doctor says you're healed," I said, gripping his shirt in my fists. I could see him ignoring the doctor's orders and sneaking out. And I suspected stowing away a second time would be impossible. He knew to look in the bed of his truck now. "Promise me."

"I promise not to go alone." The words looked like they pained him, but he'd said them, and I had to trust he'd keep his promise.

"Good. Because we don't know how many other traps he's set out there."

"I've run those woods a lot," he said. "I've been fine. Although I can't figure out why I haven't come across his scent out there before. It doesn't make sense."

"But you wouldn't have been fine yesterday."

His shoulders dropped. "I know."

My stomach growled.

"We should go down and get some breakfast," he said. When I hesitated, he brushed his lips over mine. "It'll be okay. I know it will. Out of all the things I'm concerned about, my pack accepting you isn't one of them."

Of course he'd guessed why I was reluctant to go downstairs.

And I hoped he was right, because if anyone was an asshole to him because of me, I had hooves and I wasn't afraid to use them.

He slipped his hand in mine and gave it a gentle squeeze. "Ready?"

"I guess," I lied.

We'd just stepped out of the room when a door on the other end of the hallway opened. Jeremy was chattering away to his mate and didn't notice us. They were close to the stairs, so I hoped they'd go down without realizing we were here. But then Adrian sniffed, and his gaze swung right to us. Jeremy turned to see what'd caught his mate's attention. Damn it.

"Hi, guys." Jeremy's face lit up when he saw us. "I was talking to Adrian about today's events. It's going to be a-mazing." Yes, he said the word like it came in two parts and had to be fitted together. "It sucks that Nelson, Teague, and Davie are missing it. Nelson especially. I really wanted to see how fast he can move through the shadows. But he got a lead about Morgan so he's off chasing it down. And Davie was called away in the middle of the night to one of those children's indoor playground things. Man, I loved when my parents took us to places like that when I was growing up. But some ghosts have moved into this one and they are causing problems. She's called Teague in to help her, but he hasn't left yet." Jeremy spoke at a dizzying speed, jumping from one thing to the next.

"Events?" Hayden asked when Jeremy paused to catch his breath.

"Oh! Right! You left before the details were finalized," Jeremy said. "We're holding our little mini Olympics, supernatural-style."

"Today?"

"Yep." Jeremy nodded vigorously. "This is going to be

so good. I mean, what could be better than seeing a whole bunch of supes doing supernatural things? I'm going to have so much information for my *Amazing Book of Super Supes* after today." He rubbed his hands together like a greedy villain in an old-school cartoon. "We have heaps of people signed up already, but we need to run down to Levi's and see what kind of bears are at that conference. I couldn't talk to him yesterday with Parker hanging out with him. But I hope they are the shifter kind of bears. It'd be awesome to have a few out-of-towners taking part too."

They stood at the landing by the stairs, waiting for us. By the time we reached them, my stomach was churning, and my heart was beating fast. I adjusted my glasses with a shaky hand. Any minute now, they'd see our mating marks.

Hayden looked at Adrian. "What about the mundanes?"

"Gage thinks he can keep them away, or at least unaware."

I lifted my eyebrows. "He can do that? That's pretty wild."

Adrian shrugged. "We're not sure what he can do now that he's bonded to the magic here, but he's got a strong connection to Willow Lake, and he thinks it is possible. A bit like an extension of the Eternal Magic's glamour."

"Glad to know someone gets along with the Eternal Magic," Hayden muttered. He pushed his hand through his hair. The green strands slid through his fingers.

Jeremy gasped. His eyes widened, and he pointed at Hayden's head. "Adrian!"

"I know. I saw it."

Jeremy lunged toward me. His reaction took me by surprise, so I didn't react fast enough to duck. But he didn't hit me. Instead, he wrapped his arms around me and pulled me into a bone-bending hug.

"I'm so excited for you both," he gushed as he squeezed me tight. "This is so amazingly awesome. Another fated mate pairing. And it's the alpha, too!"

When he let go, I staggered back and gasped for air. Then he did the same thing to Hayden. Hayden patted Jeremy on the back awkwardly. "Uh. Thanks?"

Adrian hugged each of us too, although he was much gentler about it. Thank Magic for that. I didn't think I'd survive a hug like Jeremy's from a wolf shifter.

When the hugging ended, Jeremy grinned at me and waggled his eyebrows. "So, werewolf sex. Pretty awesome, am I right? The biting? The knotting? No one else really knows, and I feel bad for them. They miss out on so much. Well, I guess Mercer knows, but we aren't at a BFF stage yet, so we haven't talked about it. That first time, though, is a bit of a surprise, but in the best way."

Did that mean I was at a BFF level? Because that was the first time I'd heard of it. As for the rest, I glanced at Hayden. His face was curiously blank. Me? I tried to keep my face blank too. I didn't think it mattered whether a person bottomed or topped, but not everyone thought the same way. Sexual positions were about doing what felt good to the people having sex. It was no one else's business. But other people could be weird about it. I didn't want anyone to think Hayden wasn't a powerful alpha because of something intimate that'd happened between us.

"Jer, not everyone wants to talk about sex with strangers," Adrian said. Something in his tone told me he'd figured out there had been no knotting or biting for us last night.

"We aren't strangers," Jeremy protested. "Which reminds me, I really need your number. We have this group chat and—" Jeremy's words stopped abruptly. He looked between Hayden and me. Realization dawned in his eyes. "Oh! Oops. Sorry about that! My dad always told my brothers and me not to assume things because it makes an ass out of you and me." His gaze bounced between us again. "But if you guys are vers or want to change things up, I highly recommend—"

"Jer, stop talking," Adrian said, tugging his mate toward the stairs.

"Can we get breakfast here?" I asked, eager to change the conversation.

"The dining room isn't finished yet, but the kitchen has been fully renovated with all the mod cons," Jeremy said, thankfully leaving the sex talk behind. "We all make and eat breakfast together. We tried to do lunch and supper as a group, but it was hard to get everyone together, so now we do breakfast. Oh, and we also have a weekly potluck. Jake's been organizing one for ages and it is a bit of a local tradition now."

"You cook together?"

Jeremy nodded. "We tried assigning different people to make food on different days, but it didn't really work out. Most of these guys can't cook for shit, so those people are on toast duty and stuff like that."

"Says the guy who wanted everyone to eat one of those

sugary cereals the first time it was his turn to do breakfast," Adrian said with a grimace.

"Hey! That's a rite of passage. Everyone needs to eat Froot Loops, Cocoa Puffs, or Lucky Charms for breakfast at least once. Someone has to drag you supes into this century. When I was growing up, it was always a special day when we had those for breakfast. Usually, it was porridge or some other equally boring and cheap food."

"You have six siblings," Adrian pointed out. "I can't imagine having that many kids running around on a sugar high every day. I'm with your parents on this one."

Personally, I loved porridge, but I wasn't about to argue with Jeremy. I doubted anyone could change his mind anyway. For the rest of the walk to the kitchen, Adrian and Jeremy rated various breakfast foods. Unsurprisingly, Adrian was all about meat—bacon, sausage, and steaks—while Jeremy preferred sugary junk-food type breakfasts.

The large industrial-looking kitchen was already full of people milling around, opening fridges, getting out pots and pans, and talking about their plans for the day. Hayden squeezed my hand when I hesitated at the door. I'd met most of these people already, and they'd all been friendly enough. But what if things changed now?

"Morning, everyone!" Jeremy shouted as he dove into the melee. "We need to put on a fabulous spread this morning. We have a newly mated couple to celebrate."

Everyone's head snapped toward us.

"For fuck's sake, Jeremy," Hayden muttered. Then he cleared his throat. "Yes, Ryley is my mate. Be nice to him." He scowled at them as he said that last bit.

I lifted my hand in an awkward wave.

Everyone came forward to hug us or pat our backs and offer their felicitations.

When Gage approached us, he gave Hayden a pat on his back. "Congrats, Alpha."

Hayden rolled his eyes at the demon's emphasis on his new moniker. "Are you available this morning? I wanted to head back out there after I talk to Doc Roberts."

Gage shook his head. "The doctor already sent out a text to everyone, saying that you needed to rest today."

"For fuck's sake," Hayden muttered for the second time in a few minutes. "A text, really?" He pulled out his phone and navigated to his messages. He frowned as he read the doctor's text. "I feel fine, damn it."

"Take the day," Gage said. "The pack is eager to spend more time together. Jeremy's idea for the competition snowballed last night. It sounds like everyone is planning to be together today. It'll be good to help strengthen the bonds."

Hayden frowned and shoved his phone in his pocket again. "I guess. It's just that Robbie—"

"He hasn't gone far yet; there is no reason to think he'll leave now. He thinks he's smarter than the rest of us. You finding one of his bunkers? That won't scare him off."

"One of? You think there are more?" Hayden asked.

"I think it's likely," Gage said. "But I can't figure out how he's keeping them hidden from us."

"That's enough shop talk," Jake said, and he pulled his mate away.

Teague stepped forward next.

"I knew it wouldn't be long before you bonded."

Teague smiled at both of us. "When I saw you together yesterday, your connection was already so strong and vivid. Even before the alpha magic kicked in and made Ryley part of your pack."

"Thanks, Teague," Hayden said. He glanced at me, then back to the death mage. "I'd thought we might be, but I hadn't expected it to happen so quickly."

"It was meant to be," Teague said. He offered us a secretive smile that suggested he'd known quite a lot about our bond. I wanted to ask, but it wouldn't change anything. We were bonded now, and that was all that mattered.

Well, no, that wasn't quite true, was it? There was one more thing that mattered: my sub-par lineage.

I bit my bottom lip. I didn't like secrets, and not telling those closest to Hayden felt like a lie. But what if that changed their minds about our bond? I tightened my hand around Hayden's.

My mate's gaze caught mine, and I swore he could read my mind. He leaned close to whisper very, very softly in my ear. His words were barely audible to me, probably so that no one else would overhear. "They won't care. I promise. But you don't have to say anything if you don't want to."

My empty belly roiled. I swallowed. Then I looked around at the people who'd gone back to their breakfast preparations.

"Uh, hey, everyone?"

Once again, everyone turned their attention to us, to me.

"In the interest of being upfront and honest, I…" I cleared my throat. "I want you to know, because I don't want it to get out and you think I was trying to lie or something, but my dad was a mundane human. Please don't let that change how you feel about Hayden. The Eternal Magic put us together. He didn't have a choice."

Hayden growled. "Of course I had a choice. I chose you."

"Aw," Jeremy cooed. "Our alpha is a romantic, who knew? But, uh, I'm not sure why Ryley needed to tell us about his dad. Did I miss something? Is this something I need to cover in my research?"

Everyone else looked as confused as Jeremy.

"I just thought you should know. Anyway, yeah. That's all. I have nothing else to say," I finished awkwardly.

Gage stepped forward. The demon's eyes took on a reddish hue as he met my gaze, and I knew he was tapping into his magic. He approached slowly, like he thought I might bolt. And honestly, I was considering doing exactly that. Paws followed along by the demon's feet.

"I sense you feel this is a flaw," Gage said evenly as his gaze cleared. "I can assure you it is not. No one will think less of your magic or you because of your parentage." He glanced at Hayden. "I would have thought you'd know this, Alpha. Having a mundane as a parent is irrelevant. You are a supe."

"I do." Hayden nodded. "But he thought I was blowing smoke up his ass."

"How charming," Paws said, although from what I knew of the cat creature, it sounded like something he would say too.

"Van or Dillon could confirm that, if you want some reassurance about the matter," Gage said. "They can see the strength of someone's magic when they take their beast forms. They would have assessed your strength when they met you in the woods the other night."

Jake stepped forward and slipped his hand into the crook of Gage's arm. "I don't know who my father was, but we suspect he might have been mundane too."

"But you're an oracle." Oracles were powerful and intrinsically connected to the Eternal Magic.

"Yes, I am." Jake nodded.

"I see." I blinked, unsure what to say to that. Hayden had tried to tell me the same thing, but it just seemed too fantastical to be true. Had my whole life been a lie? I adjusted my glasses again.

It looked like maybe it had.

I hated my old herd, now more than ever. I wished I could take my brother away from them before they destroyed him like they had tried to destroy me. Sure, they weren't bigoted toward him since he was a full-bred faun, but it didn't matter. They didn't deserve him.

My stomach growled again. Jake smiled and stepped forward and wrapped his arm around my shoulders. "Come on in. We'll never eat if we don't start cooking food."

And just like that, everyone went back to their tasks like no one cared one little bit about me only having one supe parent. I'd lived with supernaturals before, but Willow Lake was just so different. In a good way. In the best way. Maybe his pack really could accept me for who I was and not see me as a burden.

I sucked in a shaky breath.

I wanted that. I wanted that more than anything.

Chapter Twenty-Nine

HAYDEN

The spot in my hair with my mating mark didn't feel any different from before, so why did I keep touching it? Every time I did, someone would smile at me like they thought it was cute. It was not cute. *I* was not cute. I was a grown wolf shifter, not some pup scampering along and tripping over their paws.

There had to be a few ball caps kicking around the shop. Suppliers were always giving us shit like that. I should grab one, so people would stop looking at me like they wanted to pinch my cheeks or pat me on the head while using words like adorable or precious. Except I really didn't want to hide my mating mark from anyone. I wanted the whole world to know Ryley was my mate.

"I can't believe they organized this whole thing overnight," Ryley said.

We were standing beside Willow Lake, looking out over the water. Most of the town was out here. As far as I could tell, the only people missing were the mundane humans who lived alongside us.

The only human I'd seen today was Parker, who'd been confused and, if I read his face correctly, hurt no one had invited him. Levi ushered him away. He'd texted Gage that he'd stay with Parker, so he didn't venture out again. But was it too late? Had Parker seen under the Eternal Magic's glamour? We'd find out soon enough. I wasn't worried if he had, because Parker's resistance to Gage's magic was telling. If I was right, then Parker was Levi's mate, and this was another sign of that. I wondered how long the big minotaur could stay away. That should be Willow Lake's next pub bet.

Everyone else was acting like an impromptu municipal holiday for supes had been declared. Businesses were closed, including the garage. People kept arriving with dishes for a potluck. A teenager was making balloon animals for the few kids who were running around. And, in the park behind us, food of every description was sizzling on a long line of barbecues.

The weather this time of year was hit and miss, but we'd lucked out today. The temps were warm for a random day in September. The sky overhead was a rich blue with not a cloud in sight. The lake was calm, well, except for the splashing Brodie and Weston were doing as they shot through the water. I didn't know where Henrietta and Gary had disappeared to. As soon as they'd taken their octopus forms, they sank beneath the surface of the water and hadn't been seen since.

"I'm a little surprised myself," I admitted to Ryley.

Although I shouldn't have been. Everyone was in a

jovial mood after that whole alpha pack moment last night. It'd been a long time since they'd had an alpha. A lot of supes in the world lived outside a pack environment, but studies showed how supes were healthier in packs. It was something to do with the persistent stress of knowing you were on your own, always having to hide from the mundanes, and feeling like there was no one to take care of you if something went wrong. Of course, anyone who lived in Willow Lake, even before I accepted the role of alpha yesterday, should have known they weren't alone, but having my role formalized seemed to have everyone walking with more bounce in their steps and bigger smiles on their faces.

I almost regretted resisting it for so long.

"What do you want to do after this?" I asked.

Ryley bit his bottom lip and twisted his hands together. "I was thinking about signing up for the hide and seek competition."

"Really?"

He swallowed. "I know the doctor said he doesn't want you using your magic today, so you can't participate, but I thought this might be an opportunity to…" His words trailed off and he shook his head. "You know what? Never mind. Forget I said anything. It was a bad idea."

"Hey, this is just about having some fun. You can try if you want to, but don't feel you have to. Is someone pressuring you to take part?" I looked around to see if I could pick out who might bully Ryley into this. He didn't have to prove himself to anyone. Not now, not ever.

"Nothing like that. It's all my idea. I haven't mentioned it to anyone."

Well, that changed things. I pulled him into a quick hug, fully aware of how many people were watching us and snapping pictures like the nosey bastards they were.

"I'm proud of you," I said. "You don't have to do this, but if you do, I'll support you." I hated the idea of Ryley going off by himself to hide, but this was a safe and fun way for him to experiment with his magic.

He shrugged, and his cheeks darkened. "I saw Jeremy take part in the mage competition earlier. No one cared that he sucked or that his magic didn't do everything he wanted it to. Everyone was…"

"Supportive?"

"Yeah, I guess." He nodded and looked away. "I've never seen that before. In my herd, by the time you were an adult, failure wasn't accepted."

I tightened my arms around him. "Everything you tell me about your former herd makes me angry."

He leaned against my chest. "I didn't know there was anything wrong with it for a long time. It was just the way things were. No one thought to question their bigotry and their narrow-minded traditions. After I left the herd, I'd hear humans talk about their elections and I figure it's the same thing. They'd say, 'My family has always voted for that party, so I do too.' They never stopped to listen to what was being said, to see if those promises made sense or aligned with their beliefs. It was sad. There is nothing worse in the world than saying 'It has always been that way, so we don't want to change it.'"

"I can't imagine how difficult it was for you to leave them," I murmured against his hair. "But I'm proud of you."

His arms tightened around me.

"When does the hide and seek competition start?"

"I think it is up next," he said.

Several events had already finished. A tiny mouse shifter had won the prize for being able to squeeze through the smallest opening. Isaac had won for being able to leap the highest of everyone when in their shifted form, but one of the frog shifter competitors was trying to get it over-turned. He said it should be based on the ratio between how high someone could leap and how tall they were. Isaac disagreed, for obvious reasons.

Honestly, though, if any of the cat shifters had competed, Isaac would have lost anyway. After all, I'd seen Clive leap higher than Isaac when he was trying to outrun Van after nicking a fish fillet out of the grocery store. But after the cats had shifted this morning, a couple of empty boxes mysteriously showed up close to the competition site. Intrigued, the cats had investigated. They jumped in the boxes, plonked themselves down, and made it clear they had no intention of leaving again. I didn't think the boxes were a random coincidence, but neither Isaac nor the frog shifter had taken responsibility yet.

But the day wasn't just about sports, if you could call squeezing through tiny holes a sport. Jake and his painting ladies had set out easels early in the day and had captured the festivities in acrylic on canvas. Jake's painting had moved me so much, I'd bought it from him. I didn't know what I'd do with it. The canvas wouldn't fit in the trailer, which meant it'd have to go in the shop's waiting room. Jake showcased supes in their shifted forms, painting everything in a whimsical style. A mundane human would dismiss it as fantasy, even if it was real. I could stare at it for hours. It made me wonder what life would be like if we could live like this every day. No hiding. No fear. Just people living their lives out in the open.

Then Ryley and I watched Oak's demonstration where he worked metal scraps into garden statues. When that finished, I'd dragged Ryley over to grab some cheeseburgers for me and grilled pineapple for him. It'd only been midmorning at that point, and it hadn't been that long since I'd finished a big breakfast at the inn, but I was hungry. My alpha magic had expanded quickly last night, so maybe that was why I was trying to eat my weight in beef. Either that or Xander was right, and I needed the extra protein to heal my magic.

After that, we found our way to the registration table. Ash was sitting behind the table, looking bored. He was wearing one of his many pink sweaters, and I couldn't figure out how he wasn't melting in the afternoon sun. Beside him, Jeremy was standing on a chair with binoculars in his hand. He glanced down at something on his phone before peering through the binoculars again.

On the other side of him, but standing on the ground instead of a chair, Doc Roberts stared at the water too. As a sphinx shifter, he'd have decent eyesight, so he didn't need the binoculars, but he shielded his eyes with his hand. I'd noticed him lingering around earlier, probably staying close in case someone got injured during the events. But I hadn't chatted with him yet. I wasn't sure I wanted to, not after he sent that text to the whole damn pack telling them to make sure I rested.

"I think you're right, Ash," Jeremy said. "I think both

Henrietta and Gary dropped to the bottom of the lake and stayed there. Did they forget they were in a race?"

Sally cackled. "I bet they got frisky and decided that was more interesting."

Jeremy looked aghast at the succubus. "In the middle of a race?"

Sally shrugged. "Like I said, they have stamina. How do you think they built that up? Sex. Lots and lots of sex."

Everyone who heard that comment grimaced, and I doubted I was the only one thinking about the bakery, where, until Sally came into their lives, they seemed to spend most of their time. Surely, they wouldn't do that as much as Sally was suggesting.

Nope. I didn't want to think about that.

"How can you tell where they are?" Ryley asked Jeremy as he looked out across the water. He tugged off his glasses and looked toward the middle of the lake. Weston and Brodie were at the far end, so the middle was calm. Not even a ripple broke the smooth surface.

"The contestants have trackers so we can make sure they hit the marker before swimming back," Jeremy said. "They are on loan from the Willow Lake Police Department. They ordered in a bunch of new ones after the one Simon sent through the portal with Morgan malfunctioned. These are their old ones."

"Will you use them for the hide and seek competition too?" If that was the case, it'd ease a lot of my worries about Ryley going off on his own.

I wasn't sure why that worried me so much. Everyone in town was here, so I couldn't see anyone, not even Robbie, trying anything with so many witnesses around.

Was this anxiousness about separating caused by our mating?

"That's the plan." Jeremy nodded. "I'm the only one who can see them, and I won't let anyone else use the info to cheat. This is important research. I won't have the results messed up because someone had insider information."

"I thought it was all fun and games," Ash teased his friend.

"Ha ha," Jeremy said, sounding anything but amused. He looked through his binoculars again. "Looks like Weston and Brodie are on their way back. It is going to be a close finish, I think."

We all stopped to watch the two shifters cut through the water. As they neared the finish line, which was a yellow ribbon held between two canoes, Brodie inched ahead. Then he was through with Weston crossing the line after him, no more than a foot behind.

I'd seen Weston swim enough times to know he hadn't pushed as hard as he could to cross the finish line. Merfolk were sprinters. They lived in shallow areas close to the shore where they regularly needed to hide from humans. But kelpies were creatures of the oceans and built to endure enormous distances. There was no way Weston should have lost in a small space like Willow Lake.

But no one would hear that from me.

Brodie neighed when he realized he'd won. He lifted his head in the air, shook out his silvery mane, and leaped through the water, kicking up enough waves and water to make the canoes rock wildly. Weston smiled fondly at the antics of his competitor. Huh. Brodie's interest might not be as one-sided as I'd thought.

Weston had a reputation for sleeping around. I hoped he didn't think he could treat Brodie that way. The kid—okay, he wasn't a minor, but he still felt like a kid to me—wasn't like Weston's other conquests. I wanted to say it wasn't my business, but Brodie felt like my business because of how we'd saved him from Robbie. Weston would never intentionally hurt Brodie, but when Weston inevitably moved on to his next lover, Brodie would be devastated.

They shifted and staggered out of the water. Weston clapped Brodie on the back, congratulating him on his win. As soon as Weston touched the kelpie, the kid froze like he didn't want to move or say anything to make Weston take his hand away. Then someone shouted at the merman, which pulled Weston's attention away from Brodie. The merman's face lit up, and he accepted a consolation kiss from the guy who'd called his name.

"Hide and seek is next," Jeremy said as he jumped off the chair. He looked down at his clipboard. "We have six contestants who have agreed to hide—"

"Seven," Ryley said quickly.

"You want to sign up? That's great!" Jeremy scribbled Ryley's name on his paper. "The way it'll work is that a competitor will hide, then we'll time how long it takes for them to be found. Then the next competitor will hide."

"Where are they hiding?"

Jeremy looked around at the park. "I'd originally thought we'd do it here, but there's a lot more people than I expected. Should we move this up to Winslow Park?

We'll need to go over there anyway for the Sisyphus competition." Jeremy flipped through his papers. "Although we don't have many people signed up for that one yet."

"Go figure," Ash muttered. "Rolling a boulder up a hill is supposed to be a punishment."

"If someone goes into the woods behind the park, they could run for miles," I said. "Those woods go all the way to the mountains."

"Supes can always tell when they cross the town boundary, right?" Jeremy asked. "We'll just say they can't go past that."

The back of my neck itched at the thought of Ryley going into the woods, even the ones within the town limits. No one else seemed bothered by the idea. Was I overreacting? Gage would know if anything bad was happening in Willow Lake. And Jake would have received a message from the Eternal Magic if this was a problem. Neither of them had voiced any concerns.

So, yeah, I guessed I was overreacting. A new mate problem. Or maybe that itchiness meant something else, like I had a sunburn.

I hoped it was a sunburn.

Chapter Thirty

RYLEY

I hadn't been this close to vomiting because of nerves since I left my herd all those years ago. Why on earth had I thought this would be a good idea? Nausea was not fun. Not to anyone.

The first three competitors had already gone, with another four, including me, yet to go. Adrian, who used to hunt fugitives when he worked with the Supernatural Council, was the seeker. The rest of us were supposed to hide and evade him as long as possible. Adrian found the first two within minutes. The last one, a little lizard shifter of some kind, had evaded being caught for a full fifteen minutes. Waiting for them to return had been nerve-wracking. I wouldn't last that long. No way.

"Our next competitor is Ryley Bell," Jeremy said after consulting his clipboard.

I staggered toward the starting line. I wasn't drunk, but my limbs weren't functioning properly. It might be because I was teetering on the edge of hyperventilating. If I passed out, I wouldn't have to do this.

"Are you ready?" Jeremy asked.

I gave him a shaky thumbs up. If living in the herd had taught me anything, it was that I was stronger than I thought. I would do this. I'd hidden my magic from mundane humans for years. I could hide from a supe for a few minutes. Besides, it didn't matter if I came in last. Someone had to. It'd be fine.

"Ry? You okay?" Hayden asked from the sidelines.

I waved him off.

I needed a plan. Right. Now what?

Fuck a duckle, I sucked at this.

I just needed to break this down. First step, I'd go into the trees. Then all I'd need to do was find a pretty little shrub and sit down beside it. Yeah. That'd be fine. I could do that. Easy as pie. A piece of cake. A picnic.

I needed to quit thinking about food. It wasn't helping my stomach settle.

"Here is the tracker," Jeremy said, handing me a funny little pin to attach to my shirt.

My hands shook as I tried to attach it. Hayden finally stepped forward to help. How embarrassing. Then Jeremy checked the signal on his phone.

"We're good," Jeremy said. "Ready?"

I nodded. I couldn't do words.

"Adrian, go into your cone of silence."

Adrian grumbled something about Jeremy making it up to him later, but he put on the helmet as requested. Black construction paper covered the visor so he couldn't see out. Jeremy's cheeks flushed as he patted Adrian's back. A small smile played over his mouth.

Jeremy cleared his throat and glanced at his clipboard again, as if needing to remember what he was supposed to be doing. "Right. Like the others, you'll have a head start, then Adrian will go into the woods to find you after five minutes." Jeremy held up a large metal bell. Based on what I'd seen of Oak's work in the demonstration earlier, I thought it was one of his. And why, for the love of Magic, was I even looking at the bell? I was about to be hunted through the woods. "Do you want some music to hype you up?"

No one else had agreed to the music, but it couldn't hurt. "Sure."

"Yes! Finally!" Jeremy lowered the bell and scooped up his phone. He tapped on the screen and "Lose Yourself" by Eminem blasted over two small portable speakers. He waited until the chorus before he shouted, "On your mark. Get set. Go hide!"

He clanged the bell. I shifted and galloped to the trees. As soon as I was away from the crowd's eyes, I let out a deep breath. This would all be over in a few minutes. Then I could go drink a metric ton of ouzo and promise myself I'd never do this again.

The shrub I hid behind still had most of its leaves, so I was a little hidden from view. But that would be too easy. I wandered through the trees to find another spot. I didn't want to make it too easy. Huh. Now that I was doing it, it didn't seem so scary.

I could do this. Hide. Make it a little tricky for Adrian.

I walked a little further. They'd be sending him after me soon. I should hunker down somewhere.

What was that noise?

Shit. He must already be in the woods. Five minutes had passed fast. A twig cracked. Leaves rustled. I grinned, ready to jump out and surprise my hunter. He was getting closer and closer and...

"Oomph. Ouch. Son of a goat herder's daughter."

I staggered, reaching for my head. Then I fell to my ass. What the ever-loving fuck had hit me? It was lucky I had shifted because my horns protected me from the brunt of the hit, but I was still dazed.

"Grab him. Let's go."

Oh no. I recognized that bastard's voice. But how? I was still within the Willow Lake boundary, and Robbie was supposed to be on the run. I blinked to clear my bleary sight, as rough hands hauled me to my feet.

"It was nice of him to come out and greet us like a good little pet. Now, let's go before he tries to run away again."

Then someone came at me with something black.

I batted them away with my free hand, but they were stronger and faster. Fucking fuckity foo. There had to be a way out of here. I needed to escape. Then my gaze caught on something that made me freeze. Standing behind Robbie and his buddies was a face I hadn't seen in years.

Conny was here.

———

HAYDEN

Ryley disappeared into the woods, and it took everything I had not to follow him. A digital timer was counting down the five minutes until Adrian would go after Ryley. It seemed to flick through the numbers more slowly than normal.

Finally, the timer got to zero.

Jeremy tapped Adrian's shoulder. He whipped off the helmet and rushed into the woods. Jeremy glanced at his phone. Frowning, he tapped on the screen. Then he did it again.

"Weird."

"What? What's weird?"

"Ryley's tracker isn't showing up on my screen." He shrugged. "Must be a malfunction or something."

The hairs on the back of my neck and arms all lifted at once. "What did you say?"

"The tracker. It isn't on my screen anymore. Could it be because of his magic?"

I scanned the trees. Could that be the reason? I wanted to think so.

A portal opened beside us, and Jake and Gage rushed through it. Jake's face had a streak of black paint, and the sight made my heart sink. Jake only used black when he was channeling a vision. I froze.

"Stop everything," Gage said. "Jake had a vision. We were on our way here to tell you when I felt someone breach the town boundary."

Gasps rose from the supes gathered around us. Then people were moving. Isaac abruptly stopped arguing with the frog shifter and shifted seamlessly into his centaur form. The frog shifted too and leaped on Isaac's back.

Under different circumstances, Isaac batting at the smaller shifter to dislodge him would have been funny, but no one was laughing right now. Oak scooped Mercer into his arms and growled at anyone who got close. Jeremy's white glowing magic flickered to life around Adrian, covering him in a protective shield. Brodie pulled a trembling Dakota close. Then they were both wrapped in Weston's arms. Flames surged to life in Van's and Dillon's eyes, and a fireball burst to life above Ash's open hand.

"The vision?" I choked out.

Gage's face was grim. "It showed Ryley with Robbie."

I didn't wait to find out what else he had to say. I raced to the trees, shifting as I ran, needing to find my mate. Doc's shouts, demanding I return and warning that I wasn't strong enough to fight, were lost under the pounding of my paws across the ground.

As I ran, I tracked Ryley's scent. It meandered through the trees. Given how potent the trail was, I knew Ryley hadn't used his magic. Was it because he couldn't?

Nothing about his scent said he was frightened. He'd been anxious before the event started, but that seemed to have faded once he was in the trees. I doubted his scent would be so normal if he'd come across Robbie out here.

I didn't detect Robbie's scent anywhere, so hopefully the vision hadn't come true yet. If I thought the Eternal Magic would help me, I'd be begging and praying and promising her the world to keep my mate away from my brother. But I'd tried to do that too many times in the past and she'd never listened.

I found Adrian a few minutes later. He was sniffing and pawing at the ground, just inside the town's perimeter. The boundary hummed beside us. I'd never felt the edge so vividly before. It must have been a by-product of the alpha magic.

"What? What did you find?"

"Ryley's tracker, I think."

"Move out of the way," I demanded, and Adrian jumped away from the object. I pressed my nose to the tiny piece of plastic and circuitry. "His scent is there, but it's fainter than it should be."

I inhaled deeply, trying to find his scent again in the vegetation around the area. It wasn't there. Had he gone over the boundary? Why would he do that? And why the hell would he drop his tracker?

It had to be a joke, right?

Any minute now, he was going to jump out of the trees and laugh at us. We'd tell this story for the rest of our lives, and he'd tease me about how worked up I'd been when he finally showed himself. And I'd laugh right along with him and praise him for how amazing his magic was and...

I crossed the boundary to look for more clues. A whisper of Ryley's scent floated in the air. And...

Fuck.

Robbie. Robbie had been here too. Right here. Right where Ryley had been but wasn't anymore. My murderous brother had my precious mate. My heart felt like it'd been ripped from my body.

Then I lifted my snout to the sky and howled. I howled in anger. I howled in fear. I howled for my pack. But mostly, I howled for my mate.

The air filled with the answering cries from my pack. They would help. *We're here*, they said. *We're coming,* they said. *Whatever you need,* they said. And feet pounded through the forest toward me.

I wasn't alone.

Chapter Thirty-One

HAYDEN

Van and Gage were the first to arrive and hundreds more supes came on their heels. They crowded together between the trees. Most of the shifters had taken their animal forms. They stared at me, pacing back and forth along the border of the town, waiting for me to command them.

"What's happened?" Gage asked. He'd shifted into his alternate form, an imposing figure amid the rest of the pack. His black wings barely fit between the dense tree trunks and his red skin looked vibrant against the yellow and orange leaves of the fall foliage. By the grim look on his demonic face, he already knew what had happened.

"Robbie has Ryley," I said.

"We don't know that." Adrian sat on his haunches. "We found the tracker Ryley was wearing, but it could have—"

"I detected both of their scents," I growled. "Robbie was here with his lackeys, and he took Ryley."

Adrian ducked his head and exposed the side of his neck to me. "I'm sorry, Alpha. I was wrong."

"Where is Teague?" I asked. "I need him to do whatever he did when Ogden was abducted. He could see the bond or something."

"Teague's not here," Gage said.

"Well, get him here," I demanded.

"We will, but it'll take him time to get back."

"Open a damn portal and go get him."

"I can't." Gage grimaced. "I can only open portals to places I've been."

"My mate is missing. I need to find him. All you're giving me are excuses. If you won't help, get out of my way."

"We want to help," Van said with a placating tone as he stepped forward. No one stood too close to him with his flame-covered fur. And as he moved, the few who were closest to him inched further away. "All of us. Now, talk to me. You said you picked up his scent. Do you know what direction they went?"

I gritted my teeth. The hellhound was trying to help, I knew that, but all this talking was killing me. I needed to find Ryley. Robbie had been ready to leave me to die in that cage in his bunker, so what would he do to my mate? Did he realize who Ryley was to me? Was that why he targeted him?

Would it be better if he did? He might keep Ryley close just to torment me. Whereas if he thought Ryley was some random supe, he might try to sell him. I couldn't let Ryley disappear just like that unicorn had.

Van was watching me carefully. I didn't know if he

was trying to decide if I was going to lose it, or if he was giving me the opportunity to take charge of what would happen next. I suspected the latter. He knew I'd need that control right now. I didn't bother answering his question yet. Other things needed to happen first.

"I need all the roads blockaded," I said. "I need all the rivers and streams monitored. Call on the residents who live closest to those routes and have them set up barriers. Every person trying to get through needs to be interviewed and every damn thing leaving the area needs to be searched. I don't care if it is a canoe or a bicycle, go through it from top to bottom. They have a head start. It isn't much of one, but if they've got any brains they'll get away from here as fast as possible. I think they'll be going to their old pack lands, but we can't count on that."

Van nodded as he typed something into his phone. When he looked up, he said, "Done."

"Then I want an army of people with me. We will go over every molecule of dirt and leaf and stone between here and Robbie's old pack lands. And, if we still haven't found them by then, we'll do the same to that damn property, too."

"I'll organize the search," Van said. "We can't charge into the woods without a plan. We could miss something important."

I growled. I wanted to tell him to fuck off, that we needed to leave immediately, that the longer Robbie had my mate, the more danger he was in. But the damn hellhound was right. Sending in a troop of people with no instructions could mean important information might be overlooked. Few pack members were trained to track or hunt. And if they stomped all over the weak scent trail Ryley and Robbie had left behind, we'd be worse off than we currently were.

"Fine. Make sure the roads are covered with enough strength that they can stop whoever might try to get through. I'll lead the search from here with a small team. The rest can follow behind us and hunt for anything we might have missed. We should send another group to Robbie's old pack lands in case you are right, and they have more tunnels out there. But, again, keep it a smaller group with trained trackers."

"Okay, everyone," Van said, "you heard your alpha. We're going hunting. I want you all to gather any supplies you might need and then get back to Winslow Park. I'll organize the search parties and the roadblocks from there for now. We'll go out to Robbie's pack lands and set up there once we all have everything in motion. Meet me back at the parking lot when you're ready and I'll tell you what to do."

Mercer stepped forward, and Oak growled.

"I can fly over and see if I can find them." Mercer's eyes were hard, and his stance was rigid.

"No, Mercer," Oak pleaded with his mate. "It's too dangerous."

"I've been waiting for this moment for twelve years." The raven shifter shook his head. "I can't sit back and do nothing. Not after everything he did to us."

Oak wiped his hand over his face. "I know, but I still hate this."

"You don't have to do anything, big guy." Mercer

squeezed his mate's hand. "Stay back here. Help Van and the others. I'll be back as soon as I can."

Oak's nostrils flared, and a soft growl rumbled through him. "You aren't going out there alone."

"I won't be alone. I'll be with them," Mercer said as he waved toward us.

Oak's face contorted in a pained look. "Then I'll go with them too."

Van lifted his eyebrow. "That works for you, Alpha?"

Oak was an enormous wolf and an excellent fighter, but he hated conflict almost as much as his mate hated beige. Oak's cheeks reddened as I looked at him.

"You sure about this?" I asked the large wolf shifter. "Because Mercer is right. Van will need help. We also need people to stay in town and make sure Robbie's people don't infiltrate Willow Lake while we are out there looking for him."

"I'm sure," Oak said, lifting his chin.

"If you are sure," I said, "you can both come. Thank you."

Mercer jumped into his mate's arms. They shared an intense, open-mouthed kiss. When they pulled apart, he said, "This has been a long time coming. We're going to help finish it today."

Oak nodded. Then Mercer shifted into his raven form and took flight. The big wolf shifter looked like he wanted to grab him out of the air and haul him back to their apartment above their downtown shop. Instead, he let his shift flow over him. He was easily the largest wolf in the pack, and even though he didn't want to be here, I was still happy to have him at my side. He was loyal in all the best ways. He pawed at the ground, eager to follow his mate.

When most of the pack scurried off to follow Van's orders, I returned to the spot where I'd found Ryley and Robbie's scents. I inhaled deeply. They weren't alone.

"I'll track the scent as far as I can," I said. I looked at Oak, Adrian, Van, and Dillon. "Can any of you smell them too?"

They shook their heads. Damn it.

"Do what you can, Alpha," Gage said. "Concentrate on that. Oak, Dillon, and I will watch your back. Adrian and Van will send some people behind us. They might catch something we miss."

I almost argued that all the hellhounds and wolves stay with me, but I couldn't do that. It'd leave the other groups without the strength they'd need if they met up with Robbie. Hellhounds were notoriously vicious and deadly fighters. They were traditionally the enforcers of the supernatural world. Still, as most of the pack left us in the woods to carry out my instructions, I couldn't help but feel that something wasn't quite right.

Maybe nothing would ever feel right until I had my mate in my arms again.

"Anything else, Alpha," Van asked.

Yeah. I wanted to tell him to quit calling me Alpha. We used to argue about that a lot, but this time it wasn't because I didn't believe I was anyone's alpha. This time, I needed my friends with me. I didn't want to be the leader. Leaders were supposed to know the answers to shit, and I didn't know anything at all. This was just like when my parents died. I could only hope that I wouldn't mess everything up again. None of us would survive that a second time.

"If anyone finds Robbie, tell them to delay him, then come and get me. We don't want anyone else getting hurt."

Van's fiery eyes stared at me. "Every single person in this pack would face off against Robbie again and again for you, for Ryley, and for anyone else. It is what packs do."

My chest tightened at his words. "Just come and get me."

"Yes, Alpha." Van dipped his head in acknowledgement. He turned to go, but before he left, he glanced back at me. "We'll find them, Hayden. We'll find Ryley and we'll stop Robbie."

I said nothing, not because I didn't want to, but because a big lump of emotion had lodged itself in my throat. It was all I could do not to choke on it. If I let all that out now, I'd never be able to do what needed to be done next. I pushed the emotions down until I felt like I could breathe again.

"Let's go."

Chapter Thirty-Two

RYLEY

The black fabric shopping bag tied around my head smelled musty and a bit like rotten vegetables. Not the greatest smell, but at least it wasn't suffocating me. I sucked in a deep breath and tried to figure out if I'd actually seen what I thought I'd seen.

I had to be mistaken.

Conny couldn't be working with Robbie, because he just couldn't be. Conny was only in his twenties. No one left the herd at that age. Well, except me. But I wasn't considered a true faun. And the herd was all the way on the other side of the country.

Except.

There was no mistaking what I'd seen.

The flute-playing faun at Robbie's side was unequivocally Conny.

The last time I'd seen him, he'd been thirteen. His hair had been a lot longer and his cheeks a lot softer back then, but I knew this was him. Especially with the frantic way his eyes had locked on mine over his flute. He'd kept on playing the damn thing, barely breaking long enough to breathe, as Robbie shoved the bag over my head and secured my hands with zip ties. Until that moment, I hadn't realized fauns could use their nasty flutes to make magic, but that flute wasn't making music. So that was another lie my herd told me. How had I not realized the whole flute connection before now? I bet I would have rocked playing the flute if they'd given me the chance.

Or not.

After all, it was a fucking flute, and they were the worst.

But no one had given me the opportunity to learn. Horrible bigoted elitist herd. They were a bunch of wet whisky farts, the whole lot of them.

"Bend over," the guy who was holding me demanded.

"I don't even know your name," I said.

He shoved me forward.

My stomach hit something. It took a second for me to realize the moving thing beneath me was furry. Interesting. They were trying to fold me over someone's back. This felt like an opportunity. If my hands weren't tied up, I would have rubbed them together and cackled.

Okay. Probably not. But it felt like the right time to do something like that.

A few seconds later, the body under me moved. We were on our way. With the bag over my head, I couldn't tell if a handy shrub was close for me to hide behind. So, I just had to take a chance. I wiggled and squirmed until I started slipping.

As soon as I hit the ground, I rolled, right into someone's paws.

"What are you playing at?" Robbie growled.

Damn it.

I was back on someone's back again.

Crap on a broken cracker. I'd acted too fast that time, except it didn't go any better the next time either.

"Stop," Robbie commanded. "Everyone, shift. And you, faun, keep playing that damn flute. You know what'll happen if they find us."

I didn't know what would happen, but apparently Conny did. His magic surged.

Someone tossed me over their shoulder—their very boney, very human shoulder. I didn't think Robbie was carrying me. That barnacle licker was too lazy to carry me through the woods. Then I was bouncing like a lumpy sack of potatoes. The guy's knobby shoulder dug into my stomach with each step, making me both nauseous again, and short of breath too.

"I'm going to puke." I gasped.

Whoever was carrying me tightened his grip on my furry legs, as if warning me he wouldn't take kindly to wearing vomit on his ass. Honestly, I wasn't too keen on the idea myself because if I did lose it, most of it would get caught in the bag and that was not something I needed in my life right now. Or ever.

And the guy holding me needed to watch where he was putting his damn hands. My shift didn't come with clothes, and he was getting a little too close to the goods.

No one spoke, but magic flowed around us as Conny kept playing his magical fucking flute.

I needed a plan. Again. I was so tired of constantly needing a plan. And what was I going to do about Conny? Was he here because he wanted to be?

He couldn't be, could he? My sweet little Irish dancing brother couldn't be in league with someone like Robbie.

I needed to figure that out, but not now. My priority had to be getting back to my mate and my pack.

Ha! Wouldn't these bull nuggets be surprised when Hayden showed up on his white steed—or centaur, as the case may be—and saved me from their evil clutches?

Wait, did that mean I was a prince in peril in that scenario? Yeah. That wasn't going to work for me. I could save myself. I'd done it before. I could do it again. Or, well, I could if I had a plan.

And now I was back to where I'd started.

Hayden and the others would know I was missing by now. They had to be right behind us. I knew he was there. I could feel it. Somehow. Must be the fancy bond we had.

So, I needed to either delay us until they arrived or escape and find my way back to them. Or what if I undermined Conny's magic? If all those Willow Lakers were to be believed and I had as much magic as a purebred faun, it might be possible.

Hayden showed me I had magic. But calling it up, using it, and doing all the steps in between when my brain was panicking and struggling to get more air in my lungs? Yeah. Not the best conditions for experimentation. And I doubted whatever magic I had would be enough to counter Conny's fancy flute.

I was going to be bitter about the whole flute thing for a long while. I hoped I lived long enough to get over my anger. It'd happen, eventually. But it could take a century or two.

It was time to act. I sucked in as much air as I could with a shoulder digging into my diaphragm and focused my energy inward. Hayden had said to breathe in deep and let it out slowly. That wasn't an option right now. So, moving on. Then he'd said something about tapping into the place that warmed when I shifted. I'd always felt that in my chest. He hadn't specifically described it as the place where my magic lived, but I wasn't an idiot.

Hmm… That was going to be tricky, because with the way my lungs were burning, my chest felt like it was on fire and that had nothing to do with my magic and everything to do with lack of oxygen.

Why couldn't anything ever be easy?

Whatever. I hadn't lived through a bazillion years—yes, I might have rounded that number up by a zillion or two, but this moment didn't require exact numbers—of torment from the fauns in my old herd without learning how to survive and roll with the punches.

I was getting a touch lightheaded, though. I just hoped I didn't pass out before I unleashed my heroic escape plan, whatever that was. Oh, hey, what if I did a Vulcan nerve pinch with my stomach muscles? I squeezed and wiggled, but nothing happened. The guy was completely unperturbed. He didn't even grunt or reposition me. What I wouldn't give to have an engineer with a Scottish accent ready to beam me out of here. But at least I wasn't wearing a red shirt. Small victories.

Actually, being an android like Data would be the best. He didn't have to breathe, and he'd be able to subdue these guys, because they were the real problem. I could deal with the zip ties. I'd watched videos on how to do it, although they hadn't covered how to break them when flung over someone's shoulder. If I didn't have the bag over my head, I'd try chewing through them or rubbing them against my horn.

And why was everyone so quiet?

It was creepy.

It was also past time to do something about this knee-to-the-nuts kind of day I was having. I closed my eyes. I couldn't see anything through the bag anyway. I sucked in another deep breath, or at least as big a one as I could.

Yoo-hoo? Magic? Come out, come out, wherever you are...

It was official. I was losing my mind. But my little chant worked. A little fluttering sensation tickled deep inside me. My magic. It was there. Waiting for me. I nudged it and praised it and begged it to grow. I envisioned it as the yellowy green magic that'd poured out of me last night when I'd been in Hayden's arms. Bright. Beautiful. I remembered Hayden's magic too and how his had joined with mine. Were we still linked through that magical cable?

Just in case we were, I took a moment to think about the joy and happiness and... Yes, the love I felt for him was there too. Then I asked the Eternal Magic to connect us like an old telephone operator. The magic inside me warmed and tingled, then it was gone with a whoosh. Message sent. I hoped he received it.

Because if my plan didn't work, I needed him to know I loved him. I should have told him last night or this morning or even the moment I met him in the woods and realized I was relieved when my kick to the head hadn't killed him. If it'd been his brother I'd kicked and knocked down, I would have kept kicking until he couldn't get up anymore.

As a sign that we were fated mates, that wasn't the most romantic thing that could have happened between us, but whatever. None of us were perfect.

Now it was time for my next party trick, which I liked to call "the faun kicks some ass," which is also known as "the faun finds a way to get off this guy's shoulder and hides under a bush until my mate rides in on a centaur's back like a white knight". Because that'd be epic.

This was it.

I grabbed onto my magic with both hands and squeezed the shit out of it, metaphorically speaking, as I channeled my determination to get the fuck out of this situation.

Chapter Thirty-Three

RYLEY

"Throw him in there," Robbie yelled, betraying his sense of urgency.

Damn it. I hadn't escaped yet. Apparently, my magic wasn't much good at kicking ass.

I couldn't see anything, but I had a pretty good idea of what was happening as the smell of exhaust permeated the thin fabric covering my head. They'd carried me all the way to the road and now we'd arrived at a vehicle of some kind.

"Gently!" I shouted even louder.

The guy was not gentle.

I grunted as my captor dropped me onto what felt like the bed of a pickup truck. Yeah. That was going to bruise. It hadn't been that long since I'd stowed away in Hayden's truck like this, so the experience was jarringly familiar.

"Keep moving," Robbie said, pinching my thigh to get me rolling further onto the truck bed.

I moved away from his hand, slithering and rolling along the hard metal ridges, until I was out of his reach. The truck jostled a little as someone else climbed on after me. The tailgate slammed shut, followed by the doors on the cab of the truck. Then we were moving.

"Conny? You back here?"

"Yeah."

"Can you get this foul bag off my head?"

"Yeah. Hold on. They tied the bag's handles or whatever they're called behind your head." A moment later, the bag was gone.

"Thanks," I muttered as I peered around. Was this the same truck they'd used when they abducted me the first time? At least this time I was conscious and, even better, I knew people were coming to help me.

The truck had one of those camper shell things over the bed, so that'd make it a little more challenging. I couldn't fling myself over the side and into the ditch. But the only ones back here were Conny and me. I didn't know what had happened to his flute, but I didn't see it on him.

"Well, this sucks," I said.

I cast my gaze to the road behind us, hoping Hayden would suddenly appear, but the only thing that stirred was a flash of black against the yellow leaves on the aspen and larch trees. Was that a regular bird or a shifter? I couldn't tell. I hoped it was a shifter, specifically someone from Willow Lake.

"They made a big mistake," I said as I struggled to sit up. My hands were still secured with zip ties, and the truck was weaving erratically, which wasn't helping my efforts. "Hayden will come for me."

Conny reached for me, presumably to help me sit, but I cringed away from him. He winced at my reaction and pulled his hand back. I still hadn't figured out what was going on with him yet. I needed him to explain things before I accepted any more of his help. Once I was finally upright, I broke the zip tie and freed my hands. That was better.

I crawled to the back and tried the handle. It twisted. Yes!

"No!" Conny was on me, pulling my hand away.

The truck whipped around another curve, and we jolted apart. Robbie had put on a brave face, but he wasn't wasting time making his escape. He knew Hayden and the others would be in pursuit. I hoped he pissed his pants when he saw the army Hayden would bring.

"Please, Ry," Conny said. He was too thin, too pale, and looked years older than he should have for his age. He looked so vulnerable as he met my gaze. "Don't try to escape."

"What's the matter with you, Conny? You better get talking."

All I got was another loud sigh for an answer. Conny leaned against the tailgate.

"Why would you help that blue-balled dick sock?"

Conny shook his head, and a small almost-smile twitched over his lips. "I'd forgotten about the weird way you swear."

He wasn't the first to comment on that. But single syllable curse words, which so many of them were, had always felt inadequate to me, like they couldn't convey the depth of my ire.

"Yeah, well, I'll be swearing a lot more, so buckle up."

"I didn't know it was going to be you," Conny said.

"Would it have been acceptable if it was someone else?"

"No." Conny rubbed his hands over his face.

"Why are you here, Conny? Mother and The Ass Pimple would never have let you leave the herd. You're too young." Conny's father, also known as The Ass Pimple, was the guy who swept in to supposedly save my mother from making another mistake after my father died. Like getting involved with my father, a human, had been some terrible traitorous error on her part. TAP had timed it perfectly. She'd been grieving and vulnerable and ended up believing all the elitist bullshit lies the old-school fauns spread in the herd. They'd married shockingly fast, and Conny, their only child, had come along shortly after. Given how rare supe children were, everyone in the herd had seen that as a sign of the Eternal Magic endorsing their fauns-belong-with-fauns approach to life. It didn't matter that I'd only been born a little more than a decade earlier and no one had celebrated *my* existence.

"Fuck you," Conny muttered. "And quit calling me Conny. You know I hate it."

"No, you don't," I said. I glanced toward the cab of the truck. No one was paying attention to us, although it wouldn't matter if they were. I needed information. "Talk to me."

He heaved out a deep sigh. "I had to leave."

"Leave what? The herd? Why?"

His gaze flicked to mine before he looked away. "I met a girl."

That wasn't what I expected him to say.

"She's human." He swallowed. "And she's pregnant."

"With your—"

"Yes, with my baby." He frowned at me. "You sound like Mom."

That was a sobering and disturbing thought. "It was just a question."

"Yeah, well, it was a shitty one," he said. "I knew we couldn't stay with the herd. They treated Gretchen like she was a phase I'd grow out of, but we're fated. I *know* we are. When we found out she was pregnant, I knew we couldn't stay." He shuddered. "I remember how they treated you. There was no way I'd bring up a kid in a herd like that and she agreed. So, we left. I thought I'd look you up, see if you'd let us crash at your place for a bit. Gretchen is super smart and has all these plans. She's already got a master's degree and everything. We thought I could be a stay-at-home dad while she pursued her career."

"What happened? How did you end up here?" I thought I knew where this was going, but I asked anyway.

"We stopped at a motel one night." He wiped his eyes. "I don't know how they knew I was a supe, but they did. They said if I went with them, they wouldn't hurt her. She was just starting to show, and they held a gun to her belly. I didn't know what to do." He shook his head. He let out a shuddering sob. "I haven't seen her since... Since that day."

"I'm sorry, Conny. Truly."

"She'll be getting close to delivery now." The *if she is still alive* remained unspoken. Conny's voice broke as he covered his face with his hands.

I suspected she would be. Based on what I knew of Robbie, I was certain he'd think having a baby supe to sell would be a good money-making scheme. I couldn't let that happen. I'd wanted to hurt Robbie before, but now I wanted to kill him.

"He said," Conny continued, "that if I did as he said, she and the baby would be safe."

I hoped the liar hadn't lied. For everyone's sake.

"We're going to get out of here," I said.

When Conny opened his mouth to protest, I held up my hand to stop him.

"We will find Gretchen. My mate and friends—" it'd only been a few days, but yes, those peculiar Willow Lakers were my friends, "—they'll help us. I can guarantee they're looking for me right now."

"I wondered if you'd found someone." He eyed the lock of hair that marked me as being mated. His mouth twitched a little, like he wanted to smile, but the impulse died under his worry. Conny slumped. "But they won't find us. I've been out here for months, and they haven't found us yet. Rob likes to drag me through the woods with him and have me hide him in the forest while he watches people hunt for him. There is this one guy. Rob laughs every time he sees him."

Yeah. I had a pretty good idea who that one guy was.

"It'll be different this time," I promised. I hoped I was right.

Chapter Thirty-Four

HAYDEN

"Something happened," I said, picking up speed.

"What?" Gage asked as he lengthened his stride to match my pace. He had shifted out of his demonic form so he could move more easily through the trees, but he was still keeping up with me.

"Yeah, their trail suddenly became strong enough that I can pick it up too. It isn't as clear as it should be, but it is better than it was," Dillon said from right behind me. "There are five other wolves and someone else. A mage, maybe? I can see magic lingering in the air. And for some reason they went from being four-footed to two-footed."

Oak was silent. His gaze stayed on the sky more than the forest.

"Another faun," I said. In fact, the scent reminded me of Ryley a little. "Why would they take their human forms? They'd be faster on their paws."

"It is welcome news for us, though. We might catch up and overtake them," Dillon said.

"I'll let the others know," Gage said, pulling out his cell phone.

"Good job, Ry," I muttered. "Keep doing exactly that."

Last night, when my alpha magic had erupted and spewed over everyone, I'd seen a golden thread connecting Ryley to me. It'd faded from sight after I became alpha, but the more I concentrated on my bond with him, the more I could sense it. And through that link, I tried to let him know I was coming. That he wasn't alone.

And I swore, just for a heartbeat, that I could feel him too. A warm sensation had wrapped around me. It felt like love, reminding me of all the best moments of my life: my parents telling me they were proud of me, the first time I shifted and saw my wolf, and the moment I accepted Ryley as my mate.

That had to mean he was still okay. I had to get to him before that changed.

My heart thundered in my chest. My paws pounded against the leaf-littered forest floor. Suddenly, a raven cawed overhead. Mercer was back. I thought about stopping for an update, but I couldn't. Not when I was sure Ryley was just ahead.

Mercer ducked between the trees like a shadow. The whisper of his wings shook the yellowing leaves on the aspen trees.

"I couldn't see or hear them, and then suddenly I could. There are five wolves, including Robbie. Two of the wolves are carrying people over their shoulders. One has

Ryley and the other has another faun. That other one is playing a flute."

"Did they see you?"

"I don't think so," Mercer said as he banked around a tree trunk.

"Good. How far ahead?"

"They are almost at the road. A wolf is waiting there with the engine running on a beat-up truck. I don't recognize the vehicle, but I can describe it, and I got the license plate numbers."

"Excellent work. Get that to Van," I said. "And tell him to send a vehicle out to meet us at the road in case we don't get there in time."

"Yes, Alpha," Mercer said as he shot up through the trees and out of sight.

I was already running, but I forced my legs to pump faster. I doubted we'd overtake Robbie in time, but I had to try. As soon as I smelled vehicle exhaust, I knew we were too late. We broke out of the trees in time to see Robbie's truck veer off the shoulder and onto the asphalt.

"Damn it," I said on a panting breath. My wolf wanted to race after them, but I knew I'd never catch them.

"I'm back and I brought company," Mercer shouted from overhead. His large black wings thumped against the air as he raced down the highway after the truck. Beside me, Oak growled his displeasure, but he didn't stop his mate.

"Company?" I asked.

"Over there." Gage pointed to the blue streak undulating over the treetops along the side of the road. "Simon and Ogden are with him."

"Wait, did you say Simon is there too?" I looked at the blue dragon again and sure enough, Simon was up there, attached to Ogden's back with some kind of harness system. I couldn't imagine what'd dragged Simon out here. I hoped he didn't feel obligated to do this because we'd helped him and Ogden a while back. I'd never demand such a thing from him. This was not a tit-for-tat situation.

Still, I didn't want Mercer out there alone, either. Years ago, someone had shot Mercer out of the air. Robbie had blamed one of his friends, but even if that was true, I knew Robbie had encouraged him to do it. I couldn't let that happen again. Mercer would be safer if he had a companion in the air.

Fuck. I had to get Robbie. I had to stop him. He'd been causing problems for too long.

"Where is the damn vehicle I asked for—"

"It's coming. Over there," Dillon said, pointing his nose toward the road leading to town.

A car skidded around a curve and raced toward us.

"Who is that?" Gage asked.

I recognized that car, from its dented green roof to the ticking noise in the engine that I kept trying to get the owner to fix. I groaned. "Clive Rivers."

"One of Simon's brothers."

"Believe me when I say he is nothing like Simon." That much was obvious as Clive brought the car to a squealing stop in front of us. The back end of the car fish-tailed, but he didn't lose control. I knew he didn't always have that much luck, because he called the shop almost weekly to pull him out of a ditch.

The passenger door swung open and Warren, another Rivers boy, jumped out.

"Hi, Alpha," Warren said as he waved at us. "Here, you can sit up front."

"We can't all fit in there," I said.

"We can if I shift," Warren offered with an eager smile.

I wanted to argue with him, tell him and his brother to stay here while we took their car. But we were already losing time and an argument with those two would only waste more. I could probably command them to stay here using my alpha power, but the idea of compelling them to do something against their will made me queasy.

"I hope you know what you're doing," I said instead, as I jumped into the front seat. Dillon, Gage, and Oak piled into the back, as Warren shifted to his cat form and hopped into my lap. He was no bigger than an average house cat, so he stood with his front paws on the dashboard so he could see out the window. As soon as everyone's arms and legs were inside, Clive took off down the road again.

"Watch the sky for Mercer and Ogden," I said. "And, uh, Simon too."

"Simon? As in our brother Simon? That Simon?" Warren asked.

"He's with Ogden. They're following Robbie."

"I knew he had it in him," Clive said. He let out a yahoo and pressed on the gas harder. "He's a Rivers, after all."

"Don't kill us before we get there," Dillon said.

Clive cackled, but didn't make any promises.

Chapter Thirty-Five

HAYDEN

"Here, Alpha," Ogden shouted from the ditch.

Simon hunched over his mate's back like a jockey riding a horse to the finish line. The dragon's long snake-like body was whipping through the air alongside the car as he guided us to where Robbie had taken Ryley. When they had found us a minute ago, Simon said Mercer was keeping watch on Robbie's truck while they came to direct us.

"Turn, Clive. Turn!" Simon yelled.

Clive didn't slow. Had he not heard?

"Turn now," I yelled.

Clive hooted as he brushed the brakes with barely enough force to slow us. We almost blasted through the intersection before the car swung around the corner. Warren's front claws grappled to hang onto the vinyl dash-board while his back ones ripped through my jeans as he held on so he wouldn't go flying into Clive's lap.

I tore my eyes away from the road to grab the cat in my lap, while Warren laughed like this was the most fun he'd ever had. The tires slid over the ground as branches and leaves from overgrown trees batted at the car.

I glanced up. My mistake. That wasn't it. Clive had just driven off the road and was racing down the ditch.

"Who gave this guy his license?" Dillon muttered.

"Be careful," I ordered Clive.

"Their vehicle is up ahead," Clive said. "I can catch them."

So he didn't slow down, and I didn't try to make him. I wanted to get to that truck more than anyone. But if we couldn't stop them on the road, we needed a plan for what would happen when we finally had Robbie cornered.

"Dillon, send Van an update," I said as Clive finally maneuvered the car back onto the asphalt.

"Already done," the hellhound said.

I looked at Gage. "Are you strong enough to keep going?"

After the demon had bonded with Willow Lake, he'd complained that his magic was weaker when he left the town boundaries. I didn't want him out there if he couldn't hold his own.

"It's better than normal. Might be because you're here."

I frowned. "Why would that make any difference?"

"Because you're my alpha."

Huh. Right. I supposed I was. I hadn't known if a pack bond would work the same for a demon. Apparently, it did.

"Van and the others are a few minutes behind us."

Dillon looked up from his phone. "They were already on their way when I texted."

Oak still didn't say anything. He looked like he wished he was anywhere but here. If I could, I'd keep him out of the fighting.

"If Robbie stops and makes a run for the woods, we should wait until they get here to go after him," Gage said, even though I knew he'd never have listened to that same advice if our situations were reversed.

Because what if Robbie disappeared again? I might be able to track him now that Ryley was with him, but I couldn't risk it. I considered my options.

The Rivers boys were all the size of house cats, but they each had different colorings. Warren was a brown tabby, and I remembered Clive's fur as being orange. With the fall foliage, Clive would be less noticeable than if we'd been out here in the summer, but Warren still had the best chance of blending in.

"We think Robbie's going to another tunnel he built on his pack lands. I doubt we'll be able to stop them before they exit their vehicle. So, Clive, while we get to wherever Robbie's going, you stay here with Oak," I said. "When the others get here, they'll be able to track us."

"No way," Clive said. "I'm better at this kind of shit than Warren."

"We aren't doing anything right away. We'll look around. I don't want to confront Robbie until the others get here." It killed me to say that, but it was the right thing to do. We didn't know how many followers Robbie had out here. I thought most of his pack had disbanded and moved on, but what if they hadn't? And others might have joined him since.

Too many people were too easily manipulated by anger, lies, and bigotry, and Magic knew Robbie used those to his advantage. It was wild the shit people believed. Too often those misguided beliefs were twisted into a justification for people's heinous actions. He could have riled up a whole new mob of angry, entitled assholes to follow him by now.

Clive kept his mouth shut, but I figured he'd try to change my mind again once we stopped. In the meantime, my gaze clung to the tailgate of the truck in front of us, while my nose hunted for any little hint of my mate's scent.

"If he drops into a tunnel, that's going to be a problem," Gage said.

"I know."

If they had enough food stored down there, they could defend the tunnel indefinitely. My dad had once told me of a famous battle in ancient Greece where a small army defended a narrow passage against a much larger one. This would be no different. If Robbie's new bolt hole was like the other tunnel we'd found, the entrance would only be wide enough for one person to enter at a time. Robbie could easily pick us off one by one as we tried to get down there with him.

"A tunnel would leave us with three options," I said. "One, we wait for him to come out, which seems unlikely, and I'm not waiting around for him. He wouldn't retreat to a tunnel if he didn't think he'd be safe down there. That means he has either food or an exit strategy." I don't know why I mentioned that option. I'd never leave Ryley in his hands. As it was, I was barely resisting the urge to rip the world apart to get my mate back. "Two, we toss some kind of smoke bomb or something down there to flush him out, but if the tunnel is anything like the last one, there will be no air vents. I'm reluctant to mess with their oxygen. And, lastly, I go in and negotiate with him." That was my favorite option.

"There are more options than that," Gage protested. "Common sense says we wait for Ash's brother Birch to get into town. He's already coming here when he finishes up with the SC. As an earth mage, he could have that tunnel exposed in a day, two at most."

Before I registered what I was doing, I swung around and bared my teeth, which wasn't the smartest thing to do to a powerful demon. "I won't wait around for days. He has my mate. My mate!"

"I understand." Gage nodded. "At least wait until the others arrive before you decide on what action to take."

I would go into that damn tunnel. I didn't care what anyone else said. I needed to see Ryley. I needed to make sure he was alive. He had to be.

I swallowed. I hadn't realized my parents were dead until Van had sent someone to wake me in the middle of the night, so he could tell me. I prayed it'd be different with Ryley because he was my mate, but what if it wasn't? What if my belief that I could feel him was just wishful thinking?

I had to know.

And this confrontation was a long time coming. I

couldn't hide any longer. I'd done that long enough. Alphas didn't hide.

"Fine," I agreed. "After we know what we're dealing with, I'll wait until Van and the others arrive. In the meantime, we'll need to scour the forest for a back door to the tunnel."

"On it," Oak said.

"I'll go with him," Clive said decisively, still irritated at being sidelined earlier.

"Look for large clearings. The tunnel opening we found the other day was in a cleared area. They must have taken the trees down when they built the tunnel entrance."

"This is all just a bunch of wild speculation. We don't know where he is going or what his plan is. Hell, there might not even be another tunnel," Dillon said.

Yeah. He was right, but I needed to do something. Otherwise, I'd just feel like my life was spinning out of control. I needed some way to get control. And coming up with schemes to overcome all the various scenarios we could imagine felt like I was taking action. Who knew? Maybe one of them would actually come true and we'd be prepared.

From the corner of my eye, I saw movement on the side of the road. What was—?

"Watch out!" I shouted.

Out of nowhere, a tree fell in front of us. Clive slammed on the brakes, but it was too late. The tall aspen crashed onto the hood in an explosion of yellow leaves. The windshield shattered. Warren shrieked as he went flying from my lap. My head slammed into the dashboard.

I blinked once. Twice. The side of my face felt wet and

sore, reminding me of when Ryley had kicked me the first time we met. Damn it. The last thing I needed was another concussion. From the seat behind, I heard grunts and groans. Clive was already reaching for his brother, who'd ended up in the tree and, as far as I could tell, was still breathing. We were all alive.

I wrenched the door open and shifted before my paws hit the ground.

"Stay with them until help arrives," I said to Ogden, who'd shifted and was telling someone, hopefully Van, about the accident. Simon rushed to his brothers, muttering something about how they were running out of lives and how their mama wouldn't be happy.

I leaped into the forest by the side of the road. That tree hadn't fallen on its own, and whoever had done it was going to tell me everything I needed to know about where Robbie was going.

Chapter Thirty-Six

RYLEY

I watched in shocked disbelief as a tree slammed down on the car Hayden had been in. Then the car was lost from sight behind a wall of quaking yellow leaves and twisted branches.

"Did you do that?" I pointed at the tree and turned my narrowed gaze to Conny.

He shook his head. "Not me. They took away my flute."

"What's that got to do with anything?"

"The flute is where the magic is," Conny said slowly, like I was a child.

"No, it isn't. I can do magic without a fucking flute."

Conny's forehead squished up in confusion. "You're a hybrid—no, don't take offense at the word—I'm just saying that you don't have magic like that."

"The herd was wrong. As long as one parent is a supe, the kid will be a supe." I hadn't believed that a day earlier, but the people in Willow Lake had convinced me. I crossed my arms over my chest. "And for the record, calling someone a hybrid *is* offensive." Even if I'd called myself the same thing more times that I could count.

Conny gaped. "But that means my baby will be a supe." He shook his head. "No way. Not possible. Junior is human. Weak. Not magical. Mundane."

"They will be a faun, like their daddy."

"But that means those asshole wolves will keep them."

"Yeah. Or sell them to someone else." I grimaced.

"I... I thought... I thought they'd eventually let Gretchen and the baby go when they realized I wasn't fighting them. I told them I'd do anything for them if they let her go." Conny clamped a hand over his mouth. His face had gone white.

I doubted they would have let her go regardless. She knew too much. But I didn't say that to Conny.

Conny lunged for me and grabbed my hand, clutching at it. His eyes were wide and frantic as he squeezed hard. "We've got to get to her. We've got to save them. Oh Magic, what if I'm already too late?"

Before I could answer, tires squealed over the asphalt. The truck fishtailed, sending us rolling to the right in a tangle of limbs.

"What in the Magic happened?" I muttered as I righted myself.

Conny rubbed his head. "I think we turned around."

"Look, there is a roadblock! It's about time something went my way." I grinned. "If you want to help Gretchen and the baby, you need to trust me. Help me stop Robbie and his asshole friends. The first step is getting away from him so he can't use us as hostages anymore."

"What if they hurt her? What if Rob tells them to?"

"Robbie has other shit on his mind right now. He is thinking about how to save himself. He isn't worrying about one pregnant human."

"Is that a gamble you'd take with your mate?" Conny challenged.

"Yeah. I would," I said. I didn't have to think about it. "This is the best chance you'll get to have a better life for all of you. My mate and his friends are the only ones who can stop him."

Conny looked green, but he nodded. "I hope I'm making the right decision."

"Can we get out of here now?"

He swallowed hard, but didn't protest when I reached for the handle on the canopy.

———

HAYDEN

The strange wolf I had pinned to the ground whimpered. I tightened my teeth around his neck, letting my saliva drench his skin and my tongue flick across the spot in his throat where his pulse was pounding.

"I swear, I don't know anything. Rob didn't say where he was going." He swallowed and whimpered again. "He just said to knock the tree over."

With a mouthful of asshole, I couldn't ask him questions, so I growled, throwing all my power as alpha into the deep, menacing rumble.

The scent of tears and piss and sweat bloomed stronger. He whined. His body was slack. Everything about his body language said he surrendered, but I couldn't trust him. I couldn't trust anyone connected to Robbie. I hoped this guy wouldn't want to die, but Robbie also attracted a lot of zealots. Over the years, people had willingly sacrificed themselves to Robbie's cause time and again. Was this guy the same?

He didn't smell much like Robbie, so he must be a newer recruit. Which meant Robbie might not have indoctrinated him as thoroughly as someone who'd been with him longer, but I couldn't bank on that.

I couldn't let him go. But it also went against everything I believed in to kill a defenseless man, particularly one who was going through the motions, at least, of surrendering to me. So, what should I do with him?

My teeth dug in a little deeper. He gasped. His body went limp. I dropped his neck and sniffed at him. He'd passed out. Okay, then. That worked too.

I lifted my nose to the sky. I couldn't smell any other wolves in the area, but that didn't mean they weren't there. If Robbie had a faun, they could hide right in front of me, and I'd never know. But I doubted he was close. The truck he'd been in had sped away.

Where would he go? We'd been so sure he had more tunnels out on his pack lands, but what if he didn't?

There was only one way to find out.

I looked down at the unconscious shifter. He'd shifted into his more vulnerable human form as soon as I'd pounced on him, but I didn't trust him to stay here once he woke up. I could leave him, but the world had too many assholes wandering free as it was.

In a flurry of feathers, a raven dropped to the ground beside me.

"I found you," Mercer said. His long black wing stretched out to point toward the road. "Robbie's turned around. He hit a roadblock. He's coming back."

I looked toward the road, ready to meet my brother halfway. Then the unconscious man stirred. Son of a—

"Don't worry about him, Alpha," Mercer said. "I've got him."

"Are you sure?"

"Oak will stay with me," he said, just as a massive wolf crashed through the trees.

"Don't let him get away," I said.

Then I bolted toward the highway.

Chapter Thirty-Seven

HAYDEN

Robbie had nowhere to go. He'd taken care of this end of the road with that tree, and I had the other covered with a blockade. He was trapped, so I waited for him to come to me. In the distance, I heard an engine. It had to be Robbie. I stopped on the centerline of the road and waited. The downed tree was about a mile behind me.

My heart should be thundering so hard it bruised my ribs. Sweat should be pouring over me like a waterfall. But none of that happened. Sure, resignation warred with a deep desire for retribution. Bitter determination vied with reluctance. But in the end, my love for my mate overwhelmed any lingering sense of familial obligation I felt for my brother. An eerie calm settled over me.

How many times had I envisioned confronting Robbie? Too many to count. Now that the moment was finally here, all I felt was relief.

Predictably, as the truck neared where I was standing,

the engine revved. The pickup might look like a piece of shit that was more rust than body, but it could still do a fair bit of damage if it hit me. Luckily, I didn't plan on letting that happen.

As the truck shot toward me, I caught more and more details. The bent grille guard. The crunched bumper. The excited grin on Robbie's face as he stared at me from his spot in the passenger seat.

The driver tried to steer around me, but Robbie grabbed the steering wheel and pointed the nose of the truck at me again. The driver looked horrified—I guessed it wasn't every day someone asked you to mow down a person in the middle of the road—but he didn't fight Robbie for control.

There was nothing quite like playing chicken with a six-thousand-pound truck.

My muscles tensed as the truck got within kissing distance. I pounced. My paws slammed into the hood, caving it in with a satisfying crunch, before I landed on the top of the cab with another crunch. Windows shattered. Someone screamed. The truck lurched to the side, nearly throwing me off. I leaped to the camper shell next. This time, though, I dug my claws into the fiberglass. The rear door was up and shuddering against the wind.

"I'm coming, Ry. I've almost got you," I shouted.

I ripped and pulled at the camper shell until it cracked and buckled under my determination. The truck rocked wildly down the road. Robbie, the bastard, was trying to dislodge me, but I wasn't going anywhere without my mate. As soon as the hole was big enough, I poked my head inside.

It was empty.

Where was my mate?

I spun around, ready to break into the cab and demand answers from Robbie, except the toppled tree was right in front of us. The driver hit the brakes. I went flying.

This was going to hurt.

Then I was scooped out of the air.

"I've got you, Alpha," Ogden said. He flipped around with dizzying speed. Before I knew it, he was lowering me to the ground right beside the passenger door of the truck.

"Find Ryley," I shouted after him.

"On it, Alpha," Simon said. He sounded anxious and a little tremulous, which I expected, but I'd never heard the cat shifter speak so loudly. And the fact that he hadn't shifted into his house cat form and scurried off to hide in the trees was shocking. Finding your fated mate did strange things to people.

I shifted quickly as I marched over to Robbie's door. I wrenched it open. Robbie leaned away, so I reached in and grabbed him. He wasn't wearing a seatbelt. Did the guy think he was invincible? I yanked him out and threw him to the ground. His cohorts scampered out of the truck on the opposite side.

"Where is my mate?" I roared at him.

"What are you talking about?" He squinted at me like I wasn't making any sense, then his gaze caught on the lock of green hair at my temple. I expected him to outline conditions for my mate's release, gloat about how easy it'd been to take him from me, or demean my mating altogether. He didn't do any of those things. In fact, he shook

341

his head like I was confusing him. Did he not know what that green mark in my hair meant?

"Don't lie to me, Robbie. What did you do with my mate? Do not mess with me right now."

"Don't be so uncivilized, brother," Robbie said with a scowl as he pushed himself up. He brushed the bits of rock and dust from his jeans as he straightened. "You'd think you were the one forced to live in the woods all summer. Oh, that's right, you like living rough. Still living in that trailer, isn't that right?"

I fisted his T-shirt and swung him around. His back slammed against the truck, making it rock. Robbie rolled his eyes at me, like he used to when he was younger. For a moment, memories of us growing up together tumbled over me: watching over him during his first run with the pack, teaching him how to jump into the lake from the tire swing Dad had hung up, letting him crawl into my bed when he'd had a nightmare. But this man, he was no longer my family. He'd become my nightmare. We might share blood, but he'd severed any familial links the moment he hurt—*killed*—our parents.

"I will not ask you again," I bit out. "What have you done with my mate?"

"I. Do. Not. Know. What. You. Are. Talking. About," he shouted, pausing between each word to draw out the sentence.

I yanked him away from the truck, then slammed him against it again.

He grunted, but he still didn't seem to appreciate the position he was in. He grinned at me. "Temper, temper, brother."

"He was in your truck. Where is he now?"

He glanced at the camper shell, then back at me. His gaze popped up to my mating mark again. I wanted to shout at him to avert his eyes, that he didn't deserve to look at it. Then I saw the moment he realized what I was talking about.

"My pet? He's your mate?" He laughed, slapping his leg in obvious mirth.

"Who are you calling a pet, you shit-filled diaper?"

That question was the most beautiful thing I'd ever heard. I whipped around, letting go of Robbie.

"Ryley…" I let out his name on a shaky breath as I hauled him into my arms. "When you weren't in the back of the truck, I was so scared."

He pressed his face into my neck. "I'm okay."

The tremulous way he spoke had me pulling back to look at him. His glasses hung lopsided on his face, and one lens was shattered. Little bits of grass and twigs littered his dark hair. His clothing was dusty, but with no obvious damage. He must have spent most of his time in his faun form.

"Are you sure you're okay?"

He nodded. "Better than okay, now that you're here."

Out of the corner of my eye, I caught movement. Robbie was slipping around the back of the truck.

"Get your ass back here, Robbie."

He bolted for the trees. I raced after him. I couldn't let him get away. Not again. I called on my magic to shift. Nothing happened.

I tugged at it again. A little flutter, but nothing more.

Son of a fucking fuck.

Don't mess with me right now, Eternal Magic. Not now. Not when I finally have him.

Robbie's change rolled over him between one step and the next. Matted fur hung in clumps from his too-thin body. He was not a healthy wolf.

Good. I hoped he'd suffered.

But an unhealthy wolf was still faster than a shifter stuck in his human body. He disappeared between the trees. I followed, but he outpaced me. I tried to shift again, but still it eluded me.

"No!"

Where was the Eternal Magic? I needed to stop Robbie to protect my pack and my mate. Why wasn't I shifting? I'd done what she wanted. I had become the alpha. I had accepted my mate. What more did she want from me?

"Please," I begged. "Just, please…"

The air became unnaturally still, as if the Eternal Magic herself had hushed everything else so she could listen to me. I glanced down. My hands were still hands. No fur in sight.

"I am sorry," I said. "I need your help. I can't do this without you. Please."

I lifted my face toward the sky to scream my frustration, but what came out was a howl. A deep, earth-shaking howl. All those shimmering golden threads that I'd only seen on the night I'd accepted I was Alpha of Willow Lake glowed around me once more.

I fell to my knees. Magic zinged through the air as footsteps raced in my direction. My mate called my name as he flung his arms around me. I glanced down at my hands again, only this time, they were paws.

As people—my pack—broke through the surrounding trees, they stumbled to a halt. It looked like our reinforcements had arrived, and every single one of them was gaping at me.

"Holy Magic," Mercer muttered. "Alpha just got super-sized."

Awed murmurs of "Alpha" filled the forest. I sought my mate. His eyes were full of wonder.

"Why are you looking at me like that?"

"You're beautiful, Hayden," he said. "You always have been, but you're, uh, bigger than I remember."

"That's what he said," someone joked. It might have been Isaac.

"You think so?" I looked at my paws again. They seemed a little larger than usual.

"Oh yeah," Ryley agreed.

Ogden stepped forward. "I haven't seen one of your kind in a long time."

"Yes," Gage agreed. "The first time I saw Oak I thought he might be, but now that I've seen you…"

"Now that you've seen me what? What are you talking about?"

"You're a dire wolf, Alpha," the demon said.

"Where is my notebook?" Jeremy said, as he patted his pockets.

"That's impossible," I said, shaking my paw as if that could make it return to normal.

I looked at the others who'd gathered around me to see if they had answers. They all tilted their heads to the side, exposing their necks to me, and murmured "Alpha". For fuck's sake, not that again. I mean, I got it. This was probably an important development. But we, me in particular, had other shit to do right now. I pushed my nose against Ryley's neck to inhale his scent, making sure he was really okay. He smelled healthy and, surprisingly, a little turned on.

"You're amazing," he whispered against my fur.

I stepped back. "Stay here. Stay safe. I need to get Robbie before he escapes."

Ryley nodded. "I need you to be safe too."

I had no intention of letting anything happen to me. I had too much to live for.

"We'll be right behind you, Alpha," Van said. His gaze was full of flames as he transformed into his hellhound form. All around me, the shifters did the same.

"Let's go," I said, bounding through the woods after the man who'd chosen to be my enemy instead of my brother.

Chapter Thirty-Eight

RYLEY

As Hayden led most of the shifters through the trees in pursuit of Robbie, the two-footed supes trailed after them. As a faun, I apparently was adept at escaping, but I'd never be a hunter. That was fine. I didn't need to crush Robbie's neck between my teeth. I could just wait until he surrendered and then kick him in the balls a couple dozen times.

Because he would surrender. My badass mate would make him.

We made a strange group hiking through the forest. There were several of us, but the ones nearest to me were part of Hayden's closest group of friends. Ash had sparks shooting from his fingers, Jeremy was muttering as he scribbled in a notebook, and Jake was worrying his hands like he wished he hadn't left the inn. And then there, at my side, was Conny.

"We need to hurry," he said. We were already hoofing

it, but Conny pulled me along to get me moving faster. We were following the obvious trail of footprints, broken saplings, and crushed groundcover. "They can't kill him. Not before he tells me where Gretchen is."

"They won't kill him." I was at least sixty percent certain of that. Ish. Although Hayden wasn't the only one who looked pissed. Okay. Yeah. Maybe we should pick up our pace.

Once Conny was satisfied with my speed, he moved closer. "Was that your mate?" He shook his head. "I guess he couldn't be. Never mind."

"What are you talking about? Of course he's my mate." I frowned at him.

"But he's not a faun."

"I thought you said you met your mate. You should know our mates don't have to be fauns."

"Right." He nodded. "I know, it's just he's a wolf. Like a massively enormous wolf. I thought he was the one Rob had me play tricks on in the woods, but that guy wasn't nearly that big."

Yeah. I didn't know what'd happened there either, but it didn't change how I felt about him. "Him being big means he's the best one to put an end to all this."

Jeremy came alongside us. He glanced up from his notebook and eyed my brother.

"Can I help you?" Conny said. He sounded as snooty as The Ass Pimple.

Jeremy didn't take offense at my brother's tone. "Are you working for the forces of good or evil?"

Conny grimaced, and his face paled.

"You see, Adrian told me a faun helped Robbie abduct Ryley earlier. That was you, wasn't it?"

My first impulse was to step in and defend Conny. He was still so young as a faun; he shouldn't even be away from the herd. But the fauns might have that wrong too, because he was old enough to get a woman pregnant. So he clearly wasn't a kid any longer; he was going to be a dad. My baby brother, a father.

Conny looked at me for guidance. I nodded. Hayden trusted these people, so I did too. And wasn't that bizarre? Me, trusting a bunch of supes.

"He's holding my mate hostage," Conny said.

"Seriously?" A fierce look contorted Jeremy's face. "It looks like we're going on another rescue mission, boys!"

"Another one?" Ash grumbled. "We just finished one. That's already two this week."

"What's your name?" Jeremy asked Conny.

Jeremy then asked about his mate's name. After that, he started muttering. "Hmm... Conny and Gretchen, Conny and Gretchen. Operation: Rescue Gretchen. That's kind of boring. What other information do you have? What can you tell me about her?"

Conny was eyeing Jeremy warily, but he still answered. "She's pregnant?"

"You're having a baby?" Jeremy smiled and clapped Conny on the back. "That's awesome! We need more babies around here."

"Oh, I don't..." Conny stammered. "I'm not from here."

Jeremy talked right over my brother's protest. "With magical werewolf jizz off the table, all you straight supes need to pull your weight. Although, there are lots of ways to get around the same sex thing. Adrian and I have been talking about surrogacy, but we aren't there yet. And it isn't like we need to rush since we literally have forever to do this. And who knows, a hundred or two hundred years from now, when we are ready, mpreg might be possible."

Jeremy continued to ramble about Magic knew what, as Conny shot a look my way. I knew how he felt. I didn't know what the guy was talking about, either. What was important, though, was how Jeremy was treating Conny, like he'd already accepted him as someone who belonged in Willow Lake, someone they would fight for.

I doubted Conny understood that. I wouldn't have in his position.

"You're my brother, Conny. Of course you and your family will be welcome in my mate's pack."

"After everything I did?"

"Did you hurt anyone? Kill anyone? Maim them? Traffic them to some other asshole?"

"Well, no, but…"

"There is no but, Conny. This is all on Robbie," I said. "He coerced you into doing things. And if anyone says any differently, they'll get to meet my hooves, up close and personal."

Conny wiped tears from his face as he averted his eyes.

Shouts ahead of us spurred us to move faster, because those shouts could only mean one thing. They'd found Robbie.

We stepped into a strange clearing in the woods. It didn't look or feel natural. In fact, the area reminded me a lot of the place where Hayden and I had found that other tunnel opening. I pushed up my glasses and wished I could see better through the shattered lens, but I could still see we'd arrived at another hatch on the forest floor.

But Robbie hadn't had time to jump down it like a rabbit diving into its den. Instead, Hayden and Robbie, both still in their shifted forms, were circling one another, while all the other shifters formed a ring around them. Hayden had a gash in his side that was dripping blood and Robbie was limping. They snarled, baring their sharp, lethal teeth at each other.

It was like one of those old documentaries about wild animals that families used to watch every week on prime-time television. You know the ones. Animals were always getting killed and eaten by other animals. As a faun, I was not a predatory supe, so that show was fuel for nightmares that woke me in the middle of the night for weeks after. I couldn't understand how humans enjoyed watching that with their children.

Seeing my mate in one of those fight-to-the-death situations, I wondered if I'd ever sleep again.

I wanted him to win, of course. But how would he cope if he killed his brother?

"Surrender. I don't want to hurt you," Hayden said.

"Like you tried last night? Screw you."

"If someone tried to hurt you last night, it must have been one of your own people."

"I felt it," Robbie screamed. "When you tried to take more of my power from me last night."

"I can't take power from you or anyone," Hayden growled. "If you were a true alpha, you'd know that."

"Is that what you think? That you are a true alpha? All

you do is hide in your little dumpy trailer behind your dumpy business." Robbie sneered. "And you can't lie to me. I felt it. You sent your magic after me. You thought you could trick me and make me submit to you. Well, who is the smart one now? You can't fool me like that."

Hayden stumbled. "No, I never."

That must have been when Hayden accepted his role as alpha. Some part of Hayden had still considered his brother part of his pack. My mate had too soft a heart. Of course, I would do the same for my brother, but that was easier to justify. Mine wasn't a murderous nostril dildo. But now what? I couldn't let him kill Robbie now. How was I going to stop this?

Robbie lunged for Hayden. Hayden met him halfway. They collided in a blur of teeth and claws and fur. The smell of blood infected the air. Hayden was incredibly large now, but that didn't mean he wasn't vulnerable, particularly since he was holding back. Robbie could kill him. More blood splattered across the ground. Hayden roared in pain.

Why hadn't teleportation been invented yet so I could zap Hayden out of there?

"He'll win," Ash said, rubbing my back.

Jeremy nodded. "I think if he was truly in danger, my magic would try to shield him in my personal brand of magical bubble wrap."

I'd have believed him more if his words hadn't sounded so tremulous. And based on how wonky his magic had been in the mage competition earlier, I wasn't ready to trust his magic to do what he wanted either.

Hayden swiped at his brother, slicing along Robbie's

belly, but Robbie rolled away before the thick, razor-sharp claws went too deep. Robbie whimpered and shook his head.

"Surrender," Hayden growled. "We don't have to do this."

Robbie's frantic gaze bounced around the people surrounding him, as if noticing them for the first time. All of us were there for Hayden. Every single one of us.

"When I win," Robbie choked out between panting breaths, "you'll all answer to me. You'll be mine to do with what I want."

"It doesn't work that way," Hayden said. "The SC will never allow you to have a pack again."

"Fuck the SC." His words were full of bravado, but his quick gasps took on a panicked rhythm.

Hayden and Robbie circled one another. Why didn't Gage or Van or *anyone* jump in and grab Robbie now? Fuck it. I couldn't take it anymore. I had to act. I shifted into my faun form and waited for an opportunity.

My plan wasn't a plan at all. I just wanted to distract Robbie long enough that others could pin him down. If it involved kicking the jerk beetle in the nuts, well, that shouldn't be a surprise to anyone. When Robbie turned so his tail was right in front of me, I stepped forward. Jeremy and Ash tugged me back.

"Let me go," I shouted at them.

At the commotion, Hayden took his eyes off Robbie to look at me. Robbie seized the opportunity and lunged. I screamed. Everything was a blur of motion and limbs and fur.

When things settled, Robbie was sprawled across the

dirt. He was limp. His eyes were closed. His chest barely moved.

Hayden stood over him with his teeth clamped on his brother's neck. Then he whimpered, like he just realized what'd happened. He tore his bloody mouth away. His shift rolled over him faster than my eyes could track. One moment he was a massive badass wolf and the next he was human.

He dropped to his knees beside his brother and pulled him into his arms.

"Robbie," he sobbed and pressed his face into the bloody fur at his brother's injured throat. "Why didn't you surrender?"

I rushed forward and wrapped my arms around Hayden. I didn't know what to say, so I simply held him.

"Is Xander here? Teague? Someone, help!" Hayden shouted at his pack.

Then my brother was there with us. "Where is Gretchen? Wake him up. Please. He has to tell me where Gretchen is. Don't let him die. He can't die." Conny leaned over and put his face right up to Robbie's. "Where is Gretchen?"

Robbie's eyelashes fluttered, almost like he was opening them just enough to see through his lashes. Was I imagining that? Then his mouth twitched. Almost like he was fighting off a smile. That sweaty piece of toe lint was up to something.

"Don't get too close, Conny, he's—"

Robbie whipped his head around before I could finish. I yanked Hayden back, but not fast enough. Robbie's teeth grazed Hayden's jaw.

"No!" I shouted.

Before Robbie could try again, my chest exploded with fiery heat, almost like I was shifting, but it was so much more. Green burst through the yellowy leaves around us as shrubs and trees shot to life, knocking us to our asses. In a flurry of rustling leaves, a bunch of twigs, branches, and roots descended upon Robbie. When the whirl of activity slowed, Robbie was gone. Had the forest consumed him? Had I killed Hayden's brother? I scrambled forward and pushed at the leaves. There, encased in a cage of twigs and roots, was Robbie. He was unconscious, but alive.

Only then did the heat inside me ebb away. I fell back on my ass. What had I done?

"How did that happen?" Conny gaped at me for a moment, then he crawled toward Robbie. "Is he alive? He can't die. Please say he's alive."

Van stepped forward. From one step to the next, he shed his fiery hellhound form to take on his human one. "He's still alive. I can hear him breathing. We might need a hacksaw to get him out, though." He glanced at me. "Unless you can back this up a little?"

"That wasn't... I didn't..." I stared at the tangled cage. "Fauns can't..."

"You saved me." Hayden tugged me into his arms. "I didn't think he'd try to kill me."

"How did that happen?" I swallowed hard, unable to pull my gaze from the leafy cage. "I didn't mean to do that. I don't know what happened."

"You saved me," Hayden repeated.

Huh. Maybe I had. It was like my magic, which until recently had done little more than allow me to shift, was on steroids. Was this because I'd met my fated mate? Was it because Hayden had been super-sized by the Eternal Magic, so she'd super-sized me too? Fuck if I knew. But the important thing was Hayden was here. He was alive. And Robbie had been caught.

"I love you, Hayden." I hugged him as tight as I could.

The leafy mound by our feet shook. Robbie was awake.

"They cheated." The flora muffled Robbie's words, but they were still loud enough that everyone could hear he was still very much alive. Leaves jiggled as he squirmed within his living prison. "I demand Hayden surrender to me. His life is forfeit now. I am alpha."

"Real life doesn't work that way," Van muttered. He pulled the leaves away to expose Robbie's face. "There you are. Robert Walker, you are under arrest for crimes against supernatural beings."

Chapter Thirty-Nine

HAYDEN

The party that night wasn't planned, at least not by me. But somehow Ryley and I ended up at the Willow Lake Inn, along with almost everyone else in Willow Lake. I'd wanted to be at the police station with Van and Dillon while they interviewed Robbie and his men, but they'd turned me away at the Supernatural Council's request. Van promised I could talk to them tomorrow under the SC's supervision. I supposed their precautions made sense given the number of criminals killed during transport to SC prisoner facilities this summer, but still it didn't make a lot of sense if you thought about it. If I had wanted Robbie and his people dead, they wouldn't be breathing right now.

But at least they were in custody. Now. Finally.

The SC had also decided only they could gather evidence from the tunnels, which sounded like they just wanted to come in and throw their weight around to get credit for something they had nothing to do with. But whatever. Van didn't seem bothered. Gage was chill about it too. So, I let it go.

Really, it was just a relief to have it all over.

At least the SC had agreed to act swiftly to carry out justice after they'd gone through Robbie's secret lairs. Although no trial date had been announced, I already knew I'd attend. I wanted to see him get what he deserved, but that wasn't the only reason. There was still some tiny part of me that thought of him as my brother, my family. It was fucked up.

So, instead of dwelling on the past and things I couldn't change, I'd spent the day thinking about healing and hope for the future by spending time with some of Robbie's victims. Their relief at Robbie's capture was overwhelming, and I hated that it'd taken so long to give them their sense of security back.

Brodie and Dakota were still working through their trauma, as were Conny and Gretchen, but they were getting there. I made sure they knew they were all welcome to stay in Willow Lake as long as they wanted, forever even, and I hoped they felt a little safer now. The Jahaller was still struggling to move, but Doc assured me he was improving. Mercer and Oak were all smiles—especially Mercer, who was giving away bottles of glitter to everyone who walked in the door to their shop so they could spread the joy throughout town. I wasn't sure I equated glitter to happiness, but I could see why it'd appeal to a raven shifter. Jake was excited to discuss the renovations to the inn, and Gage just looked happy that his mate was happy. I'd found Ash and Dillon at the Flying Rowan Café on Dillon's lunch break from the police station. Ash was experimenting with a new pizza topping combination that would have set my tongue on fire but seemed to appeal to both of them. And I'd even stopped by the land Ogden and Simon had purchased to chat with them about their plans. They hadn't been as directly injured by Robbie as some of the others, but I couldn't help but wonder if Ogden would have been safe if Robbie's activities hadn't attracted kidnapping assholes to the area.

The list of those who had been hurt could have been so much shorter if I'd acted sooner. That was something I'd have to live with for the rest of my life. In the meantime, I would work to try to make it up to my pack every day.

But strangely, it also wasn't all bad. If Robbie's men hadn't stolen that whistle from the inn, Simon and Ogden might never have met. That was the same for Jeremy and Adrian. And Robbie's action was the catalyst that brought Ryley into my life too. I could never regret that. Not even a little bit. Ryley was the center of my world. I just wished he hadn't needed to endure being abducted and held prisoner for us to find one another.

"Robbie's still not talking," Van said, dropping into a chair across the table from me. He hadn't even taken the time to order a drink yet. It almost felt like he was reporting to me. And now that I was officially *the* alpha, I supposed I warranted getting my own personal update.

"Not surprising," I said.

"The SC is doing some good work," Van continued, "despite Robbie's refusal to cooperate. They tracked down the hotel where Ryley and Conny's abductions took place and found the guy who helped Robbie. He was the front desk clerk, who supplemented his income with a side hustle in supernatural trafficking. Their vehicles were his finder's fees. Unfortunately, the vehicles are gone. They were sold to someone overseas, so we can't recover them. The guy had a ledger book going back about five years, though, so that's useful. The records suggest three vampires were taken around the same time as Ryley."

"I wonder if that's who Robbie was alluding to when he talked about his pets. You don't think there are more tunnels out there that we haven't found yet, do you?" I frowned.

"The SC is bringing in an earth mage to test the entire property. If there is another tunnel, they'll find it. We've requested Birch Avery, but it might be someone else who comes."

"I wish I could say Robbie might talk to me, but I doubt he will," I said.

I honestly didn't understand how Robbie had convinced so many people to sign up to be his minions. Even all those years ago when the pack had split apart, it'd never made sense to me. Was it just luck that he'd gotten this far and found so many people to join him? I wasn't sure that it was, and that scared me, because I'd never considered him much of a strategist, and yet he'd done a lot of damage for a long time without getting caught. But maybe feeding people's anger and prejudice overcame whatever shortcomings he had as a leader and attracted the people who could make his visions a reality. Even with some of his people talking to the authorities now, I doubted we'd ever really know the full story.

But at least he couldn't hurt anyone else now.

"The others are spilling their guts," Van said. "So that's helping."

That was true. Without a faun's magic to keep them hidden, they'd been easy to round up in the woods. From the moment they found out about Robbie's arrest, they'd started talking and hadn't shut up about everything they knew, even before seeing Van and Dillon in their fiery hellhound forms.

One of Robbie's cohorts had returned Conny's flute and then he'd taken us around to all the tunnels. I swear I must have walked over some of those entrances a hundred times, but Conny's magic had kept them hidden from me.

That's when we found Gretchen. We found a few other supes down there too, but none of them had stuck around after being interviewed. I couldn't blame them for wanting to put as much distance as possible between themselves and Willow Lake. And if they found it so easy to leave, they weren't meant to stay.

That was one thing that had become increasingly clear in the short time I'd been alpha. Willow Lake chose us as much as we chose her. And everyone in this room right now, including Conny and Gretchen, had been invited to stay by Willow Lake herself.

"Has anyone said anything else? Anything new?"

Van grimaced.

"What?"

"Someone from the old pack was still with Robbie," Van said slowly.

I nodded slowly. The way Van was drawing this out was making my skin itch like it was too tight.

"He was there when your parents died. He confirmed Robbie orchestrated your parents' deaths."

I sucked in a breath. I don't know why I was shocked. I'd known... I'd fucking known. But having confirmation...

"Apparently, Robbie thought that if he was with your dad when he died that your dad's alpha power would pass to him."

My eyes stung. We sat in silence for a moment. Ryley's hand slipped into mine. He squeezed. The rest of the pub bustled with activity around us. Being surrounded by my pack soothed me in a way I'd never thought possible. I let their energy, acceptance, and love fill me until I could breathe normally again.

Jeremy brought a tray filled with drinks and lowered it to the table, pushing Paws aside until he had to jump out of the way.

"Watch what you're doing with that thing," Paws grumbled.

"Grab your drinks, people, I gotta get back up there," Jeremy said. Everyone swiped a drink.

Jake had Alice and Jeremy working with him behind the bar filling drink orders, while Dakota and Brodie were both bustling around in the kitchen prepping food. Most nights, Dakota sat on a stool and watched Brodie, but he was scurrying around just as fast as Brodie was tonight. Like last night, the doors to the parking lot had been propped open and people were sitting all over the place inside and out.

"Adrian, love, put 'Another One Bites the Dust' on the jukebox for me," Jeremy shouted over his shoulder as he returned to the bar. "Oh, and follow it up with Pink. It's time to get this party started."

I swear he said the same thing after the last time we survived facing off with the pack in the hills to the west.

As soon as the first song blasted over the speakers, Jeremy belted out the lyrics alongside Freddie Mercury while strutting behind the bar. Then others yelled requests at Adrian too, everything from Britney Spears to Taylor Swift to Lady Gaga.

"Is everyone in Willow Lake gay?" Conny asked.

He had a very pregnant Gretchen tucked under one arm, while his other hand rested on her stomach. Some of Jake's painting ladies had arrived earlier with armfuls of clothing and other supplies. They'd fussed over her, giving her a manicure and a haircut and who knew what else. Despite her trials over the last several months, Gretchen looked radiant and relaxed in a clean, flowery dress that flowed over her baby bump. I knew those smiles hid trauma, though, so Ash had already hooked her up with the same therapist that Brodie and Dakota went to.

She'd also been to see Doc Roberts. Unsurprisingly, the doctor encouraged her to rest. I swear he said the same thing to everyone. But she'd refused, saying she was tired of being alone and that it made her feel safe to be with other people. Conny was fussing over her like, well, an expectant father who'd almost lost his mate and their baby.

At Conny's question, everyone at the table laughed except Ryley.

I felt him move, his foot swinging past mine to kick Conny under the table.

"Hey, don't be a bigoted asshole," Ryley said.

Conny shook his head. His gaze darted over the group as if he thought they'd attack him. "No, I didn't mean it like that."

"There are a lot of us," Ash agreed with a grin. "That's one of the many awesome things about this place. No one cares who you love, or what kind of supe you are, or how strong your magic is."

"It's a bit like the Federation," Ryley mused with a nod.

"Yes," Gretchen said, pointing at Ryley. "That's exactly it."

They grinned at one another. They had more in common than I'd expected, and I was glad that Ryley was getting on well with her. It'd go a long way to repairing the awkward relationship he had with his brother.

"What Federation?" Conny asked. "I thought Willow Lake was part of the Supernatural Council, like the herd was."

Everyone else shrugged and looked at my mate.

"You know, the United Federation of Planets?" Ryley explained. "Has no one else seen *Star Trek*?"

It sounded familiar, but I wasn't sure. "Is that a show?"

"Is that a show?" Ryley repeated my question in mock horror, turning his attention from his brother to me. "Neither of you have seen *Star Trek*? I can understand Conny not knowing about it, the herd only allowed weird old movies, musicals, and shows that reinforced the idea of obedience and traditional roles, but you, Hayden, what's your excuse?"

I shrugged. TV shows had never interested me. There were always too many other things to do. Shows with fake laughter and stilted dialogue never held my attention for long, not when I could rebuild an engine or repair a transmission.

"What about *Star Wars*? *Stargate SG-1*? *Battlestar Galactica*? *Lost in Space*?" Ryley's eyebrows crept up on his forehead when my face stayed blank. "We need a movie night."

"Don't say that too loudly," Ash said, looking over his shoulder at Jeremy, who was eyeing us curiously from the bar as he filled a pint glass. "We've had so many movie nights lately, I need a break."

"Why? What do you mean?"

"Jeremy decided all the supes need a pop culture education, especially Jake," Ash whispered. "I love movies as much as the next person, but…"

He cut off his words when Jeremy appeared beside us and set a full pint glass in front of Van. "What are you talking about? Did I hear someone mention *Star Trek*?"

Ryley raised his hand. "That'd be me. I can't believe no one knew what I was talking about."

"No," Ash groaned.

"What?" Jeremy gaped. He shook his head and put his hand on his chest. "I'm sorry. I dropped the ball. I haven't introduced them to any of the space greats yet."

Ryley grinned. "We should plan—"

"A movie night!" Jeremy and Ryley finished in unison.

This time, everyone at the table groaned, but I could tell no one was too upset by the idea. As the conversation progressed to setting up days and times, I turned my attention to Van and Gage.

"Did any of Robbie's people know where to find the unicorn?" I asked.

Van frowned and shook his head. "Nothing yet. They weren't lying when they said they'd never heard of one."

"We'll find him," Gage said.

"Because Jake had a vision about it?" I asked.

Gage nodded. "Yeah, that's part of it, but Nelson is also one of my best. He'll find Morgan."

"I hope this is the end of this shit," I said.

"Don't we all," Van muttered, lifting his glass. Then his gaze caught on something at the door. I glanced over to see Parker slip inside. His gaze darted over everyone, then he quickly made his way to the pool table where he normally hung out.

Willow Lake Pub was primarily a hangout place for supes, but some humans were regulars here, too. Parker was one of them. It was surprising he hadn't seen under the Eternal Magic's glamour yet, given how long he'd lived here and how long he'd been crushing on our local minotaur. Levi, who'd been lining up to take his shot, spun around with his pool cue in his hand, like he could sense the other man was near. Yeah. I didn't think Parker's crush was all that one-sided. He greeted the human before turning his attention back to his game.

Parker's gaze caught on mine, and he nodded. Then he placed money on the corner of the table, a sign that he would take on the winner of the current game. I swore his hand shook, just a little, but then he leaned against the wall and started teasing Levi. Just like normal. Huh. He must not have seen anything magical at Jeremy's mini Olympics, or he probably wouldn't be that calm.

"Hey, what's up?" Ryley said.

"Nothing. Just surprised to see Parker out tonight. With this many supes in one place, most humans stay away."

"Yeah, I could see that," Ryley said. "So, what are we doing tonight? Going back to your place?"

I cringed. I didn't want to take Ryley back to my trailer again. He deserved so much better than that. "I talked to Jake. He said we could stay here for a while. I thought you'd want to stay close to Conny and Gretchen."

Ryley slipped his hand in mine. "Do we have to? I kind of want to get back to the trailer. It isn't like we can't come back tomorrow to see them."

"You'd want to stay there?"

"Of course," he nodded. "It's yours."

"I do like the idea of having you in my den," I whispered in his ear.

"It's settled then. Besides, I thought a little privacy might be nice. Jeremy keeps talking about biting and knots." He grinned. "And now I'm curious."

My blood heated at his words. "We could definitely do that."

"Let's go, Alpha mine."

"Anything for my mate."

Chapter Forty

HAYDEN

I'd walked through the yard behind my garage thousands, if not millions, of times, but tonight everything felt new. The familiar scents of grease, oil, and tires signaled I was home, but with Ryley at my side this time, I realized that home had different meanings. I supposed I'd known that all along, but it was just so damn obvious now.

Before, home was the place I slept. The place where I hid from the world. The place where I tried to heal. But now, home was so much more. Home was the place where I would spend time alone with Ryley. Where I would show my mate how much I cherished him. Where I would love and protect him. I wanted to laugh with him there, fight with him and make up, and build memories to last a thousand lifetimes. I couldn't wait to get started.

The hinges creaked as I opened the trailer door. I reached in and turned on a light, then motioned him inside. He grinned at me as he hopped up the metal steps.

"It feels like forever since we stayed here our first night together," he said as I stepped in behind him and closed the door. I dropped our bags on the built-in sofa.

He was right. We'd only spent one night at the Willow Lake Inn, but it felt like an eternity since we'd been here. As I watched him move through the tight space, something settled inside me. The blankets on the bed might still be mussed from when we'd slept there and the dining table was still made up into a bed, but it all felt like perfection.

He spun toward me and stalked across the scant distance that separated us. He poked a finger into my chest. "You better not try to sneak out again tonight."

"There is no other place I'd rather be," I said, earning a smile from him.

"Me either," he whispered as he leaned forward and brushed his mouth across mine.

I chased his lips, eager for more. I pushed my fingers into his hair and pressed my lips to his. This wasn't our first time, but it still felt like it was. Maybe it would always feel this way with Ryley because I couldn't imagine a moment when I wouldn't stop to acknowledge how blessed I was to have him in my life.

We grinned at one another when we broke our kiss to tug our shirts over our heads.

"Hi, mate of mine," I whispered.

"Hello, mate." He grinned back at me as he backed up toward the bed. He shed his clothes along the way. By the time he got to the mattress, he was naked and flushed. "Hurry. Before I get cold."

"Are you cold now? I can adjust the heater." I didn't

normally feel the cold until snow hit the ground, but if my mate—

"Hayden," Ryley said sharply. "Get your ass over here. I'm waiting for you to fuck me, bite me, knot me, and give me orgasms."

I wasn't about to say no to that. I tore my clothes off and fell into bed beside him.

"About time," he said as he pulled me into a kiss.

The kiss we'd shared at the door had been sweet and full of anticipation, but this one was passion unleashed. Heat rocketed through me as his bare skin pressed against mine. Our hands explored. Our tongues danced. My achingly hard cock rubbed against his.

"Are you sure?" I asked between kisses.

"Am I sure that I want you to top? Fuck yes. Unless you don't want to."

I pressed my forehead to his. "I do. But I won't last long. You feel like perfection. I want you so damn bad, I could come now. Already."

"I would say you're good for my ego," he said with a soft laugh, "but I'm right there with you. I'm so turned on right now."

I raised my head to look at him. His glasses were fogged up. His cheeks were flushed. His lips were swollen and wet. He was the sexiest damn thing I'd ever seen.

"I love you," I whispered as I reached between us and rubbed my hand through the slippery pre-cum coating the crowns of our cocks. Ryley shuddered and arched into my touch.

"I'm going to come if you keep—*Ah…*"

I wrapped my hand around both of our cocks and jerked.

"Hayden…"

Ryley's eyes fluttered shut as he lost himself in pleasure. His scent grew headier and more intoxicating, and I breathed in to take as much of it into me as possible. Our hard lengths slipped and rubbed against one another as I tugged faster. Ryley squirmed and bucked beneath me, chasing his own pleasure. Our combined magic sparked to life around us, making the air sing and dance with our love for one another. As his body tightened in his release, I slammed my mouth against his as I followed.

Normally, after coming, I'd feel spent and relaxed, but I wasn't done. Not yet. I didn't bother wiping away the cum that was cooling on our skin. I wanted it there. I wanted my scent marking him. I wanted this physical proof between us of how hot we were for one another. And I wanted to add to it. I wanted to cover him in my cum and fill him up. And have him cover me and fill me up, too. Until our scent was so intertwined, there was no him or me, there was only us.

"I love you, Ryley," I whispered again. I didn't think I'd ever tire of saying that.

"I love you too, Hayden." He smiled. Under his fogged-up glasses, his eyelashes fluttered.

He had a bit of a sexy nerd look going on when he wore his glasses. I hadn't known that was my type until I met him. Or maybe my type was Ryley. Just Ryley. Either way, seeing him sweaty and sated with his glasses askew was hot as fuck. Except this time, I wanted to see his eyes. I'd have to find out if there was a way to keep his glasses from fogging up during sex. I hoped so. But for now, I gently tugged his glasses from his face and set them aside.

"You still want this?" I asked. "Or do you want to sleep now? It's been a long day."

"Abso-fucking-lutely I want this." He grabbed the lube from beside the bed and pressed it into my hand. "Lube me up, Wolfy."

"Wolfy?" I raised my eyebrow.

"You know, like 'Beam me up, Scotty,' only not."

I had no idea what he was talking about.

He took the lube out of my hand, because apparently, I wasn't moving quickly enough. He opened it and squirted a generous portion onto my hand. Then he grabbed his knees and pulled them to his chest. "Get me ready."

Seeing him presented to me like that made my heart pound. My pulse raced faster as my fingers slid over his opening. When he moaned and shuddered under my touch, my cock hardened. It was already rallying again for what was coming next.

I still took my time, though, sliding my fingers inside him. Opening him. Getting him ready for me. I needed to make him feel good. I needed this to be amazing and beautiful and...

"Fucking fuck me already."

I laughed. I couldn't help it. "Such a damn romantic."

"Honey Bunches of Oats," he said in a sugary sweet tone, as he batted his eyelashes at me. "I think I'm ready for you to take your beautiful fat cock and lovingly pound me into this bouncy mattress."

I snorted, but I got the not-so-subtle message. When I

was between his legs, I locked eyes with him. My dick nudged against his prepped hole. Then I pressed inside.

"Yessss," Ryley hissed, lifting his hips to mine to take more of me.

I grabbed his hips with a bruising grip to slow him down. I refused to hurt him by going too fast.

"I can take you," he said. "I'm your mate. I'm built for you."

"Mine," I growled. My teeth were already elongating, getting ready to bite him.

Suddenly, I wished humans were right about mating bites. Someone had told me once that, according to human fiction, wolf shifters had to bite their mates to join their lives together. The bite mark would stay, a visible sign of their joined lives.

Was it greedy to wish I could mark him like that? Sure, we had matching locks of hair to show we were mates, but that wasn't something I had done. It was a gift from the Eternal Magic, not me. I wanted him to wear something to mark our union that came from me. Just me. Not a mark from the Eternal Magic and not a ring forged by someone else, like humans did.

But biting during sex wasn't about mating. It was about energy and feeling good and trust. The marks would fade by morning. But, for now, that would be enough. If Ryley was agreeable, though, I wanted to find another way to mark our union. Something that was unique to us.

I'd think about that later.

Much, much later.

Because, right now, our bodies were chasing pleasure. Our magic shimmered around us. Unlike when we had sex the first time, there was no separate color for him and me. Right from the start, it was our joined magic. A yellowy green that reminded me of pack runs through ancient pine trees. It was home.

Ryley was my home.

"Bite me, now," Ryley demanded.

He threw his head back, exposing the beautiful column of his neck. My teeth sank into his tender skin and the world exploded in a flurry of pleasure and beauty as I released deep inside him.

His body tightened around me as he came too. I pulled back, but there was a tugging sensation that stopped me. In my post-orgasmic daze, it took longer than it should have for me to realize that must be my knot.

"Oh." He shivered as his body tightened around me. "That's…"

He sounded drunk.

"Ry? I think I knotted you."

"Yes." He shivered again, like he was experiencing little climactic after-shocks. "That's… Feels so good."

I grinned. Ryley was rarely at a loss for words. I was rather proud of myself for fucking him senseless. Wrapping my arms around him, I rolled us, so I was on my back with him draped over me. I lapped at the bite mark until he was groaning and tilting his head to the side to give me more access. I didn't know how long it'd take for my knot to go down, but I was going to relish every second.

Chapter Forty-One

HAYDEN

I stepped out of the shop and closed the door. The sun would be setting soon. It always set early this time of year. Soon, it would be dark at closing time, but not yet.

My chest warmed as I lifted my face toward the sky and inhaled. Magic stirred in my blood, letting me know the Eternal Magic was right here with me, along for the ride. She'd done that a lot lately. I still wasn't sure what to think about it, but I didn't fight her as much as I used to.

I let a partial shift roll over me and the magic inside me grew more heated, sending a tingling sensation out from my chest, filling my torso, down my limbs, until it made my toes and fingers curl. I had a good feeling about tonight.

When I was sure no curious mundane eyes were watching, I crossed to the gate in the perimeter fence and slipped through. As soon as the gate clicked closed behind me, I shifted to my wolf form and shook out my fur. Every time I shifted, this new body felt more and more familiar. I stretched to loosen my muscles before trotting down the lane that'd take me to the outskirts of town.

In the few days since I'd been out here, the last of the leaves had fallen from the deciduous trees. Now that they'd fallen from their branches, the once brilliant yellow aspen leaves and larch needles were browner and duller. The dormant grasses and forbs in their various shades of beige weren't as crisp and rigid under my paws as they had been a month earlier, beaten down by paws and frost and late autumn rain.

Hidden from view now, safe within the embrace of the woods, I lifted my face to the sky again. This time, though, after I inhaled deeply, I sent a deep, inviting howl into the air.

Come, it said. *Come run with me.*

Then I listened. The few wild animals who weren't already safely tucked into the nests or dens for the winter scurried away, but they weren't who I was waiting for.

A howl in the distance rippled through the air. There. The first of my pack responded. Then another. And another. Footsteps raced toward me.

Anticipation built until the first eager bodies broke through the trees in a flurry of fur and feathers.

"Oak, Mercer." I nodded toward them. "Thank you for joining me."

"It's been a long time since the pack went on a run together," Oak said. "I'm looking forward to it, Alpha."

I didn't have the chance to respond before more people joined us. Until this moment, I hadn't realized how much

I'd worried no one would show. It'd been, as Oak said, a long time. People weren't used to it anymore.

I hoped to change that, and tonight was the first step. It was time to embrace some of our old traditions again.

The woods were filling fast with every kind of supernatural, and the more I saw, the more my magic sang. I could feel not only my own joy, but the Eternal Magic's joy too. This coming together, despite our different supernatural abilities and backgrounds, was the true magic of Willow Lake. This was the beauty of finding people who became family.

Ryley appeared with his brother, the mages, and the other human pack members. They were among the last to arrive. He'd been meeting with a few local supe business owners, talking about how he could help them create websites on Supenet and increase their business. By the look on his face, I knew it'd gone well, but I suspected the way his face was rosy with excitement had more to do with tonight's run. He cast a quick glance around at those gathered and flashed me a thumbs-up.

Everyone turned expectant eyes toward me.

"Thank you." I projected my voice, so it carried across the group. "Thank you for coming out tonight on our first pack run. When I was a pup, my parents taught me that packs are about spending time together and looking after one another. They are about family, but also friends who become family. About being a part of something that when we're all together becomes more than what we could ever achieve alone. Even when I was in denial about being your alpha, I always believed that. I also believe that Willow Lake is special, blessed by the Eternal Magic herself.

Supes aren't meant to isolate from other supes. Our magic is stronger together. I am sorry it took me so long to accept I was your alpha, but I am here now. And I love and appreciate each of you—"

From the back, Isaac's voice shot out. "Does Ryley know about that?"

I ignored him and the few snickers that followed.

"You are my pack. My family. You always have been. Even when I was too much of an asshole to see it."

"Awwww," Jeremy said from Ryley's side, then he tapped on his phone quickly before lifting it up as "We Are Family" started playing. Ogden and Jeremy did their best to get everyone to join in and sing it with Sister Sledge.

"Okay, everyone," I said when they finished. "Let's—"

"Wait," Van said as he stepped forward. He shifted from his hellhound form, and I shifted to meet him.

"Is something wrong?"

Van shook his head. "Come here, Alpha." He wrapped me in a bear hug, surprising the shit out of me. Van wasn't usually one for emotional displays. "I'm proud of you, you asshole," he said. "I was there in the beginning, so I know it wasn't an easy road to get here, but I always believed in you. I always knew you'd be my alpha one day."

I hugged him back. He was right. He had been there, right at my side, every step of the way, from that first night when he'd been the one to let me know my parents had died until now.

"I could never figure out why you were so insistent I was the alpha."

"Because I knew the truth, even when you were too

stubborn to see it," he said. "No one else but you could have been our alpha. You are the heart of Willow Lake."

Asshole. He was trying to make me cry. I patted him on the back to break our hug.

Then Ryley rushed to my side, like he knew I needed him. He smiled up at me. The way he tilted his head exposed his neck and the bite mark I'd left on him that had never faded. No one, including Doc Roberts, understood how that was possible. In the end, he'd said, "It must be magic." And I supposed that was true. Either way, I loved seeing it on him and now he was determined I should wear his mark too, so he was designing a tattoo for me. I couldn't wait to see his creation permanently inked across my skin.

"Hear, hear," people shouted around us.

"Let's run!" I shouted.

My shift was faster than it'd ever been. Jeremy had asked if he could take a recording of it, so he could watch it in slow motion and time it, but I didn't see the point, not even "for research purposes", which was the usual line he threw around to get supes to agree to his schemes.

"Are you climbing on?" I asked Ryley when I realized he hadn't shifted yet.

"Absolutely," he said as he threw his leg over my back and climbed on.

With my larger Dire Wolf form, I was tall enough that his feet dangled well above the ground. He'd recently said it was almost like riding Isaac, which had led to me growling, and him laughing. In the end, I'd reminded him, very thoroughly, that I was his mate, and showed him I was infinitely superior to any centaur.

"Hang on," I said.

He leaned forward and wrapped his arms around my neck. "I'll go anywhere with you. Always."

THE END

Want to see what happens when Ryley moves to Willow Lake? (Spoiler: they end up at the hospital and Hayden sees things he never thought he would...) Sign up for my newsletter and download the bonus scene: www.loriames.com/newsletter

———

Interested in finally finding out what is going on between Levi and Parker? Moody as a Minotaur, the first book in the new Willow Lake Pack series, is now available to preorder on Amazon.

———

Curious how it all began? Ash and Dillon find their happily-ever-after in **Hellhounds Never Lie** (Willow Lake Supernaturals #1). Get it at Amazon.

A Note from the Author

Hi!

Thank you for reading Hayden and Ryley's book!

I was really apprehensive when I started writing Hayden's book. Let's face it, he had a lot of stuff going on. And I debated a bit about what kind of mate would be his perfect match. I thought about having someone who was timid and shy, someone who'd bring out Hayden's protective alpha side, and then Ryley showed up on the page.

And I guess Ryley has some of those traits—as a faun he isn't as strong, for example, and his life with his old herd messed him up a bit. But I love that he doesn't put up with the lies Hayden tells himself. He calls Hayden on all kinds of things and I think Hayden desperately needs someone like that to stand up to him. I also love that Ryley confronts things, even when they scare him. I think we could all benefit from having a little more of that in our lives.

I hope you enjoyed their story!

Then there is Robbie. Oh, Robbie. I think Willow Lake

will be celebrating his incarceration for a long time to come. He's been hanging about causing problems from the beginning. And, now that he is gone, it felt like the end of the series. But there are still a lot of people in Willow Lake still waiting for their happy endings, so I've started a new series **Willow Lake Pack** and the first book will be Levi and Parker's. *Moody as a Minotaur* is up for preorder already. These two have waited sooo long for their story to be told and I'm having fun writing their story now.

Thank you to my beta readers Kirk Waite (Rare Bird Beta Reading) and Courtney Bassett. They both provided amazing feedback that made this book stronger. Thank you also to my editor June. As I've said before, I'd be lost without her. They have all helped me so much as I worked through the final steps on this book. But, as always, if any errors have survived to the final version, that's on me. If you spot any typos or oddities, feel free to email me (lori@ loriames.com), rather than reporting the book.

A few final thoughts... I mentioned that *Moody as a Minotaur* is available to preorder now! The preorder has a 2026 release date, but I expect to release it before then. If you join my newsletter, you'll receive all the latest news, including updates on the release schedule. You'll also receive updates about other fun news, like *Hellhounds Never Lie* being made into an audiobook with Kirt Graves as the narrator! Yay! That releases on April 15, 2025. More Willow Lake audiobooks are releasing shortly after that!

Okay, I think that's all I have for now! Wishing you a never ending supply of books you love! <3

Cheers,

Lori

PS… Reviews help other readers decide if a book might be something they want to read, so please consider writing a review of *Alphas Never Hide*. That would be wonderful. I'm sure even Hayden would smile.

About the Lori

Lori Ames writes MM romance with touch of magic! When Lori was in elementary school, she wrote a very compelling story about a girl with a prickly personality who turned into a rose. (Sounds amazing, right? She knew you'd agree.) Then she discovered romances in her teens and, well, she knew she wanted to write romances. It took her a little longer to find MM romances, but once she did, she was addicted. She lives in a small town in Alberta with her husband and an elderly black cat.

You can find out more here:

- Patreon: patreon.com/c/LoriAmes
- Facebook Group: facebook.com/groups/LoriAmesReaders
- Facebook Page: facebook.com/LoriAmesAuthor
- Website: loriames.com
- Newsletter Sign Up: loriames.com/newsletter
- Bluesky: bsky.app/profile/loriames.bsky.social
- MM Wire: themmwire.circle.so/c/lori-ames/

I also have a store with fun merchandise now! Find a link to it on my website: loriames.com

Also by Lori Ames

WILLOW LAKE SUPERNATURALS

MM Paranormal Romance

Ravens Never Fall - *Prequel* (Oak & Mercer)

The prequel is available to my newsletter subscribers as a free download.

Hellhounds Never Lie - *Book 1* (Ash & Dillon)

Wolves Always Bite - *Book 2* (Jeremy & Adrian)

Oracles Always Win - *Book 3* (Jake & Gage)

Cats Never Fly - Book 4 (Simon & Ogden)

Alphas Never Hide - Book 5 (Hayden & Ryley)

WILLOW LAKE PACK

Willow Lake Supernaturals Spin-Off Series

The first book is coming soon!

Moody as a Minotaur - Book 1 (Levi & Parker)